A Change in Course

by JD Cline

The contents of this work, including, but not limited to, the accuracy of events, people, and places depicted; opinions expressed; permission to use previously published materials included; and any advice given or actions advocated are solely the responsibility of the author, who assumes all liability for said work and indemnifies the publisher against any claims stemming from publication of the work.

This is a work of fiction. Unless otherwise indicated, all the names, characters, businesses, places, events, and incidents in this book are either the product of the author's imagination or used in a fictitious manner. Any resemblance to actual persons, living or dead, or actual events is purely coincidental.

Dorrance Publishing Co
585 Alpha Drive
Pittsburgh, PA 15238
Visit our website at *www.dorrancebookstore.com*

ISBN: 978-1-6376-4151-4
ESIBN: 978-1-6376-4788-2

Foreword

My dream has always been to be a published author. Life put that dream on hold until now. I hope you enjoy my first book as much as I enjoyed writing it. Hopefully it finds a way to be published and enjoyed and there are many more books to come. Special recognition to my niece Ellice Whatley who was my editor and sounding board and my mother Marget Hall an avid reader.

1

Ding, ding, ding the video screens wailed and people cheered as the market closed on another successful week on Wall Street. Matt stared at the screen with a smile and then walked down the rows and congratulated his team by patting them on the back. "Nice week, everyone. That's how we do it." Matt had run his team for over five years, focusing on emerging technologies and startups.

It truly was a job of Russian roulette as only 10 percent of startups made it, and sometimes it took years for them to go public, if they ever did. But if you bet correctly, there was always a pot of gold underneath those rainbows. This week culminated years of research by Matt and his team on a ride-sharing application that had just gone public and the stock shot through the roof. If that wasn't enough, a company that used sound wave technology to reduce wrinkles had just been purchased by French mega health company Perazo, and he netted $90,000,000 on their 49 percent ownership. He was riding high. It had been his team's best week ever.

Alex, his assistant, walked over and handed him a cup of coffee. He savored it as he sipped. This week was a winner, a moment in time to be cherished. "Wow, I have never seen a week like this," Alex smiled as he sat down. Matt with a sip of coffee still at his mouth nodded up and down in acknowledgment. Perazo closed on Wednesday, and they wanted to trade in shares, but they were a bloated behemoth mega company, whose shares barely moved on the markets regardless. Matt wouldn't budge, so the money landed in their funds account this morning. Next week, he would diversify those out to his next phase of startups they had been scouring and researching over for months.

The ride-sharing app had increased 10 percent since going public this morning, but Matt was sticking. It had a bullet, and the potential upside was immeasurable. Eventually competitors would enter the market in the upcoming years and would catch up unless they continued to innovate. If they didn't, he would dump it, but those worries were years away. By the end of next week, the stock would be up another 10 percent because the home investors who had little knowledge of the market and how it operated would begin to get in. They would get in because they used the service, and the man on the street usually invested in what they knew. It had a bullet.

Interrupting his thoughts, Alex spoke up. "You knew it was underpriced… how?" He was twenty-seven, but he looked sixteen, and bless his heart, he had every presence of a geeky exterior. He completed his undergrad at Harvard and his MBA at Wharton, and now it was Matt's job to bring him along, to mentor him, if you will. He was one of the partners' stepson.

Matt smiled, "I just did."

Alex's face turned into a frown. "Oh come on!"

Matt laughed. "Alex, how many tech IPOs did Brown and Fister bring to market last year?"

"I don't know."

"You should know—one," Matt shot back. He got up. "Brown and Fister have a great name, and they know a ton about commodities and basic stocks and can run an IPO seamlessly, but they don't know shit about tech, which is just about the same as most of New York." Matt waved to the windows at the sprawl of New York City that lay beneath them on the 39th floor of Wavemen Tower.

Matt stood and walked to each one of his team members and congratulated all ten of them individually. They were all kids in the big scheme of things, all under the age of twenty-five, but that was how Matt wanted it. If they were to catch the next big wave, his team needed to live it, to be in the middle of it. They were at the peak of consumerism and on the cutting edge of everything going on in tech and in life.

Not encumbered by the reality that lay below, living in efficiency rent-controlled apartments in the city, which they didn't care about because they never saw them anyway. They were either working or partying or, as today, both. They would be hammered tonight. There would be hookups via apps, or internally, but they would be back on Monday, killing it. None were married yet or had kids, so nothing weighed them down. There had been a scare last year when the twins, Chi and Wa, both got engaged within months of each other only to see it fall apart.

Chi and Wa were Asian from parents who emigrated from Hong Kong when it became clear China was going to get it back. They fled as many did and were still doing so today to avoid living under communism.

Papa Son, as the Chi and Wa nicknamed their father, decided on arranged marriages for his daughters. With neither of them having anything resembling a steady boyfriend, after being beaten down verbally, they relented. Both prospective husbands were fine, connected Asian men, but the girls arrived in America when they were five. They essentially were no longer Asian; they were American. They spoke Cantonese, but they didn't live it. It lasted about a month and ended in a blowout with Papa Son, but the girls were not receptive taking orders. They were not property. Both graduated with finance degrees from Yale at nineteen and crushed their MBAs at the #1 International business school in the country, Darla Moore in South Carolina.

Today Chi and Wa crunched Matt's numbers relentlessly. The two best finance minds he had ever seen, and when they completed their work, they checked each other's work, hammering away on each other's models until they were sure it was correct or as correct as you can be in tech.

Matt could hear his boss's, King George's, booming voice coming down the hallway. He looked at his watch, and it was almost five. It was time.

He rose and stood in front of his team as George walked in. Matt gave him a nod and George stopped and waited as Matt spoke. "Big week, team. I couldn't be prouder. All kidding aside, you are awesome." The room broke into applause. "Everyone up and out of here! Nobody takes any work home. I don't want to see that anyone has carded in on the weekend and that's an order. I will see you at 8:00 A.M. Monday for the staff meeting." A few papers were thrown in the air, a few whoops went up, and with that, they were moving toward the elevator. "And no hangovers on Monday. We have $90,000,000 to move, so get that shit out of the way in the next thirty-six hours." They all busted out laughing, which could still be heard as they were exiting the work area.

King George's mouth was gapped wide open incredulously. His Oxford-educated British accent sputtered out, "Really? Don't we think we need the weekend to work on this?"

"Not your team, George. They are mine, and they are no good to you or me if I run them into the ground. My team doesn't work the weekends."

King George had been Matt's boss since he arrived, and he oversaw all the Wavemen technology investment teams until about a month ago when he took on the operations director position. He was a good boss because he hired great people and let them run, and at the same time he ran block for all the stupid shit coming down from the partner's on the 49th floor, which would have hampered the productivity of the teams.

He was a great boss but a terrible investor when it came to tech. Matt and King George had a scheduled one-on-one each Wednesday, so George could brief Matt on what the other four tech fund teams were doing. Matt had been advising George for years, telling George to have them pull this, get this, make sure they have checked this.

Matt applied for George's old position running the tech teams, which is basically what he had been doing in private for years. George desperately wanted him in that position and had been lobbying hard even though Matt was only thirty-two. If Matt didn't get that position, there was no telling what the next tech director might do. Matt's team had figured out something that resembled a system—if you could find that in tech—and had been running circles around the other tech teams for years. George thought that this would be a no-brainer and put on the full-court press to get him promoted.

If he got the position, there would be a staggering increase over what he made today. It was life-changing money for him and his wife, Beth. Would they really give this position to someone who got their undergrad and MBA from Nebraska, while he was surrounded by Yale, Harvard, Princeton and, of course, Oxford? George had said over and over that results, not pedigree, is what mattered in America, which is why he was no longer in the UK. George was the bastard son of some Duke in the UK and his mother was his former maid who was his mistress. Being a bastard got him into Oxford but little else because it was all on the down low.

"But...," George stammered. "Are we sure?"

Matt shot him a glance. "You don't get to do that with me, George. Again, my team. If you would like to come to my 8:00 A.M. on Monday and provide input, you're welcome," Matt said, smiling at George because he never came in before 9:30 A.M. anymore.

"Shag that! Why on earth would I do that? That would be a bloody waste of time," George said, knowing he had nothing really to offer. "I think that is really just nasty of you, Matt, to infer that I waste valuable sleeping time on an endeavor that would be fruitless." They both laughed.

"Good, then. It's settled. Conversation over. Don't we have a meeting to go to?"

"Oh right, bloody promotion thing. Another waste of my valuable time."

"We think it's a promotion," Matt countered.

As they entered the elevator, Matt pulled out his phone and texted Beth. *I'll be at the train station by 7:30. Get us reservations at Albrinos and have him open our celebration bottle an hour ahead of time. The team crushed it this week. No word yet on the promotion. Text you when I know. Love you.* Albrinos was Matt and Beth's favorite restaurant in Connecticut where they had relocated from the city about two years ago into a house Matt paid off from the sale of the high-rise condo in the city.

He had toiled away for a decade at Waverman to pay it off, so he and Beth would be ready to have kids. By the time they got the condo paid off and celebrated, Beth thought it would be best to move out of the city to raise the kids and avoid paying for private schools. A remarkably logical financial assessment from his wife who he could not argue with, except that it added ninety minutes each way to his commute to the office from the twenty minutes he had before. He adjusted doing his research on the commute versus at home or office, but what a change it had been.

When he hit Send to the text it immediately rejected. He sent it again with the same response. He looked at his phone, and it had no signal, which was bizarre because cell service had been tunneled into the building Wi-Fi, so they almost always had perfect service. It had to be some kind of outage.

Matt looked up. "George, do you have service?" George pulled out his phone and showed it to Matt. His phone had five bars. "Bizarre." Matt rolled his eyes. The thought of having to deal with this problem didn't sit well, nor the possibility of being without a phone for the weekend. Matt murmured to himself "reboot" as he shut his phone off, and when he saw it restarting, he placed it back into his pocket. It would be fine.

The elevator door opened on the 49th floor, revealing the last glimmer of sun ducking below the horizon on the cool March day. They were a week away from daylight savings time, and it could not come soon enough. Matt was commuting into the office in the dark and leaving in the dark. He would go to the gym at lunch and see the mostly gloomy cold days from the treadmill, elliptical, or CrossFit class. This was one of the few things that kept him sane. Alex would have his lunch at his desk for him every day when he returned.

2

When they were summoned to the conference room by the receptionist, Matt's stomach leaped. George went to the large, metal double doors and rapped on them with his knuckle before opening them. Matt's mouth was completely dry as he stepped inside.

Matt had only been allowed in this room once in the entire ten years he had been at Waverman Investments, when he was promoted to the lead of his team five years ago. Most had never seen this room.

The entire back wall of the conference room was glass, and now that it was completely dark outside, the freedom tower glimmered in the distance. The sixty-foot-long board table was forged glass, ten inches thick, with varying edges. The rumor was the recently deceased Mrs. Waverman had it brought in, and they craned it up while the shell of the building was being built because there was no way to get it up there otherwise. They literally built the room around it. The floor was steel-looking, as were the board chairs with white cushions. All very clean lines.

In the middle of the table, with their backs to window, were four men, all of whom Matt recognized but, based on their roles, made no sense why they would be there together. The two middlemen were Albert Dean and Mark Cross, the senior most partners at the firm, both completely suited up, which was not the standard for a Friday. In fact, both of them should have already arrived at the Hamptons for the weekend, as they left via their drivers at noon every Friday. Seated on the left was the head of IT, as always in all black and no tie, Herbert Jackson, which no one was allowed to call him. He went by HJ, and he was, in the eyes of Matt, a demon. To the right of them was a good friend of Matt's, Paul Johnson, who was the chief of security. Paul and Matt would sometimes work out together at the gym. Paul was a former Navy Seal, and as an African American he had been a trail blazer his entire career in the Navy, and one of the finest people Matt had ever known. The look on everyone's faces said it all, and George saw it as well: something was very wrong.

Who was missing from the table was even more telling than their faces. Don Waverman was not there. He lived on the entire 50th floor of the building. He was incredibly hands-on with what happened at his company and was never far away from the action. There was no way that someone would be getting a promotion to run his tech teams, which amounted to billions of dollars in fund money, without him being part of the process.

Matt looked at Paul for some kind of comfort, and Paul immediately looked down. Paul looked like he was going to throw up. He just shook his head a little side to side. Albert Dean and Mark Cross looked so uncomfortable they were ready to come out of their suits, and finally HJ had a wide smile on his face that said it all. Whatever was going on in that little fucker's mind, he was enjoying this, and that would not bode well for Matt.

Sitting in the middle of the table were two files. One about five inches thick and the other about an inch thick. In Albert Dean's hand, he was holding a card.

Albert Dean started speaking. "Matt, I'm not sure where to start other than to say that I'm sorry we are having this meeting today. I know you have come in here with expectations that are not going to be met at least not today and for that we are all sorry." He paused to clear his throat, and Matt shot a glance at George, who looked totally dumfounded. Albert Dean looked around the room. "What we're going to talk about is totally confidential to a man. It's in everyone's best interest for this to NOT leave this room," Albert said firmly. He handed over the envelope in his hand to Matt, and Matt froze when he received it. It was an envelope from his wife's stationary, which was embossed with BT for Beth Thomas.

Matt stammered and looked at Albert. All the blood ran out of Matt's face. "I don't understand." Albert motioned for him to open it. Matt stammered again, "Is she okay?" The other men at the table would not meet his gaze except for HJ, who could not get enough of this. Matt could tell he was cataloging it all in his mind, so that he could play it back over and over again. Taking the envelope, Matt tore it open. Inside the envelope, Beth's matching stationary was there, and the BT on the outside could be seen as he pulled the card out. As he opened it, he immediately recognized Beth's penmanship. As Matt read the note over and over every word tore into his soul, he could feel his heart beating in his chest. Beth was leaving him for someone else. He was in total shock.

Beth and Matt had met at Nebraska their freshman year. She was the most beautiful girl he had ever seen. She wasn't just the most beautiful girl he had ever seen; she was the most beautiful girl anyone had ever seen. Time had not changed that, but instead put a brighter spotlight on her as she got older. When they went almost anywhere, every man and woman would stop to look at her. Her beauty commanded being noticed.

Matt's head tilted down farther. He was broken. They'd built a life together since deciding to come to New York from Nebraska to make it. It had been a hard ten years, but they'd done it together and eventually got to where they would be making real money. That was supposed to be today.

The room was dead silent as he laid the card down. He got up and turned to look away from them as the tears started to form. He started taking larger breaths as his mind raced and his heart followed, combatting a sick feeling in his stomach. The room fell into a dead silence for several minutes.

HJ began to reach across the table to read the card, but Albert grabbed his reaching arm at the elbow. George, not knowing really what was going on but knowing it was a very private situation they all had gotten sucked into, slammed his fist on the table between the card and HJ's hand. King George hated HJ, as most did.

It had the effect of startling everyone in the room, including Matt who spun and saw what was happening. He walked back to the table picking the card up and waved it in front of Albert Dean's face. Through gritted teeth, Matt took a deep breath. "What is going on? Why do you, of all people, have this and what does this have to do with the firm?" His eyes were visibly tearing, but there was rage in his voice. Albert visibly moved back fearing Matt might come over the table, and George sensing this put his hand on Matt's and said, "Let's all just take a breath and sit, and I'm sure we'll get to the bottom of this."

Matt turned to George with his eyes in exasperation. "Beth is leaving me." He tossed the card to George, and he immediately read it. George knew that Beth was Matt's entire life and Waverman was his second, and somehow today, in this conference room, the two had collided. George and his wife were good friends with Matt and Beth and had gone out almost weekly together for dinner until they moved to Connecticut. George's eyes met Paul's, and he understood immediately that it would take the two of them to get Matt through this meeting.

"Let's sit down and figure this out," George said, motioning to his chair.

Matt threw himself back into his chair and looked at Albert. Albert reached for his water and cleared his throat. Looking down at the table, not making eye contact he started, "It seems that Mr. Waverman and your wife Mrs. Thomas have formed a relationship and that has prompted this meeting today." With that statement all the air exited the room. Don Waverman at the age of sixty-seven was fucking Beth who was thirty-three, and it had just ended his marriage.

George exhaled, "Jesus," loud enough for everyone to hear in the still room.

Albert continued, "As I said before, we are all so very sorry, Mr. Thomas." Ann Waverman, Don's wife and the matriarch of the firm, had died just over two years ago after battling breast cancer for some time. Beth had been especially nice to them through the process, dropping in on them almost weekly. "She moved out of your home today, Mr. Thomas, and all the details have been worked out. She will not be claiming any spousal support if you agree to a no-fault divorce. Mr. Waverman insisted that all the joint assets are yours as she will be surrendering it all to you." Matt smiled. Of course, she would. She now had Don's hundreds of millions to support her.

Rage came over Matt, his entire face was red, he came out of his chair with his fists balled up on the table. With that, Paul and George both came out of their chairs. Albert again moved farther away from the table, and the other partner moved over immediately hitting HJ's chair. Matt reached his right hand in the air and pointed toward the ceiling. "Are you telling me that my wife and Mr. Waverman are above us right now setting up house on the 50th, and if I am a good boy, I get to keep what I have earned? Are you kidding me?!"

Albert began to stutter as the tension escalated. "They are not here, Mr. Thomas. They left today on vacation, and we're not sure when they will return, but to be blunt, understanding how awful this all is, eventually they will be back and yes they will be living on the 50th."

Matt fell back in his chair, he looked at Paul and George and shook his head from side to side. "This is unbelievable."

"Mr. Thomas," Albert continued, "I can't imagine what you are going through, but in the interest of the firm, we need to keep this quiet until it's time to go public."

To that Matt looked up and responded, "What?"

"If the firm gets bad press, it hurts everyone, our clients, which I know you care about, the investors, and yourself through our stock, your stock, Mr. Thomas."

Matt looked. "Or what? The founder, president and CEO of this firm is having an affair with an employee's wife."

Albert's lip got tight and with that it seemed that the whole room changed again. Waverman Inc. just went on the offense. HJ pushed the two folders over. Albert separated them and put them in front of Matt. Both were purple and purple folders only meant one thing at Waverman, an FTC investigation. Albert laid his hands on them. "Mr. Thomas, you know what these are. Two of our fund managers in this office have had incredible quarters. This manager," he patted on the five inch file, "has tons of research and work that will clearly and easily explain to the FTC how he got to his conclusions and show them and the street that he is an outstanding mind in the technology field. This other file is a manager that has cut corners and moved from operating in the gray to the red with insider information. This manager," he said, now patting on the five-inch folder, "has a promising career ahead of him, is truly gifted, and honestly we want him *here* at Waverman in the future as a director if, of course, he wants to stay." He then shifted to the other file and said, "This other manager will be exposed, lose his license, his job, his career, and his future. Both of these files have been requested by the FTC which require an investigation that will take probably sixty days." Albert put the two files back on top of each other and pushed them back to HJ. "We have decided, due to the nature of these investigations, that a sixty-day paid leave of absence to be the best course of action for these managers during this time, of course, with benefits. Mr. Thomas, under the circumstances, this would be an excellent cooling-off period, really a time for reflection for everyone involved in this other situation," he said, pointing to Beth's card.

Albert shifted forward in his seat his body stiffened and his tone shifted from a tone of compassion to being very stern. "If things were to spiral out of control here, which would again be in nobody's best interest, we would hate for someone innocent to possibly be caught erroneously in this other manager's unfortunate situation." He turned and gave HJ a nod. Everyone in the room knew what that meant.

HJ came to Waverman in a very unusual way. Matt received a frantic call from George one Saturday years ago. When he arrived at the office, he joined the partners in George's office in front of the Wall Street board. In the middle of one of the jumbo computer screens, one of the office computers output had been thrown there.

Matt had some IT when he was at Nebraska, but in no way was an expert. Knowing what to bet on for tech on Wall Street was one thing, but programming was entirely different. Arthur Sands, the CIO, and his apprentice, David, were angrily pecking away at the screen to no avail. Matt in his jeans and T-shirt sat down and read the screen. As a public service to Waverman, a hacker by the name of Death Spiral had infiltrated their system, found multiple levels of weakness and locked them out of everything other than the funds balance sheets that all showed as $0. Billions were gone. Death Spiral was willing to help them out for $10 million dollars to fix their system. They were being blackmailed with ransomware. He would send a report once the funds were transferred to the Caymans and release the system.

Don Waverman bellowed to his CIO, "What do we do?"

Arthur turned. "We need to alert the FTC and call the FBI."

George and Matt looked at each other wild-eyed and then Matt spoke up. "What this person has done here is very strategic. He waited until the market closed on Friday and then began the hack and shut everything down. If our investors get wind of this, it could cause a run on our funds to pull the money out. I think I might have a better course of action. I have a buddy in Silicon Valley who does this for a living. He is a white hat hacker who used to work for the FBI and left to make his riches. We need to get him involved before we do anything else."

They made some calls and hatched a plan that was run by Matt. They paid the $10 million, which in the course of things is really a rounding error at Waverman. Remarkably within minutes of the transfer the system rebooted itself and all was back to normal. The white hat followed the money and how the system had been hacked because no report came as promised from Death Spiral. The white hat was very impressed with how they had taken over, calling it a game changer. The system was then immediately patched.

It took three months of serious work and cost millions before white hat caught up and received the location of Death Spiral. Things then took a strange turn. Instead of then notifying the FBI, turning everything over and having the shit arrested, Don Waverman had the white hat hack Death Spiral's computer system and set up a meeting. Rumors abound over the outcome of that meeting, but at the end of the day, the hacker Death Spiral ended up being the new CIO for Waverman, now known as HJ. The other team had been fired after the initial takeover and white hat played remote interim, so everything appeared to be on the up and up. No word on whether HJ got to keep the millions, but he drove a DB9 and lived in one of the nicest buildings in the city.

Unfortunately for Matt, he and HJ had several run-ins since then. HJ liked women, but they couldn't stand him. He was greasy with bad eyes and obviously had no clue. Matt caught him after hours pinning a twenty-one-year-old intern against a refrigerator. Matt at 6′2 was much bigger and, having played football at Nebraska for a short stint, easily grabbed HJ at 5′5 and threw him out of the room. It all got reported to HR and the intern disappeared with all her student loans paid off. HJ was right back in the office the following Monday with the entire thing swept under the rug. It wasn't long until it happened again with the same outcome. The women kept quiet after being paid off, and HJ was viewed by the partners as indispensable.

HJ looked at the files, and Matt knew within an instant that with a few keystrokes of fake emails and text messages, HJ could easily implicate him in that other file, and he would be ruined along with the other manager.

Albert continued, "We are extremely confident, Mr. Thomas, that you will be exonerated completely. I have read the file myself, and it's inspiring work. We would welcome you back after sixty days in the position managing the tech teams that you have in fact earned. If not, then you will receive a glowing recommendation from George here, and I am sure that you can pick almost any firm you might want to join. In fact, Mr. Thomas, under these unfortunate circumstances I can promise you that if you don't want to return, I will make calls myself and guarantee you a position somewhere else. It's up to you on how you want to move forward. You have sixty days to decide, so please take a vacation, get your mind right, and hopefully we will see you back here in sixty days in a much nicer office than you left."

Albert then got up, which meant the meeting was over. Everyone rose, including Matt out of nothing but muscle memory. Albert didn't reach out to shake Matt's hand, most likely out of fear of getting yanked across the table and strangled. Albert nodded to Paul. "Mr. Thomas, Paul and George are going to lead you out of the building and take your cell phone and key card. Your access has already been pulled including all computer systems before you came in here today, so please don't try and access the systems before you have been cleared to return. You know that there is nothing nefarious going on here as it is all standard procedure."

Paul and George led him to the elevator which was being held by the receptionist of all people, and they went down to the 39th floor to gather his coat. When the door closed George began, "What the fuck!" Paul shut him down by quickly pointing at the cameras. Of course, everything that happened to Matt from the time he left the boardroom would be monitored through the security cameras.

3

ORiley's Irish Bar was hopping as would be expected at 6:30 P.M. on Friday. King George, Matt and Paul all sat together in the back corner. Matt was staring at the foam on the top of his Guinness quietly. O'Riley's was upscale and near the market as it would be expected to be, and on a good week, as it had been for most, it was wall-to-wall chatter singing the hymns of the brilliant work they had done.

Looking at Paul, George was the first to speak. "How long have you known?"

Paul was a very straight shooter. "Two weeks. I got pulled into a full partners' meeting two weeks ago. It was a shitshow. Somehow, they found out about the affair, and it was bad. You need to know that most of them were incensed about what was going down." Paul sighed and took a sip of his drink. "Man, I didn't know what to say. Albert was there leading the resistance. He was speaking on behalf of the partners who looked like they were attending a funeral, but Don was hearing none of it. After his wife died, he changed. And here is the thing. Albert is being completely straight with you for good and bad. You will be cleared, and you will be back in sixty days as long as things don't go bad for the firm, but I am telling you, they will circle the wagons and bury you if it does. They have their entire livelihoods bet on it, and unfortunately we all know that HJ can carry it out."

Matt got up, threw a $20 on the table and headed into the crowd without a word.

4

The train chugged through the countryside with the city in its rearview. Matt read the card over and over again. There was no doubt that it was her stationary and her penmanship. Of course, what was not on the card was the fact that the person she was leaving him for was the CEO and owner of his firm with his name on the fifty-story building. He recounted back the last couple of years in his mind. How long had it been going on and how had he totally missed it? In retrospect, it had to be easy. Waverman's secretary had access to his Outlook schedule to know when and where he was. Waverman had tons of money, so they surely never met at Matt's house or even the company building that doubled for his home.

That would have been stupid. With the death of his wife, there would have never been a spouse on the other end wondering what the hotel room bills were for and there certainly would never be wondering why he was out of the office but... Waverman? He was sixty-seven, in relatively good shape, but he looked eighty. Did his age or looks really matter, though, when it came to what amounted to unlimited money? He was sick, and the knot in his stomach churned.

The train slowed as it arrived at the station. People rushed off into the cold Friday evening, most likely to cars with their families awaiting to catch dinner out somewhere. As the train pulled away, the feeling came over him that he could have known and just didn't want to face it. Nothing ever seemed good enough for Beth. In Nebraska, her family had no money. She had barely gotten into college on a program to be a teacher to the rural areas of the state. When she graduated, she would have had to do six years in a rural area in order to forgive her college debt.

The retention for teaching in rural areas was about 50 percent, but Beth never did a minute of time in the country. She hated Nebraska, and as soon as they left, she never went back, not even to visit her parents. They always had to come see her, and eventually that got old for them. Her debt fell on her and Matt after they got married and moved to New York. He thought they would starve there for a while, but after the third year at Waverman, he got a bonus that enabled them to wipe Beth's college debt out. Beth disagreed and wanted to keep the debt to move into a nicer place from the efficiency rent-controlled apartment that was strangling them. She worked in retail at a high-end store for a while and then moved to the makeup section, but eventually her spending on the clothes, makeup, and shoes from the store outpaced what she was bringing home.

In retrospect, she'd never been happy. The apartments were never big enough or nice enough. It always had to be better. Matt hated when they went to George's place because all he ever heard for the following week was how much nicer it was than theirs. Eventually he succumbed and moved into the same building in a much smaller condo. He thought that would make her happy, but no. They had gone to Connecticut for a long weekend at a bed and breakfast, and she seemed to fall in love with the town. He had just been able to pay off the condo two years prior, and the prices had skyrocketed in the city. They tested the market, and the condo was gone in a weekend. They moved into an entirely too old and too large house in Connecticut because they were going to have kids. It was another four years of slaving away, saving every dime and hiding his bonuses from Beth until he got most of it paid off. She didn't even know.

She would get her teaching certificate to teach elementary, and he would suck it up and spend the mornings and evenings on the fucking train. Was it all gone? Was it ever real? Maybe this was all just a bad dream, and she would be there with Hank when he got home. Hank!

His heart sank. Hank. Would she have taken him with her? Hank was their two-year-old chocolate Lab Matt got when they moved out of the city. He gave Hank to Beth on their first Christmas in the house. They both loved him dearly. He was such a sweet boy. He had a big box English head and an American Lab body. He was now almost ninety pounds and just the most sweet and beautiful animal that he ever had.

Matt got into an awaiting cab. He couldn't help but to look around for Beth waiting for him, but the station was empty as it was now almost 8:00 P.M. on a Friday. There was no sign of her BMW 525. They had made love this morning and it had been special, so special that he was late and missed the first train. She told him that she had some place to be. He remembered waving back to her as he left and smiled. Had that been a tear in her eye?

The cab roared down the road. The driver was talking, but Matt wasn't listening. His heart was beating a mile a minute. Would she take him with her? She would. She loved him. He would come home to the house, and it would be empty. As the cab rolled into his driveway, his heart sank. The house was completely black inside. Nobody was home. He threw money at the driver and ran up the driveway slipping on the ice. He had those damn rubber shoe covers, but, of course, they were still at the office where he was walked out of the building with his credentials taken along with his cell phone and laptop. None of that mattered now. He scrambled with the key, and opened the door, and Hank wasn't there.

Hank was always there when a car came into the driveway. He would rumble down the stairs or from the kitchen where he was waiting for food to hit the floor to greet him, bounding up and down and throwing himself against Matt's legs. But tonight, he wasn't there. Matt threw his stuff on the floor, shut the door, and sat on the steps. For the first time today, he finally succumbed. Matt began to cry. He hadn't cried since his parents died, but this was the final straw, and the tears came. Then he heard a thud from the master bedroom. He looked up the stairs, and in the dark, he could see Hank thundering down them. Beth had to have left the bed unmade because that was the only time he was allowed to sleep on it. He ran right over Matt, laid his entire weight on his body, and licked his face. Left alone in a dark house, Hank had gone to bed.

When he couldn't love on Hank anymore and the crying and self-pity had abated, he walked into the kitchen because it was nugget time. Hank was starving as it was two hours after his feeding time. Hank ate within seconds of the food hitting the bowl. Matt opened the small wine fridge built into the cabinets and went to the bottom. He pulled out his best bottle, the one he had been saving for his promotion. It was the Jerkasky Wine specifically from the Steed Vineyard in Napa Valley. He pulled it open and poured a huge glass, and then he took Hank out into the backyard. He plopped down on the back step, and Hank ran around the yard marking his area. The plan was to drink the bottle and then figure out what to do in the morning. For right now, he was relieved at least that he still had Hank, and he was certain that Hank loved him. Beth had left them both.

5

Alexandra lay on the couch with her eyes closed half-in and half-out of consciousness. All that she cared about was that the dragon had subsided in her chest, and its thirst had been quenched for a moment. She wondered how long it would last as this was her first-time using Fentanyl. She didn't know how long she had lain there, but she felt someone standing above her. As she opened her eyes, he was on top of her. He put his full weight on her and pulled both of her hands above her head. She was trying to fight, but she was in no condition to fend him off. His hand slid up her dress and ripped her panties down. She violently tried to fend off his advances, but he was too large. He said he was going to help her. She had gone there for his help.

His legs slid between hers and forced her legs open. She heard someone screaming in the distance. No… it was her voice. She was trying. His left hand that was holding both of hers moved. He had one of her hands pinned with his elbow while his other hand covered her mouth to quiet her. He moved his hand, and she could feel him trying to free himself from his pants, so that he could enter her. This couldn't be happening. He said that he was going to help her? As he spread her legs more, he ran out of couch and lost his balance for a second. It was enough. Alexandra got one leg free and drove the bottom of her foot down on the head of his exposed erect penis. He screamed horrifically and crashed against the coffee table as he tried to get away from the next blow, but it was too late. Her foot came crashing down on his crotch again. He threw his body away from her and got pinned between the other couch and the coffee table. That was her chance.

Alexandra stumbled off the coach to the dinner table where she had left her designer purse. She could hear him behind her trying to get up but still in too much pain; she dared not look back. She grabbed her purse and was out the apartment door. She ricocheted back and forth against the walls trying to get to the elevator at the end of the hallway. That was her target, but the Fentanyl made her body less than responsive. As she got to the elevator it opened immediately when she touched the button, and she fell inside touching the button for the ground floor. She could hear his thundering steps down the hallway, but the elevator door closed before he could get to it. She took a deep breath and grabbed the wall handle to pull herself up. No one could see her like this. When the door opened, she quickly walked across the empty lobby trying to look composed and exited the building to the street. She could see her blue Jaguar XJ and crossed the street toward it, stepping right in front of a car that was fortunately paying attention and slammed on brakes. Alexandra didn't even stop; she just kept going. When she got to the car, it immediately unlocked as her hand hit the handle, and she almost fell backward into the street when the door flew open. She fell inside, closed the door and sat.

She was in no condition to drive. Her head was cloudy, her heart was racing, and this caused her body to not respond together. As she caught her breath, she saw him come out of the door of the building. He was also high and deranged. Fear gripped her, "No!" She ignited the XJ and tore out of the space and down the street almost hitting him. He said he was going to help her.

What had it been? Nine months since the surgery? She was given Oxycontin to recover, an opioid, which she honestly had no idea what that meant, but after a week when she should have been getting better, instead she seemed to need more pills. Now when she didn't take them, the dragon built up in her chest. She went back to the doctor and got a refill, but he insisted on an MRI of her knee to check to see if it was healing correctly. She never showed up for the appointment. It wasn't long before she found herself going to other doctors, trying to get more medication, and that was when it happened.

One doctor called another, and the knee surgeon called Style who told him that Alexandra had been going around town trying to get more pills. Style was so embarrassed. He tore the house apart to find the pills and poured them all down the toilet while she lay on the floor crying and begging. He then found an exclusive anonymous rehab meeting in San Francisco and got her in. For months, she snuck Oxy off the streets and went to meetings, so Style thought she was okay. That is when she had met him.

He was an anesthesiologist who had been removed from practice for abusing drugs while administering them to patients. His wife had taken his daughter and left him, and he was trying to put his life back together. He said he was recovered and convinced her after a meeting over coffee that he could help her. He was going to give her Fentanyl in the place of the Oxy to slow dose her down, so the dragon didn't rage inside of her anymore. She would have done just about anything to get better and that's how she ended up at his home. He obviously lied as after he gave her some, he inserted the same syringe in his arm and dosed himself. At that point, however, Alexandra didn't care as she lay on the sofa. The dragon was abated for the minute.

The XJ was flying through the streets of San Francisco. She just needed to get home and sleep and pretend that none of this ever happened. Her eyes felt so heavy, and her body felt so tired. She slipped out of consciousness, and in a second, she ran a light. The front of the XJ was hit by a white Suburban with a family inside on their way to Pier 29. The impact altered the direction of the car as she was unconscious. It sounded like a gun going off, so all the pedestrians froze on the street looking in the direction. The XJ was now headed toward them, and they barely scattered in time as she hit the granite building on Embarcadero and Spencer. Alexandra was not conscious to brake the car, so it attempted to do so itself, but the building took a huge impact that shattered the windows of the restaurant on the ground floor, but thankfully the car did not to go inside. People on the inside of the building panicked thinking that it was an earthquake. Inside the XJ, the airbags deployed all around. The pedestrians moved toward the car and tried to open the door but the safety system had locked it when she started moving. One called the police as the other smashed the window open just in case it caught fire. Smoke plumed out from the deployed airbags. Inside they found Alexandra, a sandy-blonde haired woman in her early thirties in the finest clothes with her face smashed and completely bloody. Sirens could be heard in the distance as they all just stood and waited.

6

The doorbell rang at 8:00 A.M. Pain shot through Matt's head as Hank flew off the bed barking. He could hear his feet scratching on the hardwoods as he desperately tried to get traction to head down the hallway. He growled and barked and slid into the wall at the top of the landing, using that to ricochet down the stairs to continue his onslaught of noise to any would-be intruders. Was there anything better for a dog than a doorbell? It was like a license to raise hell and why would you want it any other way. Homes with dogs got broken into much less than those without. Hank was harmless, but he scared the shit out of the delivery drivers. Of course, with Beth there was at least one Amazon delivery a day to the house, so Hank had a ton of practice.

Matt got up and fumbled for a T-shirt and gym shorts when the doorbell rang again. Hank, who was at the door already, lost his mind again. Pain shot through Matt's head with each of Hank's barks. "Fuck! I am coming. I am coming." As he stumbled down the hallway halfway dressed pulling on his shirt, the doorbell rang again and Matt yelled, "I am coming!" to which his head answered with stabbing pains to his temple. As he passed the table in the hallway, a sharp pain shot up his leg and he began to hop up and down in the hallway. "Shit!" He looked down and saw the glass on the floor and the shattered wedding pictures of Matt and Beth coming down the aisle. There was another picture of them on the field after his second game at Nebraska just before he got hurt.

Had he done that, broken the pictures? He must have, and he didn't even remember. Poor Hank must have been traumatized. He looked down and pulled a piece of glass from his foot and the blood began to ooze when the doorbell rang again, and the barking now moved to hysterical levels. "I am going to kill this person." Matt hopped down the stairs, so as to not get blood on carpet. On his way down, he could see that it was the next-door neighbor, Alice. She had her hands cupped over her face peering through the door. Matt unlocked it and yanked it open. "Dammit, Alice, where's the fire?" She recoiled from his tone, and she held up her hand and in it held a bag. He could smell a croissant, bacon, egg, and cheese floating out of the bag from the bagel factory in downtown. It was his favorite, and she knew it. They had been friends since they moved in. Her and her husband were much older but nice. He retired from a life of working in the city, and she was the town's most successful realtor. She knew everybody, and everybody knew her. She had all the gossip on everybody. She had sold the home to Matt and Beth when they moved in two years ago and had been an invaluable asset on the town.

He forced a half smile at her, gestured her in by pulling the door more open and took the bag from her hand. He was starving. He just remembered that he hadn't eaten anything at all last night, just buried two bottles of wine. No wonder he felt like shit. She immediately shot past him down the hallway to the kitchen with her own bag in her hand and her gray head settled at the bar where Matt seated himself next to her.

"I tried to call you last night and this morning, but your phone went directly to voice mail. I was very worried," she rebuked him. Matt and Beth both had cells, so it seemed stupid to put in a land line at the house as they both had great signals, and the only person that called home phones were telemarketers and candidates during election years.

"I must have left it at work," he responded. He wasn't ready to unleash the details of the double whammy that occurred yesterday and the fact that his company confiscated his work phone to the largest gossip in town.

"I saw," she shot a look at him.

"You saw?" he asked.

"I saw Beth packing up to leave pretty soon after she came home yesterday from dropping you off at the train station." The pain in his head hit him again, and he took a bite of his croissant hoping the food would soak up some of the alcohol. Of course, she saw. She was the biggest busybody in town, and she lived across the street. "She told me."

"She told you?" Matt again asked.

"She told me that she was leaving you. Hell, when I came home, I thought your house was being robbed. Out front was a huge black Escalade and there was a cargo van in the driveway and men were carrying stuff out and putting it inside. I grabbed Harry, and we walked over together. We saw Beth in the living room dressed to the nines, looking amazing as usual and directing traffic. Matt looked around the house and everything seemed intact other than the two empty wine bottles in the sink with the empty wine glass. It didn't look like there was anything missing. When he began to feel better, he would take an inventory and figure it out.

"She told me that you knew and that it had been decided that she would move out when you were at work." Matt hung his head. "You didn't know?" Matt looked at her with pain in his eyes and shook his head back and forth. Her mouth fell open. "Matt, oh my God! I am so sorry. I would have called you, but Harry said to stay out of it, that it wasn't our business and that we didn't really know what went on in people's marriages." No truer statement could have been said. You really didn't ever know. Matt sure as shit didn't know. "What are you going to do?"

Matt hung his head, so she couldn't see his eyes as they welled up. He was crushed, devastated. The pain roiled in his soul. He was intensely overcome with anguish. Alice, now overwhelmed, immediately went into mother mode and pressed her body around his bowed head. She hugged him the best she could, her eyes now welling up as well. Matt took a deep breath, and his voice came out in a whisper. "I have no idea at this point. All I know for certain is that she is gone and not returning. I'm probably going to take some time off and get my head straight. Right now, I am living a nightmare that includes bleeding on the kitchen floor." He took the napkin he was wiping his mouth off with and wrapped it around his big toe. He was not going to disclose to Alice the connection with Beth, Don Waverman, and work because not only did he really not want to discuss it, he was actually so overcome he couldn't. That time would come, but that time wasn't now.

"How did that happen?" she asked, looking at Matt as he applied pressure to his toe.

"Stepped on some glass getting up," he said, still not believing he had shattered those pictures and not believing he couldn't remember doing it. Who else could it have been? He heard a little whine from the pantry door. Poor Hank was sitting there waiting for his breakfast. Matt felt like shit for forgetting. "Sorry, Hankapotamas. I didn't mean to forget you." Matt went over and opened the large garbage-sized Tupperware dog food container and threw three scoops of dog food in Hank's bowl. He put it on the floor, and Hank devoured it in a second. He loved his food, and it proved great for him as he looked amazing. So many Labs put on a lot of weight, but Hank was in great shape and his coat was beautiful.

Alice nodded toward Hank. "When I couldn't get you last night, I thought you might have stayed in the city and tied one on, so I came over and fed him at six and let him out."

Matt shot a look at Hank. "You shit, you ate twice last night, huh?" Hank knew the question was intended for him, and he moved his head side to side not understanding. No wonder he was in the bed when Matt got home. He already had his dinner. Matt went over and opened the back door, and Hank shot out into the backyard trying to track down the squirrels. He was always on squirrel patrol. He never caught one but had been close several times. He wasn't twenty feet, and he was going to the bathroom in the pine straw. "Thank you so much for doing that, Alice. That was very sweet of you. I can't go into it right now, but I got the news at the office, and I was in a panic when I got off the train last night that she might have taken him with her. I was so relieved when I got home, and he was still here." He sat back down at the bar in shock. "I just can't believe she left us."

Alice placed a hand on Matt's shoulder, then got up and started to head to the door. She wanted a lot of information, and she would end up prying it out of him, but it was Saturday, her biggest day of the week as a realtor. "I have an open house now, so I have to go. As a three-time failure at marriage, I can say you need to move swiftly. Cancel all the credit cards and depending on how the bank wants to handle it shut down your accounts and reopen them. I know you're hurting, but you need to take steps to remove her from you financially, so that you are covered. The pain is going to be much worse if she hits your accounts as well." Matt hadn't even considered any of that, and under the circumstances he probably should have.

"Why don't you come over for dinner tonight?"

He nodded. "I will think about it," Matt said, which was a lie, and she knew it. There was no way in the condition he was in that he was going to be subjected to her prying tonight. He was probably going to do round two of wine and forget, but this time with takeout from Alberto's.

"Just remember things will get better. From here, they just take time. Right now, you are at the bottom. It took me three times to find my right man," Alice said as she opened the door and stepped outside.

"I'll take that under consideration."

She closed the door.

7

With a five-mile head-clearing walk with Hank under his belt, Matt thought he had a plan of action. He emerged from the bathroom after showering to find Hank crashed out on the bed with his head on the pillows. He was in recovery sleep mode after the walk. Matt knew that Beth took him a couple of times a day but wasn't sure how far. Hanks eye popped open for a second and immediately closed. Matt needed to wash the sheets—they smelled like Beth—was he ready for that? He wasn't, and he knew it. He dressed in jeans and a sweater and headed to the garage. As he opened the door, he was shocked to find both cars there, and then it hit him. Beth wouldn't need a car. She would be in the city in the building that he worked in, and if she went anywhere, it would be with a driver. The anger rose in him. He hated her fucking car, and everything that it now stood for.

Beth had insisted on getting a 5 series BMW, which they fought about. They had the Jeep, which Matt had purchased used when he was in high school. It had 235K miles on it, but it still ran. She could have just driven it, or they could have traded it for something practical because they would still need something for the snow, but "no," she had to have it. It was nice, and it drove really well, but now it was a symbol of what Beth needed and that was more. It was always more no matter what they had. No matter what he provided for her. They had eventually compromised as they leased it versus purchasing it.

He pulled his keys off the wall rack where they stayed all the time because he only drove on the weekends. There was never time during the week. He noticed that Beth had left hers there as well, and his heart stabbed with pain again. She was really gone and not coming back. He grabbed her keys, locked the house and climbed into the BMW. The plan had now changed.

After ten miles in traffic, which seemed like an eternity, Matt pulled into the BMW dealership. He popped out of the car and headed inside. He was on a mission. A young and very ambitious salesmen flew out of his cubicle and headed toward Matt. Matt threw the keys for the BMW to him when he got close. The salesmen, not expecting them, fumbled them on the floor. "It's yours now," Matt said as he spun and headed for the door.

The fumbling salesmen retrieving the keys mumbled, "I don't think I understand."

"It's a lease. It's yours now. I don't want it," Matt yelled back as he headed to the door.

"What about payment options? A new lease? Aren't you interested in buying it out?"

"No, I am not interested in any options. Bill me for what's left which should only be a few months."

"You need to sign paperwork!" he yelled.

"Email it to me!" That statement caught Matt flat footed when it came out of his mouth. That email address would be his work, which would just sit in his inbox. He would call them tomorrow after setting up a new Gmail account.

The cold air blasted him as he exited the dealership. How much longer would the winter last, and he would finally get to see the sun again? Car was gone… now what? Another coffee. Matt walked up what was dealership row Ford, Chevy, Nissan, GMC, and Infiniti. He had planned to Uber, but he could see the mixed-use development at the top of the road, and there was a Starbucks in there. It was a distance, but too short to call an Uber for, and honestly, he hadn't downloaded the app on his new phone, which had been step one of the morning—get a new phone.

The last dealership on the right was the GMC before the mixed-use, and he was getting cold. He had always wanted a Sierra truck, but that was below Beth's standards. Trucks equaled the Midwest, and she had left that life behind in her review mirror. BMW was her plan, and with him on the train all the time, it made no sense for him to get a truck. In the window of the dealership was sign: *any trade $5,000 on a new vehicle*. His twenty-year-old Jeep with 235K miles on it wasn't worth two nickels, and Beth would kill him. Beth was gone. Fuck Beth. He made an immediate right and walked into the dealership.

A young girl was standing with a few other salespeople in the corner and spotted Matt immediately as he walked in. Before the other salespeople could react, she was gone. "Hello, my name is Nicki. What brings you in today, a new car, truck, or SUV?"

Matt smiled, and he could see that she was a very good salesperson. "I am looking for a new Sierra and based on how I am feeling today, if you make the price right, I could make a bad decision and buy one."

Nicki immediately responded, "Well, let's work on that bad decision." She cradled her arm in his and walked him into the showroom. On the showroom floor was a 1500, and it looked amazing with light leather interior. "So here is a beauty, metallic gray, but don't pay any attention to the price as this one is loaded to the gills with all the options. We have many others that are much less expensive than this. We just need to figure out what's important from an option standpoint and go with that." She spent literally twenty minutes going over navigation, cell phone adaption, leather—heated and cooled—seats. Box carrier in the back with Wi-Fi and the list went on and on. Finally, he stopped her as it was becoming a little overwhelming.

"How much for this one?" Matt asked.

Nicki paused as she was worried that he would run away. "Well, it's $67,000, but again this is the loaded version."

Matt exhaled. "Nicki, go tell the manager that you have someone out here who is not stable right now and could make a bad decision if he can get a decent price on this one. Also tell him I'm not going to go back and forth all day. I need his best price, and I'm taking you up on the $5K for a trade in on my Jeep."

A big smile came across her face, and she was gone.

8

"Style, Pam Johnson is in the Bay conference room." Hope sashayed across Style's office, and he put his coffee down. Hope was tall, thin, blonde and beautiful. How many times had he slept with her? He was thinking it was at least four or five times, the last time being when she got back from her honeymoon. He watched her as she left. She was wearing a relatively see-through white blouse, which was clear enough he could see her bra underneath. Her skirt was long and form-fitting, and she had on some killer high heels. She looked over her shoulder and checked to make sure he was checking her out as she left, and he just smiled.

They had an arrangement. She did a decent job but not great, and she knew that. She took way too much time off, he let her get away with it, and he paid her way too much money and allotted her a clothing allowance, which no one knew about. In exchange, he would get a blow job about once a week in his office, and when she had too much to drink at a random Thursday happy hour, she would give in and let him screw her. Coincidentally, the next day she would call in sick, which meant she wanted a long weekend with her new husband. Luckily, they were right back at it after her return. Style had never met the guy, which Hope never wanted to happen. He heard he was in real estate, which in the San Francisco market meant big money.

"I think I'm going to let that stupid bitch stew for a while. What a mess. Tell her I'm in a deposition and will be twenty minutes."

"Right?" Hope said sarcastically. "Her file is on the left side of your desk."

"Thanks." He picked up the file and read over it. Pam Johnson was on the board of his father's company Winfield International, and he had done a prenup for her at his father's request eighteen months ago. She was a brilliant business person in her own right, and that and her working relationship with her father got her on the board. Pam was fifty-five, in great shape physically, and she had the best plastic surgeon in the city on speed dial. She was already a pretty lady but was determined that ongoing maintenance was key. Spin class, Pilates, and Botox were the norm. When she came to him last year, he told her in a nice way that it was fine to bang the thirty-year-old pool guy aka aspiring actor, hell even live with him, but it was another thing to marry him. She was having none of it. She was in love. Luckily Style's father insisted on the prenup; she relented, and the pool boy finally signed with a $1M out cap unless there was infidelity.

Pam had been on a business trip that ended early and came home to find pool boy/step daddy banging her twenty-two-year-old daughter who was home for the summer from college unbelievably by the pool. A huge mess. Mother and daughter not speaking. Pam's ex-husband incensed at Pam and his daughter, and both of them worrying he was going to hunt pool boy/step daddy down and kill him. Style thumbed through everything, and the prenup was solid. Pool boy would have gotten his million up until two weeks ago because her daughter wouldn't corroborate the by-the-pool banging, so it was pool boy's word against Pam's, but that all changed last week. Style actually had video, which Pam would never see but him and the partners watched several times, of Pam's daughter now back at college, screwing pool boy/step daddy on his car.

Pam's daughter was the spitting image of Pam but a younger version, and pool boy was taking it to her, and she was all in. He had her top open with all her glory out and was bent over the back of the car getting it from behind. She was quite noisy. They took the video and converted it to pictures for Pam's sake, so now pool boy was not going to get a cent. Her relationship with her daughter was irrevocably damaged.

Style got up and grabbed the files and headed to the door to meet Pam in the conference room. He caught his image in the mirror and smiled. He looked amazing in his vibrant Italian-cut, blue pinstripe suit, pink pocket square, and light blue shirt with a little pink in it as well.

William Harrison Bridgeway had been known as Style since his fifth birthday. That day, his parents had rented out the entire Aquarium of the Bay for his party, which is really something considering it fell on a Saturday and all his friends from school and extended family were coming for him. His mother laid out his clothes, and he refused to wear any of them because it did not match a look he was going for. He basically sat down and refused to get dressed. They finally relented and stopped on the way to let him pick his own clothes from a store for the party making them late. His father, of course, explained the delay when they arrived pretty pissed and flustered, and his grandfather turned to him and said, "Well aren't you Mr. Style." Just like that, from that day on he was Style.

His brown wingtips shone vibrantly as he strolled out of the office and saw Hope filing a nail at her desk. She, of course, gave him that knowing smile.

"Who has the filing for the Bennet divorce?" Style asked.

"Sarah is working on it."

"Blonde Sarah or Brunette Sarah?"

"Brunette Sarah, Sarah Marshal."

Style grimaced. "Well, that's fantastic," he said, which of course meant the opposite. Style grabbed the elevator and went down to the 30th floor where the talent pool lived in cubicle city. It was filled with fresh-out-of-law-school-attorney wannabes and, of course, the paralegals. The partners upstairs, mostly all men, referred to the 30th floor as the talent pool where they brought in not necessarily the best in the class but certainly the best-looking in class in regards to the women. The partners worked them into the ground and preyed upon them for sex. It was no secret to the partners' wives. They all knew the game, but they lived in nice houses and drove nice cars. The worst-case scenario is that one of the talent pool would move from the one-night-stand or mistress to taking their husband, but at that point, they would divorce and get half.

The first wives never got a prenup because they married for love. The second wives were never that lucky, so they were locked into their marriages almost all of which came from the talent pool, and they knew what they signed up for. They got sued from time to time for sexual harassment, but the partners hired a pit bull female director for Human Resources, and she was a terror to anyone who disturbed the frat house of Thompson, Peels, and Bridgeway. She was a lesbian, and she preyed on the talent pool worse than the partners.

When Style rolled out of the elevator the talent pool scurried. Style on the 30th was bad. Brunette Sarah had made the job-killing mistake a month ago of turning down Style's advances at the almost mandatory Thursday night happy hour at Bensons, the bar in their building. He had been on the warpath with her ever since. He first buried her with work and then chastised her for not getting everything done. He was going to run her out of the firm.

She saw him coming, and her heart sank. As he walked up, she pulled the top of her blouse closed with one hand and smiled. He was such a slime ball in a very expensive suit. His tone was curt and cutting when he asked, "Where is the Bennett filing?"

"I'm sorry Mr. Bridgeway. I just got it yesterday. It should be ready by noon tomorrow."

"Noon tomorrow is not good enough," he roared loud enough for everyone to hear. "Do not leave here until you get it done and put it on my desk, so I have it first thing in the morning." He spun and headed back toward the elevator. When the doors closed, Sarah was sobbing. She couldn't take it anymore. He had been so nice when she started promising to mentor her, but after Benson's when she took his hand off her side all that changed. She would have to move back home to pay the bills, but she couldn't do this anymore. How would she explain that she barely made it six months at her first firm?

Sue, who had the desk next to her, tried to comfort her. "You should have just slept with him; it would have been much easier. Usually after you sleep with them the first time, they leave you alone." Sue, of course, was sleeping with a partner on a normal basis, and she hated him, but she had job security and got regular raises.

"I can't," Sarah whispered. Her husband was her high school sweetheart, and she would never cheat on him. She got up, gathered her things and left the building not planning to ever return. Style's mission was accomplished.

9

Matt watched as his Jeep, his very first car, rolled out of his driveway with Nicki at the wheel and her manager next to her as the escort. There was a puff of smoke as the engine had ignited, but it started immediately and didn't miss a beat. With two accidents on its record from Matt's years in high school and 235K miles on the odometer, it was worth almost nothing, but today at Bill Travelers GMC, it had been worth $5,000 sight unseen. There was a pang in his heart as they drove away, but the manager had a fifteen-year-old son and decided immediately upon seeing it that they would rebuild the engine together, and it would be his first car, which was comforting.

There, of course, had been back-and-forth in the showroom no matter what Matt had told Nicki, but shortly after he started to leave after the first offer, she stopped him. The manager came out. They talked shortly. Matt was paying cash, and it was over in a matter of seconds. The paperwork lasted another hour but was efficient. When the BS was over, he got it for $62K, $57K out-of-pocket with his trade in, because it was the end of the month and they needed to move some cars. The glass doors of Bill Travelers GMC floor were opened, and the cold March air poured in. His silver beauty roared to life as Nicki's manager drove it out of the showroom where outside he relinquished control, and Matt got behind of the wheel of his very first new car. The smell of the dove gray leather and all the tech was overwhelming. It rode as good as Beth's BMW, and he trucked his way back home getting an in-service all the way from Nicki on how to take advantage of all his new 4x4 Sierra loaded to the gills with everything technology had to offer.

Instead of going inside, Matt climbed back into the truck as he had more to do. Off to the bank to close the accounts to reopen them only in his name and to cancel all the cards. He really believed with where Beth was as the now-matriarch of the Waverman tower that she didn't need money anymore, but removing her from the accounts made him feel good. There was a hole in his chest that wasn't going to go away anytime soon, but getting the truck that he always wanted and that Beth had adamantly been against was a nice start. He needed to be busy, and checking off the list in his head was a way to stay busy.

10

Style rolled into the conference room and sat down at the table next to Pam Johnson. She looked beautiful as always but rattled. The sun was overhead, and the city of San Francisco lay below them with the bay visible in the distance. It was a beautiful conference room used to inspire confidence in the firm with the wealthiest of clients, and today he had earned his money saving Pam's Pilates-firm ass. It was going to be expensive, but not nearly the damage it would have been without the prenup/clause and just the general "what the fuck are you thinking" let's put some terms around this relationship. His father had called that morning to get the update, which of course was unethical for Style to provide with lawyer/client confidentiality, but whatever. He laid it out for him, and there would be a $50,000 legal bill heading her way. In other words, pool boy/step daddy wasn't getting shit, and Style had helped his father out tremendously, which is always a good thing.

He rested his arm on her shoulder, and she began to cry. "Pam, I am so sorry that you are having to go through this."

"I am so stupid," she muttered. *Yes*, Style thought, *you are stupid.*

"It happens to the best of us, and I can assure you, unfortunately I see it a lot." Style was the most terrifying or loved man in San Francisco, depending on which side of the table you sat on for your prenup or divorce. He had gone to law school as preparation for one day taking over his father's company. When he graduated, his father wanted him to practice on his own and make a name for himself, and now he was the most feared divorce lawyer in the city. Probably not daddy's idea of making a name, but he loved his job. He was a partner now, and in his world, money wasn't really an object. Running his father's company would now be totally alien to him. He was on his own path, and it was always nice to be in good graces with the old man.

"So, we have some good news. We now have pictures of him that will enact the infidelity clause so—" Before he could finish, she finished for him.

"He will get nothing?" She looked up, her eyes puffy.

"Correct, nothing," Style said, patting the envelope with the pictures. "Do not open this. I will provide these to his attorney tomorrow, and this will be over. The pictures are egregious, and there is no doubt."

"That asshole will be penniless. Well, that makes me happy. I just can't believe another woman so soon. You would think some common sense." With that, Style realized that she had jumped to the conclusion there was another woman other than her daughter. Ugh. The door of the conference burst open, and it was Hope. There was real fear in her eyes.

"Style, I am so sorry. There is an emergency."

He looked at her inquisitively, and she gave him a look that got him to his feet. "Pam, I am so sorry; I will be right back." When they entered hall, Style asked "What?" As soon as the door closed, they heard Pam wailing, and he turned to look. Pam had opened the pictures, and she was looking at her daughter leaned over the Aston Martin DB9 convertible that she had bought for pool boy with her skirt up and him entering her from behind. Style shook his head looking at Hope. "You tell them to never open the pictures, and then they do. Fuck." They always want to know who the other person is. They can't help themselves.

"Style, Kyle just called. It's your wife. She's in the hospital. She had a bad car accident."

Style looked at his watch as it was almost noon. Alexandra was supposed to go to her meeting, which was a private underground drug user outpatient meeting for the rich and famous, and then she was supposed to be going to lunch with the partners' wives. "How bad is it? Is she okay? Are others hurt?"

"Kyle said she ran a light and got clipped by an oncoming SUV with a family in it, then jumped a curb and hit a building. He said the family was shook up and taken to the same hospital, but that it was just for insurance purposes to get it on the record, and they would be fine. There definitely will be a lawsuit. She's at San Francisco General."

"Alexandra, what you have done?" Style whispered.

Hope continued, "The police on site, when they found out who she was, called Kyle. He said to tell you he's all over it, and he would meet you at the hospital." Kyle was the firm's lead investigator and ex-San Francisco PD detective for thirty years. He was also the one who somehow got the video on pool boy.

"Call my car and have it waiting downstairs. Go to my office and pack my briefcase with my laptop and the files on top of my desk. Then, meet me at the elevator. I will work from the hospital. Let the partners know where I am." And with that, he spun and went back into the conference room where Pam was sobbing over the numerous pictures she now had spread out on the table.

"Pam, I am so sorry. I asked you not to open it up. I have a—"

She turned and looked at him, enraged, tears of makeup streaming down her face. "When were these taken?" tapping on the picture. In the picture under her index finger, you could clearly see pool boy's face along with her daughter, his DB9 and his actual vanity tag DB9JDM, which meant DB9 and his initials.

"Pam."

"I need to know this!" she screamed.

"Yesterday, Pam. We followed him up to her college in hills, and she met him outside her dorm. She willfully got into the car and went to a secluded part of the state park, and that is where this was taken."

"Where is he now?" This was spinning out of control quickly.

"They have checked into a hotel up there somewhere." Style knew, but there was no way he was telling her where.

Pam started breathing uncontrollably. "His cards have all been turned off..." and then it hit her. "I am paying for this!" She pointed to the pictures, picked up the phone, and called American Express. When the automated service picked up, she pounded on the zero over and over until a live person picked up the phone. She quickly provided her security information and asked where the last place her daughter had used her card. Style watched in horror as she took down the name and address of the hotel that he knew they were in fact staying at right now. Then she canceled her daughter's card. "If my daughter calls and wants to know why her card is not working, please tell her that her fucking mother turned it off!"

"Yes, ma'am. I will put that in the notes."

"Thank you!" She was screaming.

"Pam—" Style started. She spun and put her finger in the air toward him to silence him. She dialed away on her phone.

"Jack, she lied to us, and they are seeing each other. In fact, they are holed up in a hotel in the mountains on my credit card!" Inexplicably, she gave the address of the hotel to her enraged ex-husband, who was now going to probably kill pool boy.

Style had to get out of the room and put this fire out. "Pam, I am sorry, but my wife's been in a car accident, and I have to go to the hospital. I will call his attorney this afternoon, and this will be over very quickly."

"Oh, Style, I am so sorry." He gathered up the pictures and the files and headed out of the room.

"Hope will be here in just a few minutes to show you out and again this will be over this afternoon. I will call you." She grabbed his arm and hugged him.

"Thank you for this. I am going to tell your father what an incredible attorney you are. You saved me on the front and back of this mess." She was correct. California was no fault, so with no prenup, pool boy and her daughter could have potentially shacked up together with half her assets. Totally ludicrous.

Out of the fire, Style headed toward the elevator. Hope was there with his briefcase and his coat.

"Hope, call Kyle and tell him that Pam's ex is heading to pool boy's and his daughter's hotel room right now. We have to anonymously get that information to them to get them out of there or we are going to be dealing with, no shit, assault or murder charges, and as much as I want the business, I don't want that business."

"How?"

"Don't ask, just do it. This is spinning out of control. Tell him now, immediately, Hope, and then have him text me when it's done, and they are out of harm's way. We maybe have an hour before he could get there." The elevator opened, and he was gone.

Normally Style would take the attractive lady clients out to lunch to celebrate and to comfort them on a day like this but not today. Those who he was attracted to, he would take to Umberto's, which was in the Grand Hotel near the market. If lunch went well, they would end up in a room upstairs for a celebratory romp. It was almost always the case with the younger wife marrying older man scenario, and they took them to the cleaners. They were always ready for a romp to celebrate their newfound wealth and independence. It tended to be 50/50 for those first wives who were actually hurt with the divorce. Some would want revenge sex, and others were just broken. There were always signs during conversation at the restaurant, and Style was… well, a pro now. The women would start to probe his marriage to which he would lie and say that they were separated. "Trying to figure it out." There were always buying signs.

The elevator opened, and Style walked across the lobby. His phone dinged, and it was Kyle in his cryptic way.

"They know and are moving." Phones could always be dumped, so ALL communications were kept very cryptic.

"Thank God." He saw Peter his driver standing in front of the car with the door open. He slid in, pulled out his phone, and dialed Kim Stoddle, the second most feared divorce attorney in San Francisco. She picked up almost immediately and cooed on the phone. She was forty, pretty, and terrifying, and well, they had a relationship occasionally as well.

"Style, do you have some good news for me. When am I getting the check?"

"Bad news, Kim, we got him with the daughter in the woods having sex. The pics are dead to rights, and they even have his vanity license in them. Their faces are very clear. Sorry girl, it's a bad day for your team."

"Wow, he is such an idiot," She exclaimed with disdain. "I told him to stay the hell away from her until this was over."

"Yep, I'm beginning to think they had plans together?" he questioned.

"Yeah, well now that this is pretty much over. They are in love."

"Well, that's fantastic."

"Yep."

"Sorry girl. Hope will have the pictures messengered over for your viewing this afternoon. We will see how much she loves him after Mom just had her credit cards turned off and him having no money. This is going to be a hard fall for her. Platinum spoon up her ass her entire life."

"That, Style, is an understatement. She will probably sue her parents for abandonment or something."

"I don't want that case with the pics we have."

"Neither do I. Have them sent over. I will call the idiot."

You better hurry—he is on the run.

11

Matt rode down the street with the new car smell washing over him. He had almost definitely made a mistake with the truck, but he didn't care. Beth had forbidden it, and today that was reason enough. What the hell was he going to do with a truck if he continued to work in the city. Even if he didn't go back to Waverman, he would still be in the city. The house in the suburbs made no sense at all anymore. The ninety-minute commute each way was just stupid and with Hank—what was he going to do with Hank in the city? It would be morning and evening walks in Central Park, and he would definitely get a dog walking service for at least once during the day. His new truck would end up garaged in New Jersey for a fortune, but at this point he didn't care. The dreams of kids with Beth in the country and the time spent together as a family were all gone. This was his new normal, and it was like a dark cloud over him. Everything that he thought had been changed in the matter of twenty-four hours.

His new phone was on the truck's console wirelessly charging away. It was completely downloaded now after he picked it up at the AT&T store after what looked to be a twelve-year-old clerk had restored his data. Waverman had his old phone, but with the cloud, he had all the data back. His company email all pulled into his new phone, along with his contacts, but his email address had been suspended at Waverman. All emails that went into it delivered a leave of absence notice for the next sixty days and to call or email King

George with any pressing issues that couldn't wait. Matt pressed the phone button on the steering wheel, "Call Alex Springs." The truck's female voice came back to him, "*Calling Alex Springs please hold.*" The phone could be seen trying to connect on the GPS, and then began to ring.

"Waverman Investing, Alex Springs, how can I assist you?" He sounded so rigid it made Matt smile.

"Alex, you sound pretty professional. How's your day going?"

"Well, it kind of sucks with you not being here, really. You okay?"

"I'll be fine. Sixty days out of the rat race might be good for me."

"Probably, but I am not sure it's going to be good for us. King George had a meeting this morning about the FTC investigation and how we are all supposed to be cooperating with it. I'm not really sure what this is all about."

"Honestly, Alex neither am I," Matt said, lying, "but it is what it is, and just tell everyone to be completely honest. There's nothing for them to find."

"Okay."

"You now have my new cell in case of an emergency, but don't call unless it's real. It could be construed as collaborating stories or something stupid like that to the FTC. Give this number to King George and no one else."

"Understood. See you in sixty days?"

"Sure," Matt said to the question and then hung up. Could he really go back to Waverman? His ego was crushed.

Dark was descending outside. During the winter, the sun went down almost immediately at five. It was very depressing. He pulled the big truck into the driveway and pressed the button on the mirror. The garage door opened and exposed, probably for the very first time that Matt had ever seen it, an empty garage with no cars in it. A pretty visible oil stain was on the floor from where the old Jeep had been. Matt pulled the massive truck right into the very middle and then shut the door behind him killing the engine. The inside of the truck was still alive with lights and sounds waiting for him to open the door and kill the interior tech, but he just sat there dreading going in his and Beth's home that they made together.

He again clicked the phone button on the steering wheel, "Call Amber."

"*Calling Amber Heard.*" The phone on the dash paused a few minutes longer, and then it finally started to ring. A very calming and loving voice picked up the phone.

"Hello?" The sound of Matt's sister and only sibling made him extremely emotional.

"Amber."

"Matt? Is this a new number?"

"Yeah, it's me. You will want to save it. How are you guys?"

"We are doing great. The weather seems to be breaking a little, so Steven can start on his list of projects before spring."

"That's awesome. Are you going to be home?" Matt cut right to the chase.

"Matt, we have two babies and a farm to keep up. We're always home."

"Can I come to see you guys?"

"Matt, baby, this is your farm as well. We would love to see you." He could hear the concern in her voice. If he was calling to come for a visit in March, something was amiss, she knew it. He hadn't looked up from work in almost a decade. They talked almost every week, and occasionally they would come up, or he would go there but not very often and not in the winter.

"Should we expect Beth with you as well?"

"No," he almost whispered.

"Matty, are you all right? You've got me worried." His voice broke when he spoke up, and he sniffled and then went to silence. "Are you going to talk to me, Matt? Honey, please talk to me."

"I can't right now, Amber. I just can't."

"Okay. It's all right. When can we expect you? Do we need to pick you up in Omaha?"

"Probably two days unless I hit weather. I'm driving and will text you when I get an ETA."

"You better. You have me worried. We will make up your room, and I'll have Steven pull some good steaks out and some roasts. We will do it up, okay?"

"Okay, see you soon." He hung up the phone and burst into tears, sobbing. Amber had that effect on him. He loved her so much. Their parents had died in a car crash a few years after Matt got out of college. Her being the older sister by two years and him being new at Waverman, she had left Kansas City and had gone home to the ranch in Nebraska City where they grew up to sell it, but never ended up leaving.

12

The doors of the ER opened, and Style rolled through them like he owned the place in all his fineness, which drew quite a bit of attention. Kyle was waiting on him and motioned him back to a door manned by a security guard. When the guard saw Kyle, he gave him a head nod and then opened the door. Style wasn't sure there was a single person in San Francisco who didn't know Kyle or didn't owe Kyle a favor. His hire by the firm was money.

The ER was a zoo as one of the only level-one trauma centers in the city, and because of that, it caught all the shit from car accidents, drug overdoses to gunshot wounds. The real doctors and wannabe doctor attendants (children, really) were everywhere along with nurses and orderlies. When they got almost to the end, Style could see a police officer outside the door of room 12, which was opened but the curtain in the room was pulled closed. They slowed, and Kyle motioned to Style. "Officer, this is her husband."

The officer nodded and motioned to Style's laptop bag. "That has to stay with me, and I'm going to need to pat you down. Please pull up your jacket." Style lifted his jacket up and the officer began to pat Style down to his ankles.

"Officer this bag has legal files in it and my laptop." Style opened to show him.

The officer waved him off. "Do you want to go in?"

Kyle interceded, "He does, and we will leave his bag with you, understanding you are not leaving."

"Can't leave."

"Got it." Kyle took Style's bag and put it at the officer's feet and motioned Style in.

When they went through the curtain, Style froze, "Oh my God." Alexandra was laying on a stretcher in a cloth gown. Her face was almost completely black and blue from the accident. "Jesus, Alexandra! What the fuck have you done?" Style whispered and moved to the side of the bed where she was handcuffed. There was blood all over the stretcher around her head showing the recently stopped the bleeding.

Kyle motioned to the cuffs. "She's under arrest for DUI. According to the doctor, she was spinning emotionally out of control when they brought her in, and she has been sedated for her own protection. The air bags did all of this," he said, motioning to her face.

"Drugs?" Style asked.

Kyle moved the other side of the bed and lifted her arm. There was a needle hole there. Style mouthed the word *NO*.

"Heroin?" Style asked.

"Actually, no, but just as bad. Fentanyl. Ten times more powerful than morphine. Mass produced now by the Chinese and shipped to Mexico where the cartels buy it and move it illegally across the border."

"Is she going to be okay?"

"Remarkably they have run all the tests, and she is. Her nose is cracked but not broken. The swelling will go down in a few weeks. She was probably not even conscious when the car hit the building, which is why she will be sore but walk away. Thankfully there was enough noise during the accident that it gave the pedestrians enough warning to scatter when she went barreling into the building. The Jag is a total loss, and the building, although a ton of broken glass, is unscathed. I am sure there will be a hell of a bill for all of it not including the other car involved."

Style walked out of the room into the hallway and picked up his bag and started to head to the exit.

"Where are you going?"

Style pointed toward her room searching for the words. "I can't do this, Kyle. I have been dealing with this shit for a year now, and I can't do this. Call Will in Trial and get him to take this on. He owes me. You stay with her until her parents get here. We have got to get her into an inpatient treatment program, and I don't care how much it costs, but after that, I'm done." Style walked out of the ER and got into his waiting car.

He pulled his cell phone out of his pocket and dialed a number. The driver could hear a man pick up on the other end of the line. "Ben, it's Style. Alexandra is in the hospital under arrest for DUI. She is at..."

13

Hank in all his chocolatiness was bouncing from one end of the kitchen to the other because it was again nugget time. Matt usually fed him in the morning on his way out the door and Beth had evening shift because he got home at 7:30 on a good night. It was now just the two of them, and Hank was busting a move to nugget time, a play on the classic song. Matt was singing and Hank was reveling in it, dancing all over the kitchen. “It’s Nugget time do, do, do, do.” Matt was really not in a singing mood, but it was how Hank got fed, and he couldn’t get enough of it. The custom Lab dog food mix hit the bowl and the dancing stopped as Hank engulfed his dinner and then went to find a toilet for a drink.

Hank, as with many dogs, enjoyed the freshness of an open toilet to drink out of versus a bowl of water. It always grossed Beth out when Hank did it, but Matt found an article on how the grossest things around were gas pumps, seconded only by peoples’ desks at work for filth. Toilets—because of the way they were designed and they were cleaned weekly and flushed often—fell so far down the list. They were only measured because people thought they might be gross. Not even close. Flushing and leaving the lid up became the norm, and they eventually stopped putting down a water bowl because he would never drink out of it.

The doorbell rang, and Matt was instantly starving and looking forward to his DoorDash from Giovanni’s. Had he eaten today? Nope, shit. He could not stomach going to Giovanni's by himself and be expected to answer questions on where Beth was. At this point he could barely stand being in the house. Beth was everywhere. He was going to finish packing after dinner, get a decent night's sleep with the aid of some wine, and get the hell out of there. As he walked out of the kitchen to get the door, Hank roared past him barking insanely and then throwing his body at the door. It was not DoorDash, though. It was Alice again with a bag in her hand. More questioning. Out of a place of concern and love, but there would certainly be more.

"Hey there. How was your day?" Matt asked as he opened the door.

"Sold another house. Things are really picking up. How are you and how was your day?" And there it was, cut to the chase. The questioning would now begin. Matt motioned her to the kitchen with Hank throwing his body against her for attention. She was loving all over him and that made Hank smile. "I have some dinner for you."

"Thanks, Alice, that's very kind. I have DoorDash on the way, but let me put this in the fridge for tomorrow." She seated herself at the bar and looked at him.

"How are you?"

"Interesting day. Hank and I walked our legs off this morning, and then I went and ran some errands." He pulled the phone out of his pocket and put it on the counter motioning to it. "I now have a phone, which I haven't owned a personal one in a decade, and canceled Beth's at the same time, so she might have had an interesting day as well." Alice smiled at that. Matt picked his phone up and sent Alice his contact. "Now you have my number so that you can call—"

"Before I come over," she cut him off, smiling.

"Well… yes." He forced a smile.

"What else did you do? Did you go to the bank?"

"That was crazy easy. I forgot all the accounts are in my name, so I didn't have to shut them down. I just removed her from them and turned off all the cards." With Matt having the finance degree, he had handled all the financial stuff in their life. "I have a lot more to do like removing her from my life insurance, etc. and that takes stuff coming snail mail, but the only thing outstanding really is the house, which we are both on."

"What about the cars?"

Matt motioned to the door from the kitchen that exited into the garage, and Alice got up to follow him. He opened the door and revealed his massive new truck. "She had a lease on her car which was in my name, and the Jeep was mine from high school.

"So, you dumped both of them and bought a truck?" Alice's voice rose almost incredulous. "You have had a big day."

Matt smiled. "A new truck. Beth would hate it. She forbade me from buying one for years. It's awesome, and it has everything."

Alice shook her head. "Well, it's beautiful for a truck. Not sure what you're going to do with it other than go back and forth to the store in Connecticut."

Matt headed back into the kitchen quietly, and she followed him.

"I'm leaving for a while, Alice. I can't stay here right now. I have some time off from work, and I can get away. Taking a leave of absence." Then it popped into his head what Amber had said. "I am going to see Amber and her husband in Nebraska City. Steven needs a hand to get the ranch ready for spring planting, so this works. I'm not really sure when I will be back, but it will be good to see them, and Hank will love being on the ranch."

The doorbell rang, and Hank went ape shit again. Matt motioned Alice toward the door.

"When are you leaving?" She frowned.

"First thing in the morning."

"When will you be back?"

"I'm not sure, but you have my number, and we can talk and text."

She grabbed her coat. Matt hugged her and opened the door. She slid past the DoorDash guy, and Matt grabbed his dinner from his hand. It smelled great, and his stomach leapt.

14

The phone alarm went off promptly at 4:30 A.M. with a royal commencement theme that would have normally sent Matt charging off to conquer his day, but not today. Matt turned over and could immediately smell Beth on his pillow. He wasn't sure if it was the perfume she used or if it was the lotion she put on before bed, but the aroma filled the air, and he was heartsick all over again. His soul hurt. Day two of no Beth, and as he ran it over and over in his head, he just couldn't make sense of it. Yes, Beth always wanted more, nicer things, a nicer car, nicer house, it was always more, but to do this? Matt had actually been late to work on their last day together, missing the train because Beth had gotten up with him that morning and insisted that he come back to bed for a quick romp, which turned into an all-out throw down. Parting gift? It all made no sense. She didn't love the old man. It was all about money and status. But all the lies?

Hank assumed his normal morning position in bed laying long ways against Matt's body on the other side with his head on Matt's pillow. He would start at the end of the bed on "Hanky's pillow" at bedtime, which is where he was supposed to stay, but by morning his full 90-pound body weight was crushed against Matt's body. Some mornings Matt would get up feeling like he had been in a car accident, but this morning he threw his arm across Hank and sighed. Hank immediately flipped on his back exposing his belly for a rub, which eventually led to him jumping out of the bed and heading to the toilet for a drink.

Matt followed and brushed his teeth, took his vitamins and then closed his dock kit and threw it into his open luggage on the floor. His laid out comfortable travel clothes were on the chair, a set of jeans with the beginning of holes in both knees, a soft T-shirt that he covered with a hoody, and then he threw on his worn Nebraska ball cap and tennis shoes. Having showered before bed he was ready to go. He wanted to get out before five to beat the traffic.

Hank nervously followed behind him, eyeing his every move. Hank was too smart. He learned early that luggage was a bad thing in which one or both of his owners were leaving him alone for some extended time. Matt brushed his head as he walked next to him almost knowing what he was thinking. "Not today, buddy, you're going with me." Hank turned his head trying to understand. As they went down the stairs, Hank was almost on top of him. Matt sang the customary "Nugget Time" song, which sent Hank into the throes of happiness, ending with him devouring his breakfast in under a minute. Matt took his bowl and rinsed it out and put it in Hank's backpack he'd packed the night before full of his toys, treats, and bones.

Hank headed toward the back door to do his business, and Matt let him out. He immediately busted out the door to patrol the perimeter of the yard to clear Connecticut of invaders like squirrels, birds, and raccoons.

Grabbing up their travel bags, Matt headed to the garage and threw them in the back of his beautiful, new silver truck, which had the rest of his luggage in there, including a cooler and a new bag of dog food for Hank. Fifty-eight days is a long time, so he didn't know what he would need. Would they stay with Amber and Steven for a while or travel or just come back home? There wasn't a plan right now, just running away from the memories. His loaded GMC came with a rolling lid on the back that he pulled to the end and locked. It was supposed to be waterproof, but only time would tell. Gravity was a bitch when it came to water. To be safe, he threw all the bags into garbage bags and sealed them up. A good rain shower should let him know if the cover was going to leak.

As he walked back into the house, he remotely cranked the truck from his keys to let it warm up thinking, *this is what bad asses do with a cool new truck*. He also clicked open the garage door letting the freezing last few days of March-Connecticut cold inside for proper ventilation. He secured his wallet from the basket at the door and his cell phone from the kitchen island, then opened the back door to let Hank inside. The Keurig cranked out two large cups of coffee he poured into his Jets tumbler. They were ready to go. He set the alarm, rubbed Hank on his head and opened the door. The alarm could be heard beeping in the background as he opened the back door of the truck.

Hank looked up at him with his sad face, asking his daddy for permission. "Let's go, buddy." At that, Hank threw himself only halfway in the truck. Somewhere along the way Matt had failed Hank, and his way of getting in a vehicle was literally half-assed. He would wait for Matt to grab his back legs, and then he would pull himself inside. In Hank's defense, the truck was much higher than the Jeep, but he did it in the Jeep as well. Hank was hassling in excitement that he was going with his daddy halfway in and then finally he was inside the truck. Matt covered the back seat with a dog cover he used in the Jeep, and on the floor he placed several blankets. Hank would have a grand ride.

As Matt got inside, the new car smell bathed all over him. Then the Bluetooth on his phone connected with the stereo, scaring the shit out of him as Hootie and the Blowfish picked up where they left off yesterday with "Rollin'."

"Some days you are sitting on top of the world,

some days you're stuck in a hole

Just let it all go.

Some things just look better in the rear view."

"Hanky, Darius is preaching to us. Let's get the fuck out of here," Matt said. Hank was beside him, resting his head on the console to get his ears rubbed.

The inside of the truck was lit up like a command center on a spaceship. He was never going to get rid of this truck. Backing out of the driveway onto the street, Matt watched the garage door close. It was 4:58 A.M., just in time to beat the traffic.

15

Amber just finished doing her auburn hair in the bathroom and headed back into their bedroom. Her hair now fell down her shoulders in ringlets. She left Steven downstairs feeding the kids, so she could get ready for work. Dawn was now six and in first grade at Gerald Ford Elementary, and Lucas was just now two and was a full terror at the Lutheran Church Day Care. Now that his walking had turned into running, he went around grabbing everything in sight and pulling things over.

She pulled on her sweater and size 6 jeans, which soon would be getting tight again, but today she was still fine. She loved her kids, but not what they had done to her body. A female infection turned into thirty days off the pill where they had to be careful. Then New Year's Eve ended with clothes being torn off in the back of a truck, resulting in what will be baby number three. Were married people with kids still supposed to have a torrid love affair? Steven was thrilled. He had better be because this was on the way; a third baby would happen, but this time, the plumbing was going to be turned off when they were in there. Another year of breast feeding—here we go again.

Lady, their black Lab, met her at the top of the stairs, and Amber stopped to sit for a minute with Lady. She must have come up to check on her. The stairs creaked as she walked down them in the old farmhouse, which was the only home she had ever known.

Steven was at the head of the table cleaning Lucas's face and pulling off the bib. Lucas saw Amber and his eyes lit up, "Mommy!" Amber's heart leapt, and with that she felt excitement for baby number three. Dawn turned from the sink where she was putting her bowl on the counter and turned and smiled. Her arms still barely able to get over the ledge of the counter.

Steven grabbed Lucas out of the highchair and walked over to her and kissed her good morning. It wasn't a peck, but a long, drawn-out needing kiss that made her head swim, and the area below her belly button burned to life. She gave in completely to his body as his gripped her butt and pulled her into him. An almost whisper escaped her as she said, "Good morning." She held his strong arm to steady herself until her head stopped swimming.

She stepped back from him to keep this from getting out of control. He was such a man. A real man, not what society had now turned men into. He was in one of his many pairs of roughed up, boot-cut work jeans. He wore his blue plaid shirt. His ice blue eyes popped this morning with that shirt, and his black curly hair was all over the place. It would soon be covered with a beanie or a ball cap depending on the weather and what he was doing that day on the ranch.

"Do me a favor today?" Amber asked

"Sure anything," he purred as his loving eyes cut into her.

She looked away. No time for that this morning. She cleared her throat. "Matt's sheets are in the washer, so sometime today please throw them in the dryer, and we need to clean up tonight. He will be here tomorrow evening or by midday the next."

"It's going to be good to see him." Steven and Matt hit it off the first time they met. Matt admired that Steven was a Marine who served in Iraq and Afghanistan, and Steven loved that Matt played for the Huskers and his technology knowledge, even as a rancher, frequently reaching out to Matt for IT questions and help. There was almost always a text stream going on between the two of them, and that made Amber very happy. The men in her life were close. She had tried with Beth, but her attempts were met with one-word responses. Unfortunately, Steven and Amber became what Beth was running away from in Nebraska, and Amber thought Beth was probably running from babies too. They never saw her unless they went to Connecticut, and that all ceased with baby number two. She never came back to Nebraska with Matt, so his visits became shorter and less frequent. Beth was driving a wedge between Amber and Matt, and Amber struggled with how to stop it. He was coming home now, and as excited as she was to see him, she was worried. He sounded bad, and it kept her up last night. She stared at the celling listening to the wind whine against the windows and listening to Steven's heavy breathing next to her in bed. She had to find a way to help Matt. That's what she did for a living.

Dr. Amber Heard majored in psychology at Kansas State, and went all the way to become a full psychiatrist. She had the college loans to prove it. She left the ranch for good while Matt was in high school never to return except for holidays. She wanted no part of that hard life. Her plan wasn't necessarily God's plan.

After hanging out her shingle in Kansas City after graduation, she began to get referrals for her work. It wasn't long before she had clients in the city. She was well on her way to making a life for herself there when it happened. The Sheriff in Nebraska City left a message for her on her machine one day while she was refereeing a marriage that led to infidelity. When she called back, her heart sank.

Her parents had gone into town for supplies and stayed a little late. On the way home, the freezing rain led to black ice and her father, who was notorious for driving too fast, flipped the old F150. They were killed instantly. Amber believed they died holding hands. The old F150 had a long seat, and even when they were alone in the truck, her mother sat right next to her father in the middle, and they would hold hands.

Matt and Beth came home and met Amber. They buried their parents that weekend in the Lutheran Church graveyard next to each other. When they met with the bank, their parents weren't in debt, which was a huge relief, but they also didn't have a lot of money. They were just making ends-meet and the taxes on the house and property would be due in the spring. Matt just started at Waverman, his dream job, so he couldn't stay long, and Amber encouraged them to head back to the city. His big sister would play clean up and get the ranch ready to sell.

Amber was in the last place in the world that she wanted to be and continued to work remotely with her clients on the phone during the day, leaving the early mornings and evenings to take care of the ranch. The ranch consisted of 200 head of cattle, which were their bread and butter, along with other assorted animals, and they had to plant the fields in the spring to feed them in the winter.

Within days of Matt leaving and her juggling her practice and the ranch at the same time, she was in over her head. She met with a realtor quickly who told her that it could take years for a ranch their size to sell but recommended she meet with Bill Heard who owned Nebraska City Feed and Supply to advise her. She knew she had to get rid of the livestock because in the winter they needed constant support to stay alive with the ground intermittently covered in snow. Then there was Fumble, her parents' yellow lab, who was in a sad state grieving her parents too. It broke her heart, but what was she going to do with Fumble? Born and raised a ranch dog with free rein to run the Nebraska countryside with her daddy. To seal him up in a 1200 sq. ft apartment in Kansas City would kill him, and Matt and Beth lived in less space than that in New York City. When it came to Fumble, there were no good choices.

Everyone in Nebraska City knew what happened to her parents, so Mr. Heard was very compassionate and, as a member of daddy's church, took on the personal responsibility to help her. They laughed out loud in his office as Amber described trying to get the tractor running that morning to move hay to the livestock to no avail and then using her 4Runner to deliver three bales at a time out to the livestock for hours.

They quickly formulated a plan that she would sell the livestock in the spring, which would bring the best price. Once she had them liquidated, it would be easy to get rid of the rest of the animals, and then she could shut up the house, head back to Kansas City to her practice, and wait for a buyer for the land. She just had to figure out how to hold on until then and what to do with Fumble.

It was decided she would take a loan out from Mr. Heard to hire a hand to help on the farm and pay him back when the cows were sold. Mr. Heard was going to put the word out that she was looking for help, and in the interim he would send his son out this week to help.

Mr. Heard told her that his son was a Purple Heart recipient from Iraq and that he was just waiting on his discharge papers from the Marines. She could instantly tell how proud he was of his son and some worry.

"He's not going to talk a lot. What happened over there changed him, but he's coming around." Amber had worked with some recent veterans in Kansas

City and was familiar with PTSD. They were referred to her by a veteran's group. The scars from the ongoing war, if not present on the outside, were certainly there on the inside for many, and why not? Raised as children, violence was not inherent to most and taking another human life was not natural. It haunted many soldiers who came home, but what really haunted most were the fellow soldiers and friends they lost over there. Why were they spared when others were lost? Suicides in the military skyrocketed when the war started, so Amber decided to do pro bono work with soldiers since her father served in Vietnam. The most she could ever get out of Daddy was that it was bad. That's all he would say.

That next morning in the freezing-cold house, she sat straight up in bed when she heard the tractor crank. Fumble flew off the bed and headed down to the back door thinking that his daddy was home. He was crying there when she found him trying to get out. Looking out the window, a shadow figure was loading hay onto the back of the tractor and soon rolled out to find the cows. Around noon that day, she could hear him working in the barn, trying to fix something she was pretty sure she had broken. She quickly prepared a lunch and took it out to him. It was the very least she could do. Fumble had flown out the door when she opened it, and she found both of them in the barn together. There, on his knees, was Mr. Heard's son, loving Fumble. Fumble was throwing all his weight against him, smiling.

When Amber walked up, he looked up at her and his cutting blues eyes caught her speechless. She stopped dead in her tracks. He wore a beanie because of the cold, and she couldn't help but notice he was very attractive. Black ringlets of curly hair peaked out from under his hat, his scruffy face told a story, and his solid frame was of a real man. He was Steven. He nodded and half smiled, and Amber's attraction to him was immediate. After a moment of uncomfortable silence, Amber held out her hand to present what she was there for, and out came just one word, "Lunch?" Steven reached to take the bag and gave her a nod, and Amber took the chance to really notice his eyes. They were tired. He wasn't sleeping.

That week was interesting. Steven would show up in the dark. Fumble would lose his mind, and Amber would come down to let him out, and he would run around until he found Steven. They would spend the day together working just like Fumble did with her daddy. Amber would watch from the porch when it warmed up, working on her client notes, and when he would look up and catch her looking, she would panic and look away or muster a half wave that he would return. Which again would take her breath away. What the hell was going on with her?

At lunchtime she would prepare something and take it to him. He would thank her with a nod and a half smile. She started doubling up on the sandwich ingredients because whatever she made for him, she saw he would share with Fumble who would sit on the ground when the sun was out or inside from the barn when the weather was bad.

At the end of the week, Steven got into his beat-up truck—a hand-me-down from his father, she thought—rolled out of the driveway, and left. She waved from the porch, which he would return, and Fumble would stand next to her and whine. She felt a strange loneliness now when he left. She was alone in Kansas City in her apartment for years, and she was fine. There were relationships from time to time, but nothing serious in her life. She really didn't have the time, and the last thing that she wanted to do after a long day with her clients was talk to anyone. Truth be told, her clients sucked the life out of her, but she was helping people. A nice dinner and a couple of glasses of wine working on her notes in the evening was her life, and the next morning she would get up and do it all over again.

That Friday had been a very different day. About ten minutes after Steven had driven away, Mr. Heard pulled up at the house. Amber heard the truck come down the driveway and met him.

"Mr. Heard, good evening. You just missed Steven."

He smiled a half-fake smile. "I could lie to you Amber, but that's just not who I am, if that's okay. I'm just not good at it. I was waiting for Steven to leave so that we could talk."

"Okay." She was immediately concerned.

"Do you have a few minutes?"

Amber now really concerned, gestured toward the house. "Sure, please come in." Mr. Heard came into the house, sat the kitchen table, and was quiet.

"How about some coffee or tea?" It was met with silence as Mr. Heard was looking down. Amber sat across the table from him. "Mr. Heard?"

He looked up and there were tears in his eyes. "Amber, I was waiting in the distance for Steven to leave because I need to talk to you."

"Okay. Let's talk." She instinctively reached out and touched his hand.

"A few people have come forward that could come out and help you until spring when you can sell the cattle." Her heart sank. She and Fumble had become comfortable with her no-talking hired hand.

"Mr. Heard, you could have called for that. That's not why you're here."

He took a deep breath. "I didn't disclose everything to you about Steven." He paused. "They say in town you're a psychiatrist in Kansas City."

"I am. I have a small practice."

"Amber, Steven is hurting. We need your help." And with that, his voice broke, and he inhaled a deep breath. She moved to the chair next to him to hug him as he sobbed. Amber now started to break up herself at seeing this pain pouring from Mr. Heard.

"Tell me about it." She wiped the tear from her eye. She needed to pull it together.

"He was in Fallujah in Iraq." Everyone knew that Fallujah was where the fiercest fighting in Iraq occurred. "That's where he got hurt. He won't talk to us. He is not sleeping, and he's barely eating. All we know is that he lost most of his unit. Since he came home, he has been struggling. Physically he's lucky and recovered, but he's dealing with some bad stuff, and we just don't know how to help.

"Is he seeing anyone?"

"We've tried to get him to go to the VA in Omaha, but he won't go. I called up there for help and got a counselor on the phone, and he thinks Steven is suffering from survivor's guilt. He says he's probably struggling with why is he alive and the others didn't make it."

"Does he have friends in town that he can confide in?"

"They've reached out to him, but he's so withdrawn. He's not really talking to anyone. Even Pastor Muddle can't get through."

"Mr. Heard, it's going to take time for him to work through this. We can only imagine what he has been through."

Mr. Heard took Amber's hand. His hands shook as he sobbed. "Amber, we're out of time. We're going to lose Steven. He's going to hurt himself, and we don't know how to stop him." Dread washed over Amber.

"What happened, Mr. Heard? You have to tell me what happened." Amber was now standing holding his hand trying to help him focus.

He tried to collect himself, but the tears kept coming. "Mrs. Heard and I go to a friend's house on Thursdays to play Cribbage. We always invite Steven when we go out, but he won't go. Mrs. Heard wasn't feeling well so we came home early. When I went to his room to check on him, he was holding a gun we didn't even know he had. He wasn't expecting us home so early. The dead look in his eyes said everything to me Amber. He was preparing to kill himself."

Trying to hide the panic rising in her chest, Amber asked, "How did you stop him?"

"I got on my knees in front of him and put both my hands around his, which were holding the gun. I told him that he needed to go ahead and just shoot me now if he was planning on taking his life because his suicide would kill me and his mother as well. We would never recover from losing him this way, and we need him to hold on for our sake." Tears were now streaming down Amber's face, and she held Mr. Heard as he continued to sob.

"Mr. Heard, Steven needs professional help. I've had very little contact with something like this. I could make the situation worse." Mr. Heard looked up and held her hands in his shaking.

"Please, Amber. He's different; he's different this week. He has been better this week since he started coming here helping out."

"Oh, Mr. Heard."

"Please, Amber. We can't give up on Steven."

That night had been the worst night of her life. She spent most of it going through the internet studying, calling colleagues, and finally she reached out to her favorite professor at Kansas State at 2:00 A.M. The two-hour call ended when he said, "Amber, you are a professional, and you are trained for this. If you won't help him, and he won't get help for himself, who will? And if you don't try, we both know where this is headed." It was the gut punch she didn't see coming from her professor. The statistics for suicide for the armed forces spoke for itself, especially for those who had been in combat.

The next day at lunch, she found Steven in the barn with Fumble cleaning out the stalls. When she walked in, he looked up, his eyes ice blue with dark circles. She didn't say a word, no lunch in hand today. She was mad, at him, the situation, and that she didn't really know where to start. "Come on, lunch is on the porch," she said. And with that she pivoted and walked out of the barn. A few minutes later, he ambled out of the barn and toward the house. Fumble was now lockstep next to him. When he got on the porch, he sat down at the small table opposite her, the same table her parents ate lunch at almost every day of their lives when it was nice outside, sometimes even in the cold. He sat, not looking up. His eyes were focused on his hands, which were calloused.

"You don't have to talk to me today, Steven. You just have to listen." She paused and let that set in. "Through some weird chain of events, you and I have been brought together." Her voice cracked as she continued and cleared her throat. "Your parents love you very much, Steven, and they are so worried about you." She had to hold it together, but a tear started to well up in her eye. "I need your help with the place until I can sell it, and all of that is true. But what else is true is that I have helped many people like you where I work in Kansas City." That was a total lie. She had helped two pro bono, but she needed him to be confident in her.

"Steven, you are not going to get better until you start talking to someone about this. You can talk to me, or someone else, but you have got to start talking. Internalizing this is why you can't sleep. You are grinding away on this, and your parents feel you are not making progress." She paused again to let him process. It would now be obvious to him that his father had talked to her. "So here's what we are going to do." She was now taking charge of the situation. Steven was a Marine and what Marines did was follow orders. "You're going to come help me because I desperately need the help." With that she raised her hands out to the sides. "This, with my other job, is too big for me alone. In return, you and I are going to have lunch here every day and you're going to talk to me. Deal?" He made no motion for a minute, head still down, looking at his hands, and then finally he looked up the ice blue eyes now red with emotion, a single tear on his face as he nodded yes. It was all that Amber could do to hold it together. "Good and now that has been settled, let's eat. Okay?"

Amber glanced into the rearview mirror as the 4Runner swept across the Nebraska countryside. That was seven years ago, and even now tears were streaming down her face. She looked at her babies, her and Steven's babies in their car seats in the back and smiled. Baby three was on the way.

16

Hank became increasingly restless in the back of the truck and began pawing at Matt incessantly. When that didn't work, the ultimate guilt trip occurred, and he rested his head on the console between the seats and gave Matt the sad eyes. It was almost 11:30 A.M., now six and a half hours from Connecticut in the Pennsylvania countryside. Matt searched the GPS for a park near the interstate, and about thirty minutes later, they pulled into a small city park entrance. Hank was now up on the back seat hassling up a storm. He must have known the sad eyes worked. In truth, they both needed to get out and go for a walk.

The road was lined with trees with no leaves, but it was still beautiful, and spring would soon be around the corner. Matt looked at the dash and it read 43 degrees. It was going to be a brisk walk. The road eventually opened to a decent sized lake with a walking trail around it. Since it was the middle of week and March, the parking lot and walking trail were deserted. "Hanky, it looks like we got the place to ourselves." Hank responded by whining louder. Matt pulled into the empty parking lot and picked a spot on the front row. Opening the door and getting out, Matt felt tightness in his back, and it took a second for him to completely straighten up. Sitting in the truck for so long reminded him that his latest CrossFit back injury from last week was still there, nagging just enough to be a pain, but not enough to have kept him out of the gym today had he been at work.

As he opened the back door, Hank flung himself outside. Matt normally would have been much more careful and put Hank on a leash before letting him out, but right now, there was no one in sight. He pulled on his puffy black jacket and stretched a little. Hank ran to the nearest tree, sniffed, and threw his leg up to mark his spot, then running around to the next one. He was happy, so Matt left him off the leash for now.

Matt checked his steps on his phone, and he had almost none. "Hanky, let's get 10,000 in, and then get back on the road." Matt figured that would be about an hour. As they walked the lake, Hank would run ahead and smell until Matt caught up, and then he would run ahead again. He was having a grand time. Living in Connecticut, the only time he got this much freedom was when Beth and him would pack a picnic and ride out into the county. They would find a deserted area and let Hank roam, but that was in the warm months and they were months away from anything that even resembled those temperatures. The wind blew briskly across the lake, and it was beautiful as the sun shined on the winter sky horizon.

In the distance Matt could hear a recognizable noise, and he froze. He looked about thirty yards ahead and could see Hank. Hank heard it as well, and he was also frozen, his body statuesque, his head up. Matt could hear the flapping as a flock of ducks landed in the pond near to where Hank was stopped. They hadn't seen him for the tree cover.

"Hank, don't!" Matt yelled, but before Matt could finish, Hank was gone like a bullet to the edge of the lake, running as fast as he could until he went airborne into the lake with a huge splash. "Shit!" He was in pursuit. He was going to get a duck. Hank was all Lab. The startled ducks took to flight and flew to the other side of the lake. Hank kept going. Matt just caught up to the edge where Hank jumped off and yelled, "Hank, come on, boy." Hank was unresponsive as he was now crossing the lake, his brown head visible above the water, his legs churning away below.

Matt was filled with dread. The lake had to be freezing. He immediately turned on a dead run around the lake to the other side, all the while watching Hank continuing to churn away in the frigid lake water. He was now almost halfway across, still heading for the ducks on the opposite shore. It took almost ten minutes at a dead run for Matt to get to the other side where the ducks were amiably floating in the water, and what Matt dreaded most occurred.

When Hank got near the ducks again, they just took off and went right back to the opposite side of the lake where he just came from. Hank again spun in the water and headed that way. "Hank!" Matt decided he was going to have to do the stupidest thing ever, and go in after him. Hank was now only thirty feet from shore.

Matt pulled off his shoes and started to pull off his puffy jacket when the tennis ball fell out. Matt had intended if he found an open area on the walk to play fetch with him. Matt immediately picked up the ball and threw it as hard as he could, and it went right over Hank's head between him and the ducks. Hank made a beeline to the ball, and miraculously turned and headed back to the shore toward Matt. Hank wanted to play fetch more than he wanted to chase ducks. Thank God.

When he got on shore, he scrambled up the bank a few feet out and dropped the ball in front of him and waited for Matt to pick it up and throw it back into the water. He was soaked from head to toe and whining like a crazy. His tongue was about twice size as normal. It was a long swim across that lake, and Matt was breathing as heavy as Hank from running. The wind now gusted and cut into Matt's face. He walked to Hank and immediately put his leash on him and was relieved. When he attempted to pick up the ball Hank grabbed it. It was his trophy. Matt wasn't angry or yelling anymore, just relieved.

Matt remote started the truck to warm it up and went to the rear truck bed sliding top, unlocked it, and pushed it all the way open. There were no towels back there, and Matt was going to grab some of his clothes out of his bags to dry Hank off. When he did, he saw his emergency winter bag. His father always taught him when traveling in the winter across the Midwest to always have an emergency winter bag in case they hit a snowstorm or ended up on the side of the road for any reason. It was always a subject of concern of his father's on almost every call they had over the years. "You have to be prepared," Matt whispered and smiled.

Matt opened it, and inside there were two blankets, and candles that would light and warm the inside of the vehicle. There was also a gallon a drinking water, and Kind bars for eating. This winter emergency bag was on top of the usual emergency bag that had flares, a flashlight, and jumper cables. He heard his father's voice in his head ask, "Did you check the batteries in the flashlight? It doesn't do you a damn bit of good if they're dead."

Matt pulled out one of the blankets and covered Hank, trying to dry his body from top to bottom by rubbing him vigorously. Hank squirmed under the blanket. He loved a good toweling off. Matt opened the rear door and Hank, exhausted, half-ass threw himself in. Matt immediately grabbed his two rear legs, pushed him inside and shut the door, throwing the soaked blanket into the bed and locking it back. Matt got inside his warm truck that used to smell like new car, but now had been replaced with wet dog. How long had it been since Hank had a bath? He had no idea. That was Beth's call. She would take him to the Poodle Parlor when he would become "Rank" Hank. Hank was already lying down, still panting from his long walk and swim. He was toast. Matt rubbed his wet head and ears. "You scared the shit out me." Hank closed his eyes, and he was out.

17

Amber's day was busy. Was that possible in Nebraska City? She dropped off Lucas at the Lutheran Church Day Care, which was supported by the other churches in town, with Ms. Sue at the entrance. Lucas growled at her and grabbed her leg. Ms. Sue rolled her eyes at Amber. "How did he sleep?"

"Too good; sorry."

"Big day for us. Full-steam Lucas." She walked him inside with a wave. Too soon to break the news to Sue about baby three. Steven and her decided they would tell everyone when she started to show, and by then they would know the sex.

Amber was back in the car and heading to Gerald Ford Elementary. She and Dawn were singing the *Frozen* song together. It had been a car ride staple since the movie came out. Soon, there would be another movie, and her and Steven would make an event of it. Probably go to Omaha for the day to shop and see it at the big theater. Maybe even a birthday party depending on the timing.

When Dawn had made it inside the building, Amber turned out of the driveway and waved at Sheriff Rocky Ford, who was directing traffic in front of his cruiser with the lights going. He smiled at her and waved, and she sheepishly returned it. After last week, Rocky knew too much about Amber's personal life. It would blow over. He was a sweet man, a good sheriff, and the incident last week was full of nothing but good intentions.

She was now off to the jail to see what messes had blown into the Sheriff's office overnight and to check on Wilson. He was the local drunk unfortunately, currently jailed for twelve days for public intoxication. The judge wanted him dried out, and he would be in a vicious mood. Amber's job was to try to get him into the local AA program, or to have him admitted into a state-run facility if he proved to be a danger to himself or others. So far, there was no sign of that. His last close call with a DUI was him driving his John Deere lawn mower on the sidewalk on the way to the grocery store because he had run out of beer at home. The judge removed his license indefinitely, and Wilson had now taken to stumbling. His wife left him years ago, and his family stopped coming around. He still paid his bills, and other than the occasional run-ins with the law over drinking, he still was not a danger.

Wilson at his current pace would most likely drink himself to death, which was so sad. He had lost almost everything but his home and still just kept drinking. Her professor's words echoed in her ears. "You can't help those who don't acknowledge they have a problem or don't want help. All you can do is try to get them there." Per their discussion yesterday, Wilson had no desire to get there.

The rest of Amber's morning would be spent at the high school. She had an office, which was really a large closet, behind the main office, and she counseled kids in the morning with emotional problems, college ambitions, military service or if they wanted to stay on the path of their parents and farm or ranch. This morning, she had a session with Derek, who had just lost his little brother in a farming accident. His brother was climbing their corn silo, lost his footing, and fell to his death. Farming was dangerous work. Derek at seventeen was now an only child on the path to college, but he decided to abandon his ambitions of an accounting degree and stay behind to help his parents.

His mother was having none of that. All of them were now in counseling. Derek at school, and his parents on Thursday afternoons at her office, which she worked at after lunch. She literally had the same type of clients in Nebraska City that she had in Kansas City. She kept some of her old clients from Kansas City and had sessions with them via video calls and conferencing. It worked, and she was still helping people. The school and local police worked out a deal to put her on the county payroll for thirty-two hours, which allowed her to get medical insurance for the family. It also put her on call with the local sheriff and school system. There had seldom been knocks on the door in the middle of the night, but when they occurred, it was usually awful incidents. Steven insisted and would not let her drive the roads at night. Between the possibility of bad weather or an animal she could hit with her car, he didn't believe it was safe for her to be out there on her own. He, of course, would have to stay home with the kids. If they wanted her after dark, they had to come and get her, and she was fine with that.

Recently an online psychiatry company reached out to see if she would start taking patients from them virtually. The internet really had changed the whole world. She listened to the pitch, which was very compelling, but did she really want to open her world to the issues of New York or LA? Places where there was a lot of money, but very little she could identify with? Her rates would be the same as she charged today, but the company took 20 percent off the fees for themselves for setting up the times and clients. Something to think about if things got tough on the farm, but today, they were making it just fine, and she had a full schedule.

18

Alexandra was sitting as straight up in her hospital bed as possible. Her face was swollen and black and blue from the abuse she had taken from the air bags that had saved her life. She was almost unrecognizable. On her right was her attorney, Will, a man she had only recently met who was new to the criminal division group at Style's firm. Her left hand was handcuffed to the stretcher in her room, and there was an officer outside in the hall twenty-four hours a day. There was a laptop in front of her with a judge on the screen, a woman, who Alexandra had met several times in passing at events that Style had taken her to. Unfortunately, today she was there to judge her and to hand down a preliminary sentence.

Evidence was being given by a prosecutor in the background, a man she could not see, only hear. It detailed her toxicology report, the drugs, the history of her last year on display leading right up to the moment that she plowed into a building under the influence of Fentanyl, how she almost killed pedestrians on the street, a reality that made her nauseated. She couldn't remember the building or the accident only escaping the doctor and sobbing behind the wheel. How did she get here, how did this happen, how could she get out of this nightmare she was in? She pinched her arm the pain stinging. No, she was awake. As the prosecutor finished up his summation of the charges, the courtroom became very quiet.

The judge shuffled the papers in front of her, then looked up and appeared to be looking directly at the screen. "How does the defendant plead?" she asked.

In a shaking, cracking voice with her heart in her throat and tears streaming down her face, Alexandra said, “Your Honor, I plead guilty. I am so sorry and ashamed of what I have done.” Alexandra could hear her mother weeping outside the door of her hospital room. It broke her heart.

Before she could continue, the judge cut her off, “Your plea is accepted. It is very evident to the court that the defendant is contrite and sincere in her guilt. It is also evident in the ongoing legislation across the country that drug manufacturers crafted medications that lead to many people becoming addicted to these drugs. Based on this evidence and the fact that the defendant has no criminal record whatsoever, she will be remanded into rehabilitation under the first offenders’ program. Will we need a public facility?”

Will sprang into action and said, “Your Honor, we have secured a spot at a certified private inpatient treatment center in Monterrey, California for at least the next thirty days, and sixty if it is deemed necessary.”

The judge again cut her attorney off before he could continue and spoke directly to Alexandra. “Does the defendant understand per the conditions of the terms that you must successfully complete this rehab program? If you leave this program early and don’t complete it, you will be in violation of my order and will end up back in court and will go to jail?”

A wispy voice came out of Alexandra. “Yes, ma’am.”

“Fine. The defendant if successfully released will surrender her driver’s license for the next twelve months and do 100 hours of community service. I also want the defendant in a program for that period of time. Does the defendant agree to my terms?”

“I do.”

“Good. Based on this first-offender program, if the defendant successfully completes all the steps that I have just laid out, at the end of the year she will have her record scrubbed of this incident.” The judge laid her paperwork down and again looked directly at Alexandra. Her attorney told her she would be on a TV screen in the courtroom, and the judge would be able to see her. “The defendant is very lucky to have this chance. These circumstances had people been killed would be devastating for everyone involved. I do not want to see you back in my courtroom. Good luck, Mrs. Bridgeway.”

“Yes, ma’am.” It went down just as her attorney told her it would. It was all preplanned and negotiated she just had to agree to the terms. Alexandra was broken. Her husband had now left her, and she was on her way to an inpatient drug rehabilitation center.

19

Amber drove her 4Runner through the Nebraska countryside. It had been a beautiful day, cold and clear. The sun was almost set in the west, the sky filled with red glory dancing on the clouds. You could see for miles. They lived in a beautiful place, a place she ran from only to return and never want to leave.

In the mirror she could see that Lucas was unconscious. Another long day of terror at Lutheran Day Care had taken its toll on him. He apparently was kicking over blocks, per Ms. Sue, which was something she would take up with him later after dinner. He had been put in time-out, which was not out of the ordinary, unfortunately. He had become a handful, and that was something that she and Steven would need to start addressing now.

Dawn had her head in her games on the iPad. She had already given Amber the entire rundown of her day. Dawn was an open book, and oh-my-gosh could she read people. She was seeing things in people she really didn't understand yet, but she could see right through them, through their actions. Dawn was becoming a mini version of her mother, an Amber 2.0. The older she got, the more they looked alike except for her father's eyes.

She turned into the long driveway toward the farmhouse. It was gray with white trim with black shutters. Steven spent weeks repairing the outside and painting it in the fall, and it was beautiful. It had been built by her grandfather and father when she was a child. There was a massive front sitting porch wrapped around all three sides of the house. The almost half-mile-long driveway from the road was gravel with grass growing in the middle, Amber could hear the rocks crushing under the tires as she slowly rolled along. Off to the right of the house sat the massive white barns, and off to the right side of one barn was the steel silo that towered in the sky. It was quite the layout but the minimum they needed to be able to take care of the cattle. Where was Steven?

He was usually waiting for them on the porch with Lady, but he was nowhere in sight today. There was a pit in her stomach. Farming was so dangerous, and this time of year, there was no migrant help because there was not enough work, so Steven worked alone during the days. It worried Amber to death. If something happened to him and he called for help, it would take an hour for help to arrive. Thank God for cell phones. How many lives had been saved with cell service since it got put in? They texted each other incessantly during the day to check in, and he always let her know if he was not going to be at the house when she got there, so she wouldn't worry.

"Where's Daddy?" Dawn questioned from the back seat.

"I don't know, baby." Amber scanned the barns and the silo, which, after her day of counselling, took on a new aura of fear.

"There he is!" Dawn squealed from the back seat.

Amber's eyes cut to the house as Steven and Lady were coming out the door and walking toward the driveway. She let out a sigh of relief. He, of course having no idea of her panic, smiled his beautiful smile. His blue-ice eyes cut right into her. Lucas, now awakened by Dawn's squeal, started with "Daddy, Daddy, Daddy, Daddy!"

As she pulled up to the house, Steven met her, and Lady was running circles around the car in anticipation of them getting out. Steven opened her door, she unbuckled and immediately got out. He took her into his arms with another long drawn-out kiss; she reciprocated by putting her hand on the back of his neck and pulling him deeper into her mouth. After a long minute, she released and laid her head on his chest.

"Hey there. Did you miss me?" Steven whispered.

"I always miss you, you shit," she responded. "You know you scare me when you are not out front, and I don't know where you are."

"I was inside making up Matt's bed for you."

She looked up at him and his blue eyes. "You made the bed?"

"Yep." He pulled her close and kissed her intensely again. The area below her belly button exploded with tingling, and she felt her head swim again. Lady, eager to get in on the action, wiggled her way between their legs to get attention.

Amber smiled and rolled Lady's head in her hands. "Hey, Lady, did you take care of Daddy today?" Lady was always at Steven's side all day, every day. She loved her daddy, as did the kids from the commotion. Steven had pulled Lucas out of his car seat and gone to the other side to release Dawn. Once released, she thrust herself into her daddy's arms, and he carried them both up the steps onto the porch with Lucas singing, "Daddy, Daddy, Daddy," and at the same time Dawn doing a play-by-play of her day, repeating what Amber had heard in the car.

Amber pulled her briefcase out of the car along with the kids' backpacks and followed them up. "Let me have Lucas, so I can get him fed. You put the car away and get in the shower. You have chores to do inside before dinner."

"Chores?" He smiled at her.

"We have to tidy before Matt gets here." She immediately looked away from him and those eyes.

"Okay."

Upon entering the house, the smell of the soup in the crock pot that had been simmering all day hit her nose. She was hungry but that would have to wait. Feeding Lucas became the priority before he got cranky, and Dawn would sit at the table, do her homework, and talk about her day again. She had so many probing questions about the people in her life from such a small person. Lucas was a voracious eater, and he ate almost nonstop for thirty minutes until finally stopping by spitting up, which was his sign he was done. She placed him in the playpen in the middle of the living room and put the *Trolls* on TV, his very favorite. He was immediately mesmerized.

"Dawn, I need for you to be a big girl and watch Lucas while I change before dinner."

"Okay," Dawn replied distractedly.

Amber looked directly at Dawn and raised her voice a little for emphasis. "Dawn, I need you down here with Lady and Lucas okay? Got it?"

"Yes, ma'am."

Amber got up and hustled upstairs to the hall bath. Steven would be in their bathroom, and for an old farmhouse, it was not big enough for the two of them in their bathroom at the same time. She opened the medicine cabinet and found her second toothbrush there. She quickly brushed her teeth, checked her hair and put on a little perfume. She looked at herself with some satisfaction. People told her she was pretty. Steven told her all the time. Men looked at her, sometimes too hard.

She had thought of Steven all day thanks to that morning's kiss. She unbuttoned her blouse, slid it off, and then took her bra off. She put the blouse back on only buttoning it enough to keep her chest barely inside, her hard nipples poking through. She then pulled her jeans off and removed her panties. The bottom of her blouse covered to the top of her thighs.

Going down the hallway she could see the door to their room was closed and going by the laundry she threw her bra, panties, and pants into the hamper.

Opening the door to their bedroom, she could smell Steven through the humid-just-showered air, a mixture of his body wash and his cologne. She slid into the room, carefully locking the door and double-checking it, and then laid on the bed with her blouse barely covering the top of her thighs, and her chest almost out. She sat and watched Steven as he shaved. From the angle on the bed, she could see him, but he couldn't see her.

"Hey there," she sweetly said.

"Hey there, yourself," he responded. "How was your day?"

She could hear the tink of the razor on the sink as he was shaving. What had her daddy said when she was growing up? There were two kinds of people in this world: those who showered before work and those who showered after work. Her beautiful husband showered after work, and that left him carrying around a five o'clock shadow all day, which made him prickly irresistible. "It was not bad, just dealing with the usual stuff, nothing out of the ordinary. Oh, I forgot—your son is a terror. I blame you."

Steven laughed. "What did he do now?"

"Apparently, he has taken to kicking over everyone else's blocks at day care. Ms. Sue is all over him, and he spent some valuable time in time-out today."

"That's not good. We have got to nip that in the bud."

"I agree. He's just so damn wild."

"Yeah, we have to focus that energy in a positive direction and under some control before 'baby three' arrives. I will spend some time extra time with him this weekend."

Steven got quiet as he was shaving his neck. Amber admired him. His 6′2 frame was wrapped only in a towel at the waist. There was another tink on the side of the sink as he shaved. His broad shoulders contrasted with his narrow waist. There were scars on his back she could see from Iraq that earned him his purple heart and more on the front she couldn't see from where she was sitting. He also had scars on the inside that flared from time to time, but he was a different person than when they first met. According to Mr. Heard, he was all the way back.

She could hear him washing the leftover shaving cream off his face, and she couldn't stand it any longer. She rose from the bed and walked into the bathroom.

Steven saw her in the mirror as she walked in. Her bra-less nipples were hard and poking through her blouse and raging at her cleavage. Her legs were bare and barely covered. His eyes lit up immediately. "Whoa!"

"Whoa is right. I have been thinking about you all day. What right do you have to send me off with a kiss like that this morning?"

Steven began to respond, looking at her in the mirror. She reached up and put her finger on his lip to stop him and shook her head. She placed her left hand on his back and began to drag her fingernails back and forth on his shoulders. Looking at him in the mirror, she took her right hand from his lips and dragged across his chest. He instinctively started to reach back with his hand to touch her leg, and she stopped him. "No."

He let his hand fall back to the side again, looking at her in the mirror. Her right hand traced his hair down the middle of his chest to his stomach. Steven took a deep breath and exhaled sharply. Her left hand followed down to the middle of his back. She then loosened his towel, and it dropped to the floor. She had to touch him. Her left hand then caressed his backside, while her right hand took his penis. Rubbing and kneading the head until it was fully erect. "Come with me."

She guided him across the room by his penis to the bed and kissed him savagely on the lips. She could feel him wanting to respond, but she was in charge today. This was her show. She unbuttoned her blouse, and her breasts tumbled out. She then trailed her breasts back and forth across his body, while she continued to knead his penis in her hand. Steven again took a deep breath and exhaled. Stepping back from him, Amber lay back on the bed with her full body now exposed, her blouse falling to both sides. She signaled for him to come closer, and as he did, she guided his head below her belly button. Steven instantly responded, and his tongue was lashing her clitoris down and sliding in and out of her. His damp curly hair was clutched in her hands. Amber began to moan louder and louder, her body receiving what she needed all day. She could feel his just-shaven smooth face on her thighs, smell his body wash and cologne, and it was just too much.

She pulled his head tighter into her, and then her full body released with a wave. With that, Amber let out an exasperated moan. She exhaled and lay back on the bed. Her head was swirling as Steven grasped both of her ass cheeks in his hands and was nibbling ever so gently on her thighs. He would stay down until he was invited up, and she pulled his face in for a harder round two that ended the very same way. She then took his face with both hands and brought him up to her. Amber put her arms over her head, signaling him to hold them there. He took her breasts in his mouth, loving them until she couldn't take it any longer.

"Come up here, baby," she whispered. With that, he put his engorged body inside of her, and she immediately began to moan, her body convulsing against his, her hands still held above her head. "Harder, Steven, harder. Now, baby. Please…" The rhythm picked up, and Amber could feel her hard nipples running back and forth against his hairy chest and her body released again with a yell, and Steven continued. She could feel him harder and stronger, and with that, they both gave way in a wave, his warmth now inside of her.

Steven's full weight was now on her, very still with just his heavy breathing in her ear and on her neck. She wrapped her legs and arms around him and held him.

Steven uttered from his mouth tucked in her neck. "I'm starving."

She smiled and grabbed him tighter one more time. "Me too, baby."

They hustled and threw some clothes on. Steven wore his plaid pajama bottoms with a form fitting T-shirt, and she grabbed some black tights and threw a sweatshirt on over it.

"We are going to have to be quieter when Matt is here." She smiled at him.

"If you come at me like that again, I can't promise anything," Steven said, returning a knowing smile because she was by far the loud one.

"I can't promise that either." She popped him on the ass and headed out the door to check on the kids. On the way down the stairs, she could feel herself smiling so full of happiness. What a different world she had than what she had imagined. She could again hear her dad in her ears. "Not your plan but God's." Yes, it was, and she was so thankful for that.

20

The sun was just peaking over the dawn, and Matt was scrambling to find where in the many locations in the GMC he had put his sunglasses. He was going to have to settle on a location for his sunglasses to reduce the chaos. Hank had rousted him out of bed appropriately for his 5:00 A.M. feeding. Hank was on a schedule even if Matt wasn't. At that point there was no sense trying to go back to bed, so he quickly showered, and they snuck out of the hotel.

At the third interstate exit try in the middle of nowhere, Matt had found an "outy" hotel last night as planned. Hank weighing in at just over 90 pounds was not going to find a welcoming party to let him stay in a hotel room, so Matt had to sneak him in. An outy hotel, as Matt had always called them, had the room doors on the exterior of the hotel. It was a privately held hotel just off the interstate that looked clean enough, which was a dying breed these days with the chain hotels. The owner was half-asleep watching TV when Matt walked in at 10:00 P.M. He eagerly and quickly checked Matt in and, as Matt requested, gave him a king room on the ground floor. Matt backed into the space directly in front of his door. He got out and released the lock on the rolling lid of the GMC to pull out his suitcase and Hank's backpack, and then unlocked the door to his room.

Looking to the right Matt saw that a camera was at the end of the building near the ice machine. Matt immediately grabbed his ice bucket out of the room and went down there to grab some ice. Looking up at the camera, Matt could see that the cord in the back of the camera was not connected. He immediately walked back to the truck door, checked to make sure all was clear and opened the door. Hank bolted from the truck, peed on the outside post and then ran through the open hotel room door. It was almost as if he knew what to do. After a bone and some roughhousing in the bed, Hank crashed. He had a big day chasing ducks in the lake.

Securing a set of his sunglasses from the holder in the ceiling above the dash, he put them on just as his new iPhone began to ring. The sound startled him because it came through the truck's speaker system. Matt managed to turn the volume down for next time, and on the dash, it read King George. It was 7:30 A.M. on the truck dash, so that would be 8:30 A.M. in New York. Pretty early for old George to be coming into the office. He must have hated Matt not being there.

"Good morning, George."

"Bloody hell it's a good morning. Do you know what time it is?" His British accent spilled out all over the inside of the truck.

"I would say it is 8:30 where you are. Are you already in the office?"

"I have been here for an hour. Doing my job and yours—it sucks."

"I will let you run that up to the top of the building. Not my choice." Matt shot back with anger in his voice. Had he already moved from grief to anger? It was all raw.

There was a long silence on the phone, and Matt was not going to break it. King George was regrouping. "Matt, you know how I feel about this. I can't imagine how you feel. I'm sorry. I'm just trying to make light of this horrible situation."

Matt whispered back into the hands-free air, "I know."

"So, listen, this idea hit me yesterday when I was fielding your calls. That guy Amil Samua, or something like that, called you and left a message. He wanted you to come out to Mountain View to meet with his firm on tech startups to invest in. I know you and I have talked about this several times, but with the market going almost every day, there hasn't been a good time. Now we have time for you to do this, and see if it makes sense for the firm. It will also get you the hell out of town." Amil Samua was on the inside of what was going on in Silicon Valley, and he and his team sold themselves out to the highest bidder on new investment projects. His firm was a hired gun that aligned themselves with firms on projects for whoever would bid the highest. If it panned out, his team took 20 percent, which was stiff considering only one in ten startups ever made it. They had no skin in the game, but they did bring value because what's going on out there was in constant flux, and it felt like a million miles away from Wall Street.

"George, I am already gone."

"Where are you?"

"I am heading to my sister's in Nebraska and don't know when I will be back. Besides, I am suspended for sixty days."

"Please tell me you did not take that broken-down Jeep?"

"Sold the Jeep two days ago and returned Beth's leased BMW. I bought a new truck I wanted that Beth would have hated."

"Well, I guess that works. You showed her!" There was only silence on the other end. "Nebraska? Hell, you are halfway to California. Make a road trip of it."

"Suspended, George. Don't know if I am coming back."

"You will be back. Your team needs you. I need you." Matt could hear the worry in George's voice. Would Matt really jump ship to another firm? "Matt, your promotion is going to be waiting here when you get back. This is what you have worked for. With your looks, you will find a girl ten years younger than Beth and prettier and really screw her over." More silence from the other end. "Listen this whole thing sucks to high heaven, but sabotaging your career is not the answer. Go to Mountain View, meet with Amil, and listen to what he is selling. Then come back here and kill it. Show Beth and Waverman what a bunch of sorry fucks they are."

"I'll think about it."

"Good, good," George exploded into the phone relieved. "It is a done deal. Keep up with your expenses and when you come back to work, we will turn them into a bonus. You have my word on that. So… just one more thing."

"What?"

"Waverman's secretary called down to get your info. I wouldn't give it to her. I told her that it needed to go through me."

"What the hell does she want?"

"They have drawn up separation papers that are supposed to be in line with the discussion in the conference room. She wanted to know where to send them to be reviewed."

"Seventy-two hours, George, really? Seventy-two hours—Jesus! How long have they been planning this?"

"Apparently quite a while," George muddled.

"I don't know. I guess send them to Allen on the 11th floor." Allen was a CrossFit workout acquaintance of Matt's who became a friend. The law firm Allen worked for rented space on the 11th floor of the Waverman building. "Hopefully he can look at them."

"I'll go up there and get them from her and personally walk them down to Allen. I will do it right now and fill him in."

"Thanks, George."

"All good… now off with you to Mountain View via Nebraska. Please try to put this shitshow that's going on here behind you."

Matt hung up by pressing the button on his steering wheel and stared into the distance. This whole thing was utterly unbelievable. He was sick inside all over again. His phone dinged as a text message came in. He wondered what George had forgotten, but it was a text from Amber.

Steven and I can't wait to see you. When will you be here? Love Amber.

Matt texted back and in the process the truck corrected itself as he was going over the yellow line. "Shit. That's a feature."

Love u see you at 6. He hit the Send button and reached back to rub Hank's head. "We are going to be there this afternoon, buddy. You are going to love it."

21

Style was seated at his desk when Hope came into the office. He smiled and she returned it.

"Here are the briefs you're looking for. Mr. Burns has been divorced twice before, and both court rulings mention his infidelity."

"Really? This just got a lot more expensive for him. Wonder why Mrs. Burns didn't mention the infidelity when she came in?"

"She may not have known. There are no kids involved, so I doubt there is any contact between her and the other exes." Hope stood next to Style and laid the paperwork out on the desk. Her perfume hit his nose, and her blouse fell open as she leaned over. He immediately began to feel his pants tighten. He stayed late last night to work on his own divorce and separation papers, which of course was unethical, but he would get one of the other partners to sign off on it as their work. Honestly, who was more qualified in the city to do his divorce than himself? Hope had checked in with him when she was getting ready to leave, and he requested for her to order him dinner. She left quietly, but when dinner arrived an hour later, it was for two.

After dinner the conversation delved into Alexandra, her treatment, and what his next steps were. Style loved Alexandra in the beginning, but they were now completely different people. His professional career had taken off, and now he was a partner. Alexandra's professional career as an artist went into a tailspin after a disastrous showing, which was widely panned by the merciless

San Francisco press. She quit painting after that, and eventually her art studio in their apartment became unused. He couldn't remember the last time he saw her in there. Her days before the accident were occupied with keeping things running at home, so Style didn't have to worry about it: shopping and running with the other partners' wives. Then the drugs came into their lives, and the relationship Style was tolerating immediately became intolerable. Of all things, Oxy which eventually led to the Fentanyl. Why couldn't she just get a drinking habit like the rest of partners' wives? Two glasses of wine, and Alexandra was happy. Three and she was asleep.

As the evening wore on, Hope had excused herself to his private bathroom to "freshen up," and when she came back, all she had on was her designer underwear. Style didn't need an invitation, and they immediately went into full throw-down mode. They had slept together before, but last night was different. Hope wasn't drunk like the other times. She was sober, and she was on a mission. She was into it. Style thought things weren't that great on the home front, and with him soon-to-be-single, she had designs on being the next Mrs. Style, a partners' wife.

When Hope finished laying out the paperwork, she stood up and laid her hand on the back of Style's neck. She began caressing his neck, and it felt amazing to him. They were both startled when they heard a knock on his open door.

Kyle was in the doorway, and Hope immediately dropped her hand down by her side. "Style, do you have a few minutes?"

"Sure, Kyle, please come in." Hope took her queue, nodded at Kyle, which he returned, and then headed out the door with Kyle closing it after her.

"It is none of my business, but you may want to be a little more careful."

"Kyle, California is a no-fault state. Besides Alexandra and I have a postnup."

"You convinced Alexandra to sign a postnup?" Kyle asked.

"Yes," Style answered abruptly. There were things that Kyle did not need to know, and Alexandra had in fact not signed a postnup that she knew of. The subject of a postnup had never even come up. Style had slipped the postnup into a pile of paperwork that he needed her to sign when he became a partner at the firm. He flagged all the paperwork, and she came by the office that day at 5:00 P.M. to see his name now on the wall with the other partners above the receptionist. They stood at Hope's desk, and they both signed with Hope notarizing everything. They then took it to Alex, the lead partner, and handed it to him. He congratulated them and told them to go and expense an elaborate dinner on him. That next morning, Style found only the postnup on his desk, which excluded Alexandra's rights to his portion of the firm, and he put it in his safe as he was sure he would never need it. The entire thing had been the partners' idea.

"What did you find out?" Style asked.

"Not a lot unfortunately. We dumped her phone and all her social media. We started with Facebook and then looked at her Twitter and Instagram accounts. Other than a lot of shopping on Amazon, which is every woman in America right now, there wasn't anything."

"No idea where the Fentanyl came from?"

"She had gone to her addiction group that day, so my bet is that she got it from one of them. One of the pitfalls of groups like that is sometimes they take each other down."

"Any sign of infidelity?" Style needed to know because, in the postnup that she didn't know she signed, infidelity cut his obligation to her. All of this made sense to Style as the partners laid it out for him. When he became a partner, he was the sole breadwinner in the family. Did it really make sense for him to give up 50 percent of what he had solely earned, which is what California no-fault demanded, if he was in fact making all of the money?

"There was nothing like that. She was clean," Kyle replied.

There was a tinge of guilt because a long time ago Style had become anything but "clean." It started with a client he was representing, that he fell for. It lasted six months, and eventually, as he was unavailable, she took a transfer from work and left San Francisco. It killed him, and he had taken comfort for his loss in a member of the paralegal pool, whose intentions were to move up.

"Thank you, Kyle. Can you reach out to Digger and have him appraise my place? I am going to need that as part of the settlement."

"Sure." Kyle frowned and headed to the door.

Style did not like that reaction and immediately confronted him. "Kyle, are you and I okay?"

Kyle turned, a frown still on his face. Style could see that he was searching for his words carefully, and then finally he broke the silence. "Style, I like Alexandra a lot. She has always been very kind." The guilt was back, and it hit Style directly in the heart. Who the fuck was he to question him?

"Kyle, I like Alexandra a lot as well, but sometimes it doesn't work out. This is what we do here on this wing of the firm, and unfortunately this time it is personal." Style's voice immediately went from calm to angry-pissed levels in seconds. "Despite what you think, I can assure you none of this makes me happy. We were high school sweethearts. It has dissolved into the shit I've been dealing with for over a year. My wife is an addict."

Kyle started to turn away and head to the door but stopped halfway. "Don't you think that you need to wait until she gets out of rehab and see if you can work this out?" There was an uncomfortable pause as Kyle awaited his reply, which did not come, so he continued. "Style, I am not so sure how much of this is Alexandra's fault."

The look on Style's face said it all. He was furious. Kyle was beginning to speak again, and Style raised his hand to stop him. "Kyle, you need to get right with this. We are not talking about this anymore. We are done here!" Kyle turned and walked out. The exchange had been loud enough for many in the office to hear, and Hope was immediately standing at the entrance of the door to see if he was okay. Style waved her off.

22

Matt had taken a drive through memory lane on his way home. He went past the high school football field from his glory days and through the five stop lights of Nebraska City. Some things had not changed at all, like Peterman's Diner that was still in full swing where he had spent so many date nights with his high school girlfriend Rachel, and Bill Lanes Chevrolet with the giant rotating Chevy symbol above its building. He used to dream of the days when he would be a huge NFL star and go to Bill Lanes to buy his parents a new truck, which was something they would never do on their own.

An illegal clip on Matt shattered his knee six games into his sophomore season at Nebraska, and he put all his dreams of the NFL away. He rehabbed after surgery but could never get that knee back into shape to play again. It took years of rehab, but it finally came around, which was a tremendous relief.

Rachel had been his first love. The most beautiful girl in high school that finally relented to go out with him when he was a junior and she was a senior. She had long brown hair and green eyes, and they were passionately in love, or at least looking back on it, Matt was. She was a year older and had dated older guys, so she was quite a bit more experienced than Matt in relationships. Rachel had taken Matt's virginity in her bedroom after school one day right after the beginning of the school year.

Matt could still remember every detail of that day as they studied in her room, which looked like somebody had vomited pink all over it. Rachel had wanted a massage, so she had lain on the bed, and Matt on his knees by her side nervously began to rub her back and neck. As he massaged her back, Rachel became more relaxed. With her eyes closed, she said her bra was in the way, so she asked him to look away while she took it off. "You can turn around now," Rachel said. As Matt turned around, he saw Rachel had removed her shirt, and her bra and was lying facedown on the bed naked from the waist up. Her long hair was pulled to one side exposing her bare neck. Matt continued to massage her, but now he could feel her smooth skin and the curvature of her back. As he would draw close on her sides near her breasts or move lower on her back near the top of her jeans, her breathing would deepen and get louder. Being no fool, Matt began to focus his massage on those key areas. Then suddenly, without warning, Rachel turned over. He would never forget his first sight of her breasts, soft milk pale skin with hard, pink nipples. Matt froze. He couldn't take his eyes off her. She took his hands and guided them to her chest. Just like that, she took him to school.

His junior year and that next summer had been amazing with Rachel. They became inseparable, but then, as quickly as the spark became a flame, she left for college at Kansas. She was going to come home every other weekend because Matt couldn't visit during football season. She followed through with her promise for the first month, but Rachel very quickly found other interests at college, perhaps another guy, Matt still wondered, and she broke up with him. Matt took the breakup hard and dated on and off for a while senior year before settling for a cheerleader named Wendy, who was a year younger than him. This time, he was her first, and they were close, but not like him and Rachel. He thought Rachel was the one until he went to college and met Beth. Their relationship had been electric.

He passed the red brick Lutheran Church of his youth located just down from the Methodist Church. This intersection almost always caused a ridiculous traffic jam downtown on Sunday mornings. Matt couldn't help but smile at the thought: a traffic jam in Nebraska City versus that of New York. According to Amber, there had been a vote which was widely controversial and caused weeks of front-page news in the *Nebraska City Herald* where the Methodists voted to move their main service to 10:30 A.M. so both churches wouldn't start at the same time. Unfortunately, though, the Lutherans accused the Methodists of wanting all the parking spaces at the restaurants after church before them. The Lutherans threatened to move their time as well, and the Methodists finally dropped it.

Beside the Lutheran Church, there was a stone wall with red brick entranceways that encompassed the churches graveyard. Matt would come back and pay his respects to his parents.

The wide-open spaces of the countryside brought a calm over him he would never feel in New York. Connecticut was about as close as he could get. Hank hung his head over on the armrest and started hassling. He was getting excited for the past hour since leaving the interstate. He knew something was up, and he would soon be able to get out of the car. In the distance, Matt could see the first outline of the home and ranch where he grew up. It looked remarkable, well maintained, and he could see a small smoke rising from the chimney

As he turned off the road, he could hear the rocks under his tires, and Hank began to get anxious. As he pulled up to the house, he could see Steven outside cleaning the grate on the grill. He immediately turned, smiled his big smile, and waved. It was so great to see him. A black Lab that must be Lady stood beside Steven barking. Hank let out a whine in the back seat. As the truck came to a stop, he saw Amber come out onto the porch with Dawn, who had gotten so big, and Lucas, who was on her hip. When Lucas was born two years ago, that was the last time Matt had seen them. He was elated, and Amber was grinning from ear to ear.

Matt killed the engine, unbuckled his seat belt, and opened his door. Amber was right there to take him in her arms when he got out. She held him so intensely his eyes began to well up. He lovingly returned her embrace. For what seemed to be an eternity, they didn't let go. He needed this. Finally, Amber whispered in his ear, "I am so happy to see you, Matty."

"I am so glad to be home, Amber." As they let go of themselves, Steven approached and hugged Matt with brotherly love.

"So great to see you, Matt. Your sister has a ton of work planned for us while you're here," Steven teased.

"Great." There was always a list of work that needed to be done on the ranch, and Matt loved doing it.

"It's stuff he shouldn't be doing on his own, and your names on the lease, so it's the least you can do." Amber smiled, her eyes still watering from their hug.

"Always happy to do my part." Matt leaned over and put his arms out for Dawn. She left her mother's side and jumped into Matt's opened arms. "My gosh, who is this big girl?"

"It's me, Dawn, Uncle Matty," she said as she hugged his neck.

"Wow, you are getting almost too big to hold," he said as he gently settled her to the ground while Lady rubbed back and forth on his legs. She was a much smaller Lab than Hank, and unlike Hank, she was black. He got down on a knee and petted her until she rolled over on her back, exposing her belly. "She's got a beautiful coat."

"Egg whore," Steven immediately remarked.

Amber snapped, "Steven, please don't use that word!" and looked at the kids.

"Whoops. Dawn, please don't repeat that word," Steven said, looking at her, knowing that she would now absolutely use that word.

Amber continued, "We kept missing eggs from the coop. We were thinking snakes or coyotes, but the chickens were fine, just no eggs. Then Steven caught Lady coming under the fence with an egg in her mouth unbroken."

"Really," Matt said as he continued to pet Lady.

"Oh, it gets better. Steven secures the fence and scolds Lady. We're cooking out with the neighbors a few weeks later, and low and behold, they also have a missing egg mystery. Matty, they live miles from here. Now Lady is not allowed outside by herself, but honestly, she is always here. We have no idea when she was doing this. Steven thinks she can open a doorknob." Matt continued to rub her belly and then from inside the truck came a very jealous bark.

Elated Dawn grabbed the handle and pulled herself up on the running board of the truck putting her face to the window trying to see in through the tinting. "Uncle Matty, do you have a dog?"

"Yes, Dawn, that's Hank, the great duck hunter," he said very sarcastically. "Wait until you hear this story." He smiled at Amber and Steven.

"Can I let him out?"

"Go for it but watch out." She stepped off the running board hanging on to the door handle and used her body weight to open the door. Hank flew out the door and made a beeline to Lady. Matt looked up at Steven and Amber and crossed his fingers. The dogs immediately went in circles around each other getting the consummate good butt smell, and then Hank was off running loose on the farm, stopping every few minutes to pee. Lady would follow right behind him and pee in the same place. What a wonder it must be for him with all these new smells.

Steven smiled. "Well, that went about as good as could be expected. He is a huge Lab. How much does he weigh?"

"He's ninety pounds."

"Wow, he's almost double Lady's size."

Dawn, giving up on chasing the dogs, ran up, and wrapped her hand around Amber's leg. Steven stood next to her with Lucas in his arms. It was a picture. "Wow, look at this beautiful family," Matt said.

Amber reached out and took his hand. "It is a beautiful family, and you are part of it." She gripped his hand.

From below, Dawn's tiny voice yelled out, "And we are going to have another baby, Uncle Matty!"

In unison Amber and Steven bellowed, aghast, "Dawn!" She cowered behind her mother's leg and hid her face.

Matt, seeing their reaction, drew a big smile. "Is it true? Are you pregnant?"

Amber stuttered through the response. "Well… yes we are, but we're not even out of the first trimester, so we hadn't planned on telling anyone until I started showing. Dawn, are you listening in on me and your daddy's conversations again?"

Dawn immediately went on the defensive. "No, ma'am. I didn't listen in—I promise. Cross my heart."

"So how did you know?"

"Daddy was in the attic." Amber immediately shot a glance at Steven. He looked flabbergasted.

There was a heavy pause as Steven, wild-eyed, found his words. "There is no way that she could have known. I was just moving things around up there."

Amber looked at Dawn. "What did Daddy do that made you think there was a baby on the way?"

"Daddy moved all the baby stuff together at the top of the stairs. It made me think he was going to bring it back down."

Amber looked at Steven. He threw his arms in the air. "Yes, I did. I give up."

Amber looked at Matt. "She sees everything. Reads people. It is unbelievable."

And with that, Matt said, "She's you."

"Yep!" Steven echoed that sentiment.

Matt smiled and laughed, and it felt good. "I am so happy for all of you. It's going to get crazy around here."

Amber grasping to change the subject said, "You look tired, Matty."

"I am," he said, smiling. "But very glad to be here."

Amber returned the smile, and her heart empathized with him. Something was up, and she could see it all over his face.

"Oh, by the way, nice truck," Steven bellowed.

Coyly, Matt said to them, "It happens to be new. Very new, in fact just a few days old."

Amber needed to know. "How's Beth feel about the truck?"

"It's not her problem anymore."

And there it was. Amber frowned in pain, but knew she had to change the subject. Turning to her husband. "Well, Steven, you smell like the farm. You need to take a shower and do some chores before dinner. Matty, would you like to freshen up before dinner? It will be at least an hour before we start grilling."

"A shower actually sounds great, and I might grab a twenty-minute nap." He called Hank who came tearing across the yard. He and Steven grabbed the bags out of the back of the truck and headed up to his room.

23

Alexandra's parents had left about an hour ago. She didn't think they could stand to watch her perp-walked, well… rolled really via wheelchair, out of the hospital. All the tests came back negative, which meant she looked a hell of a lot worse than she was. Her face was black, blue, and still swollen to where she almost didn't recognize her reflection. The inside, well, that was a different story. She had destroyed her life, her reputation, and although her family would never admit it, she had shamed them as well. Calistoga was a very small town where she grew up, and with Style being from Napa, the entire valley would know what happened. How would she ever be able to face everyone there. The prom queen now Oxy addict.

She stared down at her phone at the text messages she received from the wives' group at the firm. The last message was the day of the accident, inquiring if they should wait on her for lunch.

After that they all knew what happened. It was all out there now, and Alexandra was bathing in the shame and guilt she brought upon herself and her soon-to-be-divorced husband. There wasn't a single message from any of them after the accident. She knew what was happening. If there was a falling out between spouses at the firm or a divorce, the rest of the women in the wives' group circled wagons and shut them out. She had been a willing participant before. They became conversation at the next wives' lunch or dinner, and they would take turns tearing down the separated member for their looks, their demeanor, their etiquette, anything that would make them feel better about themselves.

Now, she was being shut out. The thought hit her in the chest again causing pain. She had not come to the decision yet on whether she deserved the divorce. They had been together since high school, but it was a bad year for them, a really bad year, which was mostly her fault.

Style wasn't the same person she married. They were so in love, but the law firm, his job, his desire to move up took a toll on their marriage. The nature of the cases and what he did and the accepted practice of partners screwing around on the wives. Many wives told themselves that it was okay. Alexandra didn't feel that way. She never had, but she lied to herself when it began and told herself it would go away. Eventually Style would tire and would come back to be the person he was before.

Facing reality always sickened Alexandra, whether it was wanting, sideways looks from one of the paralegals he was sleeping with or a chance run in with a young, pretty divorcee he had recently represented. The guilt was readily apparent on these women's faces, letting Alexandra know they had slept with her husband.

And it hurt. How much scar tissue formed over her heart and soul over the past ten years?

However, in this moment, that was all secondary because the dragon continued raging in her chest. How long would the withdrawal symptoms last? When would she be over this, if ever? They had been giving her methadone, which took the raging to a modified roar, but she was physically ill. She had been able to go twenty-four hours at one point before but not on purpose; she wasn't able to get any drugs. She had been in this place before, but much more desperate then. She moved around on the bed to try to get comfortable, but the handcuffs kept her from turning on her left side, a nice reminder that she was now not only a prisoner to the chemical dragon but now a prisoner in real life.

The voices at the door drew her attention, and Alexandra saw Kyle walking in. She forced a half smile. He had always been so kind to her.

He returned the smile and came to her bed. "How are you?"

Alexandra was over lying about everything. "In a word, Yuck. Did Style send you?"

Kyle shook his head back and forth. "No, I have been keeping tabs on you, making sure you're okay. I knew you were leaving today, so I wanted to see you and wish you luck."

The pain hit her again. There, for a moment, was a thought that Style still might care.

Kyle continued. "Angela has been really worried about you and wanted to come see you, but under arrest, it wasn't possible." Angela was Kyle's wife, and she had always been so sweet to Alexandra. Kyle took Alexandra's hand and looked into her eyes. "We are both praying for you. I wish you would have come to me, I could have tried to help."

Alexandra's eyes welled up, and a tear moved down her face. "Style wouldn't let me tell anyone. He was so embarrassed and angry. He got me into the private program, but I couldn't control myself. It didn't work."

"The Fentanyl?" he questioned.

"A man in the group, a doctor who told me he had recovered offered to help me. He said that he'd give it to me and slow dose me down. Kyle, I was so desperate to quit. I believed him. I was so stupid." Alexandra teared up. "He injected me and then turned the same needle on himself. He tried to rape me, but I was able to get away. The getaway under Fentanyl put me here."

Kyle was now hugging her as the tears came. When she regained some control, he continued. "I'm glad you told me. You know my nephew overdosed and died?" he questioned.

"I didn't." Alexandra looked up. "I'm so sorry."

Kyle nodded. "I did everything I could to save him, but it wasn't enough. He was so far gone he didn't want to save himself. Alexandra, there are a lot of recovered people. You get a second chance, and I can tell you, you're not too far gone. You get to write the next chapter of your life."

"I'm so ashamed, Kyle."

"Let that go. The place you're going is great. It's near Big Sur and is very nice. Work with the doctors and call me and Angela if you need anything. We're here for you. We will come and visit, okay?"

"Thanks, Kyle."

There was a shuffling again at the door, and two San Francisco PD transfer officers were there. The same two who came to take her mugshot and fingerprints when she was remotely booked for DUI at the hospital. They acknowledged Kyle when they walked in. Kyle knew everyone. He pulled her hands up, kissed them, and then turned for the door. Stopping at the officers, he said, "Take care of her."

The elder of the two officers nodded at him. "Yes, sir." Then he was gone.

24

After a shower and nap, Matt sat in his room and felt locked in time. His room had not changed. There was the same single bed with a red and white Nebraska afghan, same posters and pictures from all those years ago still on the walls. His room was a time capsule of his time in Nebraska City, ending when he left at eighteen. The only difference today was that his Tumi luggage lined a wall, and Hank was sacked out in his bed, laying his head on a pillow. Hank loved a good pillow. How in the hell would the two of them be able to sleep in a single bed together? He would have to put some blankets on the floor bedside it and have him sleep there. It would be a tussle, but it had to be done.

Leaving his room, he could see the door to his parents' old room, now Amber and Steven's, was closed but a light shone under the door. He left Hank in bed and made his way downstairs. Lucas was in his playpen mesmerized by the *Troll* cartoons on the TV. Matt was thirsty, so he headed into the kitchen to grab some water when he ran into Dawn. She heard him come into the kitchen and smiled. She was standing at the top of a three-ladder stool, icing the top of some cupcakes. She was adorable.

Matt smiled a big smile. "Whatcha doin, Dawn?"

"I made cupcakes for you, Uncle Matty!"

He walked over and observed what could only be described as a mess. "They look amazing, Dawn. Thank you! Mom and Dad down yet?"

"Not yet. They wrastle before dinner. I watch Lucas like a big girl."

"Wrastle?"

"Yes, and I am not allowed to be outside their door anymore." She had a frown on her face. Matt almost busted out laughing but held it in with a smile.

"Well, tell me, what I can do to help you?" Matt went to the pantry on her orders and looked for sprinkles. While rummaging around, he found his vine guard suitcase and grabbed a bottle of Napa Cab from Bennett Lane out of it. They made excellent wine, which would complement the fresh-from-this-ranch-raised T-bones. He handed the sprinkles to Dawn and rummaged through the drawers until he found a pitiful excuse for a wine opener that must have been their parents' and began the arduous process of trying to get it to work. After a few minutes of goading and twisting, he finally had the cork out and only found a white wine glass. Beggars couldn't be choosers at this point, he thought.

He heard Lucas yell "Mommy!" from the living room, and he turned to see Amber swooping him out of the play pen and heading to the kitchen with Steven right behind her. They both looked very refreshed. She smiled her beautiful smile as she placed Lucas in the highchair. "I've got to get him down before our dinner," Amber said. She looked happy, and that melted Matt's heart. His plans of having a baby with Beth quickly turned into no prospect of having a child anytime in the future. It hurt.

Steven pulled a beer from the refrigerator and motioned to Amber, "Baby?"

Amber sighed. Now that she knew that she was pregnant, she would have to be careful with alcohol again. The doctor was very specific the first time around: one and only one a day.

"Since city slicker is here with his fine wine, I think I am going to pass and drink a glass with him. Did you find everything you needed?"

Matt smiled and jokingly opened the cupboard. "As a matter of fact, this is a horrible wine opener, and these are the wrong type of glasses for red."

He pulled another white wine glass down and poured it half-full. He turned to hand it to Amber and immediately saw the inside of her palm as a stop sign. "Well, Mr. Wine Snob, if you came around here more often, we might have these wonderful accoutrements for you. Now you are correct; that is a tiny glass, and I only get one now that my husband has once again knocked me up, so fill it up buddy."

"You see, you need to leave some space in the glass to swirl it and allow some oxygen to get into the wine. It will taste better. I didn't bring my aerator with me."

"I'm a doctor, and I have no idea what you are talking about, but I promise after I drink half, I will attempt this swirling exercise for you. Besides, I'm sure it's already going to taste better than anything we've been drinking around here lately." She took a draw from the glass. "Wow. And it is. That's very nice."

"Ruined on you," he teased. Whenever they were together, she always abandoned beer and drank his wine. Sometimes the two of them would stay up half the night catching up only to wake up the next morning hungover.

"Agreed. One glass a night." She clinked her glass on Matt's, and then Steven brought in his beer and tapped both their glasses.

Amber began to shove food into Lucas's mouth. He immediately devoured it. "He is an eating machine."

Matt suddenly remembered and said, "Hey, Steven, did you and Tim Cross ever connect from Skyhawk Tracking?"

Steven's eyes lit up. "Oh my God, wait till you see this," he said as he left the room. Matt recently invested in Skyhawk Tracking as a startup company, and as a favor, asked Tim to work with Steven on some uses of the technology for the farm. Matt told Tim to send him the bill for it, but doubted he would ever get one, which is how things worked when you invested millions into a new company.

"He is gaga over this thing," Amber said, waving Lucas's spoon in the air. "I have to admit it's pretty amazing and helpful."

Steven came in the room with his iPad showing a Google Earth image of the family farm. Matt knew the image instantly because he could see the river snaking through the back of the property and the roof of the house they were standing in. Steven zoomed out and Matt could see colored dots in the fields. There were a couple of blue ones, several green ones and then a ton of pink and purple ones. "These are cows," Steven said. "I can see all of them in real time. The blue ones are the breeding bulls." Steven could see one blue dot in the sea of cows, and two more off by themselves, which made sense. Only one bull could be allowed in with the cows at a time otherwise they would kill each other to dominate the herd.

"The green ones are the gilded males, the pink ones are the females, and the purple ones are the females currently pregnant." Steven double clicked on one, and a legend where he could change the status for each one appeared. There was an area to name the cow, but a number was currently entered there, and a picture of the cow came up on the screen.

"This is incredible," Matt said, amazed. "In real time, you can see the location of every head of cattle on all 600 acres?"

"Yes. This has been a game changer for me. I am not hunting for them anymore because I know where all of them are."

"How do you charge the battery of the tracker?"

"When Tim called, he asked me my biggest issue, and I told him keeping up with the cows. He said they are testing something and asked if I would be willing to be an alpha test. Of course, I have nothing to lose, so I say yes. Two days later, FedEx is at my door with 250 trackers about the size of a cell phone, but much lighter." Steven reached into his pocket, pulled a tracker out, and handed it to Matt.

"Solar?" Matt asked.

"Yep! So, I bring all the cows in, put their ear tag number in the iPad, snap a picture, and glue this thing on their existing ear tag. As long as they are in the sun for a while every seven days, it gives off the signal and the satellite can see them."

"That's frigging amazing!" Matt touched the screen and a warning popped up. "What's going on?"

Steven clicked on the pop-up, and the map moved away from the herd to a wooded section of the farm where there was a single purple blip. "Working with Tim, whenever a cow goes off 400 yards from the nearest cow on their own, we have programmed a warning. My guess is she's having her calf right now. We'll have to go check tomorrow."

"How many cows is it tracking now?"

"All 237 of them. It was a bitch getting them all tagged when we started. Hell, Tim and I didn't even know if it would work, but we tried a few and had no issues, so we expanded to the whole herd. He has been great."

"Tell him about the phone call," Amber said as she continued to feed Lucas.

"Amber's cell goes off in the middle of the night because she's on call with the sheriff's department, and she hands the phone to me. It's William, one of Tim's programmers, and he's worried because Charlie, one of the calves, and his mother are almost a mile away from the herd itself. I'm thinking, who the hell is Charlie? He says you know calf 225. Come to find out, they have all these jumbo screens in the Silicon Valley office, and these guys love watching the cows on the ranch. They find it relaxing and have named them all. I explained to William that on a ranch we do NOT name the food."

Matt busted out laughing. "So, what happened?"

Amber points at Steven. "He goes after him."

"In the middle of the night? Are you crazy?"

"I'd been startled wide awake, so I had to find out what's going on with Char—" Steven stopped himself midsentence. "—225. So, I saddle up Ghost and off we go to find these damn cows because William in Silicon Valley is upset." At that, they all busted out into uncontrollable laughter. "An hour-ride later, I get there thanks to my trusty iPad, and sure enough, as soon as I get close, I hear the calf wailing and the mother is in distress. Poor Charlie..." He again stops himself. "...225 is caught up in a mess of briars and can't get loose. It's 1:00 A.M. and I'm cutting the calf out, and both of us are bleeding."

"Did you call William?"

"Hell yes. I took a picture beforehand of him stuck and then took a selfie with Charlie after and texted it to him. He was very happy. I thanked him and tell him I am going to send him some steaks for him and his family, and he declines them."

"Don't tell me." Matt was shaking his head.

"Yep, he and his wife are vegetarians."

"Of course, they are. It's California," Matt laughed. "You can't make this shit up."

Steven grabbed the plate of T-bones and headed toward the door. "No vegetarians in this house," he said as he went out the back door to the grill.

Matt went over to refresh his glass of wine still wiping the tears from laughing from his face. It was good to be home. The kitchen was quiet except for the sound of Lucas pounding the food down, and Dawn was in living room now watching Disney.

Amber turned to him. "Do you want to talk about Beth?"

The pain was back in Matt's chest again, and he forced a smile. "I love you."

"I love you too, Matty. It's so good to have you home."

"It's so good to be here. It's been too long." Amber got up, embraced him, not wanting to let go. She could see his pain, and she wanted to take it away. After a long moment, Matt sighed and kissed her cheek.

"Well, I need to go outside and observe Grill Master Steven to take some of this technique back to New York with me." He grabbed his wine glass and headed to the door. Would he return to New York? Did he really know? Almost four days ago, everything was so clear and now it was a fucking mess. The screen door creaked open, and he escaped from talking to Amber. He didn't want to bring his mess of a life here with him. He just wanted to be happy with his family for now.

25

After dinner, Steven and Matt cleaned up the kitchen while Amber supervised Dawn's bath, which was followed by the story they were working on together. Dawn usually did most of the reading and crashed after four pages. She was way past books her age and was reading *The Box Car Children*, a classic Amber also read as a child. After Dawn was asleep, Amber checked on Lucas in his crib in their bedroom. He was a purring, sleeping angel, but such a little monster when he was awake. How were they all going to fit in this house with "it" on the way? She smiled. They would figure it out. They always did.

She grabbed the baby monitor and headed downstairs. She wanted another glass of wine but got water instead and headed out to the front porch in her jacket. It was cold. She could see her breath as she approached Steven and Matt cutting up on the front swing together. Matt started to get up when he saw her, but she motioned for him to stay. She snuggled her way between the two of them, taking Steven's hand. Matt threw his right arm around her to make extra room and pulled her in tight.

Matt cracked a funny smile at Amber.

"What's that about?"

"I assume you guys have added a wrestling ring to the master bedroom because Dawn tells me that you two wrestle every night before dinner."

Amber leaned forward, exasperated. She looked at Steven, "What are we going to do with her?"

"Don't look at me—you're the psychiatrist. I'm just the ranch hand, and I am really happy right now not to be in jail."

Matt smiled. "I'm not seeing the correlation."

Steven started to get up. "I'm going to get another beer."

Amber stopped him. "No, no, no. She's your spawn as well. You're going to have to suffer through this with me."

Matt was laughing. "I can't wait for this."

Amber started, "You know Sally?"

"Sally? I think I am going to need more."

"Sally, my friend from high school. Sally Simpson, now Sally Bergstrom."

"Oh yeah, easy Sally. She was pretty."

Steven leaned forward. "What?"

"Stop it, Matt!" Amber scolded him. "She is still pretty, and she is Dawn's teacher now. She's married with kids of her own and leads the women of the church."

"Really? I would not have seen that coming."

Steven, now intrigued, asked, "So, Easy Sally?"

Amber elbowed both men simultaneously. "Steven, stop! That does not come out of your mouth again. Matty! She had a lot of boyfriends in high school."

Matt repeated, "A lot. A ton of them."

Amber, not liking the direction of this conversation, said, "Moving on. She went to the same program at Nebraska that Beth did. She did her six years teaching in North Platt fulfilling her obligation and then moved back home to Nebraska City with her husband who's also a teacher. I'm surprised you didn't run into her while you were there. She would have been finishing up."

Matt jokingly said, "Had I known, I might have looked her up."

Steven choked on his beer with laughter.

Amber turned to Steven. "Serves you right. The Lord sees you." She then turned to Matty and said, "That would not have made me happy. Anyways can we move on with this story?"

"Please." Matt shot a glance at Steven who was red faced.

"Sally called me and said she wanted to have a parent teacher conference, which is kind of hysterical because I get a download of all the craziness my daughter has said at church every week. She said it should just be me, and Steven doesn't need to bother coming. I'm thinking, oh God it's some female thing, so I agree. I get to her class, and it's just me and Sally, and she is clearly uncomfortable, so I asked, 'What did my little angel from heaven, Dawn, do this week?'"

Matt playing on Steven and Amber's obvious exasperation says, "This is going to be good."

"They were teaching the kids to see something, say something, which is the last thing that Dawn needs to hear because so little DOES NOT come out of that child's mouth. Basically, if they saw something, they could come to Sally, and they would talk about it."

"Got it," Matt acknowledged.

Amber continued now getting louder, "So my little angel—"

Steven put his arm on her shoulder, "Easy, baby."

Amber took a deep breath. "She proceeds to tell Sally that she has seen Steven holding me down and that I am screaming in pain."

"Oh no." Matt is now laughing nervously.

"Oh yes. Apparently, my angel has been spying on us while we are having marital relations. Sally concludes on her own Steven is having issues and is hurting me. Then she proceeded to call Rocky."

"No, she didn't. Is that old man still sheriff?"

"Oh yes she did, and the two of them concoct a plan to bring me to school to confront me, and then Rocky and his deputies sweep me and the kids away to Bellevue to stay with his sister while they arrest Steven for abuse and, oh yes, try to get him some help."

"Oh my God!" Matt was looking at Steven who had his head in his hands.

"Oh, it gets better. She tells me that Rocky is in the hallway outside the door right now. Matt, he is one my bosses!"

"What did you do?" Matt was now incredulous.

"I was livid. I lost my shit. I went into full crazy bitch mode. I got up, went to the door and opened it, and I told Rocky to get his ass in the room. I shut the door and told them everything, that in fact Steven does hold me down when we are having sex, and yes I am screaming but not in pain!"

Steven, mortified, added, "I cannot believe you are telling your brother this. Can I get that beer?"

Amber, on a roll now, insisted, "No you cannot. Sit right here," she said, patting him on the leg. Steven was still not looking up.

"How does this story end?" Matt asked, eyes wide, mouth gaping.

"Well, Sally was dumbstruck, and Rocky was looking for a place to hide under a child's-size desk. I then tell them I am going to strip naked in front of both of them to prove there is not a mark on me and that my husband has never laid a hand on me in anger and never on the children. In fact, when Steven is laying a hand on me, it's because I want him to."

"Holy mackerel!"

Steven moaned, "Can I please get my beer?"

Amber was finished venting. "Go ahead, baby."

"Great!" Steven bounded up. "Matt, can I get you anything?"

"Fuck at this point just bring the bottle," he said, motioning to his wine glass.

"Roger that."

Matt turned to Amber. "What did they say then?"

Amber started giggling uncontrollably. "I began to unbutton my blouse, and Rocky falls over in the desk trying to get out of it, and Sally pops up and stops me. They couldn't believe what I'd said. Hell, I still can't believe I said that, but I was just so mad. Steven is the gentlest soul. I can't get enough of that man. Sally called that night crying and apologized to me and Steven. I told her next time to just talk to me. Rocky is still barely making eye contact."

Steven returned and poured the remainder of the bottle in Matt's glass almost to the top. "So how did this turn into wrestling?" Steven asked.

"On the way home, I confronted Dawn, distraught that she would think that you were hurting me. I didn't want her to feel unsafe. She said she knew I wasn't hurt because we would laugh and lay together afterwards. She was unconcerned, the little spy."

"So, you told her we were wresting, play fighting? Really?"

"Steven, I can't tell Dawn in the first grade what sex is. Can you see how that scenario would unfold? She would be instructing the entire first grade on what sex is. Our phone would be ringing off the hook from the other parents in the class."

Steven moaned again. "Ugh." He knew that would be exactly what Dawn would do.

Matt laughed. "I didn't see that story coming. What a pistol she is."

Steven chimed in, "She's her mother."

Amber stood up from the swing. “I am going to bed, and you two assholes need to wrap this up.”

“We’ll be up right after we finish these.” Steven leaned over and clinked Matt’s wine glass.

26

Amber again watched the sun set in the West as she pulled into the driveway. An amazingly uneventful day at work and school had gone by slowly as she couldn't wait to get home to her men.

As she pulled in, she smiled as she could see Steven on the porch waiting on them with Lady at the top of the steps. She popped out of the car and gave Steven a long kiss. "Hey there, baby." Lady immediately tried to muscle in on their embrace to share the love. Amber reached down and lovingly stroked Lady's head. Noticeably absent from the porch was Matt. "Matty cleaning up?" Steven shook his head no. Amber was immediately worried. "Where is he?"

Revealing his concern, Steven half smiled. "He's still in bed."

Amber looked at her watch. It was just after 6:00 P.M. "Is he okay?"

Steven shook his head up and down. "You told me to let him sleep, so I did. He just never got up. I checked on him several times today, but he was out."

Amber turned away from him in contemplation, looking at the kids in the car trying to get out of their car seats and Lady running around the two of them. "Steven, can you handle this tonight?" Amber asked, turning back to him and motioning to all the action.

"I got it. You just take care of him." With that, Amber was in the house, leaving all that behind her. The amazing smell of the pot roast cooking in the crock pot all day immediately hit her nose on the way in the door. She put it on before she left that morning with potatoes and carrots. She went to the pantry, pulled out a jar of canned green beans, and threw them into a pot on the stove.

She then walked up the stairs to Matt's room and opened the door. The room was completely dark with the shades pulled down and the curtains completely shut. She could see her brother's form in the single bed. Hank was beside the bed on a blanket guarding. His tail wagged when she came in, and she knelt to love on him, putting her head against his. "What a good boy you are, taking care of your daddy." He rolled over to expose his belly, and she petted him. He writhed back and forth on the floor in joy. Gathering herself, she sat on the side of the single bed and looked upon her brother. His breathing was deep and regular. She touched his forehead, moving his hair and checking for a temperature. He was cool. His breathing changed as he took in a deep breath and opened his eyes.

Amber smiled. "Hey there."

Matt smiled back and exhaled. "What time is it?

"It's a little after six."

"Okay, I'll get up and help Steven."

"Matty, it's six in the evening."

"What? Oh my God, I'm so sorry."

"There is nothing to be sorry for." Hank shoved his face in-between them and rested his nose on Matt's chest.

"Oh, Hank, buddy, I am so sorry."

"He's fine. I fed him this morning on my way out. Steven took him out to go to the bathroom, and when they came back inside, he came back up here and has been here all day. I'm going to take him down to feed him again and take him out. You need to take a shower and then meet me in the sewing room. Steven is taking care of the kids tonight. You and I can have dinner in there." The sewing room was their mom's space when they were growing up. Now it was Amber's office where she treated many of her clients via video. The room was out of earshot of the kids and Steven for clients who had to have sessions in the evening.

"Amber I—."

She cut him off. "Take a shower now, and I will meet you in the sewing room." Like it or not, Matt was going to talk to her now. She was in charge. She went to her bedroom and changed into green tights and threw on her favorite soft sweatshirt. She saw Hank in the hallway, lying in front of the bathroom door waiting for his owner. His big sad eyes looked up at her, and she could tell that he knew or at least sensed Matt's pain and was trying to help. She again stopped and loved on him. She could hear the shower stop, so she headed downstairs. "Come on, Hanky. Let's get you something to eat." He bounced to life and followed her down.

The kitchen was a train wreck. Lucas was eating, and Steven was trying to get a bite or two in his own mouth while shoveling the food into Lucas. Dawn was talking a mile a minute about school and working on her homework while trying to eat as well. Steven looked up defeated and just smiled. Could she love that man anymore? She didn't think so. She smiled back and hugged him. "Get used to it. This is what every night is going to look like since you knocked me up again."

"You know I love all of this. We will figure it out. Also, it's not fair for you to look that great if we're taking the night off." He wrapped his arm around her, and his hand rested on her hip.

"Who said we are taking the night off?" She was lying. Whatever was going on with Matt, she was going to pry it out of him. It would be a late night, and with Steven working all day and having to get up at 5:00 A.M., he would be asleep between nine and ten. She turned to feed Hank and then let him out. Lady followed Hank. She missed her fur-cousin all day and couldn't miss the opportunity to run around the yard with him. "Can you let them back in in a few minutes?"

"Sure, babe. I got them."

"Thank you." She went to the pantry and pulled out a bottle of wine from Matt's suitcase and struggled to uncork it with her awful corkscrew.

"Need help?" Steven asked.

"He wasn't kidding. This thing is awful." She finally got it uncorked and pulled down two wine glasses. She stopped and wrote wine opener and red wine glasses on the grocery list on the refrigerator door. She then pulled down two plates and portioned them with dinner for her and Matt.

Matt had already made his way to the sewing room, and when she entered, he startled her. Men were fortunate it took so little time to get ready, but even today, Matt had taken short cuts. He wore a gray Nebraska hoody, jeans and white socks. His head was down, and his hair was still visibly wet. When he looked up, he hadn't shaved, which gave a rugged edge to his handsomeness. "Here." She put the plate down in front of him. "Eat." He took the fork and started eating quickly, reminding Amber he hadn't eaten in twenty-four hours.

She got up and closed the door to the sewing room. They still called it the sewing room, but it looked nothing like that anymore. It was filled with books and shelves. Her desk had two monitors for her to meet with her clients and to take notes on their cases at the same time. She watched while he ate, and they didn't speak. She could see he was hiding within himself. She quietly picked at her food, wondering where to start to get him to open up. "Matty…"

Still looking down, Matt whispered, "I can't, Amber. You're my sister not my psychiatrist. I just need you to be my sister."

"I am and will always be your sister who loves you very much, and I am not here to be your psychiatrist. I am just here to listen and help if I can." She was lying of course.

"I didn't come here to dump this on you, especially after you haven't seen me face-to-face in two years. That's wrong. I should have come around more. I'm sorry."

"That's not entirely your fault. Look around. We would love to come see you, but with the ranch, the animals, and the kids, it's just not possible. There's no blame. Both our lives are very busy," She paused. "Tell me about Beth."

His voice was shaky. "She's gone. I had no clue what was going on." He still couldn't look at her. His head was down with his eyes on the floor.

Amber's face flushed, a sign of her anger she couldn't hide. Matt began to cry, and she embraced him as tears were now streaming down her face as well. When Matt grew quiet, she pulled back and put her hands on both sides of his face lifting his red eyes up to hers. He was so sad that it crushed her heart. "Tell me."

Matt took a deep breath and unloaded the entire sordid story. Amber was prepared because she was a professional, but this was awful, worsened by the fact that this was her baby brother.

When he finished, Amber asked, "What are you going to do? Are you going to stay at Waverman?"

"I don't know what I am going to do. I have seven weeks to figure that out, but I can't quit right now during the FTC investigation. I have to be cleared of this before I can do anything. If I leave now, it looks like I am guilty even if Waverman doesn't do anything to implicate me in that other mess. I'd lose my career."

"You can stay here with me and Steven until then. You know you are welcome. This is still your home as well." She touched his hand and smiled. "Steven and the kids just love you, and we can certainly use a hand."

"When does the seasonal help return?"

"They're expected back in two weeks."

"I'll stay until then and help with the projects, but I'm sure by then I'll be ready to go and will have thoroughly worn out my welcome."

"Matty, this is your home. We want you to stay. Where would you go? Back to an empty house in Connecticut?"

"King George wants me to go to Mountain View, California to meet with this hired gun tech-investment firm. We've been talking about it for years but could never pull it together. It's actually not a bad idea, and it gives me and Hanky a road trip, which would actually be nice." There was commotion at the door to the office. Hank was outside, butting his head against the door trying to get in. He heard Matt say his name. Before Matt could get up to let him in, Steven appeared and opened the door. Hank bounded in the room to be loved on by Matt and Amber.

"So, King George wants you to spend your suspension working for him? That sounds just like him." Amber and Steven had met King George several times in the past when they would come to the city to visit. George always insisted on throwing a dinner party, and they would come up to his place for drinks and dinner that would last into the early hours of the morning. He was always very gracious when they were in town.

"I wasn't really on board until I thought it through. I think Mountain View is only a few hours from Napa, which I've never been able to visit, so why not turn my suspension into a little vacation on King George with my wingman here," Matt said as he rubbed Hank's head.

Amber frowned. "If you are going to leave, then we need to talk through some coping mechanisms to help you through this."

"I thought you weren't going to be my shrink."

"I lied when I said that." They both broke out in laughter.

"I knew you were."

"Look, you need to be grateful. Since you're out of work, I am doing this pro bono."

Matt pointed to her glass of wine. "This does not look pro bono to me. You're drinking my wine."

"That's an excellent point. You also have to send me a case of wine from your trip to Napa. I'm going to need something to celebrate after "baby three" arrives." She rubbed her belly. "What are we going to do with another baby?"

"What you're doing now, just love them." The room went quiet.

"So, back to coping."

"REALLY?!"

"Yes, really. Please shut up and let me be the doctor. I need you to think of a chair. You with me?"

"A what?"

"A chair."

"Got it. Chair."

"A chair has four legs, and those legs are a metaphor for the stability of your life. One leg of the chair is your work life. Another leg of the chair is your family life."

"So far I'm not doing so well."

"Let me finish." She was getting frustrated. "The other leg is your faith, your relationship to a higher power, and the final leg is your physical life, your health, how you take care of yourself, eating, working out regularly, your general health wellness. In most cases, if you can fill out the legs of a chair, you can have a full and somewhat happy life. If we take a leg of that chair away what do you have?"

"Three legs. A stool I guess?"

"Correct, and you can still have stability with a stool, but you may not have the life you want to have. You can make it on a stool, but the chair is what you are aiming for. You need to work toward that."

"Well, this has been helpful. My family life and work life are shit right now, and I can't tell you the last time I've been to church."

"Your family life is not shit. You have us, and we love you. You just lost a piece of it. Your work life is on hold, not lost. Even if you don't go back to Waverman, it sounds like you have a good plan not to sabotage yourself and then you can move on from there. You're obviously in great shape, so we just need to get you back into church."

"I don't think that God would be very happy with me right now. My mood swings go from sadness to betrayal, then anger and back again."

"And all of that makes total sense. There are so many emotions that go on during a separation and divorce that you have to have ways to cope with it. It can eat you alive if you don't deal with it. Many of my clients are clients for these exact reasons."

"I don't want my sister as my shrink."

"Agreed because even if I could ethically, I can't. I have some great colleagues, people who I went to school with that could step in my place. I could reach out to them."

Matt knew this was not going to end until he acquiesced, so he had her text a couple of contacts to him. "If I need to, I will reach out."

"Okay. Agreed. In the interim, if you get overwhelmed with your feelings, write them down to get them out." Amber reached over and touched his chest. "Don't let them eat you up. Normally I would have clients write out their feelings and discuss them during session with them giving me their notes. If you don't want to talk to anyone you could always write them down and give them to God. Let Him handle them for you. I have clients who do that as well."

"How do I do that?"

"By writing them, it gets those feelings out at least in that moment. It can release you from the hold they have on you, and then you simply take what you have written and burn it. You send it to God, and by doing that, only you and God know what those feelings are. Can you do that for me? Promise?"

"Sure, I can do that."

"Thank you. Also, and this is so important. What you can't do is type it into a computer or blog it, put it on Facebook or Instagram or keep a journal. That can actually immortalize those feelings. You can't keep what you write. That will only prompt you at some point to go back and read it, stew on it, and that can take you right back."

"Write it out and then burn it. I can do that."

"Give it to God if you won't get help from a professional. You okay?" She got up and put the empty plates together.

"I think so."

"Well, some of us didn't sleep all day, so I have got to hit the hay. Another long day tomorrow."

"If it's okay, I think I'll stay in here awhile."

"Sure, you can use it as your office as well while you're here." She grabbed the dishes and headed to the door. "I love you, Matty."

"I love you too. Thank you."

"Sure." She left the office and pulled the door behind her.

Matt, alone in the quiet with Hank, reached over to Amber's desk and picked up a blank sheet of paper and a pen. "Okay, here we go." Hank tossed his head from side to side trying to understand, then rested his head on Matt's lap. Matt reached down and rubbed his head. "Hank, I think you are probably the only therapist I need right now. Thank God she didn't take you."

27

Alexandra laid in bed looking out her third-floor window of the Shadow Oaks Treatment Center nestled in the hills above Monterey, California. She watched as the morning fog moved through the branches of the massive trees outside. At some point Shadow Oaks had been a family estate with a large stately home tucked into the center of the property. A plaque on the property said the home had been built in the early 1900s by the Treace Family. Undoubtably the fortune had been squandered by the children and grandchildren of the family and had been purchased in 1980 by the treatment center. Now on both sides of the massive house were two buildings that served as dorms and the wellness center. The building to the left housed the women and the building on the right housed the men. The estate was now a full resort with a pool, workout area, and miles of walking trails all for the well-off broken people who were trying to be rehabilitated.

There were no walls, fences, or outer-locked doors at Shadow Oaks to imprison those inside. There was a daily schedule of meetings and activities for each to attend to heal. It was a voluntary situation for most, and they could come and go as they chose. There were check-in times for each activity, and if someone was missing or late, it was noticed, and word spread immediately. In Alexandra's case, if she went missing, it would turn into a warrant and a trip to jail.

It had been almost a week since her arrival at Shadow Oaks and two weeks since the accident that sent her there. The cuts on her face from the glass were almost healed, and the extensive bruising and swelling on her face had transitioned from black to a faded blue, but still prompted an occasional gasp when she entered a room. Because of that, she continued to stay to herself in her room, which was essentially a hotel room. She had her meals brought to her, and when she would get stir crazy, she would go for a walk alone on the trails or sit among the trees drawing in the sketchbook her mother brought. What was coming out of Alexandra onto the pages of the book was almost unrecognizable to her from her previous work. It terrified her, but the doctors encouraged her to continue as part of her therapy.

She had been awake since 5:30 A.M., which was a new record for her. When she first arrived, she would be awake most of the night fighting withdrawal. They had offered sleeping aids, but Alexandra didn't want any more drugs, something else to depend on. With two weeks under her belt, the physical withdrawal was gone. Now it was all mental and knowing that made her angry at herself. Having to examine the last year of her life and her life in general in daily exercises was excruciating.

The alarm came to life next to her bed and then almost immediately the alarm on her cell phone rang as well. Alexandra turned both alarms off. She looked at her schedule for the day, and she had one-on-one counseling with Dr. Moranne at 8:00 A.M. She would not and could not be late. As she got out of the bed, her body felt tight and sore still from the accident but was rebounding. She was cleared yesterday for all activities and was instructed to begin swimming and doing yoga. Both activities had now been inserted into her schedule by the staff. She slowly walked over to the Keurig and brewed a cup of coffee. One of the few joys of her day was the first cup of coffee, and she carefully sipped it. It was good with just a couple of sweeteners.

Walking toward the bathroom, she caught a glimpse of her naked body in the mirrored doors of the closet and stopped. She was thin, almost too thin, probably back to her high school thin and she rubbed her hands down her body and checked herself over, turning completely around. The bruising from her attack on her wrists and inner thighs was finally gone, and she was so relieved. She hadn't even thought of that when they cleared her to swim. She doubted that she had a swimsuit in the suitcase her mother packed for her. If not, Shadow Oaks would provide. Anything she asked for, other than drugs, was just a phone call away.

Alexandra took another sip from her coffee and made her way into the bathroom. She sighed in the mirror as she went inside and saw the closeup bruising on her face. How much longer? She had showered in the evening before her dinner was brought to her room, so that was not needed. She pulled her hair back into a ponytail, brushed her teeth, and applied the makeup her mother brought. It helped tremendously, but she was having to put so much on to cover the bruising, and that was never her. What did her mother used to tell her? Just enough to accentuate your features, not cover them up. She was looking forward to looking normal again.

The mornings and evenings were always cool in Monterey, so Alexandra pulled on a pair of jeans, tennis shoes, and a purple sweater. Her alarm went off again on her phone, which was her fifteen-minute warning, and she left her room with her coffee. The hallway was alive as it was almost time for everyone's first session of the day. Alexandra slid into the stairwell to avoid sharing an elevator with anyone. At the bottom, she walked out the door of her building towards the main house. The cool morning air hit her face, and the smell of the fog with the nature and the trees was intoxicating. It was beautiful here. As Alexandra entered the main house front door, she could smell the antique home smell and went into the main sitting area, which use to be the formal living room. It was thankfully empty, and she sat on the sofa and sipped her coffee. She was ten minutes early, and Dr. Moranne would come to get her when she was ready.

Alexandra heard the front door open and close, and she turned her bruised face away from the hallway looking outside, hoping whoever had entered was not joining. Sure enough, she heard steps behind her, and a young, beautiful brunette girl, probably in her early twenties, plopped down in a chair right next to her.

"Hi… I think I know you."

Alexandra was mortified, the shame roared back to life inside her. "Really." She sipped her coffee again.

"Yes, not sure from where, but I swear I do. Are you from San Francisco?"

Alexandra not having the strength to make up a lie nodded up and down. "Yes, I am."

"I thought so. What do you do?"

Alexandra paused for a moment. What did she do? "I am an artist." Which was her last real job that unfortunately went down in flames after a disastrous showing.

"Cool, would I have seen any of your work?"

Again, not having the strength to lie. "Probably not."

There was an uncomfortable silence, and then she stuck out her hand. "I'm Agatha. I know it's a horrible name, but it was my grandmother's, and she died a few months before I was born. Everybody calls me Aggy."

"Alexandra." She shook the extended hand.

"How long are you in for?"

"A month. Three weeks left." Alexandra was not happy with this line of questioning before the next line of questioning with Dr. Moranne.

"You must be a first-timer. What's your drug of choice?"

"This is my first time and hopefully last. Oxycodone."

"You and the whole world. That was one of my first drugs I tried, but my drug of choice now is heroin." Aggy turned over her arms and revealed the scars from all the needle hits. "This is my third trip to a treatment facility. I'm forty-five days in with two more weeks to go."

Alexandra was speechless. "I'm sure you're going to make it."

Aggy looked down at the floor. "I have to." Her voice was almost too quiet to hear. "My parents are going to cut me off from my trust if I don't pull it together. I don't have a clue what I would do then."

Alexandra said nothing. She didn't know how to respond.

"Alexandra." Dr. Moranne was at the door.

Alexandra bolted off the couch completely relieved to be ending the conversation. As she exited the room, she heard Aggy from behind. "Let's catch up later." Alexandra pretended not to hear her and proceeded to Dr. Moranne's office.

28

Amber was nestled into the back seat of the truck with her four children. She had taken the middle of the back seat with Lucas and Dawn in their car seats. Her other two children, who had now most likely made them late for church by insisting on taking Matt's new truck and transferring the car seats, were seated in the driver seat and shotgun. Matt and Steven like two little boys were playing with all the technology bells and whistles the truck had to offer. A smile came over her face as they laughed together at some ridiculous option.

It had been a full, busy week. Her men would get up early to work on projects most of the day and then run into town to get supplies for the next day's projects. Incredibly, all the dangerous projects were almost completed. They were actually hunting for projects for the upcoming week. They both worked well together. You would have thought they were brothers, which made Amber's heart swell. The evenings were filled with laughter at the day's activities. Matt would occasionally slide off to her office and write. It would eventually end up an ember in the fireplace. She told Steven just enough about what was going on, so he knew not to ask. Beth was not to be mentioned.

As they headed into town, the dueling steeples of the Lutheran and Methodist Churches could be seen in the distance towering above the tree line. Amber leaned forward and jokingly punched them both in the shoulder. "There's going to be no place to park because the two of you made us late." Matt and Steven looked at each other and smiled.

In a high voice Matt said, "It ain't no problem," something the two of them had been saying all week when they ran into an obstacle on a job. The two boys laughed, and Amber rolled her eyes and smiled. "I'll pull up front, so you guys can unload, and I'll go park." As they were pulling up to the church, the entrance was surrounded by people talking and hugging, all in their Sunday best. Steven was in the best pair of blue jeans he had. They were dark, blue, and only worn on Sunday. He had on a shirt Amber picked out that was bright blue and brought out his eyes with his dark curly hair and his suede, leather sport coat over top. Matt didn't have any Sunday jeans, so he was in his blue Italian suit, which was way too fitted for Nebraska standards, with a light blue shirt underneath and brown wing tips with no tie. Amber and Dawn were in their best dresses, and Lucas was in his second outfit of the day, having covered the first one with food.

Amber leaned forward and put her arm on Matt's shoulder. "Do you see anyone you recognize?"

Matt responded, "I see about ten people I recognize."

"How about the shorter blue dress with the older gentlemen off to right?"

Matt looked through the crowd and the words spilled out in a whisper, "Rachel." His first love was standing next to a man who had to be about fifteen years older with two children by her side. She was shapely, stately, and beautiful. "When—?"

Amber cut him off. "She moved back about a year ago when her marriage fell apart. Those are her children from the previous marriage. The man she is standing next to is Guy Benson. He is the president of The Bank of Nebraska. They got married about two months ago."

Matt smirked. "Really?"

"Really. Just wanted to give you heads-up." She was smiling, enjoying his reaction. She patted him on the shoulder. The bells of the Lutheran Church began to ring, announcing the beginning of service.

Matt sarcastically turned to her. "Thanks."

As the truck came to a stop out front, Steven jumped out and opened the back. Amber had already unlatched Lucas, and Steven reached in to pull him from the car seat. Amber had Dawn by the hand, and they scrambled out the same door. Amber was hurrying and barking orders. "Steven, you get the kids to Sunday school. I will try and save us a seat. Matty, look for me. I will try get us something on the left-hand side."

And then they were gone, scrambling up the steps of the church. Both the Lutheran and Methodist Church parking lots were full. God was still a big draw in Nebraska, so Matt drove down the main thoroughfare with no luck as both sides were filled with cars. He finally turned off a side street and found a space.

Walking toward the churches felt good. He could hear the singing inside of the sinners who had gathered, but he wasn't sure which church it was coming from. The cool Nebraska spring air was on his breath as the sun hung high in the sky threatening a rebirth for a new planting season. Matt walked inside, and the service was well on its way with the announcements being made. Almost immediately, he saw a hand shoot into the air. It was Amber as she said on the left-hand side of the church about halfway down. Several people behind her looked to see who she was motioning to.

He was now officially a spectacle, late for service. He quietly crouched down the side aisle and slid in next to her. Steven was on the other side of her holding her hand. As he sat down, two rows ahead of them, someone turned to look at him. It was Rachel. She smiled a knowing smile. When she turned back toward the front, Steven, having observed this, whispered, "Woo." Amber immediately popped his leg making way too much noise, which prompted more people to turn around. Matt snorted quietly, trying to hold in laughter. Amber started giggling, and Steven couldn't help but start giggling also, which was followed by various shushing from the congregation.

Pastor Tuddle led the flock through the service and sermon, which was on Paul, how Saul the Jew who persecuted the Christians became Paul the apostle and led the early church. Paul had a change in course and how those changes in course happen to all of us in life. Good and bad changes, we should embrace them as God leading us. Matt felt like Pastor Tuddle was talking directly to him. Amber must have picked up on it as well and at some point during the service took his hand. When the final hymn was sung, Matt's head was spinning.

"Steven, you get the kids, and Matt and I will meet you out front."

Matt, wanting to limit his exposure to the masses, said, "I'll help Steven, and we will meet you out front." They went down the halls of the church and memories came from each room they passed. This was the church where Matt and Amber grew up, and every corner had a story. Not much had changed, which in a way was nice. They found Dawn reading a book to several other young girls as the teacher was waiting for the parents to arrive. After they gathered her, they went to retrieve Lucas, but walking down the hallway, they could hear him before they could see him.

When they looked in the room, Lucas had his arms outstretched doing the airplane with full sound effects running around the room. The other kids were running in terror or laughing trying to avoid being run over by Lucas the airplane. Steven swooped in and snatched him into the air just as he was about to run down a small girl. A teenage girl who looked completely exasperated with Lucas yelled, "Thank you, Mr. Heard," as they left the room.

Steven carried Lucas on his shoulder and yelled back, "Thank you for putting up with him." They passed a random woman in the hallway who congratulated Steven and kept going. Matt looked at Steven, and he shrugged his shoulders having no idea why.

Out front of the church Amber was with Martha Stone, an older but well-refined woman who was the matriarch of the church and the leader of the Lutheran Women, discussing the upcoming food drive for the local pantry. Sally joined the conversation, and surprisingly Rachel found her way into the conversation with Wendy. It was a surprising group considering Rachel had not said more than twenty words to Amber other than hello in the past year. Amber wondered if Rachel and Wendy had any idea that they had both dated Matt in high school.

Martha nodded towards the church and said, "Amber, it seems you're turning your property into a stud farm as well." Amber turned to see her husband with Lucas tucked in his left arm, laughing, walking next to her brother. In between them was Dawn, who was holding hands with both and on every third step they would swing her into the air.

Amber sighed taking in the moment, and before she could reply, Sally said, "It looks that way to me."

With that Amber tapped her arm, "Stop." She caught a glimpse of Rachel and Wendy. Rachel's eyes were locked on Matt in his tight blue suit and wing tips. Her gaze was much more than friendly. It was obvious that Wendy had no idea Matt was in town, and she appeared flushed. Amber was analyzing these women. When Steven and Matt walked up, they released Dawn who was immediately off and running with the other children around the grounds.

Amber stood between the two men and put her arms around both. "Matt, I think you might know everyone here. You remember Mrs. Martha?"

"Of course, I do. How are you, Martha?"

"I'm fine, Matt. How is New York? I hear you're doing great up there."

"It's busy." Matt hugged her.

"This is Sally. We were friends in high school. She is now Dawn's teacher this year."

"Hey, Sally." Matt started to put his hand out to shake, and Sally moved in for a hug. Trying to hold her composure, Amber rolled her eyes in her mind. Sally pulled away giddily smiling.

Amber continued. "This is Rachel Benson. I think you might have gone to school together?"

Smooth Amber, real smooth. "Rachel, good to see you again. I hope you've been well."

"Mathew." Now that hugging was the standard, he had to hug her, and it was a little awkward as both were trying to not think about the past and memories that don't go away. In the embrace, he smelled her perfume, and it was the same. It took Matt right back to her pink bedroom after school.

"And finally, do you know Wendy?"

Wendy immediately went in for a prolonged hug. "Actually, Matty and I dated his senior year. We went to prom together." Rachel looked at Wendy with daggers in her eyes.

"Wendy, it's great to see you again. How are you?"

"I'm happy to see you. We're well. My husband is around here somewhere with our son. He's on the highway patrol."

"That's great. It's great to see you again as well." Rachel now directed the daggers in her eyes towards Matt. Amber was loving this. Matt was going to kill her later.

Rachel cut in with, "Mathew and I also went to my senior prom together." Tension was in the air as the conversation immediately stalled.

Martha was not one to be left out of the festivities and having uncovered all this dirt, she chimed, "Well, isn't that nice." Neither Rachel nor Wendy looked like they thought it was nice.

Sue, Lucas's day-care teacher, came up to the group. She was obviously looking for Amber. "Amber, congratulations. I am so happy for you. When are you due?" This prompted congratulatory reactions from all women.

All Amber could get out of her mouth was a stern, "Dawn! Steven where is Dawn?" Steven was smiling and rubbing his head.

Martha hugged Amber. "Why didn't you tell us?"

"Because it's really early. Too early to be telling anyone and yet our daughter figures it's time now, apparently telling everyone at church." Amber was incredulous. "Steven, where is your daughter?" With that, Steven was gone.

Matt saw the spotlight was off him and saw his escape. "Ladies, it was great to see you all again. I am going to go pay my respects." With that, he exited the group and walked to the cemetery next to the church. It was surrounded by a waist-high rock wall with a grand, iron gate entrance that was never closed. It was easy to find his parents' stones buried to the right of the giant Cottonwood tree in the center. As he approached, he saw something new: a granite statue of a Labrador about six feet in front of his parent's stones. At the bottom was an inscription: *Fumble. Loved by Alice and John.*

Matt then looked at his parents' stones with their deceased dates on the same day. Underneath their names was a new inscription: *Eternally together in this world and in heaven.* Matt kneeled down and inspected the statue of Fumble. He heard steps behind him and turned to see Steven. Matt pointed to the statue, "Did you do this?"

Steven nodded. "I loved that dog. I hope it's all right."

Matt stood up. "It's beautiful. Is he buried here with them?"

"Yes, right on top of them much to the unhappiness of Pastor Tuddle."

Matt turned and smiled, "Really?"

"Yeah, we knew Fumble was going downhill. It happened quickly. He had a large tumor pop up on this side, and he was thirteen, so we weren't going to take any extreme measures on him. It wouldn't be fair to him. The vet said he didn't know how long he had. I talked to Tuddle the next Sunday about doing this. Tuddle forbid it. He said the cemetery was for the people of God and not an animal cemetery. Two weeks later, we had to call the vet out for some cows. Fumble was in bad shape by then, and the vet wanted to put him down. It was awful. Amber and Dawn said their goodbyes and went inside the house crying. I lay down with him on the front porch on his rug and loved him and that was it. He was gone." Tears were now running down Steven's face, and Matt was now welling up.

"As much as your sister saved my life, Matt, Fumble did as well. Unconditional love unconditionally can heal." His voice was now breaking. He tried to regroup wiping a tear away. "Anyway, so the vet wants to take him away, and I say no. I'm balling like a little boy again out on the front porch, so we put him in a burial bag and put him in the back of my truck. It was late in the day at this point and the vet was a friend, so he wanted to know what I was planning to do, and I told him. The next thing I know it's pitch-black outside, we are here, finishing off a twelve-pack, burying Fumble together."

Matt turned to Steven and hugged him for a long minute. "Thank you for this. What about Pastor Tuddle?"

Steven wiped the tears from his face and collected himself. "Let's just say he isn't happy, but the people in the church know what Fumble meant to me, and they know what I went through. He's with your parents. I was just blessed to have him for the last seven years."

They both turned toward the exit of the graveyard and in the distance, they could see Amber with Lucas in her arms and Dawn at her mother's side. They'd been watching them. Matt smiled. "You're really blessed. That's a beautiful family."

"I truly am."

As they walked over, Amber hugged Steven and passed Lucas off to him. She then hugged Matt and held him. "Did you like the inscription? In retrospect, I probably should have talked to you about it."

Matt held her. "I love it."

"Really? There was nothing on their stone, and I really thought there should be something on there about how devoted they were to each other."

Matt responded again, "I love it, Amber."

"Good." She patted him on the chest and looked into his eyes. "We've got to get going. Steven's mom is going to kill us for being late to Sunday lunch." Amber stopped in her tracks and turned toward Steven with a terrified look. "Steven, your mom."

Steven looked puzzled for a minute, and then got it. "The baby..."

Amber pulled out her phone. "Should I text them?"

Steven smiled. "If you text them, they will read it sometime in the next two weeks."

Amber dialed the house phone, which was always the best way to get them. She pulled the phone away from her head. "It's busy."

"Come on, Dawn. Let's get the truck. We will be right back." Matt and Dawn found the truck now on the lonely street where he left it. All the other vehicles were now gone to Sunday lunch with friends, family, or at Shoney's. They drove the truck back to the church and found Amber and Steven with Lucas in the empty church parking lot. "Any luck?" Matt asked when they piled in.

"Still busy," Amber replied. "She's going to kill me."

Steven directed Matt through town to one of the nicest streets lined with trees and massive homes. As they pulled into the driveway, Mr. and Mrs. Heard ran onto the front porch and came toward the truck.

Steven turned to Amber. "They know."

Amber replied, "You think."

When the doors of the truck opened, the grandparents gathered their grandchildren and hugged them up. Then Mrs. Heard hugged Matt. "We are so glad you could come to lunch today, Matt."

"Thanks for having me." Matt realized she did not ask about Beth, which meant she knew. Surely not the whole story, but enough to know they were separated, which could mean the entire town now knew. Probably why no one at church had even asked about her.

Mrs. Heard turned to Amber and Steven with a forced smile. "I'm going to be so mad about this as soon as I get over being so happy about this. Imagine my surprise. I slip out after communion to come home to finish lunch, and the phone is ringing nonstop. Friends congratulating me on the new baby."

Amber almost speechless. "I promise to explain everything over lunch. It's really early."

"Well, then, come on. You're late. Dinner is going bad on the table."

Matt tried to chime in. "That's my—" but Amber immediately called him off with her hand and gestured toward the house where the Heards had already headed with their grandbabies in tow.

The table was set, and the food was already out when they went inside. It was a feast. The first part of lunch, Amber explained to the Heards how Dawn had figured out she was expecting. She had also explained to Dawn that pregnancies are usually not discussed in the first trimester for many reasons to be discussed later, and as a practice, Amber and Steven never disclosed a pregnancy until she was showing. Amber thought they had an agreement on keeping this secret. Poor Dawn never looked up and played with her food while the conversation was going on. When it concluded, Mrs. Heard was softening on her resolve and understanding how they had gotten there. She was now confident she could explain to her friends how they found out her son and daughter-in-law were expecting before she knew.

When the conversation took the turn for the better, Steven spoke up, "So Matt, are we going to discuss the run in with the ex-girlfriends at church?" Amber immediately choked on her food and then looked up and giggling.

"Thanks for the heads-up on that. I was thrown to wolves." His comments were directed toward Amber.

Mrs. Heard was excited for fresh gossip. "Do tell."

Before Matt could even start, Amber began, "Matty, the player here, took Rachel Benson and Wendy Anderson to senior prom, and they were together after church today when they each put that together."

Looking confused. "At the same time? Matt!"

"No, ma'am. Rachel and I dated her senior year and went to prom together. I was a junior at the time."

Mrs. Heard let out an "Oh," as if it was scandalous that Rachel has been older.

Amber was really enjoying this. "He was a junior football stud."

Matt now sarcastic, "Thank you." He continued, "We broke up when she went to college. Wendy Anderson and I hooked up and went to prom my senior year. She was a junior."

Steven, looking amused, asked, "Hooked up?"

Matt quickly and defensively said, "I mean we dated. She is a very sweet girl."

Steven again asked, "Amber, wasn't she a cheerleader?"

"Oh yes, she was. All cheerleader." Amber smiling continued, "The two of them come face-to-face outside church catching up with Matty here on old times, and they put two and two together. It was very uncomfortable."

"And Amber, you loved every minute of it, which is why you set this up." Matt was maddened.

"It was an exercise in psychology. I admit it; I can't leave it at the door, but I did not set it up. Wendy and I are on the Methodist women together, which Martha leads. I barely know Rachel as you know. I was gone at college most of your senior year. She came looking for you," Amber said while pointing at Matt.

Steven was in full agreement. "Yep. And Wendy certainly seemed surprised to see you as well. You did catch that her husband carries a gun for a living, right?"

Matt raised his finger in the air. "Yes, that was duly noted during the conversation."

Amber, not giving up on ribbing her brother, said, "Well, Rachel seemed very aware that you were there. How about that look when you sat in church?"

Steven busted out, "Agreed! That was not a normal hey-how-you-doing or good-to-see-you look."

Amber, now imitating Rachel at church in a stern whispery voice, said, "Mathew… what did that mean? Nobody calls you Mathew." Again, with a stern whisper, "It's going to take me days to analyze what just happened."

Matt agreed there was something to it and threw his arms in the air. "I'm laying low for the rest of my stay. No dinner parties for me. I'm not leaving the ranch for the rest of the trip."

Mrs. Heard now getting in on the fun, suggested, "Maybe I'll invite them to Sunday lunch next week?" That coming out of Mrs. Heard's mouth sent the table rolling in laughter.

"No please," Matt yelled as more laughter erupted.

29

The knock at Alexandra's door was expected. It was dinner time, and she was starving after swimming laps today. It had been a long time since she was in a pool, and it felt good. Her hair was still damp after her shower, and she was wrapped in her Shadow Oaks robe. The gas fireplace in her room was lit to take the cold edge off the evening air coming off the Pacific, and there was calm in the room with classical music playing from the Bose radio in the background. When she opened the door, an orderly (guest services attendant, per Shadow Oaks) brought her dinner.

"Good evening. Please put it on the stool in front of the fireplace."

"Good evening Mrs. Bridgeway." The orderly put the tray down and exited the room. The Mrs. Bridgeway comment was left stinging in air. Was her marriage really over? It had to be. She had not seen or heard from Style in over two weeks since the accident. He hadn't even returned the text, her apology to him. When she woke up in the hospital, her parents had been there to comfort her with Kyle, who had obviously been sent by Style to keep watch.

This was not uncommon for Style. When crossed by friends, associates or relatives, Style put them in the rearview mirror never looking back cutting off all communication, and if forced to spend time with them, he ignored them. Alexandra was now in Style's rearview mirror, no longer Mrs. Bridgeway. Would she change her name back to Steed?

Another unexpected knock came at the door, which startled her. The orderly must have forgotten something. When she went to open the door, Aggy was there with her dinner tray in her hands. Shit.

Sheepishly, she asked, "Can I join you for dinner?"

"Aggy, I'm not sure this is allowed." Alexandra was desperate for this not to happen.

"It is. I promise. I just can't stay after nine, so we have some time." Aggy was almost desperate in her plea.

Alexandra relented. "Just dinner, okay? I am really tired, and I need to get some sleep." She pulled the door open, and Aggy came in.

"Okay. Wow your room is pretty. My room is on the inside of the building, and it's nice, but I don't think third-time rehabbers get windows or fireplaces."

Alexandra motioned toward the stool opposite of her dinner, and Aggy sat down in front of the fire as well. They both took the steel tops off their dinner service and prepared to eat. It was very quiet. Alexandra felt uneasy from Aggy barging in, and tried to take the edge off. "So, Aggy, tell me about your grandmother who you were named after."

Aggy now seemed even more uncomfortable as if she was going to disclose a secret. "My grandmother is Agatha Hemsworth, and my family own some businesses in San Francisco."

Alexandra looked up in sadness. "Oh Aggy, we probably have met. Your family owns Hemsworth Department Store, Hemsworth Real Estate, and Hemsworth Transportation."

"Don't forget Hemsworth Imports and the Hemsworth Center for the Arts," she smiled. "I'm the baby of the family. There is a ten-year gap between my brothers and sisters and me. I was an accident."

"I'm sure they don't feel that way. We must have met at your family's annual charity ball. My husband and I went every year. It's very beautiful. Your mother, Keira, does a beautiful job with it. It helps many people. You must be very proud of that."

"I am. My brothers and sisters all work in the family businesses, and they are all very successful."

"And you?"

"I just don't fit. I am the square peg in the round hole. It's like the Hemsworth name is lost on me. I'm nothing like them. Don't get me wrong. They are not bad people, but I just feel I was born in the wrong family."

"The drugs?"

"They came along with a string of very bad boyfriends I apparently chose, according to the doctors, to upset my family. I got hooked and here I am."

"You look so much like your mother. She is very beautiful."

"She is, she really is, which makes this," Aggy said, turning her arms over again showing the scars, "even more painful for her."

"I'm the last person to be giving advice, which is why I'm sure they don't want us alone together. All I can tell you is that we can't live in the past." Alexandra reached out and touched Aggy's arms. "This past will kill us." Alexandra, makeup free, touched the blued bruises on her face. "We have to move forward past this and not look back."

"I know." Aggy let out a deep breath. "Let's talk about you."

Alexandra forced a smile. "I hate this subject. It's all I have been talking about since I got here. My husband is an attorney, and we live in a high rise on the Embarcadero."

"That's swanky."

"He's a very successful divorce attorney, who unfortunately appears to be divorcing me soon." Alexandra had no energy to lie or cover up.

"I'm sorry."

"I'll be honest with you. I'm not sure how I feel about it. That's something I'm working through here. I know I should feel bad, but really don't feel anything, which scares me a little." Alexandra covered her food in contemplation of this realization. Alexandra looked at Aggy's dinner, and it was gone as well. "Listen, Aggy, I'm beat. It has been wonderful to get to know you this evening, really. I have got to get some sleep."

Aggy got up with her empty tray, and Alexandra stopped her. "Just leave it. I'll call them and have them both picked up."

"Are you sure?"

"Absolutely."

With that, Aggy reached out and hugged Alexandra holding her for a long time. "I'm very sorry about your marriage," she whispered.

"Good night, Aggy."

30

Amber walked onto the front porch with the kids to watch her men finish packing the horses and the mule. Steven and Matt were riding the fence line to mend it before the heifers went into heat. A weak fence line in the spring would encourage a bull to walk right through to get to one of the neighbor's herd, or worse, one could come into theirs. Then there would be two bulls battling to be the alpha of the herd.

Riding the fence was dangerous. It took at least two full days sometimes longer depending on the shape of the fence, and Steven usually did it alone twice a year. Five years ago, Amber convinced Steven that they could take the year off, and it had catastrophic consequences. Their black angus bull, Shirako, got loose. There was a battle that ended with Shirako driving a neighbor's bull through their backyard fence and into their inground pool. The rival bull, unable to get out, drowned.

The restitution was costly. Shirako spent the rest of the spring breeding the neighbor's cattle instead of their cattle, along with the costs of repairs to the fence, yard, and pool, not to mention paying for the removal and destruction of the dead bull. The lesson was learned. Riding the fence was a necessity. It had to be done.

The plan was to fix what they could, and if there were areas that were really bad, Steven decided to try and use his satellite trackers to mark and document those. He would put one on the top of the post for good sun and signal, and then document what needed to be done and the supplies needed to finish the repair. He gave the team a heads-up in Mountain View on what the plan was, and they were very excited for another possible use for their technology. Amber and the team would also be able to track their trip because the horses already had tags on their head gear.

The sun was now creeping up over the horizon. Matt was riding Amber's appaloosa, Tango, and Steven was on his tan and white Pinto, Ghost. Lady and Hank were circling in anticipation of what was to come. They were going with the men today. At first, there was concern Hank would get tangled with a horse when he arrived, but he had a healthy fear of them and stayed away when Matt got on one.

Matt hugged Amber and the children, and then got on Tango. "We will see you guys tomorrow."

Dawn returned and said, "Bye, Uncle Matty."

Amber smiled and winked at him.

Steven forced a bullet into the chamber of the 30/30 saddle rifle that had once been her father's and released the trigger back to uncock before placing it in his saddle holster. Walking up the steps he wrapped his arms around Amber, and he kissed her hard. Her body instinctively gave way into his. He then pulled away in a whisper, "Love you."

Amber's head was swimming and the area below her navel came to life. "Not as much as I love you. Please be careful." She put her hand on his jacket where his heart was.

"I always am. I'm thinking we will be home tomorrow around dinner, but don't hold anything. You know how to find us."

"I do. You are going to be in trouble for that kiss." The app tracker made her feel much better.

Steven went down the steps and pulled himself up on Ghost. "Please don't forget to set the alarm tonight and the shotgun—"

Amber finished Steven's sentence and said, "—is loaded and hung by the back door. You two be safe."

Steven smiled. "Don't worry about us." He pointed to Lucas and Dawn. "You've got the hard job." Hank and Lady settled in front of the horses.

Amber immediately fumbled for her cell phone from her pocket and said, "Don't move." She snapped several pictures of the two of them on the horses with the dogs. "You boys just made the Christmas card." They smiled and started to ride away with the dogs sniffing and then running alongside them.

31

Style was sitting across from William Peels, senior partner at the firm, who was going through the separation and divorce paperwork that Style had unethically put together himself. Because Style couldn't put his own name on the work, William was going to have to sign off as lead attorney as if he prepared it himself, but William was not going to sign off on anything that he didn't meticulously go through. He had been reviewing it for three days and then called the meeting in his office. "Well, the good news is that she has no claim against your portion of the firm. Did she really sign that away?"

Style smiled, "You have the notarized original there. She didn't do it knowingly. When she came in to sign the paperwork on the condo closing, I slipped it in there, and with so much paperwork, she just blindly signed it."

"Good, too bad you didn't sweeten up the terms a little more." They both laughed.

"Well, at the time, I didn't think I needed to, but based on the last year, I probably should have. I actually drew up some amended paperwork and was going to slide it in as soon as something else came up, but the opportunity never came to fruition."

"Too bad. I see you live in the cheapest high-rise condo on the Embarcadero now."

"Yeah, I had it appraised by Digger, and he low-balled the price. If she gets a decent attorney, they will figure that one out, but I am not giving the condo up. She can't afford it anyway."

"Where do you think she will live?"

"I think she would move back home with her parents. Honestly that's where she needs to be now. I can't do it anymore."

"Where's all your money?" William asked, taking his glasses off.

"We've been living off the base, and I've been funneling all the bonuses overseas. She has no idea how much we have. Regardless of who she gets to represent her, they will never find it. We'll just pretend like we blew through all of it, which is damn easy to do in San Francisco."

"True. So, the number I am coming up with is about $1 million you will owe her, and we will fight the monthly spousal based on the drug use. We will probably end up settling for $1.2 million without spousal support, which will get you off the hook for the rest of your life."

Style smiled. "That was the number I was thinking. Hopefully she will just be happy with $1.2 and not start digging."

"When the smoke clears after that payout, what will you have left as assets all in?" William got out of his chair.

"Taking sole possession of the condo I should have about $10 million left." Style rose from his seat as well.

William grabbed his pen and signed off on the paperwork. He handed the file to Style, leaned over and patted his shoulder in a congratulatory manner. "Very smart work here managing this and keeping the firm out of this mess. What's the latest from the insurance company?"

"The Jag is completely totaled. The car she hit is going after our $10 million umbrella, which insurance will settle for much less. The good news is the building she hit is owned by one of our clients, so I am having lunch with him today. Word on the street is that he has a MUCH younger girlfriend on the side and may want me to do his divorce gratis."

William shook his head up and down. "You know the partners and I will support that plan."

"Thanks, William."

"No need to thank. Good job again with this. We must always protect the firm."

32

Alexandra lay quietly on Dr. Moranne's couch facing away from her chair not saying a word. Dr. Charlotte Moranne, from what Alexandra could tell from her wall of fame, graduated with a master's in psychology from San Diego State in the mid '80s, which Alexandra guessed put her age in the mid to late fifties. From there, she went on and received her doctorate in psychology from Arizona State in the '90s. There was an entire wall full of other awards and tributes. Charlotte Moranne was the real deal.

"Alexandra, the point of you being here is to help you. I can sit here all day."

Alexandra took in a deep breath and exhaled. "I'm tired of talking about me. I've told you everything. You know how I got here. I don't know what else you want me to say."

"I believe you, Alexandra, and I appreciate how open you have been about your story. What we haven't discussed is how you feel about it."

Alexandra turned her head to the side and was again quiet. Another deep breath, and then her voice broke when she said, "I feel shame and anger."

"Okay, that's all understandable. Who are you angry with?"

Alexandra's voice broke again. "Myself."

Dr. Moranne scribbled some notes in her notebook, excited to be getting somewhere. "So, you have decided to bear the entire burden of this on yourself?"

Alexandra's face became flush with anger, her voice now unbroken rose as she said, "Who do you want me to blame? Please let me know so we can just wrap this up."

"I don't know. Let's talk about the man who attempted to rape you."

That was a gut punch Alexandra was not ready for. She was on her feet pacing the floor still not making eye contact with Dr. Moranne. "Let's get this straight. I did that. I put myself in that situation."

Dr. Moranne, needing her to continue, kept her voice calm and steady. "Alexandra, he said he was going to help you. He was a doctor, so you trusted him."

"I went to a man's home who I barely knew from a drug rehab group to shoot up." Alexandra threw her hands in the air. "When I say it out loud, I am appalled at how stupid I was. I honestly can't believe I did that."

"A rehab group that Style put you in versus him trying to get you into a rehab center," Dr. Moranne added, while scribbling more notes.

"Oh, I get it. Let's blame this on my philandering husband. The group he got me in is full of very prominent people who are trying to keep their issues quiet. In his own way, Style was trying to help me and shield everyone from knowing his wife is a drug addict."

"Do you think his philandering played into your addiction?"

"I knew what was going on. It was my choice to stay in the marriage. I liked my life. It had nothing to do with him screwing around. I gave up on trying to change that years ago."

"You brought the philandering up; I didn't." The room fell quiet. Dr. Moranne scribbled.

"The Style of today is not the Style I fell in love with. He changed along the way, and so did I. There's plenty of blame to go around. I don't even know if I care he is divorcing me." Alexandra's voice finished quietly after that statement. There was remorse, but was it about losing Style? Sadly, she thought it was more about losing the life they built. The Bridgeways…"

"Well, the drug companies are certainly a responsible party in this. Lawsuits abound against them including from the states themselves."

"Great, let's blame them. Can I go?"

Dr. Moranne laughed. "We have plenty of time. Let's talk about your drawings."

Again, another long pause from Alexandra. "They are terrifying drawings. When I look at them, they scare me. The composition and shading are different than anything else I've ever done. It's like I am looking at someone else's work, which is even scarier to me than the work itself."

Dr. Moranne scribbled even more furiously than before. "That's interesting. Do you mind if I see them?"

"I do actually. I don't want to show them to anyone." Alexandra's voice was low.

"Okay, that's fine. Let's continue with them as long as they don't overly upset you. Let's first talk about it if you want to stop. They could prove to be a therapeutic tool."

"Okay."

"Alexandra, how long has it been since you've drawn? Been an artist?"

"It has been probably eight years since the showing."

"It didn't go well?"

"No, I poured myself into it. Style and I were going through a rough patch back then. He was working all the time trying to make partner. He wasn't around, and I could focus. I didn't sell a single painting. Apparently according to the reviews, I had nothing to say in my work."

"What happened after that?"

"Style made partner, name on the firm wall and all, and I became Mrs. Bridgeway. He had no time but to work, so I took over everything else at home. Became one of the firm wives, something I despised before. It worked, I guess. I was a failure, and he was exalted." Alexandra shrugged her shoulders.

"So, you also mentioned shame along with this anger. Is this shame also your own?"

"Dr. Moranne, I was the beauty queen of my county. Style was King, and I was Queen of our senior prom. I was a top-20 ranked swimmer in California and turned down a scholarship to swim in college to follow Style and be at a college near his. I married very well. Style's family is one of the richest in the state. We are—were—on the society circuits in San Francisco. My family was very proud of me..."

"And?"

"And I have shamed them all with drugs and worse, almost killing others, passing out behind the wheel of my car and plowing into a poor family, smashing into a building. It's a miracle no one was seriously hurt. I can only imagine the lawsuits and it's all in the newspapers. And it is my fault." Alexandra's voice broke, and her eyes welled up.

"I am glad we are talking about this."

"I'm really not. Can I please go, Doctor?"

"Just one more thing. Let's talk about Catherine. You have not mentioned her."

Alexandra turned flush with anger and for the first time today made eye contact with Dr. Moranne.

"What does any of this have to do with my sister?"

"Catherine, she is calling here every day checking on you. She is very worried. They say you won't take her calls and finally this morning they transferred her to me. She thinks you are not talking to her because you're angry with her."

"Well, Dr. Moranne, you finally found someone I am angry with other than myself, but it has nothing to do with any of this."

"Did the two of you have a falling out?"

"No, I love my little sister. Catherine is a saint."

"Let's talk about that."

"Really, she has nothing to do with this." Dr. Moranne didn't say anything, just scribbled. "Catherine is two years younger than me. While I was being all that I was in high school, she was the studious, quiet one in the family. She crunches numbers all day at some company in Los Angeles."

"The anger?"

"All Catherine has ever wanted was a family, kids. My brother-in-law Jack, her husband, saint number 2, is like-minded. He's a grocery store manager. Horrible hours, works all the time. They have been trying for kids for a couple of years, and nothing happened so they go to get checked out. Low and behold, they can have children, but they shouldn't. My sister has some medical condition that makes it very dangerous for her to get pregnant. So, what does my little sister, the Hallmark-watching, megachurch-goer do? She turns it over to God."

Dr. Moranne stopped scribbling and looked up surprised. "She's pregnant?"

"Yep, Catherine is very pregnant. Poor Jack was distraught at first. She didn't even let him in on what she decided. He was heading down the path of adoption." Dr. Moranne scribbled more. "So yes, I'm unhappy with my little sister. I love her."

"Alexandra, I think you need to talk to your sister—"

Alexandra decided she was done asking and stormed out of the Dr. Moranne's office, slamming the door behind her. The wall of fame shook at the quake of the shutting door. Dr. Moranne scribbled.

33

The creek babbled in the background as Steven and Matt finished up dinner next to the fire. They had made camp at the scheduled location completely on the other end of the ranch from where they had started. The tent was up, sleeping bags unfurled, horses and mule were watered and tied up on the line between two trees. Passed out next to the fire was Hank and Lady, recently fed and still wet. They had a big day chasing everything from rabbits to prairie dogs. When they had finally arrived at the creek to set up, the two Labs instinctively went directly for the water, chasing each other for hours. They were now toast.

It had been a long day. They reached the creek ninety minutes late, so they scrambled to get camp set before the sun set. A lot of fence had been mended by them, and there were four locations that Steven had marked and documented with the pictures on the trackers so that he could come back and fix with the correct supplies. Sometime during the day, Alice called Matt twice and then sent a text that she needed to talk to him. He decided he would call her after they got back to civilization. Cell coverage was spotty this far out. Honestly, he didn't really want to talk to her, fearing more questions about the situation, but he would check in with her. "So, another baby..."

Steven smiled a big smile. "Yeah, not really something that we planned, but I'm excited. I'm not sure Amber really is, which is understandable. I think she was ready to put diapers and breast pumping in her rearview mirror. She's got most of the work to do."

Matt stoked the fire. "The Heards are now officially a herd."

"Right? It's a lot to think about. This will definitely be the last one. We seriously considered one of us getting the plumbing turned off after Lucas, but we waffled on it. No more waffling now. Three will be plenty."

"It's going to be like *Romper Room*."

"It is. The good news is that Dawn is growing up quick. She's been great with Lucas even though he has been a terror. She's turning into mommy's little helper."

Matt motioned with his hands as he said, "Three kids and you two in a three-bedroom farmhouse."

"Yeah, I've got to figure that out. I may have to blow out the back of the house to make more room, but I love the wrap around porches on the front and sides. I really don't want to mess with that."

"Steven, with all you have going on with the ranch, that isn't going to happen before the baby gets here."

"I know. It's probably a project for next winter."

Matt put his hands out. "Look we need to convert my room for Lucas or Dawn now, and then if it's a boy or girl you can have them share a room with one of them."

Steven looked at the fire and pondered this. "Matt, this is your home. Amber has been adamant we keep a room for you here."

Matt ran his hand through his hair. "Steven, I love it here, but this isn't my home anymore. The truth is I'm not really sure where my home is going to be now, but it won't be here."

"You know you're always welcome here."

"I do and I appreciate that, but we need to be practical. This can be my gift to you and Amber."

Steven stoked the fire. "She's never going to agree to you not having some kind of bed here. She'll think that you won't come visit, and that will not sit well with her."

"Agreed, so we surprise her. I've got a plan. Wednesday after Amber leaves for work, we haul ass up to Omaha to the Nebraska furniture mart and pick out some new furniture for my room and either for Dawn or Lucas."

Steven scratched his head. "That works, but still doesn't solve the issue of you not having a bed."

"I've got that figured out. Have you seen a Murphy Bed?"

"I don't think so."

"Half of New York sleeps on them. During the day it looks like a nice wall cabinet. At night you pull it down, and it turns into a bed." Matt simulated it with his hands. "We put the Murphy in Amber's office on the wall that doesn't have anything. Hopefully we can get them delivered in time. If so, then we tear my room down when she goes to work, maybe paint and have the furniture delivered that afternoon."

"That sounds awfully ambitious."

"Yeah, it does, but we can give it a shot before I leave."

"You have decided to go?"

"Yes, I'm leaving this Monday."

"Back to Connecticut?"

"No, since I am already halfway across the country, King George wants me to run out to Silicon Valley to meet with this start-up investor guy and feel out what a relationship with him might look like."

"So, you're going back to Waverman?" Amber had apparently filled Steven completely in on the story.

Matt snorted and shook his head. "I seriously don't know the answer to that. I don't know if I can go back. Right now, I can't do anything until my name gets cleared. Then I can think next steps. A trip to California far away from New York sounds pretty good right now. I've decided to spend a few days in Napa and do some wine tasting, which is something I have always wanted to do but haven't had time."

"Those plans sound pretty definitive. Any chance we can get you to stay longer?"

"Hank and I will stop on our way back to New York whenever that is."

"When are you going to tell your sister?"

"I was hoping you were going to do that for me."

"No chance of that. I am going to let you break that news."

34

It had been several days since the blow-up with Dr. Moranne, and the guilt was weighing on Alexandra. She knew that Dr. Moranne was trying to help but felt that meddling in her family, beyond Style, which she was sure had no impact with her addictions, was out of scope.

The phone on her bedside table rang. Alexandra looked at her watch. It was 6:30 P.M. on the dot, and Catherine was punctual as always. She picked up the phone, "Catherine?"

"Alexandra, it is so good to talk to you! How are you?"

"I am okay, Catherine. How are you? How's Jack… the baby?"

"We are all doing fine. I hope you're not mad with me. The doctors wanted me to stay away from the hospital. It killed me, Alexandra, not to see you. I am so sorry."

"Catherine, I am not mad at you, just worried about you, and honestly I just don't want to talk about myself or the situation. It's all I do now." Alexandra was happy that Catherine hadn't come and seen her incarcerated, handcuffed to her hospital bed. The shame. "Let's talk about you."

Catherine sounded relieved. "All is good as I said. I don't have to worry about anything because Jack is worrying about everything. Honestly, Alexandra, he's driving me a little crazy. The baby's room is done, and we went with yellow as a wall color. It's supposed to be good for the baby. Jack read an article somewhere." Alexandra could tell that Catherine was thrilled to talk to her, and that made her sad that she had been shutting her out. Catherine outlined every aspect of the baby's room, and truthfully Alexandra was interested. "And, oh my gosh, Alexandra, I am as big as a house. I feel disgusting. I have to sleep on my side. I look like I am carrying around a basketball, and it feels that way too. The baby is keeping me awake at night, moving around. Only six more weeks."

Alexandra started laughing. "I'm sure you're beautiful. I'm just sorry I can't be there right now."

The phone got quiet. "I'm sorry about that too. I can't wait to see you. When can you leave?"

"Two more weeks if I am on good behavior or don't break out of here sooner, then home with Mom and Dad for a while. I've got to report to a parole officer, do the whole community service thing. A hundred hours."

"Oh my gosh, what will they have you do?"

"There is no telling. My life is not my own right now, which is my fault. This is part of a first-offender program. If I complete it, my record will be scrubbed of this, and I can move on."

"It's going to get better, Alexandra. We will do anything to help."

A tear formed in Alexandra's eye. "I know you will." Her voice broke. "I will be fine, just take care of yourself and that baby."

"I love you, Alexandra."

"I love you too, Catherine."

35

Amber's car rolled out of the driveway loaded down with the kids. Matt and Steven waved goodbye to them as usual and as soon as they were out of sight, Matt looked at Steven. "You ready?"

"Let's go."

It had been several days of preparation. They told Amber they had been working on the fence for the last couple of days but in reality, the fence material had not moved from the barn. When they went to pick it up from the supply store, they had also gone to the paint section and picked out paint for the kids' rooms.

After going back and forth on a plan, they decided Lucas would take Matt's room, and they would paint it a light sky blue with white trim. They would remove Matt's furniture and store it in the barn. Once completed, they would move Dawn's furniture into his room.

Then with Dawn's room mostly empty, they would paint her room a very light pink, something that she had been asking for. The men decided that it had to pass the test that the color, although pink, would not make them want to throw up when they walked in. The new furniture would arrive around three, which would be just enough time to get it installed before Amber and the kids got home at six. It was going to be a long day.

Steven and Matt had made the run to the Nebraska Furniture Mart on Wednesday without Amber knowing. The preplanned trip to the mart quickly spun out of control when they met Susan, the young salesgirl, who was standing at the door when they arrived. By the time they left, everybody in the house was getting a new mattress including Amber and Steven, along with the Murphy Bed for Amber's office and Dawn's new furniture. Matt insisted on paying for everything, but Steven put his foot down on the new mattress for their room. He paid for that. Susan did her damnedest to try to get Steven to buy new furniture for their bedroom, but there was no way he was picking that out without Amber. Susan finally relented when she found out there was a new baby on the way.

During the last couple of days, Matt had been going through his room deciding on what to keep and what to throw away. He had to be stealth about it to not alert Amber or the prying inquisitive eyes of Dawn. Matt's entire childhood was now gathered in three boxes for the attic. The rest was in garbage bags in the barn to be taken to the dump tomorrow. No time today for that. After they tore Matt's furniture down and stowed it in the barn, they covered the hard wood floors with plastic and began. First, they rolled and cut in the ceiling. They had no idea how dirty the walls were until the first paint went on. "Wow."

Steven looked on. "I know right?"

Then they taped and tackled Matt's tan walls and turned them into a light and airy sky blue, which took two coats. Finally, they moved on to the discolored white trim that actually was so bad that it matched the color of the walls. When it was completed it looked beautiful, but they were behind schedule as it was almost noon.

After a discussion that took just a few seconds it was decided to forgo lunch and move onto Dawn's room. The same progression took place in her room as in Lucas's except for the men were moving much faster this time and instead of getting blue paint on them it was now pink. They were now speed painting and running out of time.

When the Nebraska Furniture Mart truck pulled into the driveway at 3:30, the men had just started Dawn's trim. Matt looked at Steven. "Shit!"

"You go down and have them work on the Murphy bed in Amber's office and the new mattress for Lucas's room and our room. Hopefully, by then I'll have the trim finished."

Matt went outside and introduced himself to two men, explained the compressed timeline, tipped them up front $50 each, and then the three of them quickly went to work. It was a bear getting the furniture out of the truck unboxed, half assembled on the lawn, and segregated by room. This was very time-consuming, and when Steven walked outside an hour later after finishing the trim, not a stick of furniture had made it into the house, and it was 4:30. Amber and the kids would be home by 6:00 at the latest. This prompted a big smile from Steven as Matt and the men froze when he walked outside.

"What in the hell have you all been doing?" Steven asked, smiling.

Matt pointed at the ground and said, "Get your ass down here and help!"

Matt and Steven muscled the king mattress and box springs to the master and brought down the old ones. They heard drills being used in Amber's office. Thankfully this wasn't the delivery drivers' first rodeo as they were assembling the Murphy bed and anchoring it to the wall in Amber's office.

Matt and Steven then went out and fetched Lucas's new mattress and got it upstairs. They made his bed with new Space Force sheets and matching comforter that Susan at the furniture mart insisted they buy. The light blue walls with the dark blue Space Force comforter and Dawn's hand-me-down furniture looked great. It was a new room.

Steven decided to text Amber and have her stop for pizza on the way home, which would buy them an additional fifteen to twenty minutes. The Murphy bed was now complete, and the delivery team fully demonstrated it. They did a great job. All four of them were covered in sweat. It was 5:30.

Now Dawn's room. They decided the delivery team would do the installation, while Matt and Steven brought all the furniture and Dawn's mattress up. As they trudged up and down the stairs, the parts piled up in the hallway. Steven wiped his forehead. "We are never going to get this done in time."

A voice from one of the delivery drivers in the room yelled, "Yes we are."

Within twenty minutes, her bed was assembled. The drivers were so engaged in the process they started helping put up the pink curtains that Susan again had insisted on. Matt and Steven made the bed with the *Frozen* bedding, and when they finished, her room was amazing.

The delivery drivers along with Matt and Steven hurried down the stairs as it was now 6:00. They all proceeded to clean up the wreckage of boxes and mattresses that were tossed in the front yard. Hank and Lady thought this was a grand game and were attempting to play tug of war with whatever they could get their mouths on, causing Matt to trip and faceplant once. By the time they were finished, they were all out of breath and laughing. Matt again went into his wallet and gave the drivers each $100. "Guys, thanks again so much. Now, get out of here."

The truck rumbled down the driveway crushing the rocks and pulled out onto the main road at the same time Amber was pulling up in front of the house to turn in. The wide swing of the truck took both lanes to come out and she had to stop in the road and let them finish the swing. The drivers waved out the window honking the horn as the truck chugged down the road.

As Amber pulled up, there was a very confused look on her face. She opened the door to get out, and Steven went to kiss her. "No, no, no you are more filthy than normal. You stink."

"Honey, do you want me to grab Lucas."

"Do not touch my child in this state." Amber proceeded to pull Lucas out of his car seat.

He immediately grabbed for Steven saying, "Daddy, Daddy," but Amber was having none of it.

"Lucas, Daddy looks like he and Uncle Matty have been rolling around with the cows today. He can hold you after his shower."

Dawn now appeared from her side of the car, and with a stern child voice asked, "What have you two been up to today?"

Amber chimed, "Well, Dawn, that is an excellent question."

Steven smiled. "It's easier if we show you." He motioned to the house.

Matt, now starving having missed lunch, said, "I'll get the pizza."

Amber immediately waved a finger at him. "No. No pizza until we get to the bottom of this." Matt and Steven laughed, and they all went in the house and ascended the stairs to second floor. As they got to the top, Amber turned and could see straight into Matt's room. "Matt, your room—"

"Amber, it's not my room anymore. It's Lucas's room, and depending on the baby whether it's a boy or girl, he may be sharing it.

"It's beautiful, but Matt—"

Matt comforted her. "Don't worry. Come on." He motioned toward Dawn's room who ran past them and shrieked.

"Mommy look, mommy look! I am a queen!" she exclaimed as she bolted up the ladder to the top bunk. She picked up her pillow to show her mother the characters.

Amber smiled at the joy exuding from her daughter. "Mommy is the queen, but you get to be the princess."

Amber turned to both her men. "Wow, you guys, how?"

"Honey, this was all Matt's idea," Steven explained. "We ran to Omaha on Wednesday and picked it out. It all got delivered today. He insisted on paying for most of it."

"Is there more?"

Steven smiled his big smile and said, "Baby, the marshmallow is gone."

"Did you?"

"Yep! I finally bought us an adjustable bed so your side of the bed can be soft and mine can be hard." Steven and Amber's friends in town had one of these beds, which they proclaimed saved their marriage. They had been talking about getting one for years.

"Oh, thank God. I don't know how we have slept on that awful mattress for this long. This still doesn't solve where Matt's going to sleep."

"Downstairs." Steven again motioned. They descended to her office and showed her the new cabinet on the wall in her office. Amber look confused. Steven reached up and pulled it down, showing how it converted magically into a queen bed.

"You thought of everything. This is very sweet of both of you. I don't know what to say." Amber, making sure not to get close enough to touch their sweaty bodies, kissed both of them. "Thank you. Now, you both get upstairs to shower, and Dawn and I will work on dinner for you."

After showering, Matt joined everyone in the kitchen for dinner. Amber smiled at him when he entered and said, "You look beat."

"I am beat. I'm sure Steven is as well."

Steven shook his head up and down. "I am dead on my feet."

Amber started toward the pantry. "I didn't know what kind of wine you wanted."

"You know I think beer with pizza sounds really good to me after the day we've had."

"Sit. I'll get it." Amber went to the refrigerator, pulled one out and poured it in a frozen mug. Dawn had made a salad to go with the pizza and when the pizzas came out of the oven, the family tore into them.

When the food was gone, Matt leaned back into his chair and stretched. Everything hurt, and it would be worse tomorrow. "Fence tomorrow?"

Steven nodded. "Yep. We will get an early start and should get most of it done if we work into dark."

Amber put her hand up. "Look, you guys have been killing yourselves for two straight weeks. The fence can wait until next week. Steven can handle that on his own. Let's tackle the chores in the morning, and then we all will take a lunch to the meadow by the stream."

Dawn yelled out, "Yeah! Dawn's Meadow!" Lucas smiled and clapped his hands.

The meadow had become a special place for Amber and Steven. It was outside of the fence line on the far side of the property. It had become available when the owner passed away. They bought the ten acres with plans to extend the property and fence line, but it was so beautiful they never did it, so the cows couldn't destroy it. The meadow was where Dawn was conceived before they owned it. Steven would keep the grass cut down with the tractor, and it was so isolated it became their very own park and special place.

Steven smiled. "Baby, I am down with that. Let's try to sleep in. We will get the blinds hung in the kids' rooms in the morning, do the normal chores and make a dump run, but we should be good to go by eleven." Matt acknowledged that with a thumbs-up.

Dawn chimed in, "Mommy, can I be excused to go and work on my new room?"

"Absolutely, baby." They had already moved all her clothes out of her old furniture, and they needed to be put away. "You two guys are on clean up duty down here. I'll get Lucas down and meet you on the front porch."

When they were almost finished, Matt's cell phone rang. It was Alice again trying to reach him. She had been calling and texting him to call her, and he couldn't dodge her anymore. "Steven, do you mind if I take this? It is my neighbor in Connecticut."

"Go for it. I'll meet you on the front porch."

Matt walked out onto the front porch, and the cool evening air hit his nose. It felt great. "Alice, where's the fire?"

"Matt, why haven't you been taking my calls?"

"I'm sorry, Alice." He truly was. "The truth is the cell coverage out here can be spotty at times, and we've been working our asses off. What's up? House is okay?"

"It's fine. How much longer are you going to be away?"

Matt pondered for a minute. Right now, there was nothing really to go back to until he could work. "I am guessing at least a month. Why?"

"I'm working with a client trying to find a house, and they have two kids. They are living out of a hotel room. Apparently, the move was a sudden thing with no warning. There was a firing at her husbands' company, and he was told to pack and move to fill that position."

"Alice, my home's not for sale." Matt wasn't there yet. He couldn't envision staying out in Connecticut without Beth, but he hadn't even considered a future living in the city with Hank. Would he stay at Waverman or move to another company? Whatever that answer was would drive his location in the city near either Waverman or the new company. There was a lot to think about.

"Oh no, I know that." She was quick to answer.

"Then I don't understand."

Alice had planned this conversation. "Just hear me out. Let them rent it for the month while I get them squared away in a new home. You get the rent, and they get out of a hotel room. The poor woman is beside herself right now."

"I don't know, Alice. Strangers in my home? It's not like I can go and clean closets out or anything. I don't have time for that."

"Haven't you heard of VRBO. It will be just like that but for a month."

Matt couldn't think of an adequate out on this conversation. "Okay, but you are the landlord."

"Harry and I will handle everything! They want to move in tomorrow."

"You already told them yes! Damn, Alice, that's bold."

"I floated the idea to them, and they were totally onboard. I told them I'd ask you when you finally decided to call me. I've got this."

"Whatever. You are in charge, and I am holding you responsible if they burn the place to the ground." Matt hung up the phone and sat in the swing. Turning, he saw Amber and Steven there with beers. Amber handed one to him and took her position on the swing nestled between the two of them.

"What was all that about?" she asked.

"My neighbor, Alice, is a realtor. You haven't met her. She has clients that she's trying to find a house for, and they are living out of a hotel. She basically rented my home to them for the next month while I am gone."

Amber's face scrunched up. "That's bold."

"That's Alice. I'm officially homeless for the next month."

Amber seized on this. "That's wonderful. You go do your California thing, and then come back and stay with us. I have this wonderful new Murphy bed in my office." They all busted out laughing.

Amber grabbed both their legs happily and asked, "You boys got any more surprises up your sleeves this evening?"

Steven exhaled, "Ughhhh…"

Amber incredulously asked, "What now?"

Steven took a deep breath. "Last Sunday at Mom and Dad's, the old man pulled me aside. With our big news about the new baby, they are even more uncomfortable with you and their grandkids riding around in the Nebraska countryside in an antique 4Runner with over two hundred thousand miles on it. Dad's Yukon is two years old with thirty thousand miles on it, and he is ready to trade again. The car is like brand new. Anyway, he thinks it would be a good idea for us to buy it at the trade-in value, and he will get a new one. He said to just pay them when we can, or we can do something monthly."

"Steven, you know this is going to be like the meadow. We will write your dad checks he won't cash, and then for a birthday or Christmas they will forgive the debt."

"I don't know what to tell you. I'm their only child, and you are their only daughter-in-law and those…," Steven said, pointing toward the ceiling, then put his hand on her belly which immediately brought the area below her waist alive and tingling, "…are their only grandchildren. They're just trying to protect us and help, and I know we turned them down last time he traded, but I think we need to consider it this time."

Matt seeing the wisdom in this added, "Amber, Steven's right. You are going to need a third-row seat in a few months. I think Dawn is still too young to be in a front seat. It's time to retire the 4Runner."

Amber exhaled. They were right. "Okay. But, Steven, we are paying for it. None of that crap from your dad. We will invite them over to our house this Sunday for dinner and tell them then. They can also see all the work you two have been up to."

"Perfect. I will call them now, so Mom doesn't spend tomorrow working on Sunday lunch."

Amber squeezed in tighter to Matt. "Thank you, Matty, for what you did, spoiling the kids and us."

"Amber, you know it had to be done. It's a three-bedroom house and you have a boy and a girl. They can't share a room. This is yours and Steven's and the kids' home now."

"It will always be your home too, Matty."

"I know that, Amber, but my life is out there. It shouldn't impact you here, and you know that too. You just needed a little nudge from me. Besides it doesn't look like I am going to have kids anytime soon, so the least I can do is spoil yours."

That statement hurt Amber for him, and she rubbed his leg. "Any idea what you're going to do?"

Matt took a deep breath. "Other than going to a meadow with my family tomorrow, church on Sunday, and heading to California on Monday for a meeting, not a clue."

"Taken with the right perspective, that could be very freeing. It won't always be this way. Hell, Steven and I aren't going anywhere for two decades."

"But those decades will be so full of living." Matt pulled Amber in tighter for a hug.

Steven walked out on the porch with his cell phone in hand. "I just got off the phone with mom, and they're very excited to come out Sunday. Apparently, they had also been concerned about the size of our home with the new baby on the way; they are anxious to see what we came up with."

Amber snorted. "Well, that's fantastic," which was the family code for *what the fuck*. "I am going to bed. You coming, Steven?"

"Absolutely. I've got two sips left."

Amber walked into the house and wasn't gone five minutes when she came back out. She wagged her finger at them to come inside. As they followed her, she took them to her office. She must have put the Murphy bed down earlier and made it because Hank was now sound asleep on it on his back with his legs in the air. "Our first guest," she said, and they all laughed. One of Hank's eyes cracked open, but he didn't move; he exhaled and went right back to sleep. Amber then motioned them upstairs and went in Lucas's new room. He was asleep in the single bed, and his new bedside lamp shining stars all over the ceiling of the room and walls. Amber built a wall of pillows around Lucas on the bed, so he couldn't roll out. He was asleep and breathing so hard it could be heard outside his room. "Sleep of the sinless," Amber said as she moved his leg back under the covers.

"Do you want me to put him in the crib?" Steven asked.

Amber shook her head no and pointed the remote camera toward the bed. "Let's see how he does. I will keep an eye on him."

Dawn's room was quiet as well, and when they walked in, they were shocked. What had been piles of toys and clothes on the floor were all gone, and the room was spotless. They walked to the side of the bed, and Dawn was asleep with a book in her hands. Amber tucked the covers in. They all tiptoed out into the hallway and hugged each other good night.

Amber and Steven went in their room, brushed their teeth, and immediately stripped for bed. Amber was in one of Steven's white T-shirts that barely covered her butt, and Steven was in his boxers. As they collapsed into bed, Steven grabbed the remote for the bed. Amber seeing this smiled. "Do me baby."

Steven adjusted the remote and the bed filled up a little more with air and stopped. "A little more." Steven adjusted it again. "That's perfect. What am I?" she asked.

"You are a just below medium." Steven adjusted his side, and the motor went on and on until it finally stopped.

Amber turned her body sideways in the bed with her head now laying on Steven's belly. "What do you have going on over here?"

"I'm just shy of the hardest setting."

"Ouch." Amber began to drag the back of her hands back and forth across his chest and his leg. "I'm worried about Matty, Steven."

"I know, babe. We've spent a lot of time together the last two weeks, and we've talked some. He's really hurting, but eventually he's going to be fine."

Amber exhaled and found one of his nipples and dragged her finger back and forth across it. "Mr. Heard, where did you get your psychology doctorate from?" Her hand on his leg moved farther up near the top of his thigh.

"Mrs. Heard, the University of Dude."

Amber busted out laughing, her hand now so high, it grazed Steven's testicles. Steven immediately inhaled. "You know we always had our doubts about her, but he was so in love."

"Yes, he was, and I believe she was as well. I don't think that you can fake that, but somewhere she really went sideways. Money can make you do stupid things."

Steven slipped his hand up her T-shirt fully exposing her lower half. She was beautiful.

"Steven, do you think something like that could happen to us if they were so in love?"

"No, baby, you're stuck with me. We have a house full of children and love. We are both in this for the long haul."

"You will let me know if you become unhappy?"

"I couldn't be unhappy with you. What I think is what I say. You know that there are no secrets between us."

"I love you so much." Amber's hand now found Steven's erection, which was now sticking out of the top of his boxers. Her head turned on his belly away from his face, and she took it into her mouth, her hand pulling his boxers down so she could grasp him fully. Steven recoiled in the bed, his hand now rubbing her backside as she rhythmically took him in and out. When she could sense he was near releasing she slowed down. "Steven."

Steven recovering from his lack of release said, "Yes?"

"I need to go for a ride." Amber climbed on top of Steven and pulled the T-shirt off her body exposing her breasts. She then took him back in her hand and rubbed him back and forth around the outside of her wet opening. Steven was watching this, and she could see it was killing him. Finally, she slid him fully inside her, Steven again recoiling on the bed. She placed her hands on Steven's hard shoulders. His hands instinctively went to her chest, and she was off. Up and down, harder and harder, over and over until she released with a yell and fell forward onto him. Steven wrapped his arms around her and held her while she recovered. Soon, Amber was kissing his neckline her hips began to move again in rhythm. She whispered in his ear, "Steven."

"Yes, baby?"

"Come inside me, Steven. Please come inside me." Amber then plunged her tongue in his mouth and then went back to his neck. She knew how much he wanted that. Steven's hands found her hips, and he was now helping with the thrusting and it became harder and faster. Steven could feel Amber's hard nipples dragging back and forth across his chest as she took him in and out and that was it. He released loudly. Amber could feel his warmth inside of her, and she was gone again.

Steven held Amber tightly against him until their breathing slowed, his body still in hers. She slowly and carefully got off him and collapsed on her side. Steven immediately wrapping his body around hers his wet erect penis nestled on her backside.

Amber whispered into the darkness, "Steven, till death do us part?"

"Not even then. Forever." And they were asleep.

36

The afternoon in the meadow had been amazing. The meadow was the high point of their property now, and in the very far-off distance, the roof of their home and the silos could be seen as specks. Trees lined the other three sides of the meadow, and the river that ran through their property cut the meadow in half. As soon as they arrived, the dogs went to the river to play. The kids chased bubbles while they set up for lunch, and then after, Steven and Matt threw a football while Amber chased her children back and forth. It was a wonderful Saturday memory.

On Sunday, they rushed home after Pastor Tuddle's sermon on love and forgiveness. The punchline was that a lack of love or forgiveness for those who wrong you only destroys you, not them. Matt was not sure why Pastor Tuddle was tuned in to his wavelength currently, but it had become a little disturbing.

The table was set, and lunch was ready to be served. Matt, Steven, and Amber were again in the swing watching the kids play with blocks on the porch when two large SUV's turned into the driveway. Mr. Heard was in his silver, fully loaded Yukon Denali, and behind him, Mrs. Heard was driving what appeared to be a new Cadillac Escalade.

What was about to happen was immediately clear to all.

Amber turned to Steven with a look. "Steven!"

"Honey, I swear I didn't say a word to them about this other than the conversation with Dad the other day! Not a word." Steven walked out in front and hugged his parents as they got out of their cars. Matt and Amber followed suit as well. "Dad, you seem to be a little heavy on SUV's today did you get a new one?"

"I did. We got the Escalade yesterday in Omaha. Matt, you don't know this about me, but I am a little bit of a car whore."

This prompted a sigh from Mrs. Heard as she said, "Honey, we just left church."

Undaunted, he continued, "But you're not going to believe this story. So, we pull in to check out the Escalades because we aren't getting any younger, and it might be nice to have a little smoother ride now. We will all go for a ride after lunch. She's beautiful. Anyway, your mother falls in love with this one, and we start negotiating. When we get to Silvey"—he points to his Yukon and continues—"the man tells me that he is heavy on low mileage SUV's and can only give me ten thousand dollars for her. Can you believe that?"

Steven went ahead and took the bait. "That does seem unbelievable." Steven was not believing it at all.

Matt looked at Amber and she smiled, shook her head and rolled her eyes.

In response to that Matt held up four fingers and whispered, "It is worth four times more than that." It was obvious that Mr. Heard had worked very hard on his way home from Omaha spinning this yarn of lies.

"Well, I am thinking to myself with our expanding family joy"—he hugged Amber again as he continued—"that you guys might could give Silvey a good home, and I can get a better deal by selling her to you."

"What are you thinking, Dad?" Steven asked.

"Well, the man says she is only worth ten thousand, so that is fine, but maybe we could work in a fatted yearling to the butcher. We are getting a little low on beef at the house." Amber and Steven had long been the suppliers of the Heards' beef, which he always overpaid. "Also, I got this young kid, sixteen, who's now working at the store. Works his butt off but dropped out of high school and made some bad choices. He walks ten miles to and from work every day, so I thought that maybe Amber you might want to give him your car in this transaction and help him out?" And there it was, all on the table. There was silence as they waited on a response from Amber.

Mrs. Heard not being able to stand elongated silence interrupted it, "Amber and Steven, you kid's just pay us when you can, a little as you go. It will make us happy to know that Silvey's going to a good home and she will be protecting our family's precious cargo." She hugged Amber and her eyes welled up. They looked at each other, eye to eye, and they both knew this was all bullshit, but it was clearly obvious the Heards were very concerned about her and the children. They were not going to let this go.

Amber knew this was out of the sincerest of love from them and hugged her back, her eyes also welling up now. "Okay, I'm sure we will be able to work this out."

Mr. Heard, now believing he had gotten away with his poorly executed lie, put his arm around Matt and motioned toward the house. "Well, then, it's settled. We will consummate this after lunch by signing over titles." He put his arm around Matt, and they began to ascend the steps of the house toward the kitchen with the rest of them in tow. "So Matt, any more run-ins with ex-girlfriends at church today?"

"Not really. We sort of snuck out after communion to get home early and get lunch taken care of."

"That's a shame. It was the talk of the town this week."

Matt looked over his shoulder at Steven and Amber smiling. "Really?" Amber immediately nodded in confirmation.

"Oh yeah, everyone is talking about it." Mr. Heard then whispered in Matt's ear when nobody was looking, "All the paperwork is done. Just run by the attorney's office on the way out of town." Matt mouthed a thank-you, and Mr. Heard patted him on the chest. "Let's eat; I am starving."

Mrs. Heard insisted, "We will eat when we see what the boys were up to this week. I am so excited."

"Oh, that's right. Let's take the tour!"

Steven and Amber followed everyone up the steps. Amber looked Steven in the eyes and whispered, "You know they're never going to cash those checks."

Steven agreed and whispered back, "Merry Christmas."

37

Alexandra followed Dr. Moranne into her office for her weekly session and took her place on the couch looking toward her wall of fame. "Before we get started, I feel I need to apologize for storming out last week and slamming your door."

As always, a calm and cool Dr. Moranne responded, "Thank you for that, Alexandra. Let's talk about that."

Alexandra sat on the couch and placed her head in her hands. "I'm just so angry at myself it overwhelms me."

"I can see that. We need for you to have an outlet for that. I will sign the orders today. As long as you are not in a meeting or a session and you get overwhelmed, I want you to funnel that into yoga, swimming, running, working out, or drawing, whatever you need to get that out. If you had to dig deep down and put your finger on what's driving that anger, what would it be?"

Alexandra lay back down on the couch and laid her hand across the top of her head and exhaled.

Dr. Moranne scribbled onto her pad. "I want you to take your time, Alexandra, before you answer. We really need to focus on this if we are going to move forward."

Alexandra sat there for about five minutes rubbing her head looking at the trees swaying in the breeze and finally it came out. "Personal responsibility." To Alexandra, it was like an epiphany.

Dr. Moranne tapped her pen on her pad sharing this epiphany. "Yes, there it is." She scribbled furiously. "Where does that come from?"

Alexandra again looked out the window, then whispered, "My father." And immediately her voice broke. "I let my father down. I failed him." Dr. Moranne got up and pulled a bottle of water out of the refrigerator for Alexandra and herself.

"This is good, Alexandra. This is a breakthrough. Your father—"

Alexandra cleared her throat and interrupted, "My father is the greatest man in the world. I know most people say that about their fathers, but he is. My father has always preached personal responsibility to me and my sister. It isn't what happens to you. It's how you respond and react to the adversity. When I look back at not just the last year, which is a train wreck, but the last several years, I'm so ashamed." How long had she felt this way? "My father saved our family business when my drunken gambling grandfather had almost lost everything. Without my father, my mother and her sister would be penniless."

Dr. Moranne scribbled furiously now. "This would make your father a very powerful figure in your life."

Alexandra wiped more tears from her face. "He is," she said. She was having a hard time speaking now. "And I have not been… who he has raised me to be for a long time." The tears now poured.

Dr. Moranne was by her side holding her, and when Alexandra was finally able to collect herself and look up, she could see Dr. Moranne trying to hold it together. "I'm sorry," Alexandra said.

Dr. Moranne laughed. "Stop being sorry." Dr. Moranne wiped another tear away. "I think this is enough today," she said, collecting herself as well. "Did you talk to your sister?"

Alexandra smiled. "I did. She is well and excited for the baby."

"How do you feel after that conversation?"

"I thought we were done," Alexandra said jokingly and smiled. "I feel better. Thank you."

Dr. Moranne smiled and nodded in agreement. Alexandra got up, crossed the room, and stopped before she got to the door. She turned back to Dr. Moranne. "Dr. Moranne, am I going to make it?" Her face was broken, needing hope that she could beat this.

"Oh, Alexandra. I wish I knew that answer. History tells me that I really don't know. I have seen people leave here who I thought had no chance, and they go on to lead very productive lives." She got up and went to her bulletin board and pulled a picture off and handed it to her. It was a man with his family on a Christmas Card. "His name is Max, and I wouldn't have given you two nickels when he left here that he was going to make it, but he did. There are many more like him. Max stays on my bulletin board to remind me that even the most hopeless cases have a shot and to inspire me not to give up on those."

She took the picture back and put it back on the board. "And there are others, not many but a few, that you are positive they will make it, and they don't." Alexandra could feel the pain that Dr. Moranne had for those she had lost. She turned to Alexandra and smiled. "What I can tell you, Alexandra, is that in many cases I sit here listening to people blame circumstances, others, or just about anything for how they ended up here. It's always someone else's fault. Not in your case. I just need to help you find your personal strength to battle and to give yourself a break. That's a very good thing, Alexandra."

Alexandra teared up with a half smile said, "Thank you, Dr. Moranne."

"Thank you, Alexandra and please don't slam my door." They both started to laugh, as she walked out.

"Yes, ma'am."

38

Matt and Steven loaded the kids into Silvey as the sun crested in the east. Amber climbed in and cranked her up. "I feel like I am driving a tank."

Steven smiled. "My love, that would be a rural assault vehicle versus in Matt's Connecticut where it would be a suburban assault vehicle, and it is designed to protect my most precious cargo."

"I hope I can get used to it. It's just so big."

Matt spoke up. "In a week, you won't know how you ever did without it." Steven agreeingly nodded.

"Bye, Uncle Matty." Dawn was buckled in the back making a pouty face.

Matt reached in, hugged and kissed her cheek goodbye for the third time in five minutes. He then reached across and grabbed Lucas in the tummy, which had him scream and giggle. "Bye, Lucas, I will see you soon." Lucas waved goodbye to him with his hand pointed in the wrong direction, and then blew Matt a kiss. Matt's heart sang as he was grateful to be their uncle. Matt then went around to the driver's side car door. It was closed but the window was down, he reached in again and said goodbye to Amber. "I love you, sis. Please take care of yourself and the Fam."

Amber reached out and touched his cheek. "It has been so great having you here. Promise me that when you're on your way back, you'll stop and stay even if it is for just a night."

"I promise. Looks like it will most likely be longer. Thanks to Alice, I have no place to live in Connecticut for a month." The look on her face was so relieved.

"Good. I will be texting or calling you every day, and you better respond. Got it?"

"Yes, sis, I got it."

"All right, enough of this. Get back or I might run over your foot." She put Silvey in reverse and cautiously backed it up using the rear camera, pulling out of the driveway. Matt and Steven watched Silvey until she was out of sight.

"Matt, thanks for helping me load." At Matt's insistence, he and Steven woke up early and loaded the trailer that was now hooked to the tractor with all the supplies Steven was going to need to fix those four fence areas they had identified. Matt was guilty for leaving him with the work, but it was time to move on. Steven gathered himself up on the tractor and whistled to Lady. She bolted off the porch in pursuit.

"Steven, please be careful."

"I always am, Matt. I have way too much to live for." The tractor sputtered alive, and they were off down through the pasture, Lady making sure to give the steel beast a wide berth.

Hank started to run after them, but Matt called him, and he stopped. Hank looked at Matt and then looked back toward Steven and Lady seemingly trying to decide what to do. Then, his decision made, he bolted toward Matt almost running him down. They went into the house, and Matt showered and finished packing. He left after stowing the Murphy bed away, putting his towels and used sheets in the washer, and starting the machine on his way out of the door. After Hank got situated into the truck, Matt's phone dinged.

It was a text message from a number he didn't recognize. He opened it up, and it was a picture of a family: an African American woman and an Asian man with two young boys. Underneath the picture was a short message: *Thank you so much for allowing us to use your beautiful home while you are away. Please know we will treat it as if it's our own. If there's anything at all we can do to help you here, please let me know. You have my number now. Janice Yang.*

Matt typed a quick reply back, "*Thank you, Janice. You have a beautiful family. I will absolutely do that. Enjoy the home and let me know if there is something you can't find. I should be able to direct you… unless it's in the kitchen ☺. Matt."*

Matt took his time on his drive in as the attorneys office didn't open until ten. He gathered all his memories of Nebraska City as he drove around town. Nebraska City was where he grew up. It was the home to his sister and her husband and their kids on their family ranch. It was not his home anymore, and at this point he had no clue where home was. He finally pulled into Mason Cromwell attorney at law at 10:02. The cool air hit him when he got out of the truck. Spring was right around the corner. "Stay, Hanky."

As he entered the brick walls of the office, he was shocked to see Rachel, his old girlfriend, at the reception desk. "Rachel."

She looked up at him in a knowing way. "Hello, Mathew."

"I heard you worked at the bank with your new husband."

She pressed an uneasy smile. "I can't work at the bank anymore because he is my new husband. I actually don't need to work anymore, but the kids are in school, and this is just short-term gig to keep me busy. Mason's secretary is out on maternity leave for two months."

"I see."

"I understand you are turning over the family ranch to your sister. Is that something that she wanted?" Rachel could see Matt's surprise that she knew why he was there. "I'm sorry. I typed up the paperwork last week."

"Rachel, Amber doesn't know. The ranch doesn't belong to me anymore. They work so hard and have made a home out there. It's hers, Steven's, and the kids'. They don't need a silent partner in Connecticut."

"That is very sweet of you, Mathew." Rachel smiled her beautiful smile that took Matt back to high school. The girl he once knew had turned into a beautiful woman. He had to get out of here.

Mason heard their conversation from the hallway and came out. "You must be Matt Thomas." He stuck his hand out, and Matt reciprocated.

"Mr. Cromwell."

"Just call me Mason. Come on in the conference room. I have everything ready." Matt followed him in with Rachel in tow. On the table was a stack of paperwork all with little flags sticking out of the sides where he was supposed to sign. "So basically, all of this in a nutshell is you deeding over your portion of the farm to your sister. It will be hers in totality. There are no liens or loans against the property, so this is all pretty straightforward. They have done a fine job managing the property, which is a very tough thing to do."

Matt sat at the conference table across from Mason and Rachel and signed away his portion of the farm to the Heard family. As he signed and initialed, he passed the paperwork to Mason who made sure everything looked good. Then he passed it to Rachel who was sealing and notarizing it. After they had finished, Matt wrote out a check to the firm for $1,000.00 and shook both their hands.

Rachel showed him out to the still-empty lobby as Mason gathered everything. "Mathew, it was great seeing you again. How much longer are you going to be in town? Maybe we can grab a coffee or something and catch up."

"I am leaving this morning, but it was good to see you again, Rachel. Congratulations on your marriage." With that, Matt closed two doors at Mason Cromwell attorney at law.

"You as well, Mathew."

"Goodbye." And he was out the door and in the truck. Hank was thrilled to see him and stuck his head on the console to be rubbed. "Hanky, we have to get the hell out of here before Mathew gets into some trouble." He brought the engine to life, and the Bluetooth connected to his phone. On cue, Hootie and Blowfish again started singing about rolling down the road again. Matt turned the radio up on the steering wheel. "Speak to me, Darius," he said as he petted Hank's head and drove off.

39

Matt drove for three solid eight-hour days to get from Nebraska City to Calistoga, California. Calistoga, California was a small town that was about a twenty-five-minute drive from Napa. Matt found Calistoga while searching for a reasonably priced VRBO homes he could rent for a week that would also allow a dog. None met that criteria in Napa. The rental options were either way too expensive or no dogs. Finally searching up and down the valley, Matt found a small home in Calistoga.

Calistoga had one main street, Lincoln Avenue, that ran through the middle of town, and it was easy to envision at one point in history it being an old western town for settlers. Mountains sprang up on either end of the town so the view in either direction on Lincoln Avenue was spectacular. What was at one point a sleepy, farming town now teemed with visitors who came for the wine and relaxation. Wineries, restaurants, boutique hotels, spas and shops that host local artists' work now dotted Lincoln Avenue, and everything was within walking distance from Matt and Hank's little blue home for the week.

There was a thud on the bed as Hank jumped onto it, sitting next to a sleeping Matt. When Matt made no movement, Hank snorted in frustration and collapsed his full weight on Matt's chest, waking Matt up. In Hank's world, it was past time for nuggets, and he was not going to be denied his breakfast.

Matt stirred, his head again crushing this morning from way too much wine yesterday. He spent the last four days in Napa going up and down highway 128 and Silverado trail between Napa and Calistoga, wine tasting, taking tours and learning about the business. It had been a fascinating time that netted him three cases of wine, his learning variety pack, which were now stacked in the corner of the tiny blue home. He would be careful during the day not to drink too much during tasting, and later after a nap, he would wander into town for dinner. He would have another bottle, eating at the bar, chatting with the bartenders and locals. Then he would pass out in bed by ten.

Hank now moaned on the bed and again snorted his frustration. Matt reached up and grabbed his phone. More daggers shot through his head. It was time to get off the wine train and back to reality. Matt fumbled his phone and it fell on the floor. "Fuck," he mumbled. He turned over to pick it up, and through Matt's blurry eyes, he could see the time was 4:07 A.M. "Dammit, Hank! It is 4:00 A.M.!"

Hank had made the easy transition from Connecticut's time zone to Nebraska City because farm life had them waking up before dawn working. With Hank running and playing all day with Lady on the farm, he literally crashed at night. Nebraska City to Napa had not been a good transition for Hank. Another time zone, and while Matt was out searching for his wine treasures of the day, Hank would spend the day sleeping off their morning walk. Hank was still on Nebraska City's time zone, and it was morning; he was hungry.

Hank nudged Matt again with his head. "I got it; I'm getting up." The second Matt threw his legs off the bed, Hank jumped off and ran to his food bowl. Matt's head swam again. While Hank devoured his breakfast, Matt went to the tiny Keurig and brought it to life. Fumbling around in the cupboard, Matt could only find one pod of coffee left. He was going to have to hit the grocery store this morning. He had two more mornings left in his tiny blue house, and then he would head to Mountain View on Wednesday. The plan was to deposit Hank at the Residence Inn, which allowed dogs and then head for meetings with Amil Samua, which was the entire reason for this trip.

Hank finished his food and then sat next to Matt, who was at the tiny kitchen table nursing his coffee. He rubbed Hank's head and ears. "Shithead. Thanks for the early wake-up call." Hank pawed at him again. Matt looked at his phone; it was 4:37 A.M. Matt took Hank for a quick walk when he got home last night at 8:30. Hank had to go to the bathroom again, and their tiny blue home for the week did not have a fenced-in yard. Matt got up and found his jeans on the floor. Hank was turning circles at the front door. "I'm coming, Hank."

Matt found a wrinkled Nebraska T-shirt and a torn hoodie sweatshirt that had the hoodie 1/3 torn off of it from a run-in with the washer. Putting them on he went into the bathroom and brushed his teeth. His hair was everywhere, so he grabbed his ballcap that was in desperate need of washing after his time in Nebraska City. Hank still at the front door was ready. "All right, buddy. Let's go."

The cool morning air of Calistoga hit Matt's nose. It was much warmer during the days in the valley than Nebraska City, but the mornings and evenings were always cold with the air coming off the bay. Matt learned from his winery tours that those cold mornings and evenings coupled with those warm and hot days in the summer is what made Napa such a great home for growing grapes. It was all about the weather and the amazing volcanic soil. Matt and Hank walked in the dark up and down the side streets of Calistoga. Matt checked his watch. They had walked four miles. Hank would be ready for his morning nap, so they headed back. Matt opened the blue door of the house and was ready for his second cup of coffee, but there was none. It was now 5:45 A.M., and the cafes would not be open in the sleepy town for a while. Then it hit Matt—the gas stations were his only option. One of them had to be open, and he could get coffee.

Matt left Hank asleep in his bed and walked up the street. The gas station lights were on, indicating it was mercifully open and doing business. There were only two pumps, one in front of the station and one on the side. Both had vehicles fueling for the upcoming day, and there was barely enough room for a car on either side of the pumps. As Matt turned into the station from the sidewalk, he startled back to avoid a truck leaving. Four men were standing against the outer wall of the gas station. When a truck pulled up, two of the men climbed into the back of the truck and drove away. They were day workers, and this was the pickup spot. Matt went into the store and made a large black coffee, which was remarkably good. He sipped it as he paid for it.

Outside the station was again teaming with action as Matt could see the two day workers were now leaning on the wall in the vines. He quickly stepped to the side along the station wall to avoid a car pulling in when an old red Ford truck pulled up with a young Hispanic man inside. He exchanged words with the two men in the dark, and they proceeded to get into the back of the truck. Matt maneuvered to get between the wall and the truck so he could turn down Lincoln Avenue when he heard a snapping sound and turned. The young man was pointing at the back of the truck. Matt looked at him curiously and then around. The young man continued to snap. Matt realized then the young man thought he was a day worker, and as he looked down at his attire, he realized he looked the part: paint splattered worn-out jeans with holes in them, a torn hoodie and a sweat stained ball cap. The young man speaking in Spanish to Matt now broke into perfect English, “Are you coming or not?”

Matt thought for a moment. There were no plans for today. He couldn’t drink any more wine. In fact, last night he declared today a beer day.

Now really frustrated, the young man spoke again, “In or not?”

In a split-second decision, Matt turned and climbed into the back of the truck and sat across from the other two men. The old red Ford lurched when it was put into drive, and the young man turned left onto Hwy 128 toward the heart of the Napa Valley. As the truck picked up steam, the air became cold. Matt pulled his hood over his hat and gripped his coffee to keep his hands warm as he sipped. Matt whispered to himself, “What the hell did I just do?”

40

Alexandra waited in the formal living area of the big house that served as Dr. Moranne's waiting room. It wasn't her day to be there, but she wasn't there for herself. There was some noise in the hallway, and then Aggy burst into the room with Dr. Moranne behind her. "I'm busting out of here. It has been a long three months." Alexandra greeted her with a hug, and looking over Aggy's shoulder, she could see Dr. Moranne smiling at them.

"What are you going to do first?"

"Mom is picking me up, and we are going shopping, spa day, hair, nails, the whole thing and then there's a celebratory dinner with the family tonight."

"That sounds wonderful, Aggy. I'm so happy for you."

"I wish you could join us." Aggy and Alexandra had been having dinner regularly in Alexandra's room on the nights when there were no conflicts. Alexandra now knew way too much about Agatha Hemsworth and her long string of bad decisions and bad boyfriends that landed Aggy in Shadow Oaks.

"I'll take a raincheck. I don't think Dr. Moranne would be too happy about me heading out of here today." Alexandra looked at Dr. Moranne and received a wink back from her.

"You've got my number. Please text me when you get out, and we can have a normal dinner somewhere. I am going to miss you, Alexandra. Promise me that we will connect when you get out."

Alexandra smiled. "I'm sure you will be too busy, but I definitely will."

Dr. Moranne nodded toward the front of the house. "Aggy, it looks like your ride is here." They all looked at what appeared to be a new Rolls-Royce driving down the center of Shadow Oaks and pulling slowly around the front. Two large men, obviously security detail, emerged from the car and opened the rear door, and Keira Hemsworth, the matriarch of the family, emerged from the back. You could have snapped a picture of her and put her on the front of any style magazine today.

"Mom," Aggy exhaled as she grabbed Alexandra's hand. "Come both of you. Please meet her."

Alexandra resisted. "Aggy, I'm sure you mother just wants to see you."

"Please, Alexandra. I don't know how I would have made it the last two weeks without you." They all walked out together with the orderlies in tow carrying Aggy's luggage.

"Mom!" Aggy hugged her mother violently, and Mrs. Hemsworth held her daughter.

She then pulled back to kiss her daughter's cheek and held her at arm's length. "Agatha, you look so well, so beautiful."

"Thank you, Mom." Aggy then turned and pointed. "Mom, I would like to introduce Dr. Moranne, my counselor, and my friend, Alexandra." The word friend hung in the air. How many real friends did Aggy really have at this level of wealth or influence? Probably about the same amount as Alexandra, which was almost none.

Mrs. Hemsworth stepped forward and shook Dr. Moranne's hand. "Aggy looks wonderful. Thank you so much for taking such good care of her."

Dr. Moranne returned the handshake and smiled. "She has been lovely, and we look forward to seeing her again as a visitor and not a patient."

Mrs. Hemsworth shook her head up and down, and powerfully meant it when she replied, "Yes."

When Mrs. Hemsworth went to shake Alexandra's hand, she looked puzzled. "Have we met?"

"Yes, on a few occasions in passing. I have actually been to your charity ball several times. You do such a wonderful job with it, and it means so much to those in the community."

"Thank you. That's very sweet. Are you a counselor here as well?"

Alexandra's heart sank, but she did not have the strength or will to lie. Besides, it was useless. The cover-up of her addiction had gone up in smoke when she ran the light and crashed her Jag. Anyone with a computer was only a couple of keystrokes on Google away from finding out what happened to Alexandra Steed Bridgeway. "No, ma'am. Unfortunately, I'm currently a patient here as well. Your daughter and I have just become very close."

Mrs. Hemsworth's face turned flush in embarrassment as she searched for the right words. "Thank you for being a friend to Aggy. We wish you a speedy recovery as well."

"Thank you, Mrs. Hemsworth."

Mrs. Hemsworth's attention was now focused back on Aggy. "We have a big day ahead of us. Everyone is so excited to see you tonight. Are you ready to get started?"

Aggy nodded and turned again to hug Alexandra and Dr. Moranne. Aggy then got into the car, and as it pulled away, she waved from the window.

Alexandra and Dr. Moranne waved back and then she cleared her throat. "Alexandra, she made more progress in the last two weeks than the previous ten. Thank you for engaging with her when she reached out."

Alexandra shook her head happily, yet she was afraid for Aggy returning to the real world and for herself. Two more weeks, and then she would be out.

41

Matt sat on the ground under a tree with a cup of water from the jug on the back of the truck. There had been no introductions when he arrived at the vineyard where they joined other day workers. He watched what the other men did for several minutes, checking the vines and then securing them firmly against the trellises, and then he began. Soon, the dormant vines would be full of leaves and huge cloves of grapes, and the work they did today would be crucial. He was incredibly slow compared to the other men, but he wasn't going to rush and mess up someone else's livelihood.

Matt wasn't sure what his plan was when he arrived. Maybe simply to live a day in the life of another man. He figured if he was in over his head, he could disappear into the field and grab an Uber.

The morning was good. Matt managed to sweat out a lot of the wine he had been consuming the previous four days. He found the work therapeutic, and it cleared his head, which is what he needed. The valley was beautiful surrounded by the mountains. The air was clear and smelled of wine, and he was able to watch the sun rise over the valley gloriously, an amazing perspective on the Napa Valley that no tourist would every experience.

The young man who picked him up was talking to the other men in the distance in Spanish. They found a spot as well under a tree and were eating their lunch. They all looked Matt's way at the same time, and then the young man headed toward Matt. "What's your name?" he asked.

"Matt. Matt Thomas."

"Where are you from, Matt Thomas?"

"New York," he said automatically. Connecticut is virtually a suburb of the city.

"Matt, have you ever worked in a vineyard before?"

"No, I have worked on a ranch many times before but never a vineyard."

"Okay, makes sense." He looked over at the other men. "The other guys say you are very slow."

Matt laughed. "That is very true, just trying to not screw it up."

"My name is Joseph. I am the foreman of Steed Vineyard."

"Very nice to meet you, Joseph."

Joseph started to walk away and then turned to ask, "Where's your lunch?"

"I forgot it today. I'll be fine."

Joseph went to the old Ford truck and opened the door. It creaked mightily with age. He pulled out his own lunch and walked toward Matt. "My girlfriend, I think she is trying to fatten me up. She always makes me too much food." In an incredibly nice gesture, Joseph reached into the crumpled brown bag, pulled out a sandwich, and handed it to Matt.

Matt's hand went up. "Thank you, but I can't take your lunch."

Joseph reached back in the bag and pulled another sandwich out. "I told you, she makes me too much. Now eat this one." He threw it at Matt. "I can't have you any slower than you already are." Joseph then smiled. "Grab a quick siesta, and then we will start back in twenty minutes." Joseph walked away and found a tree to himself and ate.

Matt opened the sandwich and consumed it. He was starving. After, he lay back on the ground and pulled his hat over his eyes. One of Matt's favorite wines was Jerkasky Cabernet, Steed Vineyard, and Matt was out there pruning the vines. Unbelievable. A glass of it would never be the same again to him. Each glass would now be a blessed memory of his time in the valley.

Matt wasn't sure how long, but he fell asleep and awoke by the sound of another truck. Matt looked and saw a man getting out of a large white, fifth wheel, Ford F350. He was a large, older man with flowing gray hair. From the response of the other men who were now falling all over themselves to get back out into the field, Matt knew exactly who this was. It was the boss. Joseph met him and shook his hand. They were talking and pointing around and then pointed in Matt's direction.

"Shit," Matt mouthed as he got up quickly and brushed the rich black volcanic soil from his jeans. He headed back into the field to assume his pitiful position, much less farther along than his day worker comrades. Soon, Joseph was beside him giving him a class in what to do. With the two of them working every other vine, Matt eventually caught up.

The crew knocked off at 5:00 P.M. Most of the men piled into other vehicles and drove away. Matt assumed they were the normal crew. Matt and his two quiet comrades all got into the back of the truck, and Joseph handed each of them $120. Matt made $15 an hour today and a ton of great memories.

The trip back to the gas station seemed to be much quicker to Matt as the spring air was now warm, and the ride much more enjoyable. Joseph pulled into the station, and they all got out. He spoke to the two men in Spanish, and they nodded and walked away.

"Matt, I will pick you up here tomorrow at six."

Matt looked shocked. "Really?"

Joseph smiled. "Yeah, we will even take you, rookie. Shows how desperate we are." The old truck fired up, and he drove away.

Matt began to walk down the street. He needed to take Hank for a long walk, and he was exhausted. His phone vibrated and began to ring in his back pocket. When he pulled it out, he saw Amber's beautiful picture on the front of the phone, and he answered it. "You are not going to believe what I did today."

42

Hank was standing over Matt at 4:00 A.M., hassling loudly. It came to Matt's attention that Hank in fact smelled really bad. A bath was in his future this evening whether he wanted it or not. Matt rubbed Hanks head and rolled over. "What do I need an alarm for when I have you?" Hank collapsed onto Matt's chest as he grinded his head into his body. Then he flipped over to expose his belly for a rub. What was the plan? First coffee and then a walk. Would he go out as a day laborer again? The thought made him smile. Amber thought he had lost his mind.

He explained to her that it was a split-second decision, and he just wanted a completely different perspective of Napa Valley. At the end of the day this land of sprawling mountains with wineries, restaurants, spas, and shops was all backed up very simply by farmers with farms on very expensive property with a very delicate crop, and as with any farm, totally reliant on God and the weather.

Matt had dressed again in his ratty jeans and ballcap but had put on a different T-shirt and hoodie. After taking Hank on a much longer walk this morning Matt left him passed out on the bed in the tiny blue house and walked up to the gas station and got his second cup of coffee. Last night, he got his dinner from the grocery store, Cal Town, and just in case, picked up a sandwich and some chips for his lunch today, which was now clutched in his hand in a plastic Cal Town bag.

There were five guys leaning against the wall of vines, his two comrades from yesterday on one end. When Matt approached, they nodded to him and spoke, "Hola."

Matt nodded at them and replied, "Hola, Good morning." Matt took a space against the wall of vines next to them, and then he heard the awful sound of the truck pulling in. It was Joseph. He greeted them warmly, and the three of them piled into the truck. They went through Calistoga this time, turning right on the Silverado trail toward Napa. They were going to a different location.

The sky was brightening up to a light blue as the truck began to slow. Matt looked in the direction they were going as Joseph turned the truck into Steed Vineyard. The driveway cut through the center of the vines on either side of the road with a rose bush planted at the end of every vine row. The beginning of the property was on the valley floor, prime real estate, and there was a small ranch house at the base with the mountains rising behind. There was an elaborate winery barn at the base of the mountain with another vineyard behind it that climbed the sides of the mountain. It was breathtakingly beautiful place.

Matt got out of the truck and took his place in the fields with the other men. An hour later, Joseph came and got him, and they walked up the driveway toward the barn. The right side of the barn was a wall of glass with an ornate porch built around two large trees growing out of the decking, providing natural shade for the porch. There were six parking spaces out front, and a sign that said *Guest Parking and Tasting Room*. The middle of the building was a huge working winery full of steel drums, sophisticated equipment and racked, wrapped empty French barrels.

In the back of the building, there were two massive wooden doors that opened to the mountain itself, the caves of Steed Vineyard. It smelled gloriously of wine and the land it came from. Joseph showed him around and then pointed to the left of the barn where a large but much less elaborate porch overlooked the valley. "That is the residence. It's completely off-limits. Don't step a foot on this porch."

Matt nodded. "Got it."

They walked back in the working winery, and Joseph started providing instructions. Matt needed to scrub the floor, which already looked clean enough to eat off of, by 10:00 A.M. before the turistas showed up for wine tasting. He was given a large hose, a broom to scrub it down and cleaning solution before Joseph left to return to the fields.

Matt was meticulously hosing and scrubbing with great care and detail, making sure not to miss an inch. When he turned around, he was startled to see the boss standing there observing his work. He nodded at Matt, and then spoke in a very deep voice, "Where's Joseph?"

Matt pointed toward the valley floor. "He's down in the fields working with the guys." The large man turned and headed down the driveway.

Around 9:45 A.M., Matt was finished and wrapping up the hose when Joseph walked in and inspected his work. "Good. We are very short-handed, so you are with me in here today. Mrs. Steed will be bringing the winery tours through here. The goal is to do our jobs but not be seen. Smile, nod, and then continue to work. Don't engage unless engaged by the turista or the Steeds. Got it?"

"Got it." This was very interesting to Matt. Not too many turista's on the family ranch back home or in his office building in New York. Joseph mounted the forklift, and they went to work. Mrs. Steed entered the winery with about six people following her all with a glass of wine in their hand around 11:45 A.M. Matt guessed chardonnay. The group consisted of two men and four women. As they walked through the door, the group came face-to-face with Matt carrying two five-gallon buckets full of water. Matt immediately stopped in his tracks and smiled a big smile. He then nodded to the group and backed out of the way to let the group go by.

Several of the ladies in the group examined Matt as they walked by. When they got to the other side of the room, Matt heard one of the women ask Mrs. Steed in a loud whisper, "Is he the wine maker?"

Mrs. Steed smiled. "No, he is one of workers."

The lady then turned to one of the men in the group and said, "Honey I know you already purchased this year's copy of winery dogs, but the girls are going to need the winery studs addition as well." The group and Mrs. Steed laughed.

"Come along. Let's let them do their job," Mrs. Steed said as she opened the door to the cave in the mountain, and the group went inside.

When the door closed, Joseph looked up at Matt from the barrel he was working on and rolled his eyes. Matt shrugged and gave him a what-the-fuck-was-I-supposed-to-do look. He then continued washing out the drum he was cleaning. The tours continued throughout the day. About every thirty minutes, Mrs. Steed would come through with a group, talk about the winery, and then head into the caves. There must have been another exit as Matt never saw them come back out.

At 4:00 P.M., the gates to Steed Vineyard automatically closed. Anyone coming for a tasting after 4:00 P.M. had questionable sobriety. Matt had been guilty of that himself. Joseph made Matt clear all the hoses out of the walkway around 2:00 P.M. for this reason, and sure enough at 3:15 P.M. a group who poured themselves out of a limo came literally stumbling through. Their accents were very strong, and they were loud. Matt was guessing they were from New Jersey and having too good of a time.

It was time to knock off for the day, so Matt went to the staff restroom to clean up a little. It had been a glorious day, better than he could have imagined, and he learned so much from Joseph about working in a winery. When he went to wash his hands, they didn't come clean. They were stained with red wine, and this made Matt smile. When he got home, he would take a picture of them to send to Amber and Steven. He couldn't wait to debrief them on his day in the valley. When he emerged from the bathroom, Matt was confronted by Joseph, who was not smiling, and the boss, who had a roll of paperwork in his hand. He pointed it at Matt and said, "Follow me."

He and Joseph followed the boss through the tasting room to a rocked firepit away from the barn usually used by guests, but with the winery now closed, it was empty. Loose decorative rocks and four curved wooden benches surrounded the firepit. Matt hadn't felt this way since he was sent to the principal's office in junior high. The boss and Joseph sat on one bench, and the boss gestured with his paperwork for Matt to sit on the bench across from them.

The boss held up the roll of paper. "Who are you, and why are you here?"

As the blood drained from left Matt's face, he replied, "I'm sorry." Over the boss's shoulder, Matt could now see that Mrs. Steed was on the porch with another woman who had a striking resemblance to her, and they seated themselves on the deck under the trees, listening.

The boss pondered in silence for a moment. "Okay, we'll do it this way," he said while he unfurled the paperwork. "There are thirty-eight Matt Thomas's in New York City. My guess, which is not a guess at all, is that this one is you." He handed over the first couple of pieces of paper, and there was Matt smiling on the first page. It was his LinkedIn profile, and his picture from the Waverman company website.

"You looked a little out of place yesterday, and we've had some trouble recently, people coming out here for all the wrong reasons, so Mrs. Steed"—he motioned toward the porch—"did some digging this afternoon." He handed over the next paper, and it was an article on Matt from five years ago from *New York Daily Business* on Matt's promotion to lead his team, again his smiling face looked back at him from the page. "My wife called Waverman Capital and Investing today, and they say you are on leave but are expected back in a month. So, Matt Thomas of New York City and Waverman Capital and Investing, what are you doing working at my winery as a day laborer?"

Time to come clean. Matt cleared his throat and began, "Mr. Steed—"

"I am actually not Mr. Steed," the boss cut him off and nodded toward the porch. "I'm Ben Faulkner, and this is our family winery. The ladies, my wife and her sister are the Steeds."

"Mr. Faulkner, you are correct." Matt looked down at the paperwork. "This is who I am, but I can assure you nothing nefarious is going on here. I have no idea what trouble that you're speaking of. I'm on leave from work and expected back in a month."

Mr. Faulkner shook his head up and down, "So what are you doing here?"

"I have been completely honest to every question I have been asked. I came to the valley to visit the wineries for a week, and I actually have meetings in Mountain View tomorrow on behalf of Waverman."

Mr. Faulkner, now disarming a little, asked, "Then how did you come to be working for us yesterday?"

"With the time change, I was up very early." Matt thought it best not to throw Hank under the bus. "I walked to the gas station in Calistoga to grab a coffee and ran into Joseph. He thought I was a day worker because of how I was dressed. Wanting to experience the other side of the valley, the farming portion of it, I got in the truck."

Ben Faulkner looked incredulous at Joseph. "You picked up a tourist to work in the fields?"

Joseph stuttered, "He was standing against the wall dressed like that and it was dark."

"That's all true," Matt defended. "I was dressed like this and to avoid cars coming in and out of the station, I was almost against the wall when Joseph pulled in. I grew up on a farm, really a ranch in Nebraska, so it wasn't that big of a leap for me to get into the back of the truck. My sister and her husband still work the family property. I've always been interested in wine, so this seemed to be another way of educating myself."

Mr. Faulkner unfurled the last piece of paper. It was a much younger picture of Matt in his football uniform at the University of Nebraska. "Which is how you came to play college football at Nebraska?"

Matt smiled, looking at the ladies on the porch and nodded. "If I need a detective, I know who to hire." Mrs. Steed smiled back. "Correct. I played on scholarship and blew out my knee the middle of my sophomore year. I majored in business and finance and ended up in New York where I still work today. I actually live in Connecticut, but for the last two days, I've been a worker in the valley. It's been an amazing experience. Again, there's nothing nefarious here."

Mr. Faulkner relaxed and nodded his head. "Okay." He stood up and put his hand out to shake Matt's. "Matt Thomas, thanks for your work today, and good luck in your meetings tomorrow. Joseph, pay him and the other workers, and take them back."

"Mr. Faulkner, if it would be okay, can I just have a bottle of wine for today? That would equal my wages. I would like to taste the fruits of the winery I've been working on for two days."

Mr. Faulkner nodded and then turned to Mrs. Steed. "Mrs. Steed, can you get him a bottle of the Reserve?" Mrs. Steed nodded and went in the winery. She came back out with a two-bottle carrier.

Matt smiled at her knowing she spent the back half of the day digging into his life. They were both beautiful, middle-aged women with long flowing brunette hair. "Thank you, Mrs. Steed."

She smiled back and handed it to him. "You are welcome, Matt Thomas of Nebraska and New York. I included a chardonnay as well."

"Thank you both." Matt nodded to both of the women and then headed down the main driveway toward the vineyard with Joseph and Mr. Faulkner. As they neared the ranch-style home, they could hear some yelling in Spanish coming from the side of the house. Mr. Faulkner quickly picked up his pace with Matt and Joseph in hot pursuit. While crossing the front of the house, Matt could see condensation running down the inside of all the home's windows. This was going to be bad. On the side of the house were three Mexican men standing in six inches of mud. It hadn't rained the entire time Matt had been in the valley.

Matt spoke up. "There's condensation on the inside of the windows of the house. It must be coming out of the crawl space." Matt pointed to the door in the foundation. Joseph was the first down, and he flipped the wood that was holding it shut. When he pulled the door open, water poured out from under the house. When it abated, they gathered around the door. Joseph reached in to flip the light switch above the door. As he went to flip it, both Mr. Faulkner and Matt yelled, "No!!!!" Joseph stepped back from the door. Matt said, "If it's hot, you could electrocute all of us." Matt took Joseph's spot in front of the door and pulled his cell phone out for light. He crawled a few feet inside into the mud.

Mr. Faulkner spoke up, "What are you seeing?"

"It's bad. There is a major water break somewhere in the house. The water is coming through the floor into the crawl space and then out. The floor insulation is coming down." Matt backed out of the crawl space. "We need to turn the power…" Matt trailed off and saw the main power to the house was right there to the right of the crawl space opening. He pulled the tab to open it and dropped the breaker killing all the power to the house. "We need to turn the water off, but we should see if we can find the leak first," Matt said. The three of them trudged out of the mud to the front of the house.

When they opened the house, it was extremely warm, and there was not a dry spot on the floors. There was water everywhere. As Matt had seen, condensation was flowing down the inside of all the windows and walls, and with the spring heat, mold had started to grow on the walls. The HVAC must have shorted out a while ago, and with the water the house basically turned into a terrarium. They walked through the house stopping at a bathroom that was full of water, but they couldn't find anything wrong.

Matt looked at Mr. Faulkner and asked, "Kitchen?" Mr. Faulkner pointed, and they walked through several doorways to the far side of the house. Matt could hear the water rushing and see it visibly moving across the floor of the kitchen. "It's here," he said.

Joseph reached down and opened the cabinet doors under the sink. "I don't see anything in here."

Matt listened again and watched the water flow on the floor. "It's the high-pressure line going to the refrigerator icemaker," he concluded. Matt began pulling the refrigerator out, and Joseph joined to help. As soon as they had the refrigerator pulled out, water started shooting all over the kitchen. Matt reached in and turned the wall valve killing the water supply to the refrigerator, and it ceased. Matt looked at the line and showed it to Mr. Faulkner. The line was ruptured. "It should have been a braided line. I have seen these many times. There is no telling how old it is. Whoever installed it, used the wrong type of line."

Mr. Faulkner sighed, "Great."

Matt looked around and said, "We need to get all the windows in the house open to start the drying-out process." The three of them trudged around the water in the three-bedroom ranch, opening every window. When they were finished, they all stepped out onto porch.

Mr. Faulkner collapsed into a chair on the front porch. "Joseph, I told God yesterday I can't take one more thing, and he gave me one more thing."

Matt sat down as well. "Was nobody living in the house?"

"This was May and Richard's home. May is my wife's sister. You met her and my wife, Hannah, on the porch a few minutes ago."

"Mrs. Steed?" Matt asked.

"Yes, the Steed sisters. Richard ran the operations of the vineyard, and I have been the wine maker here for over thirty years. Richard died eighteen months ago of a heart attack in our Chardonnay vineyard in Napa. May is a very strong woman, but it has taken a toll. She eventually moved up to our house in the barn complex to stay with us in our guest room. Joseph here was Richard's righthand, so he has taken over operations."

Matt ran his fingers through his hair. "So, the house has been empty?"

"Yep. There's no telling how long this has been going on." Mr. Faulkner pulled off his hat and shook his head.

"I'm sure you have insurance; they will cover this."

"Insurance is not the problem. There's no one to do the work."

Matt looked up. "I don't understand."

Mr. Faulkner gripped his hat. "We are down to half staff, which is how you got picked up. The vineyards are the most important thing right now, and we must have them completed before bud break, which is very soon. We are way behind. Half the workers in the valley have gone to Santa Rosa, which burned to the ground last year. They can make more money rebuilding the town than they can working for us. Every construction company in Northern California is rebuilding after all the fires last year."

Matt pointed toward the house. "You've got to get into those walls or it's going to be an even bigger mess."

"I know. I have half a mind to bulldoze the house." He sighed. "But I can't. Our family's status right now is up in the air and I may possibly need it." Mr. Faulkner looked up at Matt. "You said you've seen the ice maker lines ruptured many times?"

Matt shook his head. "I have. After my knee was torched and it was obvious football was over, I worked summers and sometimes evenings and holidays when I was in school for a fire and water restoration company."

Mr. Faulkner gestured toward the house. "How bad do you think this is?"

"I don't care what your insurance guy tells you. There's too much moisture in there. I'm positive it's in the walls and insulation. If it's ever going to be right again, you are going to have to take the whole house to the studs. Let it completely dry out and then rebuild the inside. If they want to half-ass it, you're going to have mold."

"I have a good insurance guy. We went to school together. He won't screw me over."

They all sat in silence for several minutes reconciling what happened. Then Joseph looked at Matt and asked, "You said you had a month before you had to go back?" Mr. Faulkner looked, waiting for Matt's answer.

Matt looked at them and started laughing. "There is a ton of work in there."

Mr. Faulkner scowled. "You are the fire and restoration expert."

"I was a grunt that worked for a company. I'm not licensed."

"You said it yourself. We have to get it down to the studs and dry it out. I don't think we need a license to demo a house."

Matt motioned toward the valley. "My VRBO is up today. I have no place to stay."

"The foremen's office has a cot in it with a full bathroom. You can share the space with Joseph while you are here. He is shacked up with his girlfriend. Just tell me what you need."

"Mr. Faulkner, I don't know. I have my dog with me."

Mr. Faulkner was quiet and wrinkled up his nose. "Keep him out of the winery. The tasting room and my home are off-limits."

Matt continued, "Mr. Faulkner—"

He cut Matt off. "Tell me what you need."

Matt looked out over the beautiful valley and pondered. Shit.

Mr. Faulkner got up and stood next to him. "Matt, I have no idea what your situation is, but for some reason God brought you here just when I needed you. Tell me what you need."

43

Matt walked into the office of Samua Capital in Mount View, California. The space was very open and modern. The staff were scurrying around in T-shirts, jeans, tennis shoes, and a few people were even wearing Crocs and flip-flops. Matt originally had put his blue Italian suit on and decided to forgo most of it, thinking he would be overdressed. He left his jacket and tie in the car and was still overdressed. He walked up to a young man who was the receptionist. "Good afternoon, my name is Matt Thomas. I have a meeting with Amil Samua."

The young man jumped to his feet. He was obviously expecting Matt. "Good morning, sir. Mr. Samua is wrapping up a meeting and extends his apology. He got caught in traffic coming from one of our clients and will be fifteen minutes late. Can I get you anything to drink? Water or coffee?"

"I'm fine, thank you." Matt found his way over to a modern, weird, orange, dysfunctional chair and sat down. Since leaving Steed Vineyard, everything was a whirlwind. He returned home, covered in sweat and mud from his day. He took Hank into the yard and gave him a bath first, followed by a long walk until he was dry. He spent the remainder of the evening washing his clothes and packing to go.

Matt spent no less than an hour on the phone last night with Amber and Steven recounting his day. He sent Amber and Steven a picture of his purple hands, and his phone immediately rung with several questions of, "What have you gotten yourself into?" Matt was wondering that himself.

Packing the car this morning threw Hank into a frenzy. Hank was always concerned he was going to get left behind. He was now tucked away at the Residence Inn asleep on the bed, while Matt was at Samua Capital. The elevator opened, and two men in T-shirts and jeans exited. The receptionist who had been cordial with Matt a few minutes before now turned ice cold. "What can I do to help you?" he said as the two men approached.

"We need to see Amil. We have secured the financing we need," the first man said.

"I will let him know you came by, but you don't have an appointment, and he is completely booked today."

"Please, we need to see him. Can you book an appointment for us?"

Mr. Icy picked up his phone and dialed. He whispered into the receiver, and then looked up at them. "Unfortunately, Amil is booked out for a month, but he will give you a call."

The two men, now angry, started walking toward the elevator. They stopped, whispered to each other, and then took a seat in the teal and yellow dysfunctional chairs next to Matt. Mr. Icy looked up and started to say something but thought better with Matt present.

One of the young men nodded at Matt and asked, "Are you here to see the vampire?"

Matt was dumbstruck at the comment. "I'm sorry?"

"Amil, you know he is known as the vampire of Silicon Valley."

"I'm sorry. I don't understand."

"Nobody comes to Amil for money unless your startup is on death's doorstep. If he likes the idea, then he gives you money, but it comes with all kinds of strings that you can't get out of.... Then he owns your idea or product and kicks you out of your own company. If you have any other choices, you need to get the hell out of here." The elevator door opened, Amil walked out of the elevator, and the two men leapt to their feet. The men had secured financing and wanted their company back.

They offered him 150 percent of what he had originally loaned them, and he refused. That was when the yelling and threats started. The elevator soon opened again, and security rushed out to corral the men, pushing them into the elevator. As the door closed, one of the men yelled out, "Fuck you, Amil! We will see you in court!" Matt had never seen anything quite like this in his professional life.

Amil, unfazed, walked into the office space when the receptionist stopped him and whispered. Amil took a deep breath and quickly put a big smile on his face as he turned to Matt. "Matt, so good to finally meet you. I'm so sorry you had to see that. These young people, no manners whatsoever. Come, come—we are set up in the conference room, please."

They then spent two hours in the conference room with ten startups being pitched. At the end of every presentation, Matt finished the questioning by asking the same questions of the presenter. Who owned the company now, who was running it, and where were the people who started it? He got the same answer each time. Amil owned the startup outright. It was being run by somebody Amil assigned, usually the presenter, and the people who started it had moved on to the next big idea.

When it was over, Matt sat there for a minute. He stood up and went to get a bottle of water from the refrigerator. He turned to the group and said, "I'd like to clear the conference room except for me and Amil. Thank you for the presentations."

Amil stood up and motioned the presenters out of the room. When they left, Amil shut the glass door and turned to Matt. "Impressive, huh, Matt?" Amil stuck his hand out. "Let's do business together."

Matt looked at his hand and then stepped away to the other side of the room. Matt was raised in Nebraska and that was his disposition and personality, but every once in a while, New York came out. "Amil, this is what I think. Impressionable men and women come in here looking for money but also mentorship and guidance. What you do is feed off them, crush their spirit, and steal their companies. The worst part of this is that you're too stupid to realize that when you crush them and eventually push them out, you remove the passion, spirit, and the ingenuity that created them in the first place. From what I have seen today, any startup with a good product would stay a million miles away from you and this company unless they had no choice.

Matt picked up his iPad and walked toward the door. "We are done here. Don't ever contact me or anyone at Waverman again."

When Matt got in the truck, he clicked the Call button and said, "Call King George."

The Sierra replied back, "*Calling King George.*"

"Matt, I have been waiting for your call. How did it go?"

"George, I got to tell you, I have met quite a few assholes over the years in our business, but this fucking guy takes the cake. He is a bad guy."

"Really?"

"What's worse is that there's so much more going on out here than we even know about."

44

Matt's morning meetings had gone much better than yesterday with Amil. He ran by and scooped up Hank just in time for his 1:00 P.M. late check-out and decided to take the scenic route out of San Francisco across the Golden Gate, which was spectacular every time.

The Sierra's dash came alive with a picture of Amber and his phone began to ring. Matt clicked the steering wheel to answer, "Hey there."

Amber's sweet voice came through the car. "Matty." She sounded worried.

"Amber, is everything okay?"

"I am mad at you, Matty. You shouldn't have done this."

Matt thought he knew what she was talking about, but was going to let her explain just in case. "Amber there are a lot of things I've done, so you're going to have to be more specific."

"The ranch, Matty. You deeded your portion over to me and Steven." Yep, exactly what he thought it was.

"Amber, I love you, Steven, and the kids. I am blessed to be in a position right now in my life where I can do this for you, and I want to do this. The ranch is your family's home, you guys are working it, and I couldn't be happier for you."

"Matty, the ranch will always be your home as well, and we are your family."

"And I know that, Amber."

"Why do I feel like you're tying up lose strings? You're scaring me a little." Matt could hear it in her voice.

"Dr. Heard, you are overanalyzing this. I have been thinking about this ever since I moved to New York. I just never had the time to take a breath and do it. It's just timing, not my mental disposition." That was a true statement about timing, but Matt wasn't going to tell Amber the truth. A year after his parents died, the fights with Beth began. Amber put her practice on hold to go home to sell the ranch. Matt couldn't go because he'd just started at Waverman. The truth is if Amber hadn't done that, then they would have eventually lost the place and any value it had. Everything would have gone at auction for pennies on the dollar. When no buyers had materialized during that year and Steven and Amber married and settled on the ranch, Beth was pushing Matt to force a sell of his half of the property.

Matt was never going to do that. Matt and Beth's net worth was four times that of his sister's and her new husband. Matt knew that for a fact because he always did their taxes for them. He was never going to put his sister in a precarious financial position, so Beth could have more nice things than she already had. With Beth relinquishing her claim to his assets, he could now freely do what he wanted to do and deed the property over to Amber.

"Okay. Please don't think we are not thankful. Honestly, we are overwhelmed. We talked about selling portions of it to pay you your half over the years but just couldn't bring ourselves to do it."

"I'm so glad you didn't, and you now have Dawn's Meadow." Matt desperate to change the subject, asked, "How's Silvey?"

"Oh shit, I hit something this week." Her voice changed.

"What!?"

"It's just so big."

Matt, now laughing at her, asked, "What did you hit?"

"A pole at school, backing up."

"Amber, you have a backup camera and sensors."

"Shut up. It was still beeping quickly and had not gone solid tone yet on the screen when I hit it. I blame the sensors."

"Generally, you don't wait until it goes solid, Amber. How bad is it?"

"I couldn't bring myself to look, so I drove straight to Mr. Heard's work and confessed."

"What did he do?"

"He laughed at me and then came out and checked it. Thank God it was just a scratch. He had one of his guys come out and buff it out. Steven doesn't know yet. I plan to confess tonight. Not telling him this week has been killing me."

"You're so funny."

"Matty, what's the plan?" She changed the subject. He immediately knew that she was digging. She was worried.

"For the next two weeks, I'm doing demolition work at Steed Vineyards. Much past that, I don't know, but don't worry. I am working through it. It's a process."

"Did you call any of the analysts I recommended?"

"No, I haven't, but I have been writing and burning the pages, and it has helped." That was true. Whenever Matt would think about Beth and the situation with Waverman, a dark cloud would come over him. He would then write down his feelings, mostly betrayal and so much anger, and eventually he would burn it in a grill or somewhere safe. It was helping.

"You know I'm always here to talk."

"I do, Doctor. I love you." He was trying to get off the phone now that she was analyzing him."

"Love you too."

"Amber, pay attention to the sensors."

"Shut up, Matt." And then she hung up.

Matt was smiling. He wouldn't know what to do if he didn't have her in his life. He had been working through his situation and made some decisions. It was going to be he and Hank no matter what. Till death do they part. Spending so much time with Hank had been healing as well. Matt wasn't sure who said it, but it couldn't have been truer: unconditional love, given unconditionally, was what you received from a dog.

Matt touched the steering wheel again. "Call, Alice."

"Calling, Alice." Matt decided his time in Connecticut was over. It just didn't work. He couldn't handle Hank with a ninety-minute commute both ways. It wasn't fair to Hank to have him locked up in a house fourteen hours a day. If he went back, he would move to the city. Those three hours he got back would be the time he needed to take care of Hank, and he would find a doggy day camp for him a couple of days week.

Alice picked up the phone. "Hey, Matt, how are you?"

"I'm good, Alice. I hope you are." Now that a decision had been made, Matt was ready to cut to the chase. "Listen, Alice. I have decided to sell the house. Can you please put it on the market?"

Alice cut him off. "Matt, let me call you right back."

About five minutes passed, when his phone rang again, and it was Alice. "Alice?"

"Matt, I just got off the phone with Janice Yang. She is very excited. They want your house. They are willing to work out a deal for whatever you are willing to leave behind as far as furniture. They are moving out of 1800 square feet in Chicago, so you can imagine they don't have too much."

Every room in the house had been Beth's except for Matt's office. "Alice, I just need my clothes, paperwork in my desk, and personal stuff out of my office. If we can work something out with the Yangs, they can have it all."

"I will get to work on it in the morning. I'll do the comps and get it appraised just as if we didn't already have a buyer. Matt, are you sure you want to do this? As happy as I am for a sale, I want to make sure you are doing this for the right reason."

"Alice, honestly if I don't have to walk back into that house again, and it is going to a nice family, I'm good with it."

"They are very nice. I just wanted to make sure. I'll take care of everything. Janice and I will start packing your stuff. She already offered to do that. I will send you the paperwork via E-sign in the morning, so I can be your broker."

"Thanks." After hanging up, a sense of relief and freedom came over Matt. He hadn't realized, but the house had been a burden on him since this all unfolded.

Before he knew it, Matt was on Silverado Trail heading in the direction of Calistoga. He cut over from Hwy 128 after he got through Napa and was enjoying the drive. Now off the phone for the duration, he rolled the windows down and opened the sunroof. The smell of the valley blew through the inside of the Sierra, and in his rearview mirror, he could see Hank's head shoved out the window, gleefully taking in the breeze. It was about to be spring in the valley, and it was beautiful.

Matt slowed down when the Sierra's GPS showed he was getting close. Around the bend was Steed Vineyard and the amazing driveway that rolled up to the house. Matt looked at the dash. It was 3:00 P.M., so the fence would still be open. As he pulled in, he took it all in. "Hanky, this is our home for the next two weeks. Don't screw it up." Hank started hassling in excitement. When Matt pulled up to the ranch house, he could see that his request had already been met. A construction dumpster was now in the driveway, which was on the backside of the home.

The winery parking lot was empty as it was late in the day, and Matt realized he didn't know where they wanted him to park. He decided to pull into the winery, run in and ask one of the Mrs. Steeds. As he got out of the truck and stretched his back out, Mrs. Steed, Ben Faulkner's wife, stepped out onto the porch and smiled. "Mathew Thomas of New York," she greeted him.

"Mrs. Steed. I'm sorry I just parked here for a moment to see where you wanted me to park."

"My name is Hannah, Matt. Only Ben calls me Mrs. Steed," she said as she pointed to a far building where the farm equipment was kept. "There are spaces behind the building where you can park after you get your stuff out of the truck, but come in for a second. You look nice. You really clean up." Matt was again in the slacks of his blue suit with a blue dress shirt on and his brown wing tips.

"I've got Hank in the truck and Mr. Faulkner said—"

"I can only imagine what he said," she cut him off. "He's not a fan of dogs, but he's not here. Bring him in."

Matt opened the rear door, and Hank jumped out making a beeline to Hannah. He threw his full chocolate-Lab body weight against her for some love. "Oh my gosh, Mathew. He is so beautiful and sweet." She loved all over Hank and then opened the glass door to the winery and went in. Matt sat at the bar across from the wall of glass as Hank smelled every inch of the room. Hannah pulled out two wine glasses and filled them with Chardonnay. "It looks like I got stood up on my 3:00 P.M. tour or they're late, which happens this time of the day. Matt, why don't you tell me about yourself."

"Based on your detective work, I'm not sure there's too much you don't know."

"Well, let me see. My research said you were married, but I don't see a ring."

Wow, incredibly direct, Matt thought as he forced his answer out. "Yes, my wife and I are separated. Part of the reason I am out here. Needed to get away for a while."

"I'm sorry."

"That's okay. I'm sure it would have come out at some point." Matt desperately wanted to change the subject. "Where is the other Mrs. Steed?"

"May, my sister, is down at the house collecting what little there is left. What a disaster that place is. Thank God she had her picture boxes up here. She committed to Mr. Faulkner to have it done today, so you could start throwing everything else out tomorrow. Thank you for staying for a while to help us."

"It's not a problem." A car pulled up outside, and four mid-twenty-aged girls spilled out of it.

"Oh boy. It's my three o'clock at 3:15." Hannah reached below the bar and pulled out four glasses and started to pour Chardonnay in them when the four young ladies busted into the tasting room.

The driver, a very attractive brunette with long hair, appeared to be the ringleader. "I am so sorry we are late. I'm Anastasia; I made the appointment," she said. Hank saw the four girls and bounded across the room before Matt could stop him and threw his weight against them to get their love.

One of girls squealed, "Winery dog," and joined Hank on the floor and let him lick her face. "What's his name? Is he a chocolate Lab?"

Matt looked at Hannah and mouthed, *I'm sorry*. She immediately waved Matt off. Matt responded, "Yes, he is. His name is Hank."

The girl, who was obviously close to hammered, began singing, "Hanky, Hanky, Hanky." With that, Hank excitedly danced around the girls, who were now showering him with attention.

A blonde in the group joined Matt at the bar, and although there were ten stools, she plopped herself right next to him. She put her hand out and purred, "My name is Samantha."

Matt, uncomfortable, shook her hand and replied, "Matt."

"Well, Matt, what brings you to the valley?" She thought he was tourist.

"I'm actually doing a little work here."

The blonde immediately ran her hand through her hair, locking her green eyes on Matt's blue eyes, and purred, "Are you the wine maker?"

Hannah snorted a little and cleared her throat. "Here's your wine, ladies," she said as she pushed the glasses toward the girls. She then smiled at Matt and shook her head. "We need to get moving on our tour. We don't want you to miss out, and we close at four."

At that Matt was moving toward the door. "Come on, Hank."

45

Her last two weeks at Still Oaks crawled for Alexandra without Aggy. She had no idea how much she would miss her after she left. Her days consisted of yoga, swimming laps, long walks, drawing and group therapy classes, and every three days, Dr. Moranne would poke around in her head.

Today, all of that was over. Alexandra woke up early, showered, and packed. She was sipping coffee looking out at the morning fog floating through the trees. Today, she would be free. Free was a relative term as part of the terms of her release. At least she would be free from here.

She had to report in a couple of days to her parole officer. She already surrendered her driver's license for a year. There would be random drug testing to make sure she stayed clean and 100 hours of community service. She also had to go to a meeting at least five days a week. If Alexandra did all of that for a year, all this mess would go away, scrubbed from her record. There was light at the end of the dark tunnel she was in currently. She just had to keep her shit together and stay clean. Did she want the drugs? Yes, she did, still. That was the addiction. Did she need the drugs? No, she didn't, and the farther she got away from them, the easier each day seemed.

Alexandra sprung from her chair when she heard a knock on her door. It was 7:50 A.M., and it was time to go. She followed the orderlies through the hallway as they steered her bags. As she passed one of the staff lounges, she could see many of the counselors inside in deep discussion with a few of them crying. Something was up. Whatever it was, it wasn't her problem, and she was happy about that. It would be good to get home to her family. She missed them terribly, more than she could ever have imagined, and soon there would be a baby, which made Alexandra smile.

The orderlies stood outside Dr. Moranne's office, and one of them nodded for Alexandra to go in. As Alexandra entered, the greeting she received was not what she expected. There was a heaviness in the room, and Dr. Moranne was turned away, looking out her window. When she turned back, she forced a half smile and pointed toward the couch. Alexandra sat, but didn't break eye contact with Dr. Moranne. "What's wrong, Doctor?"

Dr. Moranne's eyes welled up. She sat and took Alexandra's hands. "Alexandra, I am so proud of you. You have made such progress here over the past month. You've been so open and willing to face your issues. Truly, you have been a star patient." Dr. Moranne was doing her best to keep it together, but the problem that brought the heaviness in was all over her face.

Alexandra took a deep breath. She couldn't take it any longer. "But?" she asked.

Dr. Moranne patted Alexandra's hands searching for the words. "There are no buts, Alexandra. You have done amazingly well here, and I believe strongly in you."

"Dr. Moranne, what is wrong?"

"Normally I would never tell you this. This conversation would never happen, but it's all over the news, and you're going to find out. Patient confidentiality is out the window at this point."

Alexandra gripped Dr. Moranne's hands. "What? Dr. Moranne, please tell me."

Dr. Moranne sighed, and no longer able to hold it in, a tear streamed down her face. "Alexandra, Aggy is dead."

Alexandra ripped her hands from Dr. Moranne's and put them to her mouth. The sound that came out of Alexandra's mouth next was nothing short of a guttural cry. "Nooooo! No!" Dr. Moranne tried to put her arms around Alexandra to comfort her, but she pulled away, and was sobbing on the other side of the couch.

After a few minutes, Dr. Moranne sat next to her putting her hand on her back. "I am so sorry, Alexandra. I know how close the two of you were."

"How? I thought she was with her family."

"The details aren't important."

Alexandra looked up; her blood shot eyes meeting Dr. Moranne's. "How?"

"I'm not telling you anything that's not on the news right now. The family has been looking for her for a couple of days. Security footage from the front gate of the house showed her climbing onto the back of her boyfriend's motorcycle in the middle of the night. They tried to trace her phone, but she turned it off. Last night, they caught up with the boyfriend, and he took them to an abandoned home in Oakland where the two of them had gone to score. She overdosed. The family is devastated. We all are. She spent so much time with us."

Alexandra got up and walked to the window, tears still flowing, and whispered, "Oh sweet Aggy. What did you do?"

"Based on the circumstances, I would like you to stay with us for a couple more weeks to work through this. This would be voluntary on your part, but I spoke with your parents this morning, and they are supportive. This would be your decision."

"Where are my parents?"

"They are here. They're in the waiting area."

Alexandra walked straight to the door of Dr. Moranne's office and pulled it open. She ran down the hallway to the entrance of the waiting area. Inside, her parents were waiting for her. They immediately stood when they saw her. Alexandra ran to them and collapsed in their arms. "Take me home," she cried. "Please, take me home." Alexandra's father scooped his daughter into his arms, picking her up in complete desperation to protect his child. Dr. Moranne entered the room and nodded to Alexandra's father as he carried her out of the building to the waiting Suburban and gently put her in the back seat.

46

Matt and Joseph carried a load out to the construction dumpster. It had been this way for the past several days as the two of them had worked out a system. Matt would work in the house and remove all he could carry. Joseph would assist him twice a day before lunch and then again at 4:30 P.M. with the things Matt couldn't carry on his own. It was working, and tremendous progress was being made.

The dumpster was picked up on Friday for the first time, full of contents from the house, furniture, and other belongings, and then replaced with a new dumpster. May delivered as promised and retrieved what was important. Everything else was now in the dumpster or soon would be there. Now, the hard part came, removing soaked carpet, padding and warped hardwood floors. Tomorrow, Matt would start to get into the walls. Getting the flooring out was key as he was not able to have Hank in the house with him until he could get the floors dried out. Hank was living in the wine office during working hours, and he was not at all happy about it.

As they threw the load in the dumpster, Hannah Steed's blue suburban roared up the driveway past them with Ben Faulkner at the wheel, parking in front of their home. Joseph grabbed Matt by the arm excitedly and said, "Come on. I will introduce you."

As they made their way up the driveway, May Steed stepped off the porch of the tasting room and cut them off. "Don't," she said. Matt could see Mr.

Faulkner now carrying a woman into the house with Hannah in front of them opening the door.

Joseph was visibly upset. "Alexandra."

Matt looked and asked, "Is she okay?"

May motioned them to the tree-shaded porch of the tasting room. The spaces out front were empty, so no visitors were there now. They all climbed the stairs and sat in the shade as May brought out bottles of water.

Joseph broke the silence. "They said she was doing great. I don't understand."

May patted his knee. Matt could tell she was hurting as well. "She was, Joseph. Everything was great. Her treatment was going very well. Hannah texted me on the way back," May sighed. "She became very close to a young girl at the treatment center and found out this morning as she was being released that she OD'd and died."

Matt whispered, "Ouch."

May turned to him and forced a smile. "Matt, now that Alexandra is home, we need to bring you into the circle of trust. Can we count on you?"

Matt nodded up and down in agreement. "I am so sorry."

May forced a smile. "I knew we could trust you. We have been on an emotional rollercoaster around here for eight months now. Catherine, Alexandra's younger sister, and her husband are pregnant, which normally would be wonderful, but Catherine has a condition which makes this a very high-risk pregnancy for both her and the baby. Thankfully everything has gone well so far, but rightfully we have all been worried. The other day when Mr. Faulkner questioned you and was suspicious of your presence here, he talked about trouble," May continued as she pointed in the direction of the house. "This unfortunately was the trouble he was speaking of. Alexandra was in a terrible accident that could have killed her about six weeks ago in San Francisco. When they took her to the hospital, they found out that she was under the influence of drugs, and she was arrested. The accident made the news and for weeks reporters were coming around the winery pretending to be visitors to ask questions."

Matt shook his head up and down. The conversation with Mr. Faulkner was making complete sense now.

May continued, "As part of the terms of her release, she was committed to a treatment facility, and from everything we were told, it went very well." She patted Joseph on the leg. "We were all looking forward to her release today, to bring her home, when she got the terrible news. She is just so fragile right now; her husband is filing for divorce. She is hurting for many different reasons."

Matt looked at the house and asked, "How long has she struggled?"

"About fourteen months ago, she and her husband went skiing in Lake Tahoe, and she was wiped out by another skier and had to have knee surgery. Her doctor at the treatment center said that the pain killers they gave her after surgery are highly addictive, and she couldn't get off them. The doctor said this is very common today. Nobody had any idea except her husband. The last time those two girls got into any trouble was when they were ten years old and wrote their full names on a wet concrete sidewalk in Napa." They all laughed at that. "And then on top of all this, the damn flood in the house." Two cars were now rolling up the driveway, and May checked her watch. "My next tasting," she said, and they all stood up. May reached out and hugged Matt. "Matt, the reason I am telling you all of this now is with Alexandra out, reporters, people may try and come around again to see her. She is just too fragile to handle it."

"That makes sense. If something like that does happen, please text me 911 and your location, and I will come."

"Thank you, Matt. I will let Hannah know as well. We appreciate your discretion with this."

"Absolutely. I won't say a word to anyone."

The cars pulled up to the tasting room, and eight people got out. May smiled. "Welcome to Steed Vineyard. Welcome. Come on in, and let's get a drink."

47

Matt and Joseph helped load the last of the green kitchen appliances into the truck, and two Hispanic men then drove away. Mr. Faulkner donated them to their church thrift store, along with several other items that could be salvaged from the house. It was decided earlier in the week that Matt was correct, and the house would mostly have to be taken to the studs and rebuilt. A full remodel would eventually be underway by a contractor after Matt finished, and it was completely dried out. Matt figured he had about three or four more days of work which would get him on the road to Nebraska and eventually New York. Would he go back to Waverman? He wasn't sure yet.

It was almost 4:00 P.M. on Friday. Matt decided to go wine tasting tomorrow. He then planned to find a church on Sunday and head over to scenic Hwy 1, so Hank could swim in the Pacific. He may pack a picnic for him and Hank. This was something that had been on his bucket list since he arrived in California.

Joseph leaned back and stretched. "Matt, I know you don't have any plans tonight. You need to go to dinner with me and Rosa." Matt had not yet met Rosa, but he heard all about her from Joseph. Joseph was in love. Unfortunately, Joseph's parents were not. They were Catholic and did not approve of the relationship, which only turned worse when they moved in together nine months ago. Rosa was not a US citizen and was in the country on a political visa. She came to the US last year when the Venezuelan government collapsed. Her parents used her mother's jewelry to get her and her sister out of the country and later escaped themselves to an uncle's home in Brazil.

In Venezuela, Rosa and her sister owned a store that sold clothing and high-end home items. In the US, Rosa and her sister worked as housekeepers at a hotel in Napa. It was not the match Joesph's parents had imagined, and of course they were unsure of Rosa's intentions.

"I'm good. Honestly, I am exhausted after this week."

May came down the steps of the main house and greeted them. "Good, you're both here. We need you both at the house right away." As they walked by the winery, Matt went inside and put Hank in the office. He knew that Hank was not welcome in the house. As they walked up the steps, Matt saw Ben with a woman in jeans, an oversized sweatshirt, and white casual shoes. She had hazel eyes, wore no makeup, and had medium length hair pulled back in a ponytail. She was beautiful. When she and Matt made eye contact, she quickly looked down to the floor and didn't look back up. May went and sat in the swing and put her arm around her. She was Alexandra. Matt had not seen her out of the house the entire week.

Mr. Faulkner stood stoically but very concerned. "We just had a phone call, and we have a problem. Catherine has been rushed to the hospital. At this point that's all we know. Mrs. Steed is upstairs packing. She's a wreck. We need to go to LA now. I will come back as soon as I can, but I don't know when that will be. May is going to be doing double time in the tasting room, which is crucial because we don't distribute our wine. Between stocking, handling tastings and paperwork every day, that's a dawn-to-dusk job for one person. We are suspending all tours until Mrs. Steed gets back. Joseph that leaves you in charge of the vineyard. You know what to do. You worked with Richard all those years."

Joseph nodded. "Yes, sir, I will take care of it."

Ben patted him on the back. "Thank you, Joseph. We will stay in contact while I am gone. Matt, I don't think you have met my daughter, Alexandra." She looked up with her hazel eyes, forced a smile and nodded at Matt. He returned her nod, and she dropped her eyes back to the floor. "Matt, I am going to need your help here with both of us gone. Alexandra can't drive right now but must get to community service no later than 8:00 A.M. in Napa, and she needs to be picked up by 3:00 P.M. She also has a meeting every day during the week from 5:30 P.M. to 6:30 P.M. in Calistoga. I need you to make sure she is where she supposed to be. It's very important."

"Absolutely. I totally understand."

"Thank you. You have made amazing progress on the house the last week and a half, and I know you were planning on heading out for home next week after you finished. At this point, the house is secondary to getting Alexandra where she needs to be. Also, May could possibly call on you from time to time in the tasting room with Mrs. Steed gone."

"Yes, sir."

Mr. Faulkner exhaled relieved. "Good, thank you all. I will get back here as soon as I can." He went into the house, and Alexandra was right behind him. May got up and hugged Matt and Joseph mouthing, "Thank you."

48

The alarm went off at 6:30 A.M. Matt turned over in the cot he was not going to miss when he left Steed Vineyard. He was undecided whether his back was hurting from the manual labor, sleeping on the cot, or both. Hank was immediately there, hassling. It was nugget time. Matt crawled out of the cot to Hank dancing around in circles. Was there anything better to Hank than breakfast? Matt poured Hank's food, and then went to brush his teeth and wash his face. He then threw his working clothes on with a ball cap. He was going to fix some coffee but decided to wait. He was going to Napa, so he could grab a Starbucks after he dropped Alexandra off for community service.

Matt started the truck as he walked up to it. The morning was cool as were most mornings in Napa. He helped Hank into the backseat and then pulled the Sierra out of the space to the front of the house. He looked at the clock, it was 6:50 A.M. Motion caught his eye on the porch. It was May, motioning him to come inside. He turned the truck off and got out. "Stay, Hank."

May was standing on the porch in her night clothes. "Come inside and get some breakfast."

"I'm fine," Matt lied. He was starving. The work lately increased his appetite.

"I've already made it. Come on."

Matt, realizing he wasn't going to win this conversation, climbed the steps and entered the home. It wasn't elegant, but it was functional. He followed May into the kitchen where Alexandra was sitting, nibbling on a piece of bread with an empty plate in front her. She looked up and nodded at him, which he returned, and then he sat at the table opposite of her. May grabbed the coffeepot and poured him a cup. Matt brought it to his mouth, and it was good. She then pushed a plate of scrambled eggs, bacon, and hash browns toward him. "Any word on Catherine and the baby's condition?" Matt inquired.

May shook her head. "They're still doing tests. We should know a lot more today."

After he devoured his breakfast, he went to take his plate to the sink to rinse it and May stopped him. "Leave it. The two of you got to go."

Alexandra got up. She was makeup-less again and wearing loose khaki pants and a shirt that completely covered her arms. She had a ball cap in her hands and sunglasses. They walked out to the waiting truck and got in. Hank was thrilled that there was someone new to give him attention, and he nuzzled her arm on the armrest. She pulled away and looked out the side window.

When Matt cranked the truck, the Bluetooth kicked in and Hootie began to sing "Miss California" Matt reached over to turn it off. "Sorry."

She waved him off. "It's fine."

The drive to Napa was a quiet one. Not a word. Alexandra just stared out the side window, not making eye contact. When they pulled up in front of the police station, there was a small bus there with bars on its windows. It was pulling a trailer that had lawn tools, a water jug, and a portlet on the back. There were two guards, a man and a woman. Alexandra was mortified. She wanted to run away.

They were a few minutes early, and Matt could sense her angst. It was understandable. "So, listen," Matt said, breaking the silence. Alexandra turned to look at him in total fear. If Matt could have taken her place on the crew, he would have. "The treatment center that you stayed at I am guessing was very nice?" Alexandra nodded in agreement. She had no words. "The people you're going to meet today will be different. Don't provide your name, where you live, or anything personal. You have no idea what these people did. It could be anything." Alexandra again nodded. "And… be careful. Make sure you don't put yourself in harm's way." Alexandra seeing other people milling around the bus started to get out. "Wait." Matt reached back and pulled a green hat out with a brim that went all the way around it. "You will get cooked today with a ball cap. This is new. I just bought it." Alexandra took it and left her ball cap on the front seat. She put it on with her sunglasses and walked across the parking lot to one of the guards. He checked his list and provided her with a fluorescent vest, which she put on before boarding the bus of barred windows.

Matt had never met Alexandra until a few days ago, but he had a pit in this stomach as he drove away.

Matt had to swing by the hardware store and pick up a list of supplies for Joseph and the crew. They were hitting it hard in the Chardonnay vineyard, which was just outside of Napa. By the time he dropped off the supplies and got to the house, it was just after 10:00 A.M. He would have four hours to work before he would head back to get Alexandra. As Matt was pulling into the vineyard, he got a text from May: "911 tasting room." Shit. Matt drove to the tasting room, and there were two stretch limos out front. He hustled across the property with Hank in chase with excitement.

Matt heard them before he saw them, and it was loud. When he opened the door, there were no less than twenty twentysomething-year-old girls inside. May gave him a wide-eyed look as he came in the door. Matt seeing she needed help made his way behind the bar with her. Hank on the other hand was making the rounds of the room, being loved on by the girls who were snapping selfies with the winery dog. "I guess the 911 is not a reporter," Matt said.

May smiled. "Worse, a bachelorette party," she whispered. "I have their money just start pouring chardonnay." May motioned to a young, beautiful shapely brunette who walked over to them. "Mackenzie, this is Matt. He's going to be helping us today."

She smiled and with a raspy deep southern accent she put her hand out and said, "Hey, Matt. I'm the maid of honor, and the leader of this shitshow."

Matt smiled, put his hand out and noticed the dirt on it from when he had been in the vineyard with Joseph dropping off the supplies. Mackenzie shook it, "Very nice to meet you, Mackenzie. Welcome to Steed Vineyard."

She turned to the crew. "Ladies, let me introduce you to Matt."

In unison, the crew yelled out a very sweet, "Hey, Matt." Matt started loading the glasses up with Chardonnay. The girls came one by one and got them. May was manning the register as the girls were buying Steed Vineyard T-shirts, coasters, and winery dog books. Matt looked for Hank, and he was surrounded by four of the girls being loved on. Matt smiled as he was never going to get him out here. A stunning, busty redhead plopped herself at the bar across from Matt and put her hand out. "Hey, Matt, I'm Sandy."

Matt started to reach out and stopped halfway. "Sorry, I just came from the vineyard. My hands are a little dirty."

Sandy reached out and took his hand in hers and looked deeply into his eyes and said, "That's okay. I can get a little dirty myself." That prompted a wide-eyed look from May, and four other girls at the bar busted out laughing, which drew the attention of Mackenzie.

Matt, cleared his throat. "May." He needed to know what to do next.

"Go ahead and take twenty of those glasses out on the porch and pour about an inch of Merlot in them. Open three bottles of the cab and leave it out there. I will serve them on the porch. You stay here and man the tasting room, while I take them around."

"Okay."

"Girls, everyone has a glass of Chardonnay. Great. Let's take a quick tour of the winery, and then we can continue your tasting on the porch." As they filed out, the redhead attempted to stay behind with Matt, but Mackenzie saw what was going on and grabbed her up and led her toward the winery.

The redhead looked back. "Matt, you're not going with us?"

"Sorry, I have to stay here."

Mackenzie gave Matt a look. "Come on, Sandy, and I won't tell your boyfriend what you just did."

The redhead again gave Matt another inappropriate look. "He doesn't have a wedding ring on, and I'm not the one getting married. Matt, we are staying at the hotel in Calistoga with the hot springs. We are in the bar every night. Why don't you stop by?"

"I'll see what I can do." All Matt could think was if he was looking for trouble, he just found it as the two girls left the tasting room with the group.

Another car pulled into the parking lot, and two middle-aged couples got out and came in the tasting room. "Hi, we don't have an appointment, but can we do a tasting?"

"Come on in. Up front warning, we have a bachelorette party on a tour, but I think they are going to finish it on the porch. You will probably want to stay in here." The group looked at each other, nodded, and sat at the bar. Matt looked around for Hank, but he apparently slipped out with the girls.

The morning was a steady stream of visitors but a nice change of pace from house deconstruction. At lunchtime, Matt slipped out to take a quick shower and returned to the tasting room. It was a busy day.

Around 1:30 P.M., May's cell rang. "Hello, how is it going? What did they say? When are they going to decide? Oh no she didn't. How's Hannah? Well, listen, we are good here so don't worry. Joseph is working the chardonnay vineyard with the crew. Alexandra is on her community service. We shined Matt up, and he is in the tasting room. We are having a weekend-type day on Monday, which is great news. Okay. Love you too."

When she hung up, Matt looked at her. "What's the scoop?"

"Catherine and the baby are both okay from what they can tell from the tests. She's staying in the hospital as they don't want her moving around. The baby is almost full term, so they're going to give them both a couple days to settle down and then most likely do a C-section."

"That's great news. What was the 'oh no'?"

May sighed, "When the doctor came in to provide the update a few minutes ago Catherine told him if it came down to her life or the baby's, he was to save the baby."

"Oh no."

"That threw Hannah over the edge, and she ran out of the room. Ben had to find her and calm her down. Ben reminded Catherine after Hannah left that what she felt about the baby was the same way her mother and him felt about her."

Matt wiped off the bar. His cell phone alarm went off. "Alexandra. Come on, Hank." The trip to Napa was much slower than this morning because of the tourist traffic. Matt learned if someone was still out driving in the valley after 3:00 P.M., they were probably DUI or on the edge of it, and he had to be careful. As he pulled in front of the station right on time, Alexandra was out front on a bench. She got up and got in the truck. As he drove away, she pulled off the hat and sunglasses.

"How was your day?" Matt was trying to make conversation.

"We are picking up garbage on Hwy 128 this week." Alexandra forced a smile.

"Okay."

"And oh, by the way you were dead on this morning with your instructions. DUI man who drives a Moped tried to pick me up."

Matt started to laugh. "You okay?"

"Yeah, the female guard caught on pretty quickly and separated him. Fourteen more days of this and counting. It was a humbling day. Any word on Catherine?"

Matt recounted the story that May provided, including what Catherine told the doctor.

"Wow, I'm sure Mom is about to lose her shit."

Matt agreed. "It sounded like that from the call."

"Daddy has always said that Catherine and I are exactly like Mom in personality, so he's always been the mediator. What Catherine told the doctor is exactly something she would have done." Alexandra looked Matt up and down. "You're clean. I don't think I have seen you clean before."

Matt laughed. "There haven't been too many occasions lately I've been clean. As I was pulling into the winery, I got a 911 text from May to come to the tasting room. It was a bachelorette party with twenty girls."

Alexandra rolled her eyes. "What time was it?"

"Ten o'clock. They must have been waiting when the gates opened."

"Oh wow. That's a huge group."

"May knew there was one coming but wasn't provided a head count, so it pretty much threw her day into a tailspin. I ran over and got cleaned up at lunch and had to come right back. No work on the house today."

"I'm sorry. Alexandra strikes again." She clapped her hands.

"I don't know what you mean."

"My life is such a mess, which is my fault, and it impacts everyone. I should've been home helping May, but I'm picking up garbage on the side of the road. You should be working on the house, but you're babysitting me because I can't drive."

Matt smiled. "I'll tell you what. When I become perfect, I will start judging you." That statement made Alexandra ponder for a while. When they pulled up to the house, Alexandra got out. "I'll meet you at that tasting room when you are ready to go." She smiled, nodded and headed up the steps.

When Alexandra walked into the tasting room, there were about eight people still there at 5:00 P.M. They made it in just before the gates closed. Matt was dutifully explaining how to join the wine club, when they would receive shipments and that Steed winery didn't distribute, so this was the only way they could get the wine other than at the tasting room. He was a pro. When he looked up and saw Alexandra, he smiled, and she returned it. She was stunning, her hair was down and done, with just the right amount of light makeup to accentuate her features. She was in tight blue jeans, a very light designer sweater that fell off one shoulder, and pink flats with a small pink purse. She nodded at Matt and he looked at May.

May smiled. "Get going. I got this."

"I need to lock Hank up in the office." Hank, the Steed Winery dog, was dead asleep in the corner. It had been a big day of frolicking with the guests.

"Go. Leave him; he's fine. I'll put him in there when I close up."

Matt walked out from behind the bar and up to Alexandra. "You look nice."

She smiled. "You're not the only one who can clean up." They small-talked their way over to the Calistoga and found the Methodist Church. Her meeting was upstairs in one of the classrooms.

Matt parked out front. "I will be in the sanctuary unless something is going on, and if not, I will be right here. See you in an hour."

"Thanks," Alexandra said as she got out and walked up to the white church. She opened the side door and went inside. Matt felt much better about this drop off. Matt killed the engine of the Sierra. Being back in Calistoga, his old stomping grounds, he decided to walk to the grocery. He bought a day-old *Wall Street Journal*—they were always a day behind for whatever reason—and then walked back to the church. When he went into the sanctuary it was dead quiet. A wood ceiling with large wood beams led to white walls and then red carpeted floors. The pews were wood as well with red padding on them that matched the color of the carpet. Matt walked up the center aisle in the silence and dropped his paper on the end of one of the pews. He continued to the alter and knelt. He took a deep breath and looked up at the massive wood cross suspended in the air above him on wires. He then dropped his head to pray.

After a few minutes, he got up and went to the aisle where he dropped the *Journal* down and sat to read. He abstained from his daily research on the market while in Nebraska, but it was time to get his head back in the game. The *Journal* was a good starting spot. He wasn't sure how long he had been there when he was startled by a woman who was standing in front of him. "Hello."

"Hi." She threw her hand out, and Matt shook it. "I don't think I recognize you. Are you new in town?" She was casually dressed and probably the same age as him, in her early thirties.

"I am actually just visiting, waiting on a friend who's in a meeting upstairs."

She smiled. "You know reading the *Wall Street Journal* in church could be construed as a sin. Greed is a sin." She sat in the pew in front of him, so they were face-to-face.

Matt started laughing and thinking about Beth. Greed was indeed a sin. "What about the bag of gold parable? Burying the master's gold in the ground and not investing it is also a sin. I think he got thrown out for being lazy."

The woman was visibly impressed. "I'm in the midst of a Christian. I'm pastor Ann. What's your name?"

"I'm Matt Thomas, very nice to meet you, Pastor. If you had come in a little earlier, you would have caught me praying."

"Very nice to meet you as well. My husband and I both pastor this church together. We would love to have you attend while you're in town." Matt attended a Methodist Church in Napa last Sunday but was open. "Thank you. I think I'll do that." About that time Alexandra came into the sanctuary and drew their attention as she walked up.

"Hi, I am Pastor Ann." She put her hand out.

Alexandra smiled and shook it. "Hello."

"Well, it's settled. I guess I'll see you two in church on Sunday. Services are at 9:00 and 11:00 A.M." Alexandra shot Matt a wide-eyed look.

Matt smiled. "I will certainly be here. Thank you, Pastor."

49

The alarm went off again at 6:30 A.M., and Hank was on top of Matt almost immediately. He had a big day yesterday and was very excited.

Matt threw on the same jeans from yesterday that were not dirty, a new T-shirt and hat. He cleaned up and made his way over to the house to pick Alexandra up. He again was motioned into the house by May. When he walked into the kitchen, Alexandra was again dressed in the same outfit as yesterday, just a clean one, with the hat Matt gave her on the table with her sunglasses inside of it. She smiled when he came in, and he returned it.

May pointed at the table, grabbing the coffeepot. "Sit and eat."

Matt did as she commanded. "What does the day look like in the tasting room?"

"It should be slower than yesterday, which is a good and bad thing. I'll do my best to handle it, and let you work on the house."

"Just let me know if you need any help. It was a nice change."

"I would say so. You were very popular in the tasting room yesterday." May smiled at Alexandra. "Matt has been in the tasting room twice and hit on twice."

Alexandra gave Matt a smile. "Really?"

"Oh yes. What did that busty red hair girl say to you?"

This piqued Alexandra's attention. This was going to be fun. "Busty red head?" she asked.

Matt flushed. "I'm not repeating that."

Now Alexandra had to know. "What did she say?" Matt just shook his head.

May couldn't stand it any longer. "Well, she wanted to shake Matt's hand, and he started to pull it back because his hands were a little dirty, and she told him she had been known to be a little dirty herself." Matt immediately looked down.

Alexandra's eyes got wide and her mouth fell open. "Oh my gosh, how forward. What did you do? Was she pretty?"

May pointed at Matt's red face. "What he's doing right now, and yes, she was very pretty. Then, she invited Matt to meet her for drinks at that hot springs hotel in Calistoga."

Alexandra sat there with a coy smile on her face. "Poor Matt had to go to church last night instead of meeting the hot redhead." And then it hit Alexandra. "Oh yeah, he also told the minister, who we met yesterday, that we would come to church on Sunday. Matt, I think five days a week in that church is going to be enough for me."

May started laughing.

"I told her I would be there. You're welcome to attend."

Alexandra got up. "Come on. Let's go."

The day went quickly. Matt worked on the house most of the morning after dropping Alexandra off at community service. He was shocked when his alarm went off at 2:00 P.M. to go pick her up. The traffic was lighter in the middle of the week, and he pulled in just as the bus was pulling up. The first person off the bus was Alexandra's would-be-suitor from yesterday. He climbed aboard his Moped, fired it up, and drove away. Alexandra was almost last off and walked over to get in the truck.

"How did it go?" Matt asked.

"Okay, pretty much the same as yesterday. Another section of Hwy 128 has been rid of the scourge of garbage. It's kind of shocking that people are such pigs." Hank nuzzled up to Alexandra's arm on the armrest, and she turned and rubbed his ears. "Hey, Hanky."

"I saw your boyfriend get off first and drive his Moped away."

"The guards have been great; they're onto him. He has to sit near one of them now, and they are in the front."

As Matt navigated out of Napa, the Sierra came to life with a phone call. Matt could see on the screen it was Joseph. Matt clicked the steering wheel and took the call. "Hey, Joseph, what's up?"

"Hi Matt, we've got a little bit of a problem." Joseph did not sound well.

Matt and Alexandra exchanged looks. "Can you be more specific?"

"I think we need your help."

Matt looked at the dash, it was 3:10 P.M. and he was only ten minutes from the Chardonnay vineyard. He turned the Sierra around and headed in that direction. As Matt pulled into the vineyard, he could see most of the team and the day workers in the field but found Joseph and two other guys near the river. As they pulled up, it was evident what the trouble was. The tractor was stuck in a low point next to the river. Occasionally in the spring, the river would flood, and now the rear tractor wheels were half-buried. There was a chain hooked to the tractor and attached to the back of Joseph's truck, which was now stuck in the mud as well in the process of trying to get the tractor out. Matt and Alexandra got out of the Sierra and surveyed the scene. "Joseph, I would say you have a problem," Matt said. Joseph covered in mud looked defeated.

Matt went into the lock box of the Sierra and pulled out his roadside emergency kit, the one his father had hammered into his head that he always needed to have and pulled out his weaved tow straps. He looked at Alexandra and gave her one of the blankets. "Why don't we find a place for you to sit while we do this. It will be safer. If something breaks, it could come back at the truck." They walked up to a spot out of harm's way and put the blanket on the ground. It was warm, so Matt took off his overshirt and dropped it on the blanket and went with just his T-shirt.

"Joseph let's get the chain unhooked from the tractor, and we will get your truck out first." Matt looked into the back of the Sierra, and there were a couple of two-by-fours in there. He took them out and handed them to the other men. "Wedge these under the back of the tractor tires while we get the truck out." The two men immediately went to work.

Alexandra sat on the hill on the blanket. The men below were trudging around in the mud, making preparations. Outside in the sun was the last place she wanted to be after being outside all day, but Matt was right. It was a mess down there. She pealed out of her sun shirt revealing a sports bra underneath and pulled off her tennis shoes, socks and dropped her loose kakis off in favor of her running shorts she had on underneath. Hank looked up and saw her sitting there. He bounded up the hill and took a spot next to her. She rubbed his head. "Good boy. You don't want to be down there either." There was a noise next to her, and it was coming from a pocket in

Matt's shirt. It was his cell. Alexandra took it out to make sure it wasn't May or her parents. Instead on the ringing screen was a beautiful woman. The ringing stopped and then restarted almost immediately. Again, the beautiful woman on the screen. When it stopped, it restarted again for the third time. Alexandra looked down at Matt. He was in his truck, and he was pulling Joseph's truck out of the mud. Whoever the woman was, she obviously needed to speak with Matt. Alexandra picked up the phone and answered it. "Hello, Matt's phone."

There was an immediate pregnant pause on the other end. "Uhhhhh, is Matt there?"

"Matt's got his hands full right now. Is this an emergency? If it is, I can get him?"

"No, have him call his sister as soon as he can." Alexandra thought: *new information; Matt's got a sister.*

"Are you sure? I can get him."

"No, that's fine. Just have him call me as soon as he can."

"Okay, I will." Alexandra hung up and looked down. Matt was unhooking the straps from Joseph's truck and was now taking them out to the tractor where the other men were trying to get the wood under the back wheels. This was going to take a while. Alexandra leaned back and put her hat over her face to shield it from the sun closing her eyes to rest.

Matt checked the straps on the tractor and then looked up at Joseph giving him the thumbs-up. That was when he heard it. It was an audible growl from the gut. It began again, and the growl escalated. Hank began barking. Matt turned and saw the much less dressed Alexandra lying on the hill in the sun with Hank next to her. Two of the day workers saw her as well and made their way down to where she was to get a better look, which sparked Hank into full defense mode. "Joseph!" Matt yelled.

As Joseph turned, Hank was now on his feet, and he had positioned himself directly between Alexandra and the men. His growl escalated into vicious barking. Hank didn't have a mean bone in his body, but he was not having any of this. Joseph was now standing on the tractor. "Hijos de puta vuelven al trabajo!" Matt had heard a lot of Spanish the past couple of weeks and was pretty sure that "motherfucker" was in that stream of obscenities. The two men scurried up the rows of vines and out of sight.

Matt looked at Alexandra. She was now up on one elbow, understanding what had just happened. She looked at him and shrugged as if to say she was sorry. She called Hank over, and he plopped down next to her but remained facing the vineyard in watch mode. She lay back and put the hat back over her face.

After a few more minutes of work, Matt got back into the Sierra and cranked it. He looked back at Joseph in the rearview. The tractor was running as well. Matt put the Sierra in 4-wheel drive and eased forward until the strap was tight. One of the other men on the team gave him a thumbs-up. Matt motioned the other two Hispanic men out of harm's way and then accelerated the engine. Matt could feel the Sierra's tires slipping in the dirt. He looked back at Joseph, who had mud flying all over him, and then the tractor broke free. They all came to a stop safely out of the mud. Matt got out and congratulated the Hispanic men and then shook Joseph's hand. He looked up on the hill, and Alexandra was applauding. He motioned her down and unhooked the strap from the Sierra. "Joseph, I will get this back from you tomorrow. We have to get cleaned up and get Alexandra to her meeting."

As they pulled away Alexandra was visibly excited. "That was awesome."

Matt, covered in mud, laughed. "Hopefully we don't have to do that again tomorrow."

Alexandra rifled through the blanket she was sitting on and handed Matt his overshirt. "Your sister wants you to call her. I wouldn't have picked up, but she called three times in a row, so I was concerned something was up. She wanted you to call her as soon as you could."

Matt was now concerned. Amber calling three times in a row was not a good thing. He clicked the steering wheel. "Call Amber."

The Sierra responded: *"Calling Amber."*

The phone rang only once when Amber picked up. "Who's the girl?"

Matt and Alexandra smiled at each other. In the background, Matt could hear an intercom say, "Code blue ICU."

"Are you at the hospital? Is everything okay?"

"You didn't answer my question."

Matt was now exasperated with her. "Amber, why are you at the hospital?"

"Can you face time? Someone wants to speak with you."

"No, I'm in the truck driving."

"Okay, I'm putting you on speaker"

Dawn's sad little voice came through the truck. "Uncle Matty." Alexandra looked at Matt and made a sad face.

"What's wrong Dawn? Are you okay?"

"I broked'd my arm."

"Dawn, how did you broked'd your arm?"

"I fell off my bunk bed when I was playing with a friend."

Matt looked at Alexandra and mouthed, "Shit." He felt awful. "Oh baby, I am so sorry. Uncle Matty will buy you another bed when I see you again."

"NOOOOOOOO! I love my new bed."

Amber was now back. "Matty, I blame you for this." She was being sarcastic. "So does Steven."

Matt could hear Steven in the background say, "No I don't."

"We just wanted to call and let you know what a mess you made."

Dawn was now back scolding her mother. "Stop it, Mommy. I love you, Uncle Matty."

"I love you too, Dawn. Please be careful. I don't want to get any more calls like this.

"I will. I promise."

Alexandra gave Matt a sad face when he hung up. "I just bought her that damn bed."

Alexandra smiled. "That was an incredibly sweet call, Uncle Matty."

"Amber is my sister. She has always called me Matty, so Dawn does to. Her and Steven, my brother-in-law, live on our family ranch in Nebraska and raise cattle. They have a terrible two-year-old boy named Lucas and another baby on the way."

"They sound very sweet."

Matt agreed. "They are."

Alexandra got quiet. "You didn't tell your sister that you were chauffeuring a drug addict around the valley when she asked about me."

Matt gave Alexandra a pained look. "I think that's incredibly harsh, Alexandra. You need to know that I don't think that way about this at all. I am just helping some friends out." Alexandra didn't say anything else and just looked out the window.

50

With all the excitement of the day, the turnaround at the house was very quick. When Matt pulled up out front, Alexandra came bounding out of the house. Her hair was wet in a ponytail with a white sleeveless top and a pink just above the knee skirt on. Matt wore blue shorts with skiffs and a designer white T-shirt. He was tired of being warm today, and it looked like she was as well. Alexandra also had a black portfolio folder with her, and she put it in the back seat. "I hope you don't mind. I have a quick errand to take care of after the meeting. It won't take but a couple of minutes."

"No problem."

They followed the same pattern as yesterday, and Matt was in the sanctuary when Alexandra finished the meeting. "No Pastor Ann today? You haven't committed us to Sunday school, have you?" Matt smiled and shook his head no. "Okay, give me fifteen to twenty minutes, and I will meet you at the truck."

"Sounds good," Matt replied.

Alexandra headed out of the church, relieved Matt did not ask to go with her. She was very anxious about this visit, but it was one that she needed to make. She needed to see an old friend and needed to do it alone. She walked a block to the main street of Calistoga and turned right. It was 6:45 P.M., and she was hurrying. Pretty much everything in Calistoga other than the restaurants closed at 7:00 P.M. She walked through the sea of tourists and found the shop she was looking for. It was a gallery that represented artists of the area.

As she pulled open the door, a bell rang, and she found the person she came to see. There in the sea of paintings was a very distinguished older man.

He smiled and got up slowly. "Alexandra, come see me. What a wonderful surprise."

Alexandra walked up and hugged him. "Mr. Stone, it's been so long." Harrison Stone had been Alexandra's high school art teacher who had encouraged her to follow her passion of art in college. When he retired, he followed his own dream, opening his gallery in Calistoga and painting.

"So, what brings you in? Have you been well?"

"Well… sort off." She didn't know where to start.

He stopped her. "I know all about it. What I meant to ask is, how are you today?"

"I'm okay." Alexandra sat down and patted her portfolio. "Can I show you some things to get your thoughts? And before you say yes, they are disturbing."

"You have me intrigued, Alexandra. I definitely want to see them now."

Alexandra opened the portfolio and took out her sketchbooks she had been working on. "I'm very nervous to show you these. No one has seen them."

Mr. Stone took the books and flipped through the sketches one by one observing them. When he got to the last one, he left it open and put it down. "You are correct. These are both disturbing an intriguing. The imagery is upsetting. How do you see them?"

Alexandra's hands were now between her knees rocking a little. "The colors are bright and vivid."

"Have you moved any of them to canvas?"

Her answer came out in a whisper. "No."

"And why not?"

"They scare me. They come from a place of so much pain."

"I can feel that in them, but art is supposed to invoke emotion, Alexandra, and this certainly does. Think of Edward Munch's, *The Scream*. A fabulously famous painting that is also disturbing."

"I don't know if I can put it on canvas."

Mr. Stone pondered the last picture in silence. "Here is what intrigues me. If I had seen this in a gallery, I would absolutely have stopped and taken it in. What I wouldn't have known is that it was yours. This is not a style I have seen from you before. How long have you been doing work like this?

"I haven't been practicing since the failed exhibit. I never went back after that. I told myself I was taking time off, but soon my life was taken over by Style's life."

"So, you haven't picked up a pencil or brush since then?" Mr. Stone had been there the night of the opening. Alexandra shook her head no. "Alexandra, regardless of what happened then, you should continue your work. This style is inspiring. If not this type of work, then something else, but I believe you have had a breakthrough here."

"What if this is all I am? What if this is all that I have to give?" She put her hand on the terrifying picture her eyes welling up in tears.

"Alexandra, we are all many pieces of a puzzle."

Matt moved out of the sanctuary to the truck, and it was running. Alexandra's fifteen to twenty minutes had turned into thirty. He decided to wait outside. He was worried. Should he have let her go alone? His job was to drive her, not to babysit her. He was pondering putting it into drive and start looking when his phone rang. Matt looked at the dash, and it was King George.

"George, it's awfully late to be calling from New York. What's up?"

"I've got good news and bad news, Matt."

"What is up, George?"

"We got word today from the FTC. I was waiting on the official letter to send to you before calling, but I think now is a good time. They found absolutely no wrongdoing in your venture capital and investing practices. They were able to follow the dots on how you drew your conclusions. You're free to come back anytime." Matt was relieved his career was intact.

"What about Henderson's investigation?" Matt remembered his thin file in front of HJ.

"He's fucked. They are banning him for five years. We fired him today. Matt, the cloud over you about this is gone."

Matt was now bracing. "Please tell me that's the bad news."

"I am afraid unfortunately no. Matt...." George trailed off, trying to spit it out.

"For God sakes, George please tell me."

"Matt, Helen and I are at the Gala with Albert Dean and Mark Cross." Matt thought *Okay, you are hobnobbing with the partners*. "Matt, Waverman is here with Beth. They just got back from a month on a yacht in the Mediterranean. Beth is sporting at least a 10-carat engagement ring. Waverman is introducing her as his fiancée."

"Well, that's just fantastic. I've got to go."

"Matt, just know that partners are incensed about this lack of decorum."

"Imagine how I feel, George." Matt hung up, and he felt a hole in his chest. Any thoughts he had in the back of his mind that she might come to her senses were gone. She was lost for good.

There was still no sign of Alexandra. She had been gone for forty minutes. He tried her cell, and she did not answer. He slammed the truck into reverse, backed up, then threw it into drive and headed up the block toward town. When he got to the corner to turn onto main street, she rounded it and saw him and the look on his face.

She opened the back door and put her portfolio in. "Is there something wrong?"

He pointed toward the clock. "Forty minutes Alexandra. I was worried. Then you didn't answer your phone."

She nodded. "I'm sorry." Alexandra got into the truck visibly upset and pulled the door shut. Matt quickly pulled out onto main street and accelerated toward Silverado Trail. Alexandra was very quiet and sat clenching her fists over and over again.

51

The ride back was quiet. Matt pulled up, Alexandra got out and went in the house with her portfolio. Matt went to the winery and got Hank to take him on a long walk around the vineyard to think. When he got back to the winery office, he sat down and poured out his emotions on five pieces of paper. He thought about calling Amber, but she had her hands full with Dawn's broken arm.

When his pain and fury with Beth was all on paper, he walked up to the tasting room, which was very quiet in the evening, with a bottle of wine and a glass. He cranked up the gas firepit. The sun had just set, and the air immediately become cool. The light of the fire felt good on his face. Matt was rubbing Hank's ears when his head popped up, and he ran up to Alexandra and crashed against her for some love.

She started, "I hope I am not disturbing you. I can leave if you need to be alone."

Matt, uncomfortable drinking in front of her, moved the wine bottle and glass out of direct site. "Please sit, Alexandra. This is your home."

She saw what he was doing. "Matt, please." She pointed. "We are at a winery. I honestly would be shocked if you weren't drinking a glass in front of the fire on a beautiful evening. Wine is not my problem." She walked over and took the seat next to him on the bench. "I need to talk to you if that's okay. I need to apologize for today."

Matt frowned. "Alexandra, you're going through so much. You don't need—"

"It is not an excuse," she cut him off. "It's not okay, Matt. I'm sorry for being late and what I said in the car today...."

"I just don't see you that way at all."

"I know. The truth is I'm embarrassed right now, and I am so angry with myself for how I got here. I'm struggling with it." Matt stopped talking; she needed to get this out. She teared up a little, and he could see it in her eyes as the light of the fire danced across her face. "I can assure you I just went to see a friend today and nothing else. I am drug tested every Thursday, and if I slip up, I go to jail. Matt, I'm not going to jail. You have been incredibly kind to me, and for that I'm so thankful."

Matt reached down, picked up his wine glass and took a sip. They sat in silence for a while watching the fire. Matt took a deep breath. "I'm sorry I was short with you today when I picked you up. I was very worried but some of that emotion had nothing to do with you. You deserve to know that. I had just received a phone call from New York. My wife left me six weeks ago for another man, a much older man than me."

Alexandra's mouth opened in shock. They all noticed that he didn't have a wedding ring and talked about it, but there are many reasons for that. "You're kidding? You seem so kind. We can't leave you alone in the tasting room without a chaperone. I don't understand."

Matt rubbed his fingers together showing the sign of money. "She needed more than I could provide."

Alexandra was appalled. "You work on Wall Street. How much more did she need?"

"The man that she left me for is the Founder, President, and CEO of the company I work for. My leave from the company was just a trumped-up way to get me out of the way for a few months. The two of them showed up back in New York today with an engagement ring on her finger."

"I'm so sorry. That is horrible. Do you have kids?"

"No, it never happened. I guess now I know why. Alexandra, please don't take my troubles on. This isn't your problem. It's mine. I'm only telling you so that you understand that a lot of today, my reaction, is not on you; it's on me. I got the call a few minutes before I picked you up."

Again, they sat in silence. Alexandra pointed to the papers. "What are you writing?"

Matt smiled. "This is my personal therapy." He picked the five pages up. Amber, my sister, actually Dr. Amber Heard, a psychiatrist."

Alexandra recoiled. "No, not a psychiatrist. The next time I see another psychiatrist will be too soon." They both laughed, easing the tension in the air dramatically.

"Amber thinks I should be seeing a psychiatrist to deal with my emotions."

Alexandra nodded. "Of course, she does, and she's probably right."

"If I won't go to a therapist, which is where I am right now, according to her, I am to write out my feelings on paper to get them out of me. Then, I burn them. I am in essence giving them over to God to let him handle it. These pages are my feelings about today." Alexandra watched as Matt let the papers slip from his hand and fall into the firepit.

Alexandra smiled. "Does it work?"

Matt nodded. "For me, shockingly it does. It seems to help."

When the papers were thoroughly consumed in flames, Alexandra cleared her throat. "If my father was here, he would wax some philosophical platitude like, *everything happens for a reason*."

Matt forced a smile. "That sounds very much like my father. The last time I can remember being this down, I blew my knee out in college." Matt put his right knee out. There was an eight-inch scar right down the middle. Alexandra put her right knee out, and there were four puncture scars on each side of hers. Their eyes met and they smiled. "I was laying in the hospital bed with my parents there," Matt continued. "The doctor had just left the room after saying my football career was probably over. Any chance of the NFL was gone. I was devastated."

"What did your father say?"

"He stood up and took my hand. He said, *Matt, life is chicken shit or chicken salad. The choice is yours*. And he was right. I picked myself up, finished my degree, and made it on Wall Street. And I am going to pick myself up again."

They were both silent for a moment. Then Alexandra asked, "Are your parents still around?"

"No, unfortunately not. They died about five years after that. Their truck flipped in icy weather, and they both died instantly."

"I'm sorry."

"Don't be. We are very comforted to know they died together. They were so much in love to the very end." Matt got a little choked up and took another sip of wine.

Alexandra sensed he was desperate to change the subject, so she said, "Well, Uncle Matty, you have the Heard family in your life."

"Yes, I do," Matt laughed, and the mood immediately changed. He pulled out his phone and flipped through for a picture he took of them a few weeks ago in Dawn's Meadow, and he handed the phone to Alexandra.

"They're such a beautiful family. This looks like something you would see when you buy picture frames. Dawn is as cute as she sounds and look at the little boy."

Matt shook his head. "Dawn is exactly like Amber, and it's terrifying. They both can see right through you. There are no secrets you can keep around either of them."

"Did you talk to them tonight? How is Dawn's arm."

"I knew they would be busy, so I texted. She is fine, but my sister finished the text with *I blame you*." They both laughed. "Speaking of sisters, what's the latest on Catherine and the baby?"

"I talked to her tonight. She is nervous and excited. They're both doing well, and they decided they are going to do a C-section sometime tomorrow. They think that will put much less strain on Catherine and the baby to do it this way."

"That's exciting. Prayers tonight for them."

Alexandra got up and stood next to the fire. It was getting colder. "Matt, I hate to ask you this, but I need more of your time." Matt looked at her. "I have had some anxiety issues since the accident. I was really struggling today when I got back into your truck in Calistoga." If Matt didn't feel like a total shit already, he now did. "My therapist Dr. Moranne thinks that my fear comes from a place of thinking I'm not going to be able to stay clean. It comes on from time to time, and I have been managing it through exercise. I thought my new career as a garbage collector would be enough exercise, but it's not. I need to swim. I was on the swim team in high school." Matt nodded, listening. "There's a community center in Napa where we are members, and I can swim there. If we can go right after you pick me up, then I can get showered there, and we can go directly from there to my meeting."

"Absolutely, whatever you need."

"I feel like I'm taking over your life."

"Alexandra, I'm so glad you told me."

"Okay, I'll go and get a travel bag ready for tomorrow. Thank you, Matt. Good night."

"Good night, Alexandra."

52

Matt didn't wait to be invited up to the porch. He climbed the stairs and rapped three times on the door. May waved him in, and he entered. Alexandra had draped her clothes on hangers over the chair at the end of the table and then there was a small travel bag there as well.

"Good morning, Matty." Alexandra smiled, jokingly.

May's head perked up when she was pouring him some coffee. "Matty?"

"That is what Matt's sister and her daughter call him."

May looked at Matt. "That sounds sweet."

"They are darling. Matty, show her the picture."

Matt pulled out his phone and again pulled up the one from Dawn's Meadow, handing it to May. "Oh my, it is like a postcard," May said.

"I know. They're perfect, and there's another baby on the way."

"Oh, what a blessing."

Matt smiled. "You should have your blessing today as well."

May and Alexandra looked at each other and smiled. Alexandra crossed her fingers. "What if it's a boy, May?"

May shook her head. "Don't speak of it."

"Were they hoping for a boy?" Matt inquired.

May topped Matt's coffee cup off. "I don't think they care, and we shouldn't either but there hasn't been a boy born in the Steed family in many generations. The last was my great grandfather. He was a Congressional Medal of Honor winner in World War II. Each generation since then has had two daughters who survived, and at least one of the daughters has carried on the Steed name to keep it alive and to honor him. He was the one who bought the property we live on and farmed it after the war. The whole name thing is no big deal today, but it was very sordid back several generations. There were a few marriages that didn't happen due to it, which is sad. It would be nice to have a boy to pick it up."

"That's very interesting. Jack's cool with it?" Matt asked.

"Jack is the baby of the family, and he has three other brothers. His parents already have six grandchildren, three of which are boys."

"Come on, Matty. We have to go." Matt got up and instinctively picked up her bag and clothes, and they walked out the door.

May smiled as they exited.

Matt spent the morning helping May restock the tasting room to prepare for the long weekenders. Thursday to Monday tended to be very busy this time of year, which left Tuesday and Wednesday to prepare. May did all that she could on Tuesday and needed Matt today. Hank wasn't disappointed as he greeted all the visitors at the doors receiving *ohhs* and *ahhs* in the morning. After grabbing a quick bite, Matt went to the house and was able to finish another room, stripping out the drywall and insulation. The house was coming along, but it was a slow progression now. What was important was that it was dry.

When the bus pulled up, Alexandra exited and headed to Matt's truck and opened the door. "Any news?"

Matt shook his head. "Not yet. May talked to your mom, and they were waiting on a specialist that worked at another hospital who was going to come over after his rotation, so it was expected to be later in the day. How was your day?"

"Twelve more days. It's 3:00 P.M.; how much later in the day is that?"

"Come on. Let's get you in a pool." Matt Googled the rec center last night after he talked to Alexandra. It had an indoor Olympic swimming pool and a full workout area with weights. He hadn't seen the inside of a gym in six weeks. He was going to be there anyway, so Matt changed into his workout gear and planned to hit the weights while she was swimming.

They divided at the check-in desk and planned on meeting up in the lobby at 4:45 P.M. to head to Calistoga. As Matt entered the workout area, there were a few older, retired gentlemen there, but it was largely empty. Most would use the facilities in the early morning and late afternoon. They would be walking out as the second wave of the day was arriving. There was a wall of glass that separated his area from the pool, which was smart. The best way to make sure nobody drowned or nothing bad was going on in a pool area was to make it in full view of the entire gym.

Matt was doing pullups when Alexandra came out of the locker room in her blue one-piece suit that was made for swimming laps. The suit began at the top of beautiful legs, exposing her womanly shape. She had a swimmer's cap on with goggles strapped on top her head. She saw Matt doing pullups and made muscle arms at him before jumping in the pool. Matt found it comforting that he could watch her, keep an eye on her. She glided across the pool doing a freestyle stroke. She then flipped at the end changing into the breaststroke, then into the butterfly, and finally a slow backstroke. She repeated this stroke rhythm, gliding through the water with ease. Matt was impressed at how well she could swim.

A few minutes after 4:00 P.M., Matt's phone dinged with a text message. He smiled and headed down to the men's locker room, walking straight through following the smell of chlorine to the other side that opened into the pool area. Alexandra had just flipped into the breaststroke and was coming back down the lane toward him standing at the end of her lane. When she got close, she stopped and looked up inquisitively. Matt held up a picture of a naked, new baby boy. Alexandra squealed drawing a lot of attention as it echoed across the pool. She threw her hands in the air.

"Get me out," she commanded. Matt took both of her wrists and easily hoisted her into the air onto the deck. She took his phone and sat on the starting blocks, looking at the pictures and reading the text for herself out loud. "Mother and baby are both doing well. Eight pounds, three ounces," she said, looking at the message. "Oh my God, he is so beautiful." Finally, at the end of the text stream was a picture of the baby on Catherine's chest, and she read his name, "Jackson Garrett Steed." Alexandra smiled at Matt and then hugged him getting them both wet. "Jack's last name is Garrett, so they used it as his middle name," Alexandra explained.

Matt laughed. "I like it. It's a very strong name."

Alexandra called May for the details and then ran into the locker room to clean up and call Catherine.

May decided the tasting room was ready for tomorrow and cooking was out tonight. They were celebrating. She made reservations for Romero's, the Italian bistro, at 6:45 P.M. to meet them in Calistoga. At dinner Matt's, phone dinged again. He looked and saw it was George. He'd called several times today, but Matt ignored them. There was no way George's call was good news, and he was avoiding it.

The three of them finished the evening at the firepit with May and Matt sharing a bottle of wine in front of the fire laughing, and the evening ending with Alexandra having to help a hammered May to bed.

53

The morning was rough so far. Matt woke up to a well-deserved headache from the wine. When he got to the house, there was no May and, thus, no breakfast. It was still very early. Alexandra had to meet with her parole officer this morning before community service.

Alexandra threw a protein bar at him when he walked into the kitchen and had two to-go cups of coffee waiting. Alexandra smiled at Matt. "You look like shit," she teased. "This sobriety thing sucks most of the time, but you get a great night of sleep, and you wake up without headaches or in a hospital. Come on."

Matt laughed, picked up her bag, and they headed out to the truck. When they pulled to the end of the driveway, they could see workers going into the fields of Jerkasky Vineyard to begin their work. Alexandra pointed to the fields and said, "Only twenty-two more years, and it's ours again."

"I don't understand," Matt said.

"My grandfather was not a good guy. He died before we were born and left my Grandmother Evelyn, my mother, and May in terrible financial shape. If it hadn't been for my father, they would have lost everything. My grandfather was a gambling alcoholic, which is a terrible combination. Those twenty acres out there on the valley floor are my family's. He gambled away a lease for the land in a poker game to Sam Jerkasky. What's worse, he did it tax free. It's our land, but Peter, Sam's son, holds the lease to some of the best vineyard acreage in the valley for a dollar a year."

"This is how I have been drinking Jerkasky Cabernet at Steed Vineyard," Matt said as he pieced it together. "How long was the lease?"

"Fifty years"

"Holy shit." Matt was appalled.

"Yep. Back then, it definitely hurt paying those taxes, but when the valley took off and the property values skyrocketed, my family was screwed. You are looking at 5 to 6 million dollars in property today that costs us $100,000 in taxes annually."

"Oh no," was all Matt could say. "How did your father save the family?"

"It's a crazy story. When my grandfather, who was the winemaker, finally died, my grandmother was in poor health, so my mother being the eldest took over. She found this young brash winemaker who recently graduated from UC Davis and hired him. We couldn't afford an established wine maker."

Matt smiled. "Your father?"

"Yes, my mother said he was a talented asshole, and it wasn't long before he brought his best friend on who ran the vineyard."

Matt guessed, "Richard, May's husband?"

"Yep. These two young arrogant bucks toiled away with their passion for making wine and courting the Steed sisters, but still couldn't make enough wine on the property we had left to make a profit. Each year, we fell further into debt. My father is a great winemaker, so in a last-ditch effort, he and Richard leveraged all they had and built the winery and tasting room you see here today. The idea was for my father and Richard to help those who couldn't afford modern winemaking equipment to make their wine here under my father's guidance. They would then store their wine in our caves, which were oversized for the property we had left. In exchange, we got a percentage of their sales every year. It was a win-win for everybody involved. My father also met with Peter Jerkasky and renegotiated the lease."

"How do you renegotiate a one-dollar lease?"

"Peter agreed to pay the annual taxes every year in exchange for us adding five more years on to the end of the lease. Steed Vineyard is now out of debt and has made a profit every year since except for 2011 vintage, which was a horrible weather year. Dad and Mom eventually added their home to the other side of the winery. It was the easiest thing to do, and it didn't take up any more of the winemaking property. May and Richard took over the original house and the rest is history. Then along came me and Catherine."

"May wasn't able to have kids?"

"No, I'm not sure why. I know they tried. It was a sore subject for a while, but her and Richard were in love, and they had us. May and Richard were our second parents, and May says they were blessed for that. It was devastating eighteen months ago when we lost Richard. May moved into the house with Mom and Dad."

Matt pulled up in front of the law enforcement complex and Alexandra got out. "Time for some more humiliation. My female parole officer stands outside my stall while I pee into a cup... then I get to go pick up garbage for the rest of the day," Alexandra joked with heavy sarcasm. "I'll see you at three."

Matt laughed. "Be careful." Alexandra waved him off and headed into the building.

Matt spent the morning in the tasting room with May and was restocking during a lull when May's cell rang. "Hannah, how are they doing?" Matt searched May's face for an answer. When a glowing smile appeared, he exhaled and thanked God. "Hold on, Hannah." May put her phone on mute. "Matt, I know you need to get back. How long are you planning to stay? They are begrudgingly getting ready to come home."

"May, there's no need for that. There's time. Just tell them to come back sometime early next week. We can handle it until then." Matt thought ten days to get home was plenty of time. At that thought, he couldn't help but ask himself: Then what are you going to do? He didn't have an answer.

"Hannah, listen to me. Matt is right here. Just come home early next week. We are all doing well here." May listened to the other end. "She has her ups and downs as to be expected, but you would be shocked. She is doing remarkably well. Matt is doing a great job helping her and me. Please stay with Catherine. We've got this." When May hung up, she was smiling. "Thank you, Matt." He nodded.

After lunch, Matt finished the room he was working on and then picked up Alexandra.

"How did it go?

"Eleven more days to go, and I successfully peed in the cup. Extra cup of coffee this morning did the trick." Alexandra retrieved her cell phone and began looking through her messages. There were more pictures from Catherine of her and Jackson. "I can't wait to hold him," she said, scrolling through the images

They arrived at the community center where Alexandra swam, and Matt worked out. Then, they cleaned up and drove to Calistoga Methodist for her meeting. Matt met her in the sanctuary again, and they got in the truck to head home. As Matt pulled up to Main Street in Calistoga to take a left toward the Silverado trail, Alexandra reached out and touched Matt's arm. "Can you turn right? I need to see my old friend for a few minutes. You can sit outside if that's okay? I promise, this time it won't be long."

Matt nodded. "Sure, as much time as you need."

The visitors to Calistoga were mulling up and down the sidewalks, going in and out of the tasting rooms, eateries and stores. As Matt slowly drove down the street, a car backed out, and Matt slid into the parking spot. "As much time as you need."

Alexandra got out and walked past a few stores then into the gallery. About twenty minutes later, she emerged visibly shaken and got into the truck. Matt was concerned and asked, "Are you okay?"

She nodded yes, but she was clearly lying. The drive was again another quiet trip home to the vineyard. When they pulled up to the house, Alexandra got out of the truck and asked, "Matt, can you meet me at the firepit in an hour?"

"Sure, I'll be happy to." Matt fed Hank for nugget time and then warmed up his leftovers from last night. After eating, he made his way to the firepit with a glass of wine and Hank in tow. He kept mulling over the day, how it all went well until she went into that store. What could have happened in there that set her off? As he arrived, Alexandra was already there with the firepit going wrapped in a blanket with her feet up on the bench. She looked up and smiled at Matt. She was so beautiful. Hank upon seeing her there jumped onto the bench and loved all over her as if he hadn't seen her today. "Hanky," Alexandra said, petting him. Hank plopped down in front of her, so she could rub his ears.

"You okay?" Matt asked.

Alexandra shook her head no. "Thinking about a friend who passed away."

Matt looked at her and nodded, understanding. "I so sorry about that, Alexandra. I haven't brought it up deliberately because I saw how traumatized you were when you arrived home that day from rehab. I figured that when or if you wanted to talk about it, you would."

Alexandra cleared her throat. Matt could see her eyes welling up in the firelight. "Her name was Aggy, and she was this sweet, young girl who had this amazing life in front of her, but she was trapped in her addiction. She couldn't break free from her past." Alexandra reached down and picked up her portfolio. Matt did not see it leaning against the bench. She reached inside and pulled out her sketch book. "These represent the last year of my life. My addiction, my pain, my personal failure. They are terrifying pictures; they scare me." She laid them on the edge of the firepit.

Matt could feel her anxiety in the intensity of the conversation. "What happened in the store today, Alexandra?"

A tear streamed down her face. Matt wanted to hold her. She had her arms wrapped up around her legs that she pulled against her body. Her head was resting on her knees, and she was rocking. "The gallery owner… he was my high school art teacher."

"What did he say?"

She shook her head, the tears now coming more freely. "Nothing really. He's the only person who has seen these. He asked me to move a few of these to canvas, so he could display them in the gallery."

"So… this upsets you?"

"If I do this, then the past year of my life, my pain, will be out there. Even if it sells and I never see it again, I will know it's out here, and knowing that will take me back to where I was again. It could lock me in that place." She pointed to the sketch book. "This is who I was, my past. This isn't who I am or who I want to be. I don't want to go back and relive those emotions, that pain, again. I can't."

"Then don't do it."

Alexandra picked up the sketch book her hand shaking; Matt could see what she intended to do.

"Are you sure?"

"Yes," she whispered, and with that, she threw the sketchbook into the fire. It immediately ignited, and the fire raged in the pit. Relieved, she started to cry. She reached out for Matt, and he moved closer to her. She unfurled her legs across his, and he took her into his arms as she sobbed.

From the porch, May watched the two of them intertwined, their silhouettes outlined by the light of the fire.

54

Alexandra got out of the truck, and Matt yelled, “Go save Napa from those damn litterers!” Alexandra turned and stuck her tongue out at him. She then headed over to the bus, checked in and boarded. She’d been in an exceptionally good mood this morning. The weight that was lifted from her last night was visible. They worked with May on a schedule for the weekend, and it was going to be busy. There would be no work on the house for the next three days. Matt went back to the winery to clean up and went to the tasting room for the day. He and Alexandra were going to work there all day on Saturday to give May the day off, and then May and Alexandra were going to work on Sunday to give Matt a day off.

The Sierra came alive ringing, and Matt could see on the dash it was Alice. “Hey, Alice, what’s up.”

“You’re closing! That’s what’s up! When are you coming in?” Matt just looked at the dash. “Where are you and Hank staying? Have you found a place in New York yet where the Yang’s can ship your belongings?”

“Alice, I am lost. Let’s start over.”

“You’re closing. I texted you about it two weeks ago. It’s a week from today.”

Matt panicked. “I don’t have a text.”

“Yes, you do.”

Matt fumbled with his phone and sure enough, buried in five consecutive texts in a row with the last message asking about Hank was a text with the date for the closing. Matt began to run off the road looking at his phone and the Sierra autocorrected itself. “Alice, I don’t think I can get there by next Friday. I totally missed this text.” He wasn’t going to leave Alexandra and the Steeds in a lurch. “I wasn’t supposed to be back for two weeks. Can we move it?”

“If you read the other texts, I sent you, you would see that’s not possible. The Yang’s are selling their place in Chicago to afford yours and moving that week.”

“Well, that’s fantastic. I am going to have to make some calls and get back to you.” Matt hung up before she could respond. Why was he so upset? Going back was inevitable, wasn’t it? Matt hit the steering wheel. “Call King George.” The Sierra replied, *“Calling King George.”*

The heavy British accent picked up, “Matt, are you back? When are coming in?”

“George, I am not supposed to be back for two weeks.”

“It was an estimate on how long the investigation would take. We need you back. You’ve been cleared. The paperwork just came through!”

“George.” Matt’s voice was stern. “Two weeks, and it may take a little longer.”

Matt could hear the disappointment in George’s voice. “Okay well, I’ve moved, so your office is ready. I even had them paint it and put new furniture in there.”

“I appreciate that, but I need help now.”

“Sure, what’s up?”

“I’m selling the house in Connecticut, and I guess I’m moving back to the city. I’m going to need those three hours of my life back to take care of Hank.”

“You plan to shack up with your ninety pound Lab in the city. What’s that going to look like?”

“I haven’t figured that out yet. I don’t even know where I am going to live because my house is closing next Friday.”

“Congratulations and don’t worry about it. I will talk to the partners, and we will put you up in one of the corporate apartments until you can get settled. That’s easy. Let’s have dinner next Friday to celebrate.

“Here’s the problem. Although I have the separation agreement where Beth is turning the assets over to me, it doesn’t mean anything until the divorce is final. Beth is going to have to provide me her power of attorney to sign for her or show up and sign at closing for me to sell the house.”

"Wow, you do have a problem. Let me make a few calls."

About twenty minutes later as Matt was pulling into the vineyard, his phone again rang, and it was King George. "George, what's the word?"

"It took a little doing, but I got it figured out. Waverman's personal assistant says she will not provide her power of attorney but will sign except it has to be here. She's not doing it in Connecticut. We can set it up in one of our conference rooms. Waverman is willing to cover any additional expenses."

Matt was furious. He was having to go through Waverman's personal assistant to deal with Beth. "You have got to be fucking kidding me. The gall of her."

"Calm, calm." George was now whispering, and Matt could hear him scampering to a location to not be heard. "Listen, I know this is fucked up, but revenge is easy. This building is full of twentysomethings looking for somebody just like you. You're their fucking dream. Come back and start shagging the whole building for all I care. It will drive her crazy, and she will be spending her time with dusty balls Waverman. Hell, most of us can't stand to be in the same room with him anymore."

"George, I'm not doing it in Waverman offices. Call Allen and see if he will host the closing in his law offices and tell him to charge the hell out of Waverman for the time. Then check with Waverman's personal assistant and find out if my ex-wife is willing to put her ass in the private elevator and ride down to the 11th floor. Just text me, and I will try and set this shitshow up!" Matt hung up. Probably not a great way to talk to your boss, but they were friends first, and Matt knew just how bad King George needed him. He would find time later face-to-face to apologize.

Matt was in the tasting room when his phone dinged. It was George, and it was all set up. Matt called Alice and gave her the scoop. The closing had to be in New York or Beth wasn't going to sign, but extra expenses for this would be billable to Waverman. About an hour later in the tasting room, his phone dinged again. It was Alice confirming that the Yang's and the closing attorney agreed to conduct the closing in Allen's office. Matt exhaled loudly and texted George.

May came over and put her hand on his back. "Are you okay?"

"Yeah. Just work."

"Matt, listen I made a phone call after you guys left this morning. I have a friend coming over to help me cover on Sunday. Alexandra needs a day off as well. I think you committed her to church already." May smiled. Matt started laughing. "Why don't the two of you do something after church. I am sure both of you need a break. You have been talking about taking Hank over to Hwy 1. Let Hank swim in the ocean. Take a picnic. She needs a break and so do you, I think."

"Let me think about it."

"Okay." May turned away and smiled. She walked out of the tasting room and sat outside on the steps. Who could she call to help her? It took three calls, but she was able to solve that problem.

55

Matt and Alexandra strolled down the streets of Calistoga. They only had thirty minutes before the shops closed, and Matt was looking for a present for the Heard family from the valley. As they walked from shop to shop looking at the beautiful artistry of the valley, Matt was coming up with nothing, and Alexandra was teasing him relentlessly. "You don't understand. Amber analyzes everything that you give her. She can be quite annoying."

"I see." Alexandra picked up a hot pink wine opener that had Napa Valley on the handle. "What do you think? You were bitching about her wine opener."

"Very funny."

A woman heard them talking and came from the back. "Good evening. Please let me know if I can help you."

Alexandra smiled at her. "Thank you."

The women gazed upon the two of them. "Aren't the two of you a beautiful couple."

Matt froze. He didn't know what to say, and he wasn't making eye contact with Alexandra. Before he knew it, she responded. "Thank you. That's very kind." He wondered what she meant by that.

As they walked back to the church where the truck was parked, Alexandra reached out and said, "Give me your cell phone." Matt did as he was told. She opened the picture app and started flipping through his pictures. "You do love that dog. You have a thousand pictures of him."

"Don't mess with my dog."

"I love Hanky. You know that." When she found what she was looking for she clicked on several pictures and texted it to herself.

"What did you do?"

"I texted some pictures of them to me. I am just trying to get a feel for them and what they would like. You know, they have some nice stuff on Overstock.com."

"Very funny." As they rounded the corner, the mountains that surrounded Calistoga were ablaze with purple as the sun was setting and the wispy clouds were flowing past the top of them. "It's so beautiful here," Matt said as he stopped to take it in.

"Stand over there and let me get a picture of you with the mountains in the background." Matt stood back, and Alexandra took the picture.

Another couple approached, and they looked very affluent. The woman reached out. "Do you want me to get a picture of the both of you?"

Alexandra smiled and handed the phone over. She walked up to Matt and put her arm around him, clutching his side. Matt draped his arm around her, resting his hand on her bare shoulder. He immediately felt tingles down his spine. The woman took the picture and then looked at it. "Here you go. It's beautiful."

Alexandra squeezed Matt's side and then released him to get the phone. "Thank you." Alexandra showed the picture to Matt. They looked beautiful together. "Wow, it is great," Matt said, looking at the picture. "Thank you so much." They walked back to the truck in silence. Matt opened the passenger door, and she got in.

The quiet of the ride back to the vineyard was interrupted by his phone ringing on the dash. It was Amber.

Alexandra smiled at Matt, knowing he didn't want to take the call.

Matt clicked the steering wheel. "Hi, Amber."

"You are avoiding me, Matty." Alexandra rolled her eyes at Matt.

"Amber, avoiding is a strong word. Let's call it dodging."

"I don't give crap what you call it. It's happening. Tell me about the girl."

"Don't you have a husband and children you should be spending the evening with?"

"The kids are down, and my husband is asleep in his chair with his mouth wide open. Don't change the subject. Tell me about the girl. Is she pretty?"

Alexandra smiled a huge smile, loving he was put on the spot and waiting to see what his response was going to be.

Matt exhaled now squirming, his face flushed. "Amber, she is very pretty, and she is sitting next to me right now listening to this conversation."

"Oh, well… hello." Amber's entire voice and demeanor changed.

"Hi, Amber. It's very nice to meet you." Alexandra picked up Matt's phone and started clicking away. "I'm texting you a picture we just took."

A few seconds later, they could hear the ding on Amber's phone. "Oh, you are beautiful."

"Thank you. That's very sweet. You have such a beautiful family. Matt has shown me a few pictures."

"Thank you. Are you—"

Matt sensing this conversation was heading somewhere he didn't want it to go butted in and said, "Amber, we got to go. I will call you tomorrow. Love you." Before she could answer, he hung up.

As they pulled into the vineyard gate and up to the house, they noticed May's car was gone. Matt walked with Alexandrea into the house, and there was a note on the table that Alexandra picked up and read. "May has gone to Healdsburg to spend the night with her friend. She will be back tomorrow with her friend, and they are working at the winery on Sunday, so we have the day off," Alexandra explained with excitement.

All that Matt could think was *Oh shit*. May had taken the decision for Sunday out of his hands. "Well, if we had known this, we could have grabbed dinner in Calistoga."

Alexandra opened the refrigerator. "It's okay. I'll throw something together and meet you at the firepit. Take Hanky out for his walk. We have the place to ourselves, so let's go casual."

"You mean winery dog Hankington of Napa Valley."

"Excuse me. Yes, Hankington of Napa Valley."

When Hank and Matt finished surveying the vineyard, he found Alexandra by the firepit in black leggings, a dark purple sports bra, and an unzipped black hoodie. She was on the bench across the firepit from where they normally sat, sprawled across the expanse, drawing with a pencil in a new sketchbook. She looked happy.

Matt wore shorts with tennis shoes and a Nebraska pullover hoodie. He sat across from her in their normal spot and watched her. There was a massive charcutier tray next to the firepit with olives, meat, cheese, and crackers. On each side was a wine glass, his with Chardonnay and hers with what looked to be sparkling water. "Something for the fire tonight?" he asked.

She smiled at him. "No, this one is a keeper." He got up to see what she was drawing and she quickly stopped him. "No, no, no. Back over there."

"Is it a secret?"

"My work is always private. I don't share it unless I love it, and if I love it, it goes on canvas. Did you hear again from Amber?"

"Yes, she texted. I should read it to you. It's hysterical." Matt pulled out his phone. "*Woke up S to go to bed. Showed him pic u sent of your FRIEND.* Friend is in all caps," Matt explained and continued reading. "*S's response was WOW. S is in time-out.*" Alexandra laughed.

Alexandra smiled and drew some more. "They both seem very nice."

"Oh my gosh, they cannot keep their hands off each other. Thats how they got baby number three. I'm done talking about my family, though. There is not a lot you don't know now about me now. Tell me about you."

Alexandra sighed. "It is not very interesting."

"That's up to me. I think you're very interesting."

"What do you want to know?" She was furiously drawing now.

"Whatever you're comfortable telling me."

"I was the queen of the July Fourth Fair a couple of times. I went to Napa Valley High where I was a cheerleader in the fall, and I was on the swim team in the spring." She looked up at Matt for comments and there were none; he was just listening. "That's where I met Style senior year, who I ended up marrying. His family had just moved to Napa."

Matt couldn't resist. "Style?"

"A nickname, but trust me, there is no better name for him. He has more clothes, shoes and jewelry than I do. I think he has like twenty watches. His father has this huge company, and he was ready to slow down, so he moved to the head of his board and promoted his replacement and moved here. The property they live on is gorgeous with gardens, views, and a vineyard but the soil is not very good, so the wine isn't either. He bottled for a few years but sold very little. He hired some of the best winemakers, but you can't fix bad soil. That's where he came up with his next big idea. He brought in a specialist and they patented a system. He started to sell it as inexpensive box wine. Wine for the masses."

Matt had seen it, tasted it and it was good, but nothing compared to a regular bottled Napa Cabernet.

"Well, as you know his idea took off and soon, he couldn't keep up with the demand, so he started buying up other not so good winemaking property and any available juice. Everybody in the valley does business with him, including my father. If you get too much of one varietal, and it can't stand on its own to be bottled, you sell it off to Style's father. If you have a bad year like 2011, he gets his wine for pennies on the dollar, but his price to market doesn't change." Alexandra made the money sign with her fingers. "It's a tragedy for us during those years, but Style's father softens the blow of a total wash. They just mix it together juice it up or water it down and come out with something palatable for the masses."

"So, Style? You don't have to tell me if you don't want to?"

"It's fine. Style and I started dating almost immediately when he arrived. His parents were nice to me. I was really surprised when they didn't reach out when I went to rehab. I assume they just cut ties, not their fault, mine. I was the one taking drugs." Her voice sounded sad. "At that point in high school, I was swimming and painting. I got a scholarship to swim at a D2 school, but passed on it to go to a college art program near Stanford where Style was studying law. The idea was that he would get out one day and run his father's company, and I would be a famous artist," she scoffed.

Matt smiled. "Sounds like a good plan."

"It was, and we were happy in the beginning. After graduating, I taught art at this little school for kids and worked on my paintings, which was easy because Style had thrown himself completely into law. He was working crazy hours, desperate to prove himself to his father. And then it all changed." She paused and her hand stopped drawing.

"Alexandra, you don't have to go any further," Matt said. She looked up at him, and her hazel were eyes emblazoned by the light of the fire. Matt's soul came alive, and he questioned what was happening to himself.

"Matty, it's fine, really. Style landed this massive divorce that everybody was trying to get. There were hundreds of millions of dollars on the line, and he won big. I think that was the first time he cheated on me, with the wife, and there has been an endless string ever since. Somewhere along the way, I think I just gave up caring." Alexandra got quiet. "It's funny. I think I just realized that." She took a deep breath. "Style made partner right after that. I decided to throw myself into my art and had my first showing. It went badly. I told myself that I needed to take time off, but I never went back and eventually got sucked into the vortex that is Style's life as a partner. Alexandra of San Francisco: shoes, clothes, cars, and penthouses."

Matt picked up his wine glass. "I think I like Ali of Napa Valley much better."

Alexandra suddenly stopped drawing and looked up. "Do you?" Matt had to look away. He wanted to get up and take her into his arms. *This was your plan wasn't it May?* "You can call me Ali," she said as she returned to her drawing.

Out of nowhere Hank jumped up and was flying. He saw a rabbit. As he took off with surgical accuracy, his tail hit Alexandra's wine glass, sending it flying and shattering on the ground "Dammit, Hank! Don't move let me get this glass up," Matt said, springing to action. Alexandra was laughing hysterically.

Matt came back with a broom and swept up the glass. Alexandra watched him from behind her sketchbook. Matt left again and came back with a new wine glass filled with sparkling water. As Matt sat, Hank emerged from the vineyard and ran up to them. "Nice job, asshole."

Alexandra put her sketchbook down and rubbed his ears "Hanky." He threw his full body weight against her. "We probably should eat something."

After they cleaned up from eating, Matt went to get a glass of red. His last glass of the evening. When he arrived back, Alexandra was again making sweeping motions in her sketch book with Hank sitting right against her in protection mode. "Look at the two of you." Alexandra rubbed Hank's ears and went back to drawing. "You are a dog stealer." She just smiled.

"Matt, I know you have to leave soon, but if you are going to be here next Saturday, there is this thing."

Matt didn't have the heart to tell her. There was a pit in his chest. "A thing."

"In the spring, we have the Budd Break Ball."

"Budd Break Ball?"

"I know, it's a terrible name, but it is a charity event for the Children's Hospital. All the vineyard owners get together and somebody hosts it every year. There is an auction, massive amounts of money are thrown around, so it's fun and for a good cause. My mother really wants me to go."

"Are you ready for that?"

"You know if you had asked me that two weeks ago, I would have said no but maybe. It would be easier if I didn't have to go alone. You could escort me, as a friend."

Matt was sick. He didn't have the heart to tell her he would be gone.

She continued, "There's music and dancing. It would be fun."

"Dancing. See right there is the reason you don't want me to go. I am a terrible dancer." Matt was searching for a way out.

Alexandra's mouth gaped open in mock disgust. "Wait a minute. Superman has a flaw? The heartthrob of Steed Vineyard can't dance."

"Total kryptonite. I blame my parents. There was no cotillion in Nebraska City."

"I don't believe it. Get up." Alexandra closed her sketchbook and stood.

Matt stayed seated and did not move. "I am so bad."

"Come on." She was now standing in front of him with her hands out. He took her hands and got up. She took his right hand and guided it inside of her open zip up hoodie, around her body on her bare midriff in-between her leggings and sports bra. Alexandra took a deep breath. Matt's hand now on her bare side, he could barely stand it. His body was alive. She held her left hand out, and he took it. "I will lead," she said, and they slowly rotated in a circle together in front of the fire. "See. You're not that bad. Where's your phone?" Matt let go of her left hand and pulled it out of his back pocket.

"We will even do this to country for you. Put that wild song on that you keep playing in the truck." Matt fumbled through his phone and soon Darius Rucker and Lucie Silvas were singing about wildfire love. Alexandra took his phone and tossed it gently onto the bench. Matt put his left hand back out, but she didn't take it. She instead wrapped her other arm around him and moved into his body putting her face on his chest. It took his breath away. He could smell her hair, skin, and perfume. As they turned in the firelight, Alexandra's hand found her way up to the back of Matt's neck. She started stroking her finger up and down his neck, and with every stroke, it sent tingling shock waves up and down Matt's body.

When the song ended, they continued their embrace, circling. Matt took a deep breath and pulled away enough, so he could see her face. Staring eye to eye at each other, Matt breathlessly spoke, "Alexandra, I have to go to bed." She nodded and broke their embrace. "I'll see you in the morning," he said, and she watched as he walked away. She knew… he felt the same way too. Her body was on fire.

Matt went back to the office and poured himself another glass of wine. "Hank, what am I doing?" Hank turned his head side to side not understanding. Should he go into the house and take her into his arms? She was too fragile; he was too fragile. This shouldn't be happening. ***May, have you lost your mind?*** Matt put his glass down and walked back out toward the house. He saw that the light to her room was not on, and just then a light in the attic appeared. "Go back to bed, Matt," he said to himself and turned and went back into the winery. He was going back to New York, and this would not be fair to her.

56

The sun rippled off the water of the bay making the sky a deep pink hue. Hope floated around the conference room table and poured everyone a cup of coffee. "Thank you, Hope," Style said. He cleared his throat. "If everyone can open up your folders, I think we should be able to knock this out very quickly, and everyone can enjoy the rest of their Saturday."

"As you can see per our last negotiation, we have updated 3.1 required marital relations from four times a week to three times with requested exclusions if the couple is separated during that calendar week, there is no makeup required, which is now 3.1.1. Also, we added 3.1.2 that if they separated, part of the week relations will take place the day before the absence and the day upon return. Everyone good with that?"

Style looked across at Kim Stoddle, the second most feared divorce attorney in the city after him, and the soon-to-be Kendra Swan. Kendra's blonde hair fell upon the shoulders of her firm twenty-nine-year-old body, which was barely covered in a short, blue dress with a plunging neckline. Through the glass table, Style and his client could see her amazing legs and heels.

"Style, we have a couple of requests. We would like to put some gates around the types of acts during the marital relations," Kim said. Style turned to the almost bald but in decent shape fifty-eight-year-old Patrick Swan, who shook his head no. She continued, "Okay, let's hold on that for a second. If that is the case, we would like to look at 5.1 on monthly allowance fees. If we can move that from $10,000 to $15,000 per month and in 6.2 reduce the required personal trainer workouts from four to three per week, I think we have a deal."

There was an extended silence in the room, and then Patrick Swan, used to being in charge, looked directly into Kendra's eyes and spoke, "No gates in bedroom, four times a week for both relations, the personal trainer of my choice, and $14,000 allowance."

Style and Kim looked at each other waiting for Kendra to respond. She smiled an evil smile and said, "$15,000."

"Done."

Style laughed inside. Kendra Swan was the one now in charge. He looked at Hope and nodded. She was already in the process of typing the changes. Hope pressed print and four copies came out of the printer hidden in the table next to her. She passed them to the attorneys to read. They both nodded to their clients to begin signing, and then Hope notarized them.

Style handed half the documents to Kim and the other half to Hope. He stood up, which was the signal the meeting was over. "You guys have a wonderful weekend in Big Sur celebrating."

As the room cleared, Kim stayed behind with Style while Hope walked them to the elevator. "Style, available for lunch today?"

"Unfortunately, I can't. I have this sailing thing, but next time." He did have a sailing thing, but it wasn't unfortunate. Hope's husband was out of town at a realtor convention, and he chartered a boat and crew for them for the rest of the weekend. "Kim, did you get the word out?"

"Yes, everyone is very clear on this. Anybody that is a reputable divorce attorney in the city knows that if your wife calls, they're too busy to take the case. None of them wants you representing their spouse against them in the future.

"Good. Thank you. Have a great weekend."

57

Matt felt a hand on his back, and he instantly knew who it was as tingles shot through his body. When he turned over, a fresh-faced, freshly groomed Alexandra was there sitting on the edge of the cot. She was stunning.

"I'm sorry. I must have slept in. What time is it?" Matt asked.

"It's fine. It's 7:45 A.M. The crew is going to be here at 8:00 A.M. Breakfast is almost ready. Bring your things to the house, and you can shower there after we eat. She got up, crossed the room and opened the bin of Hank's nuggets. "How may scoops?"

"Three."

Hank was sitting right next to Alexandra now. She bent her slender body down, kissed Hank right on the nose, and then filled his bowl with three scoops. She looked back at Matt and caught him staring at her. "I'll see you in minute."

All Matt could do was nod. As she walked out, Matt threw his legs off the cot and looked at Hank finishing his food. "You're a great guard dog. Where was my wake-up call that you're so notorious for this morning?" Hank crossed the room and laid his head in Matt's lap. "I know. I like her too, but we have to go, buddy." Matt was doing the math, and it didn't work. He was there at least through Monday and would have to make it across the US in three fifteen-hour-driving days. He and Hank would be dead when they arrived, and he would have lied to Amber, Steven, and the kids that he would see them on his way back. Nothing about this worked out. He didn't know how to tell her.

Matt's stuff was in his travel bag in the corner. He had been bathing at the community center most days, so he just had to get his clothes. Not tough to pick because there wasn't much clean except for a pair of jeans and a blue shirt. He passed a mirror as he walked out of the office, his hair was long, and it was all over the place. As he crossed the property to the house with his stuff, the old Ford truck was pulling up with Joseph at the wheel. He yelled out the window, "Nice hair."

"Fuck off," Matt laughed and yelled back.

Joseph laughed and drove into a parking space. As Matt entered the house, Hank busted by him and ran up to Alexandra making scrambled eggs at the stove. The house smelled of sausage. "Dammit, Hank. Outside buddy, on the porch."

Alexandra looked up at him and smiled, "He's fine. It's just us. Nice hair."

Matt rolled his eyes at her. "I slept too well, and my alarm clock there didn't get me up for once."

She smiled. "It's fine. Sit. You needed to sleep."

Matt threw his stuff in a chair at the table, grabbed the coffeepot, and poured a cup. "Alexandra, do you want a cup?"

"No, I've already had my two this morning."

"What time did you get up?"

"I painted last night, so I was up until two and then got back up at six to finish." Alexandra seemed so different this morning, so calm, so content and happy.

"Wow, you didn't get much sleep."

"Actually, those four hours are probably the best I have had in a long time." She walked over, put the eggs down, and sat across the table from him. She looked him in the eyes. "Eat." Matt made his plate and then began to devour his breakfast. "You were sleeping so soundly. I didn't want to wake you up. When you sleep, you look like a little boy." Matt couldn't make eye contact with her.

After breakfast, they cleaned up the kitchen, and Matt went to the hallway bathroom and showered. When he came downstairs Alexandra and Hank were gone. He headed over to the tasting room, and he found them together stocking for the day. She smiled when he walked in. "There he is, the heartthrob of Steed Winery. What girls are you going to make swoon today?"

"I just want to point out I am not the only one I've seen being checked out."

"Touché." Alexandra's cell rang. She looked at the number inquisitively. It was San Francisco, but a number she had not seen before. "Hello?"

"Hi, Alexandra, I'm sure you don't remember me. It has been a long time. I'm Gabriella Morales. Is this a good time to talk? I am sorry to call you on a Saturday."

"Of course, I do, Gabriella. It has been a long time. How are you?" Gabriella Morales worked at the firm many years ago and had been an associate attorney who worked for Style. Style said she was a brilliant attorney, but she suddenly departed the firm. Alexandra had no idea why. The firm was a revolving door, as Style put it to her: They want to be attorneys, but they don't want to put in the work and the billable hours to be successful.

"I'm good, actually we're good. My partner, Isabella, my sister who is also an attorney, and I opened our own firm a few years ago, and we're doing well. We're very small, but are making ends meet."

"That's so great. I'm glad to hear it. How can I help you?" There was a long pause on the other end. "Gabriella, are you still there?"

"This call is probably a mistake. I hope you are well. Hopefully I'll see you in the future."

Alexandra laughed. "Gabriella you called for a reason. Come on."

There was a long pause. "Alexandra, Isabella has a case against the firm. Four young ladies, a secretary, two paralegals and an attorney two years out of law school have come to us. They're alleging sexual harassment, a hostile work environment, and retaliation."

Alexandra moved away from Matt, walked outside, and sat on the steps. Matt watched her go. "Gabriella, I never saw any of that at the firm, and people say a lot of things these days. I'm not sure how I can help you."

"We are in discovery for the case, and we have a conference room full of boxes of paperwork. The firm is burying us in paper and there's no way we will find what we need in these files and more keep showing up every day. That's their plan." Alexandra knew from many dinners with Style that this was just one of many tactics he and the firm would use in situations like this. They had more manpower and time, and eventually the case becomes too much for the smaller firm, so it goes away or settles for little or nothing.

"Gabriella, again I'm not sure how I can help you. I had little to nothing to do with the firm."

"The rumor is Style has put the word out on the street that none of the big hitter divorce attorneys is allowed to take your case. My hope is that you will let me represent you in your divorce. Your divorce coupled with our suit will scare the hell out of Style and the partners, and they will move to settle."

"Gabriella, I honestly don't have an axe to grind against my soon-to-be ex-husband. The reason for my divorce is as much my fault as his. I have no place for any hate or anger in my heart. That's not who I am or who I want to be. I just want to move on, and I hope you can understand that."

"I do, Alexandra. I totally understand. I hope you find a new happiness in your life. I have nothing but blessings for you."

"Thank you, Gabriella. You as well. Before we go, I just have one quick question. You were such a star at the firm. There was even talk of you making partner one day. Why did you leave?"

There was a long silence on the other end of the phone. "Alexandra, I left because of your husband."

That answer took Alexandra's breath away. "Goodbye, Gabriella." Alexandra hung up. Who in the hell was she married to? Would Style really do all of that? She knew the answer: of course, he would. She turned and looked at Matt. He smiled and nodded to her, and she smiled and nodded back..

58

At 10:05 A.M., their first visitors arrived. The two middle-aged couples piled out of the car and walked up the steps of the deck into the tasting room. As they walked in the door, Alexandra spoke up, "Good morning. Welcome in."

"Good morning, we are the Clines from South Carolina. We had an appointment. Hopefully you don't think too badly of us. It's 1:00 P.M. back home." The two women immediately went mulling through the tasting room looking through the items to purchase, and the men immediately came to the bar to drink.

Alexandra smiled. "No, not at all. I'm Ali, and this is Matt. We are so glad you decided to stop by." Matt looked at her and smiled remembering the conversation from last night. Hank bounded across the room, and the Cline's loved all over him.

Alexandra pulled out four glasses, filled them with Chardonnay, and pushed them forward to the group. The men immediately tasted while the women continued to go through the shop. One of the men spoke up, "This is good. Are these grapes grown here?

"Actually, these are grown in our vineyard down near Napa. Everything grown here on the estate is red." The women now made their way to the bar with items to purchase, and they smiled at Matt.

He reached out and said, "Here, I will take those and keep them behind the bar for you."

Alexandra pushed the two women's glasses forward, and they took them. "Would you guys like to take a little walk around the property? Matt can set us up for some red when we get back."

The women smiled. "That would be wonderful. Am I tasting apricots and melon in this?" one of the women asked.

As Ali passed Matt behind the bar, she dragged her hand along his back and sparks flew up and down his body. She whispered under her breath to Matt, "In ten months, I will let you know." Then she turned to the group. "Absolutely," she answered, and they were gone, off into the winery. Matt looked for Hank, and he was now passed out in the corner for his morning post-nugget nap.

When the tour finished with the Clines, they decided to finish the rest of their tasting on the porch in the morning air. When Ali went looking for Matt, she saw him chatting it up with two young girls who were seated at the bar. "You guys have a seat, and I'll come back with some red." As Ali walked in, she smiled and winked at Matt when he looked up. She came behind the bar and put her arm around him. "Hey, babe, can you start the Clines with the reds and take them an application. They want to join the wine club." The two women who were leaning in toward Matt immediately pulled back a little. "Hi, I am Ali," she said to them.

Matt grabbed the Merlot from behind the bar and made sure his hip caught her back side on the way as she was pouring for the girls. She gave him a look as he walked out.

The day flew by. Hankington the winery dog of Steed Vineyards would greet all the visitors when they walked in. Matt took care of the bar area, and Ali would take them on a tour of the vineyard. When the gates closed themselves at 4:00 P.M., the tasting room was full. It wasn't until 5:15 when the on-the-edge-of-being-hammered visitors cleared out, and Ali and Matt collapsed into chairs after cleaning the bar.

Ali reached out and tapped Matt's arm. "We were a good team in there today." Matt smiled and nodded. "What's the plan?" she asked.

Matt leaned back. "I'm going to wash my truck and clean myself up. I feel like I am covered in wine."

"No, I mean what's the plan for tomorrow?"

"We're going to go to *church*," Matt said emphasizing church. Ali responded with an eye roll. "And then I want to drive Hwy 1. It is on my bucket list of things to do. I was hoping we could take a picnic and maybe let Hank swim in the Pacific if that's okay?"

"Sounds wonderful. I definitely need a day off."

59

1 Corinthians 13:1

Love is patient, love is kind. It does not envy, it does not boast, it is not proud. It is not rude, it is not self-seeking, it is not easily angered, it keeps no record of wrongs. Love does not delight in evil but rejoices with the truth.

Pastor Ann was in the pulpit delivering her sermon as Matt and Alexandra sat almost shoulder to shoulder. Matt had chosen his blue slacks from his suit, light blue shirt without a tie and brown wingtips. Alexandra was in a very conservative long white dress that buttoned all the way up the front.

Based on where the two of them were in their lives, love was a heavy, confusing subject, and they both sat swirling in their emotions.

Pastor Ann shook their hands as they exited the sanctuary. "I am so glad you guys came today."

Alexandra shook her hand. "It was a beautiful sermon. Thank you."

"You guys come back. We have Sunday school now, and then the sermon again at eleven. We would love to see you guys again."

Matt smiled. "Thank you, Pastor."

Matt cranked the truck and backed out of the space. "Let's go home to change and grab Hanky and then head out." As they drove back, Alexandra didn't say anything. "You're awful quiet over there. Have you changed your mind about the picnic today?" Matt asked.

Alexandra immediately turned and touched Matt's hand for a second and then pulled it back. "Oh no, not at all. I'm very much looking forward to our day."

"You just seem to be in deep thought."

"I am. I'm just thinking about the sermon."

Matt smiled. "That's a good thing. Anything in particular?"

"I'm ashamed to say. You're going to think it's stupid." She frowned at him.

"Try me."

"The sermon and the reading today. I have heard that read a dozen times at weddings, but I guess I just missed that it was from the Bible. It's such a beautiful verse, and it says so much. I thought it was a poem somebody had written."

"Ali, that's not stupid. A lot of people don't know that it's from the Bible. It was written by a man who had a massive change of course in his life at the hands of God. He was a Jew and Roman citizen that persecuted the Christians after Jesus was crucified. God blinded him to stop him and then gave him his sight back. He went on to start and guide the first churches."

When they got to the house, Matt let Ali out. "I will be out in five minutes," she said as she ran up the stairs.

Matt headed into the winery office and found his shorts, T-shirt, and sweatshirt. "Come on, Hank." Outside, he helped Hank into the truck and rolled all the windows down opening the sunroof. The air was still a little crisp, but he planned to drive slowly today. He had no specific place to go, and that was nice.

Alexandra threw on her frayed, probably way-too-short jean shorts, a pink sweater, and sandals. When she went back down the stairs, May walked into the house. Alexandra ran up and hugged her. "Hi, May, did you have a good time?"

"I did. It looks like you did too."

Alexandra went into the kitchen and grabbed the picnic basket she put together this morning. She pulled the prepared cold things from the refrigerator and put them in a small cooler. May was trailing behind her, watching her frenzied pace with a smile.

Matt's voice came from outside, "Ali, you need help?"

She yelled back, "I got it. Coming!"

"Who's Ali?" May said coyly.

Alexandra kissed May on the cheek. "Love you, May," she said, and she ran through the screen door down the steps to Matt who opened the truck door for her. Hank had his head shoved out the back window, hassling in excitement. May followed her out as Matt shut her door and got in on the driver's side. May could hear the discussion inside the truck.

"Ali, did you just put your feet on the dash of my clean truck?"

Alexandra ignored him and left them in place. "Drive please." As the truck started to move, she turned to look at May and made an excited face sticking her tongue out.

May smiled as they rolled down the drive. She could see Alexandra through the side window scooping her hair back and putting it in a ponytail and Hank's head out of the back window. Out loud to herself she said, "God, they're cute together."

60

Matt and Alexandra lay on the blanket in the cove, exactly where she said it would be about three hours up Hwy 1 in near Gualala. The sun was high in the sky, and the air was thankfully calm. If the wind had been blowing off the ocean, they would have been freezing, but it was a beautiful day. Hank was passed out next to them on a blanket of his own. He was soaking wet and had been in and out of the water almost the entire time since they arrived retrieving a tennis ball.

Alexandra was deep in thought again. "Matty, the sermon reminded me of something a friend said one time. She told me that when a couple consummated a relationship, that an invisible string was created connecting the couple together forever, and it could only be broken by infidelity."

Matt stared into the sky. "That's pretty deep, but I would say the statistics would show that's accurate. I think only half of marriages survive after infidelity."

"She also believed that when that invisible string was created, all the things that would normally bother you about a person, traits that would drive you crazy, you could overlook because you were purposely blinded by love. It was done by design. When the line was severed, it all becomes visible again."

Matt turned toward her on the blanket. "Does Style look different to you?"

"I guess so. When I suspected the first time, I told myself it was probably only once, and it happens in all marriages, but then it continued. Now that the marriage is really over, I am like, what the hell was I thinking? When I heard that passage in church, he was nothing like any of that, especially the, *Love does not delight in evil but rejoices with the truth.* The truth to Style is whatever he can twist and manipulate the facts to be or create an illusion of facts that he could turn in favor of his clients. He reveled in it. The best divorce attorney in San Francisco. What about you and Beth? Does she look different now?"

Matt rolled back over and looked into the sky. "Well, I was sure as shit the blinded by love part." He half laughed and shook his head back and forth. "When I look back now, all I can see is the greed and me killing myself trying to feed that need for her, to make her happy. Whenever she got what she'd been pining for, there was always the next thing. In a way, when I can step away from my anger for a minute, I feel sorry for her. She's never going to be happy and certainly not with Waverman."

Alexandra picked at the blanket. "I know you have to leave soon, but what are you going to do? I'm worried about you."

"Ali, I have no idea. Whatever I do is going to impact the rest of my life." Matt decided to tell her tomorrow he booked his ticket. The last thing he wanted was to ruin her day. She had been so looking forward to it.

He was leaving on Tuesday at noon out of Sacramento and heading to Omaha where Amber was picking him up. He would stay there until Thursday morning and then fly to New York. He decided not to go into the city and just stay in a hotel at the airport. He would go to the city Friday morning to close on the house. Matt called a realtor friend who was setting up showings for him on Saturday and Sunday to look for a place for him and Hank. His return to Sacramento would be Monday morning, and he would get Hank and begin the weeklong trek back home. It made Matt sick to think of kenneling Hank for a week, but he found one in Napa that was a doggy version of the Ritz. It had video links so he could check in on him remotely. After getting this planned last night, he texted both Amber and George.

As they pulled back up to the house, Matt put the truck into park. "I had a great time today. I'm going to try and get to bed early tonight and hit the house hard tomorrow. I'm going to skip the firepit tonight. If I focus, I think I can get it done."

Alexandra frowned and reached out to touch his hand. She squeezed it for a second. "Thank you for today. It's been the best time that I've had in long time."

Matt just nodded as she got out. He felt sick.

61

Matt opened the door of the house and walked into the smell of french toast and bacon. "Good morning." Alexandra was back in her gear for another day of litter pickup. It was completely jarring as it was the exact opposite of what she looked like yesterday in church and at the beach in her clothes.

Matt forced a smile; today was the day he was going to have to tell her, and his heart hurt. He sat across from her, and May dropped two pieces of french toast from the pan on his plate. "Thank you, May."

Matt, grabbed a few pieces of bacon and was shoveling one in when the booming voice of Ben Faulkner broke the silence and startled everyone. "What in the hell?" Ben asked. It was obvious that Mr. Faulkner was not happy with Matt's presence at his kitchen table. Matt immediately got up, started choking on his bacon, and grabbed his coffee up to drink to clear his throat.

"Daddy." Alexandra bolted out of her chair to hug her father. He was taken aback. Alexandra made huge strides in the week they were gone. He grasped his daughter and held her. "When did you get back?" she asked.

"Late."

May's stern voice cut through the air. "Matt, sit and eat. Ben, Matt was invited in by me, and he's eating breakfast. What would you like?"

Ben unhappily waved her off and headed over to the coffeepot when Hannah walked in. "Good morning, Matt," she said, having the opposite reaction.

She walked over and put a hand on his shoulder. "It's good to see you." It was apparent that Ben had been left out of the loop.

Alexandra let go of her father and went to hug her mother. "Mom, where's your phone? Let's see some more pictures of Jackson. How is Catherine doing?"

Hannah paged through her phone and handed it over. "Start there." She was beaming. "He's such a joy, and Catherine and Jack are over the moon in love with him." Alexandra was paging through the pictures cooing. She flipped them back and handed the phone to Matt. He started to page through. Ben cut a look toward May and Hannah inquisitively. They both looked away from him. Matt then handed the phone to May.

Alexandra plopped back down in her chair. "When are we going to see them?"

"Jack's mother and father are there now. There was no sense in all of us falling over each other to help. We got them settled at home, and when they leave, Catherine and Jack will come up or we will go down."

"I can't wait to hold him. Only two more weeks of community service. Speaking of that, we have got to go, Matty. I have to rid the Napa Valley parks of refuse this week." Matt got up and instinctively got her bag. Alexandra hugged her parents again and kissed May on top of her hair. "See you this evening." Matt followed her out the door with the three elders of the family watching.

They rode together in silence. The tension in the car could be cut with a knife. Matt couldn't look at her, and he was searching for the best way to tell her, dreading the conversation.

Finally, Alexandra turned to him. "When are you leaving?"

Matt cleared his throat, and it came out as we quiet whisper. "Tomorrow. I have to be in New York on Friday morning for the house closing."

Alexandra turned toward the window not looking at him. "Matt, you can't drive across the country in three days with a dog."

"I'm going to fly to Omaha tomorrow and spend a couple of days with Amber and Steven as I promised and then to New York Thursday evening to make the closing on Friday morning."

Alexandra turned to him with dread on her face. "You can't put Hanky in the belly of a plane!" She embraced Hank's head which was on the armrest.

"I found a nice place in Napa that I can board him for a week, and then I'll come back and get him."

"Matt, no! You are not boarding him. I will take care of him. It's the least we can do."

"Alexandra, your father hates dogs. He will never go for that, and he can't stay locked up in the office all day."

"You let me worry about my father! Cancel the reservation; Hank is staying with me, and that's the end of this!" The truck fell into silence. They were having their first fight. Matt wondered how much of this was really about Hank.

They pulled in front of the law enforcement center, and Alexandra got out. She stopped just outside the truck. She turned back toward Matt, her eyes red meeting his, and said, "I have the present for your family."

Matt was taken aback, "Thank you. Just let me know…"

She raised her hand to stop him shaking her head to say no and then closed the door. She slowly walked across the parking lot and boarded the bus. Matt whispered under his breath, "Ten more days, Ali. Stay safe."

62

Alexandra got off the bus at 3:00 P.M. and looked for Matt and the truck, but he wasn't there. She was immediately filled with dread that he was already gone, and they had parted on a fight. She couldn't stand the thought of that. The sound of a horn caught her attention, and she saw her mother's blue Suburban in the parking lot with her at the wheel. Alexandra walked across the lot and opened the passenger door. "Where's Matt?" she asked.

"He asked if I could come and pick you up. He is working like crazy on the house trying to finish the demo as he promised."

Alexandra frowned at her mom. "Matt and his promises. He's leaving for New York tomorrow."

Hannah shook her head up and down. "He told me."

"He can't drive back fast enough with Hank, so he's flying. He was going to board him in Napa, but I told him we would take care of him."

Hannah laughed. "Your father is going to love that."

"Will you and May help me?" She was now pleading.

"Of course, we will. He's so sweet. Come on. Let's go." Alexandra got in, and Hannah pulled out and headed toward the community center. She reached over and grabbed Alexandra. "You look so good. This morning you seemed like yourself but different."

Alexandra turned. "How different?"

"The Alexandra we knew before Style. Before the two of you got together."

Alexandra looked out the window and pondered this statement because she knew it was true, "I know. I need to talk to Daddy. Did you and daddy not like Style? Why didn't you say anything?"

"We were concerned about the relationship. Your father and I talked about it right before the engagement when we could see it was coming. We decided against it because we figured you would marry him anyway, and it would just drive a wedge between us and you."

Alexandra sighed. "You're right. It wouldn't have stopped me."

"Your father despises him now and how he handled the entire situation." The car got painfully quiet again, and Hannah wanted to change the conversation. "Did you make the decision about the ball on Saturday?"

"I don't know, Mom. It's a lot at this point."

"Listen, your father and I are very proud of you, and instead of us going and telling everyone how great you are doing, you can go and show them yourself. We can get our hair and nails done like the old days. You know that Eric will fit you in. He loves you. No pressure, of course."

"Mom, this does not feel like no pressure. Let me think about it, okay?"

"Sure, baby."

"Mom, don't let me forget to stop by the gallery in Calistoga on the way home. Mr. Stone has asked me to put some of my sketches on canvas. I need to pick some up."

"You're painting again?"

"Yes."

Hannah smiled. "I can't wait to see them."

63

Alexandra scraped the remaining food off her plate and put it in the dishwasher. It had been a relatively quiet dinner. A recap of the day in the tasting room from May and her mother. Her father was buried all day working on his wine and that of his customers tasting and blending. It would take him weeks to catch back up. May had taken over Matt's dinner before they returned from Calistoga. He continued to bang away in the house and could be seen dragging sheet rock out to the dumpster. Alexandra knew he would continue working until he was finished. That was who Matt was. "Mom, can you come up to the studio and lend me a hand in a few minutes?"

"Sure, baby. I will be up as soon as May and I finish clearing."

Alexandra walked up the stairs to the third story of the house. Her father had taken a section of the attic and walled it off for her as a studio when she was in high school. It had a single dual window that overlooked the property and had the best view of the valley. On the easel was what she had been working on the last few days. She picked up a piece of cardboard, measured, and cut it so that if fit just inside the edges of the frame but did not touch the painting itself. She then put several pieces of blue painting tape on the cardboard and overlapped the edges of the frame. Last night Alexandra wrote a note for Amber and left it by her bedside table. She needed to retrieve it to tape it to the carboard. She went down the steps to her room and found the note. As she climbed back up the stairs to her studio and walked in, her mother was there. Alexandra's sketchbook was open, and her mother had laid out her drawings on the bench table. Alexandra whispered, "Mom…"

Hannah turned, knowing she had been caught. "Alexandra these are so good, so different than anything I've seen you do. When did you start?"

"Mom, please don't go through my stuff." Alexandra moved around the table, gathering up her work.

Hannah reached out and gently touched her arm. "Alexandra, does he know?" All the sketches laid out were some aspect of Matt and Hank in the valley. The vines, the sky, the weather, and the essence of Napa.

"Mom, I don't know that I really know in my current state, and I'm not sure how he would know in his. All I know is how I feel, and it's pouring out of me in the work."

Hannah hugged her daughter and held her as Alexandra took a deep breath and tried to stop the well of emotions flowing from her. Hannah's voice was soothing. "What would Dr. Moranne say if she was here right now?"

Alexandra started laughing and wiping her nose. "She would lose her shit over these sketches. Mom, it's not like I ever intended this. Again, I don't think either of us is in a condition to understand this."

In the background, they could hear the sound of more drywall hitting the dumpster. Hannah motioned her head toward the direction of the noise. "He's a good guy."

Alexandra nodded. "He is. I'm scared I'm never going to see him again."

Now it was Hannah's turn to laugh. "Alexandra, you have his truck and his dog. Two things that a man truly loves. I can assure you that you will see Matt Thomas again. There have been far too many country songs written on far less material than that. So, what am I doing here?"

"I need for you to help me make a bubble wrap sleeve around the painting so that it can slide in and out in case the TSA want to see what's inside when Matt goes through security."

Hannah looked at the painting covered with cardboard and blue tape so the contents couldn't be seen. Alexandra taped Amber's note on the cardboard. "Can I see it first?"

Alexandra turned and smiled. "No, it's for Amber, Matt's sister."

When they finished, Alexandra carried the finished product out and put it on the cot in the winery office with a small note to Matt.

64

The landing of the plane in Omaha jilted Matt back to reality. His thoughts weren't here or in New York. They were back in Calistoga, back with Alexandra. He had finished the house at midnight last night and literally crawled to bed after a shower. He found the large, covered package on his bed; a picture frame covered in front by cardboard in a bubble wrap sleeve with a small note:

> *Matt, this is your present for Amber and her family (Fragile, please don't open it). Be safe on your trip. Leave Hanky with May in the tasting room when you leave in the morning. We have a plan to care for him so please don't worry. We need to talk when you get back.*

He had woken up at eight this morning very sore and gave Hank a bath. He slung the large leather knapsack across his body and carried the package to meet the black Yukon car service at 9:30 A.M. that May had set up for him. Hank was sound asleep in the tasting room office, totally sapped as well from the huge day they had yesterday.

Matt hugged May as he closed the rear of the Yukon. "Please take care of them."

May had forced a pained smile as he got inside.

It would be another big day at the vineyard. May and Hannah in the tasting room. Ben was booked from dawn to dusk catching up, and Alexandra doing her community service, swimming and meeting.

Matt's thoughts drifted to their dance at the firepit. His arm wrapped around her bare body, the smell of her hair and skin as they circled, and her finger gently stroking up and down his bare neck. The tingles again rolled down his spine.

"Mr. Thomas." The senior stewardess was in front of him. He was in 1A in first class. It was the only seat he could get on short notice, and it cost Waverman dearly when they booked it for him.

"Yes, ma'am?"

"Let's allow first class to get totally out, and then I will get your package out of the closet." Matt nodded to her. The flight attendant team had been great when he boarded, finding a place to stow it safely. Matt also had the driver wait for him at security just in case they wouldn't let him board with it. It didn't fit through the scanner, so they pulled it out of the bubble wrap, wand scanned it with no issues, and gave it back to him. Matt gave the driver the thumbs-up, and he left the airport.

"Thank you so much," he said as she handed it to him. Matt was going to be very happy when he delivered the gift safely into Amber's hands with no damage.

Matt strolled through Eppley Field, by far the largest airport in Nebraska, and smiled when he saw Amber holding Dawn's left hand because her right had a cast on it. Steven was also there, but in fast pursuit chasing a hysterically cackling Lucas, who apparently had broken away from him. When Amber saw him, her face lit up, and he could hear Dawn in the distance yell, "Uncle Matty!" Matt smiled, and his heart sang. He loved Dawn and Lucas so much that he could only imagine how much he would love his own children. When he cleared security, Dawn broke away running toward him and grabbed his leg. He wanted to scoop her up, but he had the gift clutched in both of his hands.

Amber hugged him and looked at him inquisitively. "What is that?"

"A gift for you and Steven." Steven was now there. He gave him a hug and took the picture from him, so Matt could scoop Lucas up and hug him.

Amber inspected it in Steven's arms. "What is it? I mean, I see a frame, but what is it?"

"Honestly, I'm not really sure. I was asked not to open it but to give it to you to open."

"It's from her, isn't it? The girl, Alexandra." Matt nodded up and down and forced a smile. "What is going on between the two of you?" Amber asked.

"Amber, that's a long story."

"Great news, we have thirty-six hours, so let's hear it." Matt started laughing.

Steven gave Matt a wild-eyed look. "I'm so glad you are here. She's been driving me crazy talking about this girl she's never met."

"Uncle Matty! You need to sign my cast!" Dawn squealed.

Amber jumped right in and said, "Yes please. You are sitting in the back on the way home and signing this poor child's cast, which you are responsible for. That's all she has been talking about since she heard you were coming home."

Matt leaned down with Lucas in his arms and inspected Dawn's pink cast that was full of signatures except for a prominent section in the middle that was left open. Dawn pointed to it. "I left this section for you."

"Thank you, baby." Matt hugged her. "I am so sorry that you fell. Does it hurt?"

"Not anymore."

"Good, I'm glad. I feel bad about it." He did. He really did. He felt like shit.

"It's okay. Don't feel bad," Dawn's little voice whispered.

Amber again chimed in, "Oh no, Uncle Matty needs to feel bad. He is now responsible for two incidents that have resulted in broken family members' arms.

"Really?" Steven asked.

Matt nodded yes. "When we were little, I found a bull snake in the garden and was chasing Amber around the yard with it. She was screaming her head off. She tried to get to the house and was running up the stairs. She missed one and came down on her arm breaking it around the same time Mom and Dad were coming to see what was going on."

"Wow! What happened?"

Amber sighed and continued, "Daddy grabbed Matty up by one arm, dragged him in the house, and beat the crap out of him with a rice paddle while Mom was tending to me."

Matt agreed. "I couldn't sit down for a week and my arm was black and blue where he had picked me up by it."

Amber nodded. "Daddy felt so horrible about it that he never laid a hand on either one of us ever again. Mom was left to dish out the corporal punishment."

Matt laughed. "And she beat us harder than he did."

"Yes, she did, and we are thankful for it. Let's get home. I can't wait to open this up." Amber was pointing to the picture. "I have the crock pot going with a roast."

The entire ride home, Matt was dodging questions about Alexandra. He was not ready for this friendship (if that's even what it was) to be analyzed by Amber. He kept changing the subject, so most of the conversation was about the winery and what it took to make wine. Steven was enthralled in the farming conversation as Matt was on his fourth color outlining *Uncle Matty* on Dawn's cast.

By the time they got home, it was dusk, and the sun was setting. They all piled out of the car, and Matt retrieved his bag and the picture and went inside. "Matt, you want something?" asked Steven as he was heading to the fridge for a beer.

"Absolutely, beer sounds good. There's been a little too much wine lately."

Amber put Lucas in his play area, and she immediately turned and took the picture out of Matt's hands proceeding to the living room with it. Matt threw his bag in her office and returned to see Amber intently reading a letter. She was deep in thought and shook her head pointing toward the frame that was now out of bubble wrap. "You haven't seen this?" She pointed again to the still covered picture with cardboard over the frame."

"No, she asked me not to."

Steven and Matt took a seat on the couch as Amber intently and carefully peeled back the blue painter's tape off the frame. When Amber got the last piece free, she pulled the cardboard off and stepped back with her hand over her mouth. Amber was speechless and tears began to stream down her face. Dawn came into the room at an angle that she could see what her mother was looking at and froze. "Wow," Dawn whispered. Amber embraced Dawn, and they just stared at the frame.

Amber having lost all composure turned to Matt with the letter clutched in her hand. "Matty, who is this girl?" Amber carefully turned the frame in their direction where they could see the painting, and both his and Steven's mouths fell open. It was an impressionist-like painting of Dawn's Meadow. The painting was stunning. In the painting Steven was throwing Lucas in the air, and he was laughing. Dawn was running, turning bubbles lose in the breeze, and Amber was laying on a blanket watching them all propped up by one arm with the other wrapped around her midsection. Steven and Matt were speechless. "Matty!" Matt snapped out of the trance he was in and looked up at Amber who was in tears. "Matt, who is this girl?"

It came out of his mouth in a whisper, "Alexandra."

Amber held the letter up and began to read:

Dear Amber,

Please accept this gift from me.

It's the very least that I could do having had you share Matty with me for this very short time. He has been a blessing to me and my family.

I hope you don't mind me taking creative privilege in painting your beautiful family in Dawn's Meadow. Your hand on your midsection represents the next love of your life. I wanted to make sure that the future baby wasn't left out of the painting.

The picture of your family moved me to what I want the next chapter of my life to be.

Thank you for putting that in my heart.
Ali

When Amber finished, she put the letter down and looked at Matt. "This girl is in love with you. Who is this girl, and what happened in Napa?"

Matt dropped his head into his hands and sighed, "Ali."

There was an uncomfortable silence, and then Amber cleared her throat. "Dawn, go set the table. Matt, I need to call her and thank her." Matt fumbled through his back pocket and held out his phone not looking up. Amber found her contact and dropped it into her phone. "After dinner, you and I are on the porch talking about this. Understand?" Matt nodded without looking.

Steven was still looking at the picture, dumbstruck. "Unbelievable."

"Steven." Amber was in charge mode, and he looked up. "Hang it over the fireplace now, not later, before something happens to it." Steven was up and out the door to the barn to get what he needed. It was not a stretch to imagine Lucas ramming something through the canvas, which would be devastating.

Most of dinner consisted of Dawn discussing everything that had happened in her life since Matt left. He didn't mind because he got a small reprieve from the upcoming interrogation that was about to take place. After they finished, Matt and Steven cleared the kitchen. They grabbed another beer and headed out to the swing while Amber put the kids down. When she emerged from the house, she had in her hand her one beer for the day. "Sit over there while I sit on the swing with Steven." Amber pointed to a chair across from the swing.

"You're not just going to join us in the middle?"

Amber shook her head. "No, I want to look in your eyes while we're having this conversation."

"Damn, am I being interrogated? Steven, are you participating in this as well?"

Steven smiled and toasted Matt in the air as he got up and moved. "There's nothing that would make me miss this. I've got to find out if there were grounds for your sister obsessing over this."

Amber began and asked again, "What is her name?"

"Alexandra." Amber gave him the stink eye because he was holding out. "Steed," he added.

"Is she the daughter of the people who own the winery?" Matt nodded. He felt this was the best way to not to divulge much information and not get dragged down a rabbit hole if possible. "Married?"

Matt again nodded up and down, and Amber frowned. "But separated," he added. Steven and Amber shared a look.

"Did you meet at the vineyard." Matt again nodded. "How did you get to know each other? Did you work together?"

"A little." That was true. It was one day, though, he thought.

"You guys seem awfully familiar with each other to have only spent a little time together. Have you spent a lot of time together?" Matt nodded up and down. "How?"

Matt's mind was calculating how he could answer this. "Riding together."

Amber's patience was waning. "Why were you riding together?"

Matt rolled his eyes because he could see the entrance to the rabbit hole. "She was in a bad accident and doesn't have her license, so she needed someone to drive her."

"Why did she lose her license? Where were you driving her?"

Matt thought, here we go. "DUI. Community service and her daily meeting."

"Matt, are you kidding me?" She looked at Steven incredulously.

"It's not what you think. She had a skiing accident and got hooked on opioids post-surgery. She didn't go to jail. She just got out of rehab, and she is doing great. Awesome really."

Amber nodded. "That does make me feel better. Half the country got hooked on them. Matt, you realize that she's not supposed to be in a relationship. She's too fragile."

"We are not in a relationship."

Steven couldn't stand it. "Are you sleeping with her?"

Amber's elbow immediately caught him in the stomach, which made him double over coughing. "Well?" she asked.

"Well, what?"

"Are you sleeping with her?"

"I am not. We are friends."

At that Steven and Amber were both rolling their eyes. "Matt, come on. That painting is dripping with the emotion of what she imagines her future life to be with you. I can see it all over your face. You care about her."

"I do care about her. I think she's wonderful, but the timing as you have pointed out is awful for both of us. We're both emotional wrecks right now, and I am heading back to New York. It's just not meant to be."

"Really?" She looked at Steven. "Where is Hank? Where is the truck?"

Matt sighed. *Here comes the psychoanalysis.* "Her parents just got back on Sunday night, so I had to stay until then. Hank and the truck are with the Steeds until I can get back and drive back to New York."

Amber again looked incredulously at Steven. "He actually believes this shit." Steven hung his head and nodded back and forth in agreement with his wife. "Matt, your subconscious is having a field day with you. Don't get me wrong. I agree with your assessment; you two have no business being together right now. I'm on your side, but you left them there because you knew that you would have to go back and get them, and you would be able to see her again."

"Amber, I think you are overselling this. She's an amazing girl who has had a hard time, and she wanted to do something nice for you. We were out together trying to find a present. I am going back to New York to live and work."

"Really?" Amber pulled her phone out and hit a number. "Let's call her. I need to thank her anyway."

On the third ring Alexandra picked up. "Alexandra, this is Amber." Amber's entire body language and voice changed. "I hope it is not too late to call." Matt thought to himself, oh no. "Steven and I are so thankful for the painting. It's amazing. We are speechless and not just because we're in it. We're blown away by your talent." It was again quiet on this end. "Really, I would love to talk to you sometime on that. Oh yes, he was really blown away. Yes, he's right here." Amber shot Matt a look and hit the mute button and handed him the phone. Amber whispered, "It took her thirty seconds to ask for you." Matt immediately took the phone and unmuted it and walked off the porch away from them.

Amber, shaking her head, said, "And he walks away from us, so that he can have a private conversation with her. Steven, this is a mess, and there is no way to win. They shouldn't be together, so if he goes back to Napa, which he has to for Hank, he's screwed, and if he stays in New York, he's really screwed working with his ex-wife in the building."

Steven cradled his wife in his arms. She was so upset. He whispered into her ear, "Once upon a time there was a warrior void of war with no purpose and a damsel in distress that he made his new mission to save. The patient and the doctor. The injured and the healer. They shouldn't have been together either and yet they will be together forever."

Steven's words hit the depth of Amber's soul, and she melted into his body and whispered, "God's will, not our own."

Steven brought Amber closer if that was even possible his lips dragging next to hers, his steel vibrant eyes into hers. "Amen," he said. The kiss that followed sent shock waves through Amber's body. The intensity of his love for her was overwhelming, and it consumed her. Steven cradled her body, picked her up, and carried her to bed.

65

Alexandra was walking around the porch with the phone intently in her hand. "I am so glad you like it, Matty." The trio of elders watched her every move as Hank followed behind her as she walked.

"Like, is the understatement of the century. Amber burst into tears when she saw it. You are so talented and amazing."

"I'm amazing?"

Matt exhaled on the other end, his heart aching. "You are."

Alexandra caressed the phone and whispered, "When are you coming back?"

"I am coming back on Monday after I wrap up everything here. I will grab up Hank and head back to New York."

Before he could say another word, the connection was gone. She hung up. There was no call back. Matt took the end of the phone and pounded it into his hand. "Fuck!!!"

Alexandra crossed the porch to go into the house. Hank was behind her. Mr. Faulkner's voice broke through the silence. "Alexandra, that dog is not to be in the house. Lock him up in the winery office." Alexandra stormed off the porch with Hank running behind her. She went to the office and collapsed into the cot where Matt slept. She could immediately smell him on the cot. "Oh, Matty." Hank's head rested on her stomach to comfort her. "What are we going to do, Hanky?"

About thirty minutes later, Hannah walked into the office and sat on the side of the cot. "You okay?"

"Yes."

"Do I need to be worried? Should we set up a time to call or go meet with Dr. Moranne?"

Alexandra smiled. "I'm fine. I'm just worried about Matt."

"Come on to bed."

"I'm going to stay out here. I can't leave him alone. He's already without his daddy." Alexandra continued to stroke Hank's head in her lap.

Hannah sighed. "You're not staying out here alone. Bring him to bed with you."

"What about Daddy?"

"It will be a fight in the morning, but it's three against one."

66

When the alarm went off, Alexandra scrambled to silence it. She turned over and searched the bed for her furry sleep mate, but he was gone. They had gone to sleep last night spooning in bed with Alexandra rubbing his ears. She shot straight up in bed and whispered loudly, "Hank." There was no response. She looked around the room, and he was nowhere to be found. Panicked Alexandra bounced out of bed, threw her robe on, and quickly and quietly moved around the house looking for Hank to make sure she didn't wake her father, whispering loudly, "Hank." As she got downstairs, she saw the light was on in the kitchen and smelled the bacon cooking. As she dashed through the doorway, there was Hank sitting just below her mother while she was cooking.

May was sitting at the table and smiled at the panicked looking Alexandra as she flew into the room. "Missing something?"

Alexandra exhaled, relieved that she found him. "Hanky." Hank turned now seeing her and bounded across the room into her legs to be loved on.

Hannah smiled. "Good morning. You sleep okay?"

"I did. Until I woke up and my bedmate had disappeared." Alexandra crossed the kitchen and poured herself a cup of coffee and then joined her mother at the stove, hugging her. Hank not wanting to miss out on the attention sat on the floor, his full body weight against both of them.

Hannah rubbed her daughter's arm that was wrapped around her. "He was not going to miss out on breakfast. The second the bacon hit the pan, he was down here." She was now working on the eggs.

"Why is that dog in my house!?" The booming voice startled all three women. "What did I say?" As if on cue both Alexandra and her mother raised their hand in a stop sign toward Ben.

Hannah's voice was calm but firm. "That's enough. The dog stays. It's the very least we can do for Matt." Ben stormed out of the kitchen and headed toward the winery.

May smiled. "That went well. What does our day look like?"

Hannah brought the eggs to the table. "I checked last night. It's not crazy, but steady, which will be nice, and you shouldn't be overwhelmed while I am gone."

The three Steed women sat at the table sipping their coffee and eating. "Mom, I think I am going to skip swimming today and do some painting."

Hannah reached over and took Alexandra's hand. "Do we get to see this one?"

"I don't know. What I am doing now, what's coming out of me, is so different. It's flowing out." May and Hannah looked at each other as she spoke.

May put her cup down. "Did you hear anything else from Matt last night?"

Alexandra looked down. "No, I kind of hung up on him."

Hannah squeezed her hand. "Alexandra, why?"

"We were talking about Amber's painting, and he said my talent was amazing, I was amazing. Then we talked about him coming back, and he said it would be Monday, and then he and Hank would head back home."

May and Hannah again shot looks at each other while sipping coffee. "Honey listen, Matt is a wonderful man, and we have all been blessed to have him here, but his life is back in New York. You know this. You've got to cut him a break. We have to be thankful to have had him as long as we did when we did."

Alexandra nodded. "I know."

The door to the house opened, and an angry Ben Faulkner walked back in and plopped down in his spot at the end of the table to make a plate for himself. He was apparently too hungry to let his anger keep him away. The Steed women all looked at him, but he was not talking or making eye contact. Hank who was by Alexandra laid his head on her lap and looked up at her with his sad eyes. Alexandra broke off a piece of bacon and gave it to him. Her father catching this out of the corner of his eye froze his fork halfway to his mouth. He immediately dropped his fork onto the plate and stormed back out of the house and slammed the door. Alexandra looked wide-eyed at May and her mother, and all three of them busted out laughing. Hannah was laughing so hard that she was covering her mouth. She could barely get the words. "Looks like your daddy is going to be on a diet this week." With that, they were rolling out of control. "He might just fit into his tux on Saturday."

The day went by quickly, and after group, Alexandra went down to the sanctuary and forced a smile, looking at the pew where Matt would sit reading the *Wall Street Journal*. She walked up to it and gently rubbed her hand on the top of it. Finally, she sat her purse down there and went to the alter, knelt at the base of the cross, and prayed. When she finished, she got up and was startled to see Pastor Ann sitting next to her purse in the pew. "That was some pretty intense praying you were doing. Do you want to talk about it?" Alexandra frowned and shook her head back and forth for a no. "That's okay. Where's your gorgeous man?"

That was all it took, and Alexandra was tearing up, her face distraught. Pastor Ann was immediately moved. "Oh, Alexandra, I'm sorry. Come here." Alexandra sat down, and Pastor Ann hugged her. "Is he okay?" Alexandra sniffled, pulled back, and unloaded the entire past year of her life on Pastor Ann leading up to today. When she was finished, she was exhausted. Pastor Ann rubbed her hand. "You had a tough year. I'm so sorry you have had to go through all of that, but, Alexandra, my impression of you is that you're so strong. The intensity of your soul overflows from you." She pointed toward her chest.

Alexandra sniffed. "Right up until it comes to Matt."

Pastor Ann nodded. "Listen, God sends angels and people through your life when you need them. You need to come to a happy place that Matt may be one of those people. Be thankful that God sent him."

"I know. It's just so hard."

"I know." Alexandra got up and gathered her things, put her hand on Pastor Ann's shoulder, and started to leave. "Alexandra." She turned back to Pastor Ann. "You may consider that we may also have this completely backwards."

"How so?"

Pastor Ann pointed at Alexandra. "You may be an angel that was sent to Matt to get him through his turmoil."

The thought floored Alexandra as she looked down and pondered that.

"But Alexandra all you can do is pray about it. You can't force it. God's will, not your own."

Alexandra nodded and walked out the sanctuary door.

When they got home, they found May and her father sipping wine on the front porch waiting on them for supper. Alexandra was getting ready to plop down in a seat when she heard a car come up the driveway. When she turned, she froze. The car was a long black Bentley completely polished up. She immediately knew who it was, and all the color drained from her face. "Style."

Mr. Faulkner saw the sheer panic on his daughter's face and saw the car as well. "That motherfucker!" He balled up his firsts and started toward the steps. Hannah came out the door of the house with a glass of wine and appraised the situation.

Before she could say anything, Alexandra signaled her father to stop. Her voice was calm and cool. "Please sit, Daddy. Don't say anything. You and his father still have to do business together. I've got this." She walked to the top of the steps as Style, dressed to the nines, got out of the Bentley and closed the door. With that sound, a sleeping Hank was now on his feet and heading over next to Alexandra to greet whoever was there, his tail wagging. When Hank saw Style, the hair on the middle of his back went straight up and a guttural growl erupted from his entire body that culminated in five rapid and intensely terrifying barks. The Steed elders all looked at each other in shock. Hank hadn't growled and barely barked the entire time he had been there.

Style froze at the bottom of the steps looking up at her. "When did you get a dog?"

Alexandra's voice was calm but firm. "Style, what are you doing here? You should have called first." Hank was back to his terrifying growl. Alexandra placed her hand on his head, and Hank moved his body between the two of them never taking his eye off Style.

"Dad asked me to bring some things out for the ball from the city. It made sense for me to come by. We have some paperwork that we need to go over." Style moved forward and put his foot on the first step, and Hank lost his shit. His two front paws descended onto the first step down, and a rapid-fire barking, fierce growling combination erupted. Style recoiled back in fear and backed into the Bentley. "Jesus, Alexandra, can you put the dog up so we can go over this?"

Again, very stern she replied, "No, I can't. What paperwork?" Hank descended two more steps toward Style and unleashed another volley of anger that was so fierce it moved his entire body.

"For God's sake Alexandra, put him up!" Hank went down two more steps closer and lost it all over again. Style was now backing away to the other side of the car. "I have paperwork here allowing us to use one attorney, which saves us both a lot of money. Separation paperwork that allows us both to move on with our lives, and I would like to go over a settlement offer."

Hank was now at the bottom of the steps between them, and Alexandra was not calling him off. Style, not taking his eye off Hank, opened the driver-side door if he needed a quick getaway. "Listen please, we won't have to liquidate any assets. I will take the burden of all of the debt along with the penthouse and write you a check for $1.2 million. You can be free and clear of all this mess and start over."

Hank was now crouched and moving toward the front of the car erupting over and over again, moving in for the attack. Style was wide-eyed behind the driver-side door. Alexandra crossed her arms. "If that's the case, that's fine. Please send it to my attorney. I only want what's fair, Style. Nothing more."

"Alexandra, please be reasonable. I'm trying to protect you in your fragile state. We are being sued by the people in the other vehicle and the building owners. This litigation could drag on forever."

The fragile state comment threw Alexandra over the edge, she didn't yell but her voice was even more stern. "Style, our insurance company is being sued. I am not stupid. Send the paperwork to my attorney, and if it's fair, I will sign it tomorrow. Now leave." Hank turned the corner of the driver-side bumper and went crazy.

Style was now in multiple levels of fear. "Fine. Who am I sending it to?"

"You know her. Gabriella Morales." Styles' mouth fell open, and he froze. The look said it all.

Style threw his hands in the air. "Alexandra please—"

She immediately cut him off. "Send it, Style!" Style threw the paperwork across the car to the other side, and it crashed against the closed window and fell against the seat. He climbed in and shut the door. "Hank, come now!" Hank stopped, turned and bounded up the stairs but kept his body firmly between the two of them. Style fired up the Bentley, threw it into drive and spun down the driveway.

Alexandra turned to see the elder Steeds all on their feet. They had moved to see if Hank was going to kill Style and if their daughter was going to let him do it. Hannah broke the silence. "Hanky, come here. Good boy," she said as she patted her legs. Hank bounded across the porch to her, tail wagging as she bent down to love all over him. Mr. Faulkner looked at him incredulous still analyzing what just happened.

"Mom." Hannah looked up.

"Yes?"

"I want to get my hair and nails done if that's okay, and I would like to join you at the ball."

"Yes, we would love that."

"I'm not hungry. I'm going to paint. Come on, Hanky." Hank fired across the porch and into the house with her. The Steed elders looked at each other speechless.

As she headed up the stairs, she searched through her numbers and found the sole San Francisco number easily on her phone. She texted, *you're hired. Only what is fair and nothing more. The less I know about it the better.* Within a second her phone dinged with a thumbs-up response.

Alexandra texted back: *He should be sending you the paperwork.*

67

Matt looked out the window of the plane as it circled and finally made its way down the Hudson to land. They sky was overcast and gloomy, mirroring the way Matt felt. There was a sense of impending doom. He was forced to change his plans and cancel his room at the airport. Waverman put him up at the corporate apartment.

Matt thought back to yesterday. The family declared it a holiday with Matt home and took the day off to spend half of it in Dawn's Meadow. Matt had snapped a picture of them there and texted it to Alexandra last night when they returned home. *Almost as pretty as your picture,* he texted with the image. She returned a smiling face. *Hank?* he inquired. He got a picture back of Hank passed out on a tile floor with his head on a pillow. He didn't recognize the floor, but Matt assumed they were in her studio as he saw a few various colored paint droplets on the floor.

Matt checked his watch. It was almost 4:00 P.M. in New York, so it would be 1:00 P.M. back in Napa, and Alexandra would be getting off the bus soon. *Only six more days, Alexandra,* he thought. *Hang in there.*

When he got the text from King George yesterday about the apartment, he was not happy, but admittedly he needed a haircut, so he texted Stan who agreed to stay late and fit him in.

The plane taxied to the gate and Matt was one of the first off the plane. The pungent smell hit him when he walked out the door. He was back in

New York. With his leather bag hitched to his side, he made his way through the throngs of people in JFK to the exit in baggage claim. Matt was shocked to see a driver waiting for him. King George was really rolling out the red carpet.

Matt directed the driver to drop him off at Dul Vassa Salon, and Stan smiled when he walked in. "Wow, Matt, what have you been doing? You look so ruggedly handsome? Is this a new workout? If so, my partner is going to want to know what it is."

"It's the being a rancher and home construction worker workout for the past two months."

Stan held out his hands. "Matt, these are sacred instruments. That's never going to work for me." Stan waved for a young lady to come over. "She will wash you up, and I'll meet you in the chair. I am inspired by how your hair has grown out. I am seeing something here." After they caught up during the cut, Matt checked his phone. It was Alexandra, making sure he landed safely. He texted her back and asked about her day. Her response was six days to go. He sent a smiley face and thumbs-up.

As Matt weaved in and out of the crowds of people on the street, he was trying to envision navigating them with a ninety-pound Lab and was coming up with no good answers. Also, after seeing Hank thrive on the ranch and the vineyard, it made him sick to think of him being locked up in a small apartment all day. He had to come up with a plan, and he knew it. When he reached the building with the corporate apartment, a doorman swung open the door and welcomed him inside. He walked over to the security desk, and an imposing bald man was there in a suit. He immediately looked up with no smile. "Sir?" he asked.

"Matt Thompson. I am staying in the Waverman apartment on the 22nd."

The man nodded. "Yes, sir. 2210. The young lady came by about two hours ago and picked up the keys. I think she's waiting on you."

Young lady? What young lady? "Thank you, sir." Matt went to the elevator and hit the up button. What woman was waiting on him? The bell on the door rang as it opened, and Matt entered hitting 22. The sense of doom was getting worse for Matt. Please God, it better not be Beth. He could barely stomach seeing her tomorrow, let alone tonight. As the door opened, Matt exited and walked down the hallway to 2210 and hit the bell. He held his breath when he heard the clicking of heels coming to the door. When it opened, Matt was shocked to see it was Sandra.

"Hello." He stuttered out. She immediately reached out gave him a hug that lingered for too long.

"Welcome back. It feels like you have been gone forever. My God, look at you. You look even more handsome than when you left. Are you hungry? George thought it might be nice to have a friendly face meet you tonight versus you coming to an empty apartment." She turned and walked down the hallway, and Matt followed her. Sandra was a beautiful, tall, slender brunette , and her body seemed to float down the hallway as her high heels clicked on the floor. Her dress was form-fitting and the back had a gold zipper that extended from the top of the neck down to the very bottom, which was midthigh. Sandra was an attorney at Waverman who served as his teams' legal liaison. She graduated in the top ten percent of her class at Georgetown and was brilliant.

What the fuck George? Matt thought. There had been an incident last year at the Christmas party when she was hammered. She tried to corner him in his office and kiss him right after her divorce. Matt sent her packing and rejoined Beth at the party. King George was the only one who knew about it. When they walked into the living space, there were two glasses of wine poured on the bar. The lights were down in the room, and there was light jazz playing in the background with a fire dancing on glass beads. Sandra walked to the bar, picked them up, and turned and gave him a wicked smile. "So, do you want to go and grab something to eat out on George, or we can just order in?"

And there it was. George had set this up. He wasn't stupid. Handling people, knowing people was George's talent. He could talk to any client who was getting ready to dump them and bring them around. George referred to it as handling them. Right now George was handling Matt. He knew tomorrow was going to be very difficult for him, and maybe just maybe if he got laid tonight, he would feel much better about tomorrow.

"Sandra, it's great to see you, but let's just sit and talk." Matt walked over and turned the lights up a little and sat in a chair making sure not to sit on the couch, sending a message. Sandra looked visibly hurt. She walked across the room and handed him his glass and sat opposite of him on the couch. She wasn't giving up as she kicked off her heels and brought her long legs up across the couch. "What's going on at the firm? How's the team?"

She nodded, seeing where this was going; it was business. "The truth is it's not going well. The moment you got walked out of the building, your absence was felt. It is very evident that George was leaning on you to make a lot of his decisions as things have started to move sideways. He was right to promote you to his former position because you were doing the work. They're rolling out the red carpet for you because they need you back, badly."

"And Don and my soon-to-be ex-wife?"

Sandra rolled her eyes and leaned back on the couch. "God what a mess, Matt. They rolled back in here three weeks ago like they thought this was going to be okay. Everybody knew she was your wife. She's hard to miss whether you're male or female. Waverman was parading her around the building as his new fiancée." Sandra, now angry, set her wine glass down and pointed at him. "Your ongoing suspension, everyone immediately at that point knew it was bullshit."

Matt nodded in agreement. "It was."

"Matt, here's what I can tell you. Things are not the same at Waverman without you running technology, and the winds are blowing in the wrong direction for Don. A lot of people in the dark corners of that office building are questioning his stability and reasoning based on what has happened."

Matt shook his head and then got up from the chair. "Thank you for the information and coming to meet me. I have to prep for tomorrow. It's going to be a long day."

Sandra looked at her half-drank wine glass and forced a smile. She was being shown the door. She got up, went to the dining room table, and closed her laptop where she had been working, waiting on him, and threw it into her bag. "Matt, you need to know that George didn't ask me to come over here. When I found out, I called him and volunteered. I think you're a great guy, and what is going on is horrible. I think that maybe we could spend some time together and see what happens, but I understand it's probably too soon. When you are ready, give me a call and know I have your back in the building."

Matt walked her down the hall and opened the door. "Thank you for that and for coming over. It was good to see you." She again went in for a lingered hug and then walked away. Matt closed the door behind her and sighed. He felt like he'd just dodged a bullet. He walked back into the empty apartment, picked up his wine glass, and sat down at the bar. He looked at his watch. It was 7:00 P.M. He texted Ali, *What are you doing?* He knew she would be in the pool and wouldn't respond, but it was nice just to reach out and know she was there. A little sanity, an anchor in the stormy seas he was walking into tomorrow.

He was shocked when the phone immediately dinged back. *Painting. What are you doing?*

Sitting alone in a 22nd floor apartment prepping for tomorrow.

He immediately got a text back emoji of an unhappy face.

How's Hank? Driving you crazy?

Again, immediately she responded, and he got a picture of Hank eating a rawhide bone on the tile floor of what again must have been her studio. *He's wonderful, missing his daddy, though. I catch him looking for you.*

Matt studied his phone, typed, then deleted, then typed it again. *How are you?*

There was a pregnant pause this time, no immediate response. Finally, she answered, *Ok. Worried for you tomorrow. Prayers for you.*

Matt looked at his phone and sighed, *It will be fine. Please don't worry. Have a good meeting today.*

Another thumbs-up appeared on his phone.

Matt walked across the room, got the bottle of wine and poured another glass. He then went to the phone and ordered dinner. Walking over to the floor-to-ceiling windows looking out at the city he thought to himself, what are you going to do?

68

Matt walked out of the building in his blue Italian suit he had been dragging around for two months. He put a tie on this morning as well, which was the first in quite a while, and he'd forgotten how uncomfortable it truly was. The jacket was noticeably tighter on him as his body has changed with all the manual labor he had been doing. As he walked the streets, there was a confidence in him thanks to Sandra that he was needed at Waverman, but also there was dread and anger of being in the building with Beth and Don.

Matt walked up and through the doors of the glass spiral that was the Waverman building shooting into the sky and blotting out the sun. He took a deep breath on entry and forced a smile. One way or another, this day would finally be over. He had no key card to get past security, so Allen was waiting on him in the lobby. "Good morning, Matt." They shook hands. "You look great, so fit and tan and rested. Good for you. Come on, everybody is already here, and we put them in a conference room. They arrived around eight and seem to be very nice people."

Matt nodded and followed Allen through the turnstile with a badge he brought for him. "Thanks for setting this all up. I know it's unusual."

"No thanks are needed. As ordered by you, we are charging the shit out of Waverman for it. The partners love it because he just hiked our rent again, so it's a little redemption for us." They entered the elevator, and Allen again tapped the reader.

On the 11th floor, the doors opened, and Matt followed Allen through the law offices to a glass conference room, which held the Yangs, the closing attorney, and a smiling Alice. She jumped out of the chair when she saw him, met him at the door, and hugged him. "Wow, you look so good."

He smiled back at her. "Thank you. You look great as well."

Alice then turned. "Matt, let me introduce you to Janice and Bruce Yang, and their closing attorney, Michael Bennett."

Matt crossed the room and shook their hands. "Thank you all for coming all the way to New York for this. I apologize for the unusual circumstances, but this situation couldn't be helped."

Janice stopped him. "Please don't apologize. We understand it's not your fault, and we're just so appreciative that you allowed us to buy your home." She shot a look at Alice, and as expected, Alice had been talking.

Matt assured her, "I am thrilled that you love it so much. I want you to raise your children there and live out your dreams." Matt painfully thought to himself, Please do what I couldn't.

Allen broke the silence and asked, "Matt can I get you anything?"

"Please, Allen. Coffee, black."

"Absolutely, everyone else okay?" Matt looked down and they had already been served.

They all sat, and Matt walked the Yangs through some of the intricacies of the house. He started discussing the master with the jacuzzi tub fault breaker being in the side cabinet and if it wasn't working to start there. He finished discussing the basement with the door sticking during the summer months that they would need to shave off. It was something that had been on his list to do. The Yangs were furiously taking notes the entire time. When Matt finished, he looked at his watch and it was 8:45. He shot a glance at Allen who gave him a look. Beth was late. They chatted for another ten minutes about the schools and best restaurants near the house when Matt, now pissed, got up and excused himself. "Let me walk out in the hallway and check on Beth's ETA. I'm so sorry for the delay." He was furious.

He tapped the phone and put it to his ear. George immediately picked up. "Matt, congrats. Is the closing over?"

Matt's voice was filled with quiet anger. "George, she's not here. I flew across this country, and she forced these poor people into the city for this closing, and now she decides to not show up?"

George quickly responded, "I'll call you right back."

Matt walked down the hallway and found the bathroom. He was fuming. As he was washing his hands, his phone rang. "What's the story?"

"She's coming down now."

"Thanks." Matt walked out of the bathroom and back to the conference room. "I'm so sorry. She's on her way down now." As if on cue the young woman who Matt had seen at the reception desk rounded the corner, and there was Beth following her. She was dressed to the nines in a black suit that he was sure cost thousands, and she was covered with jewelry. What threw him off was the makeup. Beth didn't need makeup she was beautiful without it and used just a little to accentuate. This Beth looked like makeup had been spackled on her face. She looked very different and not in a good way. She was followed by a little twerp who Matt recognized to be Don Waverman's personal assistant. Next to him was another young girl who must have been hers, and then in the rear was possibly the driver/bodyguard. It was a ridiculous display to ride down an elevator. Matt looked at Allen and then at Alice who was shaking her head back and forth as they entered the room.

Beth walked in and put on a fake smile. "I'm so sorry to be a late. I was meeting with my decorator." There was an elitist tone in her voice. Matt thought to himself, who is this person? She didn't introduce herself to anyone. She just sat and looked at the closing attorney. "Shall we begin?"

He was a little taken aback but began passing out documents immediately. "This is the home inspection that was paid for by the seller. Please initial that you have agreed to not ask them to fix any of the things found and then sign and date below." The Yangs signed and then passed it to Matt and Beth, and they signed as well. It went on and on for almost twenty minutes, and then finally everyone was finished.

When it was over, everyone stood and shook hands, Beth participating this time, again with the same fake smile, and then they began to file out of the conference room with Alice taking the lead. Beth then turned to Allen and asked, "Can I have the room for a few minutes? There are a few things that I need to speak with Matt about before we leave." Allen looked to Matt for confirmation, and Matt, hoping to avoid a confrontation, knew that it was unavoidable and nodded to him.

"Sure, let me see if I can move the next meeting." He was gone, leaving Matt and Beth with her entourage who did not move.

Beth nodded to them. "I will meet you in the lobby."

The twerp began to speak, "Mrs.—" It was obvious he was here at Don Waverman's request.

"Lobby now. It's not a request," she snapped. They all got up and followed in the direction Allen went. When the room was cleared, Matt sat back down in the chair and watched Beth pace the room slowly, searching for what to say. She was looking out the window when the words finally came. She sounded like the old Beth when she asked, "How's Hank?"

Matt's tone was very icy. "He's doing incredibly well considering his mother walked out on him."

Beth spun and shot Matt a hurt look and then looked back outside. "Will you let me see him?"

"He's not here, Beth. He's in California with some friends, so no. I had to fly out here to make this meeting."

Beth now turned and looked at him inquisitively. "What friends, Matt? You don't have any friends in California."

"I do now. I have been there for a month. George sent me there for a meeting."

Beth now looked very concerned. "When is he coming back?"

"I don't know, Beth, but you can't see him then either. It would be too confusing for him, and I don't want him around Don. You chose to leave us for this." Matt held his hands out motioning around the building. Matt could see the 10-carat ring on her finger. "And that," Matt said, pointing to her finger. "Your choice, not ours, Beth."

She again turned back toward the window. "I made him promise me that he wouldn't do anything to hurt you."

Matt snorted. "Beth, I guess you haven't figured this out, but I have been suspended and under a cloud of suspicion by a manufactured FTC investigation to get me out of the building. Basically, blackmailing me and keep me quiet.

Beth crossed the room and sat across from Matt at the table. Under the heavy makeup on her eyes, Matt thought he could possibly see the old Beth. "But you're back now, and you've been cleared. If I could go back and…" Beth started to reach across the table to touch Matt's hands, and he immediately recoiled pulling his hands out of reach. His actions caught her off guard, and again she went to stand, looking out the window.

Matt now felt very sorry for her. She was trapped in a world that she created. His next words came out in a whisper with compassion. "Beth, I don't know what's going on inside your head, but we are over. You have obviously moved on, and so Hank and I must move on as well." In that moment of clarity, Matt knew he would never work in this building again. He could not come back here, and with that realization, the tremendous weight he had been carrying around since he left California lifted. He made his decision, and he could breathe again.

He heard her sniffling at the window. "I understand. It's just... he can be so cruel sometimes." Matt now immediately understood the heavy makeup. Waverman had been abusing her.

Matt hung his head and again whispered, "Beth, it's the difference between being loved and being owned. You are property. You need to run, Beth, while you can." That statement sent her bolting out of the conference room in the direction of the lobby. Matt watched her leave and felt awful for her. He pushed back from the table and took a deep breath. He now knew what he needed to do. He called the Waverman travel desk. "Hey, Sattie, it's Matt. I need to head back to Sacramento ASAP. What's the next flight that I could make? Yes, today if that's possible. She was clacking away at the computer. Matt looked at his watch. It was 9:30 A.M. "Yes, perfect I will take 2:00 P.M., which with the time difference has me landing at... great 6:00 P.M." He would be back in the valley no later than 7:30.

Matt clicked on George's number next. George picked up. "Please God, tell me it is over, and she came?"

"She came, George, and you're right—it's over. I need my letters of recommendation and my letter clearing me. I am resigning from Waverman, effective immediately."

George, frantic, stuttered, "Maaatttttt, please reconsider this. I know you're upset, and I know this is very unusual, but in a year we will all be laughing about this, and you will have a new girlfriend or wife. Matt, every woman in this building has been inquiring about you."

"George, I won't be laughing about this ever. I'm gone. I want my recommendation letters as promised and the FTC letter clearing me. It doesn't have to be today, but the company needs to follow through. You owe this to me, George. The company owes this to me."

"Matt, where are you?" George's voice was low.

"I am down in one of Allen's conference rooms."

"Give me ten minutes, and I will be right down."

Matt hung up the phone and turned to see that Allen had walked in witnessing the entire conversation. He cleared his throat, "Wow, Matt, I have to say that I'm proud of you. That took real balls. This whole thing is bizarre. I just came back to let you know that the wire transfer went through, and the money for your house is in your account."

Matt sat back into a chair.

Allen came and sat across from him, "You want to talk about it? When did you decide you weren't coming back?"

"About five minutes ago."

"Really? What are you going to do?"

Matt tapped a pen on the table. "Allen, I need you to do me a favor. While I was out, I ended up in California to work on a partnership with a tech firm out there to help Waverman invest. It was an awful meeting and we, Wall Street, have no idea what is going on out there. I am going out to set up shop either solo as an intermediary for investors or as a subsidiary of one of the big firms. Can you leak that out for me?"

"Sure, that's awesome, Matt. Good for you. Do I have your permission to give them your number?"

"Absolutely." Through the glass wall, Matt could again see the young girl receptionist leading a group down the hall toward the conference room. As expected, it was George but close behind was Albert Dean and Mark Cross, the two most senior partners at Waverman. Sandra was not kidding last night. Matt had been missed.

They all walked into the conference room and nodded to Matt and Allen as they sat. The worry on all their faces was palpable.

The young lady chimed in, "Can I get you gentlemen anything? Coffee or water?"

Albert Dean took over. "We are good, thank you." He then looked at Allen. "Can you excuse us? This is a private conversation."

Allen started to get up, but Matt shut it down. "He's my attorney, and he's staying."

Albert nodded, not happy. "Matt, I understand you're angry. We would like for you to reconsider staying. Your promotion is baked. It's yours, and we will throw in a substantial bonus that will enable you to live comfortably in New York. We understand you just sold your home."

Matt looked directly at them. "Mr. Dean, I came to the realization a few minutes ago that there's no amount of money you could offer me that would keep me in this building with them." Matt pointed upward. "I respectfully request you provide me with the recommendation letters I was promised."

George pulled out an 8½ by 11 manila envelope with three very formal looking letters, and passed them to Matt. Matt read them, and they were three glowing recommendations from the men across from him.

Albert reached over and tapped the letter. "Matt, please check the date. We put these together the Monday after you were walked out in case this meeting ever came to be. You need to understand that none of us agrees with what has happened. In fact, the entire situation has called into question the choices Mr. Waverman has been making. What I'm asking from you is time. I need another month, and things could change very quickly around here."

Matt exhaled. "I'm sorry. This time off has given me a lot to think about, and New York is now in my rearview mirror. I'm leaving the city."

Mark Cross now chimed in, asking, "Matt, can we ask you what your plans are?" The tone of the room changed.

"Sure. George sent me to meet with a firm in Silicon Valley that we've been considering partnering with to provide more insights on the startups out there. It was a disastrous meeting; the guy's a real parasite, but there's a need for Wall Street to get somebody out there that they can trust to set up shop. We need to help by providing capital and guide some of these startups, and in turn funnel some of that revenue back here. We're missing a huge chunk of this."

There was silence on the other side of the table. Matt could see the wheels turning, and Albert finally spoke. "Matt, you plan to set up shop out there?"

"Correct, either as an independent that will funnel what I believe to be winning ideas to the firms with the best terms or as an independent subsidiary of one of the larger firms."

Albert clapped his hands together. "Regardless of this situation, this is a great idea. It fulfills an obvious need that we have, and it also solves your New York and this building problem."

"Mr. Dean, please understand I am not comfortable working where HJ at the whim of Don Waverman with a few keystrokes can destroy my career. If I were any of you, that would concern me as well."

With that Albert grew silent. "You have your letters. That's your protection. You also now have my word that won't happen. Please give me another month." He then turned to his left. "George, Matt stays on the payroll, and we are covering all his expenses until further notice."

George nodded. "Got it."

Albert then turned back to Matt. "Everything will become clear in a month. Just give me that month." Matt nodded, and the partners got up and left the room. Allen got up with them and showed them out.

George lingered behind. "I knew you would never come back here."

Matt gave him a hug. "Really? Because I didn't know until about ten minutes ago."

"It's not you. This situation is not you. Albert is shooting straight with you. I can't say more about it, but he is being straight, and everyone feels awful."

Matt smiled. The weight having been lifted. "Hey, I need a favor."

George smiled. "Anything, really anything."

"Does Helen's sister still run that high-end evening dress store on Fifth Avenue?"

George laughed. "Yes, she does, and it costs me dearly every month."

"Can you call her and let her know I am on my way? I need to pick up a dress on my way out of town."

"Sure, I will make certain you get the family discount, but it will still cost you a fortune. What's the girl's name?"

"I got to go, George." Matt hugged him again and headed toward the elevator. He was determined that this would be the last time he ever set foot in the Waverman building. He typed furiously on his phone on the ride down.

69

Alexandra bounded down the steps of the house and flew into the kitchen startling the three elders. Hannah looked up from her breakfast at her ecstatic daughter. "Where's the fire?"

"Matt just texted, and he is flying in today. He's going to escort me to the ball tomorrow."

Ben looked up from his paper. "I don't remember inviting him." The Steed sisters immediately shot him a dirty look.

Alexandra, totally ignoring her father, was bouncing across the kitchen with Hank excitedly following behind her. "You didn't; I did, but then he had to go, but now he is back!" She leaned down and hugged on Hank. "Hanky, Daddy is coming home." Hank started dancing as if he knew exactly what she said. Finally, she sat down with her cup of coffee at the table, her phone in her hand rereading the text. *Business in NY ended early. If the offer is still open, I would be honored to escort you to the ball tomorrow night. Catching early flight home and will land at 6PM. Meet you at the firepit?* Alexandra responded by sending a gif of a person yelling yes and then people dancing. "Can someone take me and Hanky to Sacramento tonight to meet him?"

Ben immediately stopped eating. "What about your meeting?"

"I have to go five days a week. It doesn't say which five days, and there's a meeting every night the same time. I can go on Sunday evening. I will call the leader and give her a heads-up."

May and Hannah exchanged looks. Then May said, “I will take you.”

“Thank you, Aunt May!” She bounced up the stairs to get dressed for community service. Hank was in full pursuit. As she pulled up her pants, she caught a look at her slender self in the mirror. She almost didn’t recognize the person. Her nails were cleaned and done and thanks to the trip to the salon yesterday her hair was cut and feathered. She smiled to herself. Matt is coming back, but for how long? She wasn’t going to go there. Even if it was just for the weekend, he cared enough to come back early to take her to the ball, and for now that had to be enough. She pulled her hair back into a ponytail, grabbed her hat, and was out the door downstairs where Hannah was waiting to take her.

The day seemed to drag on forever. All that Alexandra could think about was seeing Matt. She wasn’t allowed to have her phone to get messages, so it just went on and on. Finally, they were loaded into the bus and returning back to Napa for the drop-off. She raced off the bus to the waiting car of her mother. Without a word, she pulled open the door and found her phone where she left it in the console. There were two messages waiting on her. One of them was from Matt, and it just consisted of *plane taking off*. She smiled at her mom. “He’s in the air.” Then she looked at the other text, and it was a stream from Catherine that consisted of many people. In it was a new picture of Jackson, which were now being received daily by the group. “Look at that cutie!”

Hannah smiled. She was on that text stream as well. Alexandra’s phone dinged again, and she anxiously looked it. It was from Gabriella Morales. *Can you talk now? We have an offer*

Alexandra immediately called the number, and Gabriella picked it up on the first ring.

“Alexandra, thanks for the quick response. Is this a good time?”

“Yes, I’m in the car. What’s up?”

“So, the fact that our firm had both these actions had the exact effect we expected. They want both to go away badly.”

“Gabriella, what’s the bottom line?” Alexandra didn’t want to be a pawn dragged into the mud with two firms raging against each other.

“Alexandra, did you know that you signed away any claim against Style’s ownership in the firm?”

“I didn’t do that.”

"Actually, you did last year in August. Did you sign anything for him back then? It's notarized."

Alexandra thought back to what happened in August of last year. Then it hit her. It was hot as hell, and she remembered them sweating their asses off moving into the new penthouse. "We bought the new penthouse in early August."

"He must have slipped it in with the paperwork."

"What does that mean?" Dammit, Style.

"The firm is off the table, but all is not lost. We did a quick check, and you have a $10-million umbrella policy."

Alexandra shook her head. "No, it's only $3 million."

"Five years ago, Style increased it to $10 million. Alexandra, you don't get a $10 million umbrella policy if you don't have $10 million to lose. We sent offers over last night that included a $7 million settlement for you." That number was mind-boggling to Alexandra. She couldn't imagine them having that much. "They have countered with $3 million. I think we should counter back at $5 million." The phone went silent on her end. "Alexandra, are you still there?"

"Take the offer."

"Are you sure? I think we can get more."

"Gabriella, at what cost? We discussed this at the onset. I have no place in my heart for hate, anger, revenge, or anything else. Please take the offer, so that I can move on. Please remember there's plenty of blame to go around. Style didn't destroy a car and almost kill people under the influence of drugs. That was me. It was on me, and for that, I accept my portion of the responsibility."

"At least let me tack on the attorney fees on so that you are free and clear with the $3 million."

"Whatever, just let me know when it's done."

"Okay, you should have the separation agreement, which is the standard you do what you want and he does what he wants, and the final paperwork within the hour if they agree. I will send an e-sign for it."

"Thank you, Gabriella, truly." Alexandra hung up the phone and put it down on the seat.

Hannah reached over and took her hand. "We are almost home."

Alexandra smiled. "Matty."

When they pulled into the driveway there was a strange van in front of the house. Alexandra pointed to it. "Who's that?"

Hannah shook her head. "I am not sure."

As they pulled up, Mr. Faulkner emerged from the winery to meet them.

Hannah pointed to the van and asked, "Who?"

"Harrison Stone, Alexandra's old art teacher, was down the road delivering a painting and stopped by to check on Alexandra's work. He said you guys went by the other day to pick up some canvas and paint? I sent him up to the studio and told him you would be home in a minute."

Alexandra got wide-eyed and raced into the house, up the stairs and found Harrison in front of the five foot by five-foot paining she had just finished last night. He was in deep thought in front of the work. When she walked in, he turned to her with a concerned look on his face. "Alexandra, has anyone seen this?"

She was visibly upset. "No, and I wasn't ready for anyone to see it."

"Alexandra, this is staggering work. It's amazing and intricate. The emotion is pouring out of it. How long did it take you to paint? You were just in the shop for the canvas."

"Just a couple of days."

Harrison pointed to it. "And no one has seen this?" She nodded no. "Alexandra, I have some people coming by the gallery today. These are very important people. Do you mind if I take this and show it to them?"

Alexandra thought *no*, but she replied, "That's fine."

"I noticed that you didn't sign it yet. Any reason?"

She shook her head no. "I guess if someone wants me to sign it I will. That would make me an artist." She looked longingly at the painting. "Harrison, I'm sorry. I have to get cleaned up and meet someone at the airport."

He immediately pulled a sheet from the table and put it over the painting to protect it, "Please accept my apology for intruding unannounced." He started to leave with it. "Alexandra, again this is amazing work. I am very excited for other people to see it." She followed him down the stairs opening the doors for him, and then watched him put it in the cargo van carefully. He closed the doors and waved, which she returned. She looked at her phone and booked it back upstairs to get cleaned up.

As she climbed the stairs, she got her answer as her phone dinged again. It was Gabriella. The offer of $3.3 million was accepted by Style, and the paperwork was now in her inbox to be e-signed. She would have to do it on the way to the airport. In ten months, her and Style would be officially divorced, but on paper and in public, it was over.

May was waiting downstairs when Alexandra came flying down with Hank right behind her. She was dressed in a yellow and white sun dress that buttoned from top to bottom in the front. She had dumped the ponytail and her hair was done up with a little makeup. She pulled a clean bandana from beside the door and tied it around Hank's neck and kissed him. He was hassling excitedly. He didn't know exactly what was going on, but he did know that it included him.

May now motioned for the door. "Let's go, Alexandra. We are going to be late." They all went out and piled into Hannah's suburban, drove down the driveway, and out onto the main road. May punched the accelerator. If she sped, they would make it just in time. Flights from the East Coast usually landed just on time because they had to fight the jet stream the entire way.

Alexandra opened her iPad and found the e-sign email from Gabriella. She started to read it and got lost about five paragraphs down. She finally gave up and clicked through, initialed and signed. When she finished, she texted Gabriella and let her know it was signed. She immediately received back a thumbs-up.

They were lucky the traffic going into Sacramento was light, and May skid the Suburban in front of Sacramento International exactly at 6:00 P.M. Alexandra had been tracking Matt's plane on the trip over, and it just landed. She jumped out, opened the back door, and leashed up Hank, "Come on, Hanky. Let's go see Daddy." Hank jumped, out his bandana on display. "I will text you as soon as I get him. Thanks again, Aunt May."

May smiled. "Go on."

Alexandra busted through the sliding door with Hank. He was excited, and he was dragging her tiny frame across the airport. She rounded the corner and found the waiting area where people came up from the flights. There were two security guards in place and a red line on the floor with signs on both sides that said do not enter. She stood with Hank in the middle and told him to sit, which he did. There were droves of people coming up the concourse from flights, and they went to either side of them.

She leaned down and kissed Hank on the head and whispered, "Look for Daddy." Hank looked up at her and then back at the crowd, hassling loudly.

Alexandra caught the reflection of herself in the short sun dress in the window and decided to unbutton one more button at the top.

Hank stopped hassling. His head peaked up, and he bolted. Alexandra wasn't sure if he saw Matt or smelled him because she hadn't seen him, but Hank was gone, and it was so sudden the leash popped right out of her hand. She tried to go after him but one of the security guards caught her wrist and held her behind the line. She panicked and cried, "Hank!" The people walking up the concourse toward them parted like the red sea as they saw a ninety-pound chocolate Lab barreling straight at them. The security guards put out an alert but manned their positions as the alarms were going off. Suddenly in the middle of the parted sea of people, Matt was walking toward her smiling, and Hank was barreling toward him. Hank tried to stop when he got to Matt but started sliding on the waxed floor and went right into Matt's legs almost taking him out. Then he began jumping around him in a circle of absolute joy. Matt leaned down, and Hank was kissing all over him in excitement.

A woman walking past Matt smiled at him. "That's what I call a homecoming."

Matt laughed, picked up his leash and searched for Alexandra. There she was, being held back by a security guard and looking relieved. He walked up the long hallway, and Alexandra jumped into Matt's arms and hugged him for too long. She whispered in his ear, "Welcome back."

When she let go, he smiled at her. "Glad to be back. You look so beautiful. Missing something?" he asked, holding out Hank's leash.

She looked down. "Hanky, you scared me to death. He must have smelled you. I never saw you." She immediately noticed that Matt was now carrying a white garment back with him along with the leather crossbody bag he had left with around his back. "What's that?" she inquired.

Matt shook the bag. "That's my tux and maybe a gift for you."

"A gift for me!"

"Maybe a gift. There is no obligation to wear it, and you might even hate it, but I saw it and thought you would look stunning in it."

"What is it?"

"A dress for tomorrow night. I know it's really an out on the edge type of gift. I gave you so little notice that I didn't think you would have had time to buy one, and you might not want to wear an old one."

"I didn't. Can I see it? What if it doesn't fit?" She was now frowning.

"All good questions. May sent me your size, so I have my fingers crossed, and no you can't see it until we get back to the house."

Alexandra frowned. "I'm not really good at waiting." She reached up and brushed her hand through Matt's hair and fireworks erupted in his body. "Your hair looks great. You must have gotten it cut. How was the trip?"

"Much better than expected. You and I need to talk."

Alexandra turned and stopped him. "Please don't. I understand it's inevitable, and I just want to enjoy the weekend together, okay? Then we can talk."

Matt thought for a moment and then stopped himself from telling her. He would let it come out naturally. "Sounds good." They exited the airport, and May picked them up.

70

As they pulled into the vineyard, Matt smiled. What a difference seven hours made from the urban jungle of New York to the paradise of Calistoga. Matt sat in the back with Hank who had buried his head in Matt's lap to be rubbed on most of the way. As they pulled up in front of the house, Hannah and Ben walked out on the porch to greet them. Hannah walked down the steps and hugged Matt as he got out. "You were missed." He smiled back at her.

"I missed being here."

She then greeted Hank who jumped out the open door, and then he ran up the steps to Ben who shockingly patted Hank on the head to say hello as well. Matt exchanged a look with Hannah who smiled. Hank managed to break down that barrier while Matt was gone. He would have to get that story later from Alexandra. Hannah whispered to Matt, "Thank you for coming back early. She's very excited about tomorrow."

Alexandra rounded the other side of the car smiling with the wardrobe bag. "Matt brought me back a dress from New York for the ball tomorrow. I can't wait to try it on."

Matt immediately cut in. "Only if you like it. There is no obligation to wear it." Matt went to the back of the Suburban and pulled out his crossbody leather bag.

Hannah motioned everyone toward the house. "First we eat. Dinner is on the table getting cold." They filed into the house, and Matt left his leather bag on the porch before following them in. Dinner was literally on the table, so they immediately sat and began passing the dishes around. Hank made his way under the table on patrol if anything happened to drop.

Dinner was filled with laughter as Alexandra recounted Hank's airport adventure. Matt was caught up on the week's work in the tasting room, and Ben was making progress on his winemaking but still far behind. Then discussions turned to Jackson with this week's onslaught of baby pictures being shown and how Jack decided to take matters into his own hands and scheduled a vasectomy. Catherine wasn't thrilled but understood. As they were finishing up, Ben cleared his throat and asked the inevitable question, "So, Matt, when are you heading home?"

Matt looked across the table at Alexandra. She had stopped midbite and was staring at him. Her eyes begging him not to answer the question. He could see she just wanted a weekend without the impending doom.

Matt started to answer, and Alexandra shook her head back and forth her eyes filled with emotion. "Well, it looks like I'm going to be staying and setting up shop." Everyone at the table stopped eating, and the silence was deafening.

The next noise was a quiet whisper from Alexandra, "Really?" Her eyes were welling up.

Matt smiled at her. "Yes."

Hannah's voice cracked a little with emotion. "That's wonderful news, Matt." She reached out and patted his hand. "Tell us your plans."

"You know I had that meeting in Silicon Valley, and we discussed how badly that went. New York needs a good person out here to be their eyes and ears, filter through the startups and be advised on what to infuse capital into for a piece of the company or what to invest in if and/or when something goes public. It was very apparent in that meeting we didn't have a good partner prospect. We also need to lend some business expertise to those who we invest in. There are so many wonderful ideas, but 90 percent of them die because they're either managed poorly from a business standpoint or not fully explored for their full potential."

Alexandra and Matt had not taken their eyes from each other since he said yes. She needed more information. "Are you staying with Waverman?"

"I actually resigned, and they refused my resignation. They have asked for a month, and we discussed my terms to stay. For now, I'm still on their payroll.

I have almost eight years there, and until recently, they've been very good to me, so I owe them this month. In the interim, I've received four requests from other New York firms that would like to talk to me about working with me out here." When Matt turned his phone back on after landing in Sacramento, he had two text messages from the heads of two firms requesting a meeting and two voicemails from two others as well. He was right. The need was recognized by the street, and this interest from the other firms would give him the autonomy to run it his way if he decided to stay at Waverman. If not, he was out.

"Are you going to move to Silicon Valley and open your offices there?" May asked.

Matt shook his head no. "Actually, it's not necessary anymore. The concept of the office building where employees gather is dead. Eighty percent of the work can now be done remotely as long as you have a stable and strong internet connection. Your office is where your phone and laptop are. There will still be face-to-face onsite meetings, but that's no longer the rule on how to do business. You can set up a virtual building with some of the new programs out there and increase productivity by not having staff commute. They just have to be disciplined, and it's easy to see when someone starts getting distracted. I will probably start looking for a place in Calistoga. I would also like to dabble in the wine industry as well. For the next month, I'll just find something to rent and expense it to Waverman and then go from there."

Mr. Faulkner looked at him confused. "I will just tell you I'm lost." Everyone at the table started laughing.

Matt smiled. "That's okay. When we are out there in the vineyard and the winery, I'm lost as well, but that doesn't mean we both can't learn. I'm happy to help from a technology standpoint if we can talk wine from time to time."

May and Hannah shot a look at each other, and then May said, "Matt, Hannah and I have some ideas that we have been throwing around but don't understand how to execute them. We would love to get your input."

"I would be thrilled to help."

As dinner wrapped up, Alexandra asked impatiently, "Can I go try my dress on now?"

Matt repeated, "If it doesn't fit or you don't—"

She reassured him. "I know, I know. You know I will be honest with you. Now, I'm going to go try it on." She darted out of the kitchen with the garment bag. Everyone else got up and cleared the table as May loaded the dishwasher. It only took a few minutes, and they were settled out on the porch with a glass of wine waiting for Alexandra.

The wait was killing Matt. "She must hate it."

"I'm sure she doesn't." Hannah laughed at him.

The door of the porch opened, and Alexandra walked out in the white dress. There was an audible gasp from the Steeds. It fit perfectly, and it was stunning. It was cut just above the knee with a subtle slit in it, and the dress contoured her body, coming together with delicate, braided metal shoulder straps. Her feet were bare when she walked out.

"What do you think?" Matt asked nervously.

"I love it. It is so beautiful. I've tried on every pair of shoes I have and can't find something nice enough to wear with this. Mom or May, do you have anything?"

Hannah broke the gaze she had on her stunning daughter. "I will have to look."

Matt got up. "I think I have it." Matt opened his leather duffel and reached inside. "Sorry, I had to throw the box away. I didn't have enough room for it." From inside, Matt pulled out two delicate, black high heels. They had a single row of shiny stones that started between the big toe and went and wrapped around her ankle. Alexandra was speechless as she took the seat Matt vacated, and he knelt down in front of her. He took one of her ankles with his hand, which sent shock waves through her body, and slid the shoe on, locking it in place around her ankle. He repeated this for her other shoe as well. When he finished, he rose in front of her and put his hands out to help her stand. When she did, she hugged him and whispered in his ear, "Thank you."

Alexandra did a runway walk across the porch for all to see. "What do you think?"

Her normally stoic father choked up with tears in his eyes as he spoke, "Baby, you look amazing. I am so proud of you. So proud of how far you have come in such a short time." He got up and hugged his daughter

Alexandra began to lose her composure and whispered in her father's ear, "Daddy, I am so sorry. I am so sorry I let you down. I don't even know how it happened." They were both now fighting back tears. The pain and fear of the last two months was pouring out of them both.

"Oh, baby I thought I lost you." He was desperately trying to pull himself together. "It's okay now. You're back, and it's going to be okay now."

Matt looked across at May and Hannah in the swing, and they both had tears rolling down their faces. Hannah looked back at Matt through her red eyes and mouthed, "Thank you."

Matt nodded to her.

When they finally broke their embrace and gathered themselves, Hannah, spoke, "Alexandra, that dress is white. Get upstairs right now and hang it up. Don't put it back on until we get ready to leave tomorrow. Let's pray we can get through tomorrow night without somebody spilling something on you."

Alexandra wiped the tears from her face and smiled. "Yes, ma'am." She opened the screen door of the house and stopped turning to Matt. She smiled a smile that melted his heart. "Meet at the firepit?"

Matt nodded, and then she was gone in the house. He got up and picked up his duffel. "Mr. Faulkner, would it be okay if I stay here for a few more days until I find a place." He grunted a positive acknowledgment back to Matt as he used his handkerchief to clean his eyes and wipe his nose. "Hannah and May, thank you so much for dinner." They both smiled back at him. As he passed May, she put her hand up to him. He took it and let his grip slide away as he continued toward the winery. He looked back to call Hank but no need. He was just a few feet behind him as always, and Matt was looking forward to a walk with him in the vineyard after a quick shower.

Matt hung his new tux up in the office and checked to make sure that it was not out of sorts in any way. It looked to be fine. His suit tailor, Fabrizio, who had immigrated just a few years ago from Italy, had been riding Matt about getting a new tux. He was ecstatic when Matt called, and he had it completed by the time Matt left the dress store.

Matt washed the seven-hour plane trip off and found a lose pair of shorts, a T-shirt, and a hoodie for when it got cold. He walked the vineyard with Hank who seemed to be ecstatic to have his daddy back. Every now and then, he would chase a rabbit or run the birds out of a row.

As they finished up their walk, he found Alexandra at the firepit in her tights with a loose sweater over her. Her legs were crossed and extended across the length of the bench. He saw her before she saw him, and she was staring into the fire, mesmerized in thought. The light of the fire was dancing off her beautiful face. When Hank saw her, he ran up to her and brought her back from where she was in thought. She smiled her incredible smile at Matt. "I thought you stood me up."

He smiled back at her. "Never." He sat across from her and looked in her eyes.

"It sounds like you had a good trip to New York. Does Amber know what you decided?"

It all happened so fast he forgot to tell her. "Not yet. I will call her tomorrow and let her know. Better yet, we will send her a picture of us dressed up."

"When did you know what you were going to do?"

"Honestly, it wasn't until I got into the meeting that the clarity came to me. I couldn't see myself there anymore. They made a full court press for me to stay in some type of capacity, so let's see how the next month turns out."

Alexandra looked into the fire again, and then looked back up at Matt. "I love my dress. How did you pick it out?"

"When you accepted my invitation, I had about three hours before I had to get to the airport. I didn't really know if I would find anything. George's wife had several dresses hung up for me, but the dress I picked was on the mannequin. The instant I saw it, it looked like you."

This statement sat with Alexandra for a minute. "What did you see in that dress?"

"It's white and that reminds me of the purity and honesty I see in you. I know you said it wasn't you before the accident, but Alexandra I see it in you now. The creativity of the lines, the beauty of the dress reminds me of your beautiful artistry in your paintings. Don't get me wrong. It can't come close, but I think that it's as beautiful as you can get with fabric." Matt continued to look into the fire. "And the braided metal shoulder straps. That is this incredible strength I see inside of you to overcome what was thrown at you. You're an incredibly strong woman."

Matt was quiet, still not looking up. "Matty, what about those heels?"

Matt smiled, and still not looking up, he blushed and finally spoke, "Sexy." His face flushed red.

Alexandra's voice came out in a toying playful whisper, "Do you think I'm sexy?"

Matt realized he dug himself into a hole. He looked up from the fire at her. "I think you are an incredibly beautiful, talented, and attractive woman."

Again, she immediately replied in the playful, toying whisper, "That is not what you said. You said sexy." Matt's face was beet red.

Alexandra decided to let him off the hook. "I talked to Mom and May before I came out. They're shutting down early to get ready for the ball, so I asked for the day off and thought we could take Hank for a picnic to Gualala. We just need to be back in enough time to get ready. Daddy and Mr. Jerkasky split a limo, and it will be here at six to pick us up. It officially starts at seven, but the drinks start rolling much sooner. What do you think?"

Matt nodded. "I would love that."

She stood up and looked at him. "Pick me up at ten, Matty?"

"Absolutely." She turned and made her way past the tasting room and winery and entered the house.

Matt rubbed on Hank's ears. He was in real trouble here. She was all he could think about. Had he opened up too much about the dress? Neither of them was in the right frame of mind to be seeing someone, and he could be reading all of this wrong. He went to bed recounting and regretting their conversation.

71

In the morning, Matt got up late and cleaned up the truck. He was out front at 10:00 A.M. exactly waiting on Alexandra. May emerged from the house heading to the tasting room for their first appointment. "We missed you at breakfast."

"With the flight and the time change I was dead on my feet last night. Sorry."

"It makes sense. You two have a good time today and don't be late. We will be leaving at six."

"Got it."

Matt waited for another fifteen minutes and wondered if Alexandra had forgotten or changed her mind. He didn't want to push it. When he started toward the other side of the truck to leave, Alexandra came out the front door. She had white tennis shoes, pink shorts, with a white button up sleeveless top on. She must have seen him getting ready to leave and was in a panic. Matt smiled. "I thought you stood me up."

She smiled at him. "Never. I can't wait to go."

Matt took the basket and small cooler from her, put them in the back of the truck, and then opened the door for her. Hannah had walked out onto the porch and waved goodbye to them as they rolled down the driveway.

When they pulled out on Silverado Trail, Alexandra kicked off her shoes and put her feet on the dash. She pulled her hair back into a ponytail. Matt just looked at her and smiled. That wasn't a fight he was going to win. Darius was on the radio singing about Miss California, and it made him smile looking at her. Matt reached down and rubbed Hank's head positioned on the rest.

Alexandra was strangely quiet in deep thought. Matt was wondering where her head was when the tingling started at his neck and settled to his feet. Alexandra had reached over and taken his hand. He looked at her and smiled, and she smiled back at him. Whenever Matt would need both hands, they would release but as soon as it was free, she would take her soft hand and place it into his. Thinking back to last night's conversation, maybe he hadn't gotten it so wrong.

When they got to Gualala the cove was strangely quiet for a Saturday. There was no one around, and they quickly dispensed with lunch. Matt then took Hank and walked up and down the cove, throwing the ball into the ocean, Hank jumping into the cold waves to retrieve it. This went on for about thirty minutes until Hank was spent and came to drink fresh water by the picnic on his blanket. He would fall to sleep in minutes. When Matt walked up, Alexandra was sitting up covered in a blanket, and Matt lay down beside her and looked into the sky. "Cold?"

Her hand appeared from under the blanket and took his. "Not really. We need to talk." Matt rolled on his side and looked at her, nodding. It was time. "Matty, I have played this conversation out a hundred times in my head this week. I know this doesn't make any sense, but I am in love with you." Matt started to say something, but she stopped him. "Please, I have to get this out. I know this is a tough time for you as well with what is going on in your life, but I do love you. I can't hide it anymore. Somehow being together has reached inside me and activated my soul. It's on fire, and I am so scared right now that telling you this will make you want to run away."

She could see that he wanted to say something, but thankfully he just listened. "Matty, there are so many reasons that I shouldn't allow myself to be in love with you that I have lost count, but… I am. It is not something I can control." She released his hand for a moment and collected herself. "I want you to know that if you want to leave, you can. I will be miserable, but I will be okay. You are not responsible for my happiness. I had to get this out today before the whole world see's it tonight. I can't hide it, and they are going to see it." Alexandra took Matt's hand she was holding and brought it inside the blanket and placed it on her bare chest over her heart. Lightning exploded through

Matt's body. Her delicate breast under his palm, he could feel Alexandra's heart beating a mile a minute. "Matt, do you feel my heart? My body is exploding for you. I want that invisible string between us. Even if it's for an hour, a day, a year, ten years, or forever. I want that connection with you for however long we can have it." Her other hand released the blanket and it opened in front of her, and Matt could see that she was completely bare underneath the blanket.

Matt couldn't hold back any longer. "Oh, Alexandra, I love you too. You are all that I thought about when I was gone." Matt's eyes were welling up. "If I touch you now, I'm afraid I'm never going to be able to let you go."

Her voice was a whisper, "Don't Matt. Don't ever let me go."

Their mouths met gently and immediately became forceful. Matt climbed inside the blanket with her, her naked body pressing against his. It was like oxygen for his soul, and he needed more. He could feel her hands tugging up on his shirt, but his body wouldn't release her lips. He forced himself to break away for a second and pull it off. As soon as he was free, her mouth was back on his, her tongue searching for his. Her firm nipples now rubbing against his bare chest sent shock waves through his body.

Alexandra's body was on fire, the constant tingling of the last few weeks had culminated into a crescendo she could not stop. Her hands went for the button on his shorts, and she could fell him beneath. When she broke the button open, she pushed the shorts down on his body, and she could feel his stiffness against her body taking her breath away. Matt pulled away for a second again to finish what she had started and got his shorts all the way off. His mouth found its way to her breast. Alexandra moaned as he took her nipple in and out of his mouth, his tongue lashing against her body, rocking it, and then she let loose in a yell.

She couldn't wait any longer. Her hand went down and took ahold of him, which provoked a moan from Matt, and she pulled it toward her open legs. She exhaled sharply at his size and breathlessly mouthed, "Easy." She barely got the word out, and his mouth was back onto hers as he gently entered her. Every delicate stroke became deeper each time. She had to break away from his mouth to breathe. His body thundered against hers, her body convulsing against his, and she came over and over, losing all control of herself.

The speed of Matt's body increased, and she felt his warmth cascade inside, sending her over the edge again. Matt's weight was on her now, his breathing was rapid in her ear, and he began to pull away, but Alexandra refused to let him go wrapping her legs and arms around him pulling him in deeper. "Don't," she breathed. "I didn't know it could be like that." Her body was trembling in the aftermath of the shock waves, and tears flowed on her face.

Matt felt her tears and pulled up. "Are you okay? I didn't hurt you?"

Her hands found his face to reassure him. "You didn't hurt me. It's just never been that way for me. I love you so much." Her mouth found his, her hands stroking his hair, his body, and then his neck. Almost immediately, Alexandra felt Matt growing inside of her, and her body was not going to pass on it. It involuntarily convulsed against his, and he let out a whispered moan.

She was not the only one who could not control themselves as Matt now again stroked violently inside of her now. They were now both out of control. Her hands found his rear, and she was now pulling him into her, harder and harder each time, her mind now spiraling, and she came again. Matt did not let up until his warmth filled her again. They collapsed on the blanket, both bodies shuddering against each other. Alexandra pulled Matt's head to her bare chest, her hands shaking. In a few minutes, Matt was asleep as she could feel his breathing deepen on her chest with the ocean waves thundering away in her ears. She held him tightly and then drifted off into a blissful sleep.

They awoke together their bodies interwoven in each other, and Hank was standing over them hassling. Matt grumbled a laugh. "Go away, Hank." Hank did not comply and instead let his entire body fall against them and started rolling around.

Alexandra started laughing. "I don't think he's going to go away."

Matt's head was still on Alexandra's chest, and he pulled back just a little and kissed her nipple. She immediately recoiled and inhaled. "Stop unless you plan on following through." He moved up and kissed her mouth, and she melted into his.

Matt, pulling back, looked at her. "Did you sleep?" She smiled and nodded. "How long have we been here?"

"No clue." She fumbled around and found her phone. "Oh God, Matt, we got to go or we are going to be late." They rolled around under the blanket laughing trying to find their clothes and put them on. Hank thought it was a game and joined in, rolling around with them. Finally, when they had their clothes on, they gathered everything and went up the hill to the truck.

As they were pulling out of the parking lot, a policeman pulled up next to them with his window down, so they stopped. "We got a report of two kids making out in the cove. Did you see anyone down there?"

Alexandra replied, "No, sorry. We didn't see any kids down there."

"Thanks." He pulled down into the parking lot.

Matt shot a wide-eyed look at Alexandra, which she returned.

Then she turned and loved on Hank. "Good boy, Hanky."

Matt started laughing. "No kidding."

72

May was standing on the front porch looking at her watch. It was 5:30, and Matt and Alexandra were still not back. Finally, she saw the truck pulling up to the gate and speed quickly up the driveway. She gave them both a look as Alexandra flew out of the passenger door and mounted the steps to the top. "Cutting it a little close, aren't we?"

"Sorry, Aunt May." Alexandra gave her a huge joyous hug as Matt sped away to park the truck. May looked at Alexandra puzzled when she released her. "What?"

"Do I smell Matt on your clothes?"

A wide grin crossed her face. Alexandra leaned in and whispered to her, "Not possible. We didn't have any clothes on." May gave her a wide-eyed look as Alexandra gave her a peck on the cheek and then ran into the house.

Matt cleaned up quickly, then fed Hank and put the new tux on. When he left the bathroom, Hank was asleep in the cot, exhausted from his day at the beach. As he walked out of the winery, the limo was already out front, and he could see the elder Steeds on the porch with a glass of white wine speaking with Peter Jerkasky and his wife. As he walked toward the porch, Mrs. Jerkasky spotted Matt. "Who is this gorgeous man?" The comment had everyone turn.

Hannah smiled and put her arm around her. "This is Matt. He has been doing some work for us here and is going to escort Alexandra tonight."

"Good for her! Come up here, Matt, and tell us about yourself. You know I have two daughters myself who are single. We should get a picture and send it to them."

Matt caught a smirky look from May. "Yes, Matt, please come up here and explain why the two of you were so late getting back from Gualala today. We have zero chance of Alexandra getting ready in thirty minutes."

He shot May a look, which she returned. Damn, she knew.

Matt discussed his background, and then the work he had been doing on the house all while nervously checking his watch. Finally, Alexandra emerged from the house at 6:15 in the white dress, and she was stunning. She did an impromptu runway walk up and down the porch, which elicited *oohs* and *ahhs* from the elders. Ben spoke up after and said, "Let's go."

Alexandra stopped them. "Wait," she said as she gave the phone to Hannah. "We need to get a picture of us to send to Matt's sister." Hannah quickly snapped a few pictures and then handed the phone back to Alexandra. She rapidly attached it to a text, which within seconds received a line of hearts back from Amber. Then Matt heard his phone ringing in his pocket. He knew exactly who that was and fished it out. It was Amber. He turned the ringer off and gave Alexandra a look. There was no time for this conversation today.

It took them a solid thirty minutes to arrive at Santego Vineyard. As they pulled in the gate, security was very tight. Soon, they were released, and the drive through the property was stunning as the sun was just beginning to set in the spring sky. The driveway was lit with candle holders, but Matt recognized they were battery operated to take out any chance of a fire. The limo meandered through a property and stopped at the base of two gigantic wooden doors in the side of the mountain. There were no buildings anywhere to be seen on the property, and they all filed out of the limo. Matt looked at Mr. Faulkner and asked, "Where is everything?"

"At Santego, everything is underground to protect the beauty of the property."

"Wow." Matt was stunned. Mr. Faulkner made the money sign with his fingers, and Matt nodded. "No kidding." They walked to the massive doors that were manned by two attractive young ladies in plain black cocktail dresses who were handing out literature on the auction. Beside them were Napa police officers.

Matt put his arm around Alexandra and she reached over and moved it down so that it rested lower on her hip giving him a dirty look. He whispered into her ear, "Stop, you are going to make this a long night."

She purred back, "You have no idea." They quickly went inside the mountain, and they could hear a string trio playing classically. It sounded as if they were in the same room, but the acoustics in the cave were outstanding. As they meandered through the underground winery, Alexandra became very nervous. The valley was a small town, and she was sure most people knew what happened.

Matt pulled her in closer. "Are you okay?"

"I am nervous. I feel a little sick. This is my first time out, and I'm sure people have been talking about me."

Matt started laughing. "Wait until tomorrow. They're really going to be talking about you. You look stunning, and you're very recently separated, and have the audacity to show up to this charity event with another man."

Matt and Alexandra broke into laughter and were still laughing when they walked into the grand ballroom inside the cave filled with the well-to-do of Napa Valley. Out of the corner or her eye, she saw Style and a few of the partners of the firm with their dates and wives standing next to his parents. They were all staring directly at her and Matt, and Style looked furious. She received the countersigned agreements from Gabriella on Friday evening. Style was no longer her problem and the look on his face made this entire evening worth it. She was having a great day. They followed the elder Steeds around with Hannah making sure they met everyone. Hannah was having a grand time. It was her victory lap of showing off her incredibly strong daughter and her date.

Matt and Alexandra broke off and went down one of the cave tunnels to review the silent auction items. Matt tapped on one. "Alexandra, here's the use of a private house, skiing in Aspen for a week February. What do you think? It comes with a chef and a maid?"

Alexandra punched him in the shoulder. It would be a long time before she considered putting on another set of skis, but it wasn't out of the question.

They continued down the row. Alexandra picked up one and handed it to him. "This is more like it." It was the use of a private home in Bora Bora for a week that was a hut out over the water. Matt looked at it and the latest bid. "I'm in." Matt put it down and wrote his name down and put $10,000 above the last offer of $7,000.

Alexandra looked at him surprised. "Really?"

"It says we have a year to use it, and there's nothing more I want to do than lounge together in our bathing suits for a week. If by some miracle we get the trip, we can use it to celebrate the end of your probation."

Alexandra turned and kissed Matt passionately right when some people turned down the row they were on. "Hello, Alexandra. It's so good to see you again. You look wonderful."

She composed herself, her body tingling again. "Yes, great to see you as well."

"Who was that?" Matt asked as they walked away.

"Shit. The vineyard operations manager for Style's father."

Matt laughed. "Scandalous."

"Come on. Let's eat before we get into any more trouble." They meandered around the room gathering food from the stations that were set up. They found her parents at the Jerkaskys' table, and Matt excused himself to get a glass of wine and sparkling water and lime for Alexandra.

By the time Matt returned, the festivities had started by announcing the winners of the silent auction. "The winner of the week in Bora Bora is Matt Thomas."

Loud clapping erupted, and Matt got up in his regal tux and went to the front of the room to gather the packet of information on the trip, then returning to the table. May was eyeing them the entire time and smiling as Alexandra leaned in and gave him a big hug on his return. "I can't believe that $10,000 held up."

Matt smiled. "It didn't. I checked on it when I got up for the drinks and someone outbid me, so I upped the ante a bit."

When the actual auction started, Alexandra excused herself and went looking for the ladies room to freshen up. As soon as she entered, she went to the mirror and opened her pocketbook. As she looked up and saw herself, she was shocked. The woman standing in front of her in the mirror was so happy and joyous. How did she get here? A realization swept over her. Had God reached down and set Matt and her on paths toward each other? She whispered to her reflection, "A change in course." There was no other alternative explanation for something so dramatically impactful to happen to both of them that would change their lives forever and bring them together. Her eyes welled up in happiness, searching for a breath, overwhelmed by this realization. All she could say to God was, "Thank you," as she reached down and touched her heart.

The door of the bathroom opened, and this extremely stylish older lady walked in. It was someone she had not yet met, and she smiled at Alexandra. Alexandra gathered herself and smiled back as they both fixed their makeup. The older lady spoke, "Are you enjoying yourself?"

"I am. It's wonderful. I'm so blessed to be here tonight with my family, and the children's hospital is such a good cause. How about you?"

"I am as well. Hopefully we can wrangle some more money out of these rich people's pockets." They both laughed. Alexandra closed her pocketbook and went to the restroom inside one of the floor-to-ceiling stalls.

When she was preparing to leave the stall, she heard the bathroom door open again, and a very loud female voice entered saying, "Oh my God, I can't believe she is here. Do you believe the audacity of her? Style says she's working on a chain gang during the day."

Another woman's voice chimed in that Alexandra immediately recognized as one of the partners' wives. "Do you think they checked her arms for track marks on the way in?" They all busted out laughing.

Another unidentified voice said, "Can you believe she's over there drinking gin and tonic and who's that guy with her?"

"Probably her probation officer." Again, more laughter.

Alexandra's head dropped and her heart hurt. She had two choices. Stay in the stall and wait them out and pretend she didn't hear it or walk out to confront them. It wasn't really a choice. She watched as her hand moved forward and unlocked the stall, and she walked out into the main area of the bathroom. The women all froze at the mirrors when they saw her.

"Good evening Hope, Emma, and I am sorry I don't know your names." They were all speechless. They were frozen. Alexandra held out her arms and turned them over. "Emma would you like to check my arms for track marks? You can see there are none. My drug of choice was Oxycotin, which I got addicted to after knee surgery. A needle was only used on me once, actually the last time." Emma didn't move. "Hope, I am doing my community service, which is incredibly humbling. You should try it. When you see those orange bags of garbage on the side of the road, you have me to thank." Alexandra smiled.

"And my drink of choice this evening is sparkling water with lime, but please come check it, I invite you. And finally, that man, that gorgeous man, he doesn't know it yet, but I am going to marry him and have his children and spend the rest of my life with him. You see God rescued me from the life you're living, a life that I was miserably trapped in and didn't even know it."

The door of another stall opened and out walked the extremely stylish older lady that Alexandra had been talking to at the mirror a few minutes earlier. She nodded to all of them and then motioned toward the sink. "Alexandra, let's wash our hands and get back out to the auction."

Alexandra wasn't sure how the woman knew her name. She smiled. "Yes, ma'am." Hope, Emma, and her crew, still not breathing, moved away from the sinks, and they quickly washed and toweled. As they moved toward the exit the older lady stopped and said, "Ladies, I don't really know you, but I hope you've had a good evening here tonight because when you leave my home and my winery you're never to come back here again for any reason. Do you understand?" The shock on their faces showed their devastation. A couple of them nodded. "Good."

As they exited the bathroom, Alexandra took a deep breath. "Mrs. Santego, thank you so much for that."

They turned toward each other, and she pointed toward Alexandra's heart. "When I saw you tonight, I thought to myself, there is such a light inside of you that it outshone everyone here." She pointed toward the bathroom. "Don't let them extinguish that. They see it and are envious. That is what that was about in there and nothing more. Now, let's go join our families before one of them makes a fool of us." They hugged, and as Alexandra turned, she saw Matt looking at her and smiling. Her heart swelled with joy. She couldn't help but return the smile. She was so happy.

She held up a finger to let him know one minute, and he nodded to her. Alexandra crossed the room and found the DJ who would take over after the auction. As soon as it was over, the ball would spiral out of control into drunken dancing. She spoke with him for a minute and then went and sat directly in front of Matt. She leaned her body into him, and he wrapped his arm around the front of her body and held her tightly. She took her hand and gently stroked it back and forth on his arm. This intimate embrace caught the attention of Hannah and Ben who then looked at May, and she smiled and nodded confirmation.

The emcee for the auction returned to the stage. He was a retired actor who had settled in the valley and purchased a winery. "Ladies and gentlemen, for our final auction item of the evening... you know we always save the best for last. We have to make sure we drain every very last dollar out your pockets." The crowd busted into laughter. "Every year the ball committee has the very same argument on what the final item is going to be. A ten-year vertical of the best wine in the valley or some outrageously expensive sports car." Again, more laughter from the audience. "Well, ladies and gentlemen, I am proud to say this year the committee was unanimous on what the final selection would be, and it is neither of those things. I would like to invite to the stage an artist in his own right, Harrison Stone, who is the owner of Calistoga Gallery, to introduce us to this final item." The room broke out clapping. Harrison mounted the stage with two men behind him carefully carrying a very large, draped painting.

Alexandra's fingers dug into Matt's arm. He leaned down and asked, "What?" She was speechless.

Harrison began. "Thank you all for your time this evening. I am very proud to be able to introduce this work. It's one of the first pieces of its kind from an unknown, budding new artist in the valley. I can assure you they will not be unknown for long. When the committee saw this work, they were overwhelmed by its power as was I. The new artist has not been paid for this work but agreed to sell so half of what we receive this evening will go to the artist and half will go to the Children's Hospital."

Harrison turned and nodded to the men, and they carefully pulled the sheet off the painting. An audible gasp rose in the room as it dropped. The five-foot by five-foot painting in a huge frame was an encapsulation of Napa Valley from the top of one of the mountains looking down. It was unbelievable, and Matt knew instantly from the style of Dawn's Meadow, it was Alexandra's painting. "Oh my God, baby, that's unbelievable," he whispered in her ear.

Matt could feel her nails digging into his arm. She turned and looked back at him. "He came to the house the other day and said he just wanted to show it to some people. Then he texted this afternoon when we got back and said that it had been sold. I had no idea," she explained.

Matt was still mesmerized, taking in the masterpiece he saw. There at the very bottom center of the painting was a man in jeans, white T-shirt and work boots walking down a row of vines with a large brown dog, who was looking up at him. Matt whispered in her ear, "Me and Hanky?"

Alexandra looked up at him and smiled. "Yes, that painting was my prayer. When he called this afternoon and said it was gone, I didn't care because my prayer had been answered." Her eyes welled with tears. Matt leaned down and kissed her passionately. When they broke away from each other and collected themselves, they realized the entire table was looking at them. Alexandra smiled at them and looked back toward the painting.

The emcee now took over again. "I got to tell you, when I saw this, I was blown away and that doesn't really happen. I want this painting for myself, so I am going to start the bidding at $25,000." Another gasp came from the room as it was immediately answered with $30,000. Matt started to raise his paddle at $35,000, and Alexandra stopped him. "No, Matty. There's so much more where that comes from because of you." She gently took the paddle away from him and laid it on the table wrapping his arm around her.

Hannah saw and overheard what happened. She gasped putting her hand to her mouth and grasped her heart. Ben moved into comfort her not understanding what had happened, and she whispered in his ear. There was shock on his face, and he began to raise his paddle, and Alexandra reached her hand toward him and whispered, "No, Daddy." He reached his hand out to meet her hand, and his eyes welled up. Now the entire table began to understand what was going on.

"Oh my God, Alexandra," Peter Jerkasky exclaimed.

Matt pulled Alexandra in tighter, and she leaned up and kissed his neck.

The bidding was now out of control. It was now going up in $10,000 dollar increments, and the bid had just crested $200,000, which brought another gasp and stir from the audience. The bidding was down to two men, and they were not giving an inch. Art Bridgeway, Style's father, and Logan Santego, the owner of the winery, were dueling. "Do I hear $210?" Art raised his paddle. Logan Santego immediately yelled, "$225." They were taking the emcee out of it. Art answered across the room with "$230." Style's mother was now tugging at his jacket and shaking her head no. Logan responded $250,000. Another gasp from the room, then dead silence. Art understood Logan was not going to give up an inch, so he sat down. The emcee then said, "Going once, going twice, sold for $250,000." The room erupted in applause. The Santegos got up and went to the front of the room to get a better look at their new painting.

Matt was clutching Alexandra. "Wow." She again turned and kissed his neck, and then turned to their table, which was now in shock. Her entire body was exhilarated by the touch of Matt and what had just occurred. Everyone at the table was smiling at them.

Logan Santego could be heard on stage, as he was close enough to the emcee to be caught in his microphone, asking, "Who is the artist? It's not signed." The room immediately got quiet. "It's not signed. Who is this artist? I must know." He was now pleading with Harrison Stone who reached back and picked up a microphone. The room was dead quiet waiting for the answer. "Ladies and gentlemen, when I picked this painting up from the artist, I asked why it had not been signed. I was told that if someone wanted them to sign it, then that act would make that person an artist. Mr. Santego would you like the artist to sign it because if so, the artist is here tonight?" The room gasped again.

Alexandra's nails were digging into Matt's arm. She was shaking and couldn't breathe. He leaned down, and whispered in her ear, "It's okay."

Mr. Santego took the microphone from the emcee and turned toward the crowd. "Please come forward and sign your beautiful work. Take credit for your masterpiece because you are an artist." The entire room was now looking around and waiting for the artist to emerge.

Alexandra didn't move. Matt again leaned down. "Come on, Alexandra. We can do this together." Matt started to move, but Alexandra was dead weight in his hands. He pulled her up, and they took a few steps forward, which caught Harrison Stone's eyes but no one else.

Harrison brought the microphone to his mouth, "Ladies and gentlemen, I present you your artist, Alexandra Steed." Shock and gasps erupted from the room and then immediately turned into raucous applause.

Matt walked her forward to where the sea of applauding people stopped and said, "Go, baby." This was about her, and he wanted to stay out of her spotlight, but she didn't move. Mrs. Santego who had just been so kind to her in the bathroom saw her fear and took her by her arm forward to Mr. Santego who hugged her. Alexandra had a tear streaming down her face when Harrison Stone handed her a brush and a palette. She gathered herself and took it from his hand. She chose a color, and leaned in signed it, Ali Steed.

When she handed it back to Harrison, the room erupted in applause. She leaned in and said something in his ear. He questioned her back, and she nodded in the affirmative. "Ladies and gentlemen, I have one final announcement. Mrs. Steed is declining the royalties from the painting, so the entire $250,000 from the Santegos will be given to the Children's Hospital." The applause was so loud in the cave it was deafening. Matt turned back to the table to see the proud Steed and Jerkasky families. He nodded at them, and they returned it.

The crowd now moved forward to congratulate the Santegos and Alexandra, and Matt stayed back with the family at the table. The lights in the room dropped as they prepared to turn the rest of the evening over to the DJ. Alexandra appeared from the crowd, hugged everyone, and then sank into Matt's waiting arms. He looked at her. "You are so incredible."

The music started, and Alexandra's eyes lit up. She grabbed Matt's hand and pleaded, "Dance with me, Matty. It's our song." They were the first to the floor, and with Alexandra being the lady of the hour, everyone saw them enter and stayed seated to watch.

Matt immediately recognized the song from Hootie and the Blowfish's latest album they had been listening to. Darius and Lucie Silvas sang of wildfire love.

Sunday morning and I'm waiting for a train, darling, I'll be gone for a while

Don't know how to ask but baby, will you wait, you know the world gets lonely sometime

A rolling stone in the desert, a wind that blows in the trees

Through the storms and bad weather babe, the only thing that we need

Matt and Alexandra circled the floor, embraced in each other's arms. The entire room remained seated, mesmerized by them. Each time the song got to the chorus they sang it to each other:

Is love, burning love, well it's a wildfire love

Taking everything it sees

And, it's a love, red hot love, well it's a wildfire love

Baby, that's just you and me

Baby, that's just you and me

As the song finished up, Matt and Alexandra went in for a kiss, sending the room into applause.

73

The inside of the limo was raucous with adrenaline from the festivities of the night. Peter Jerkasky and Ben Faulkner were slur arguing on who was the best winemaker. Peter leaned in and slurred, "We need to go to our house. I will show you."

Ben responded, "You're on."

"Us sober people are going home. We're exhausted," Alexandra said. Matt reached back and pulled the window open between them and the driver. "Sir, please pull in the driveway up ahead. You don't need to go in. We will walk the rest of the way."

"Are you sure, sir?"

"Absolutely. There's a full moon. It will be a lovely walk." The limo pulled off laterally into the driveway of Steed Vineyard. Matt opened the door and helped Alexandra out. She had her high heels in her hand. "Good night. Thank you so much for a wonderful time." Matt took the shoes from her and scooped her into his arms as the driver shut the door. Alexandra laid her head on Matt's shoulder and with her hand, stroked the back of Matt's neck.

The window on the door where they exited opened, and the Steeds and Jerkakys watched as Matt hit the keypad for the fence, and it opened. He carried Alexandra up the road to the house in the moonlight. Hannah leaned forward and took Ben's hand. "We need to get the house finished." He smiled and nodded back to her.